THE TITANIC DECEPTION

AN EDEN BLACK THRILLER

LUKE RICHARDSON

PROLOGUE

Cervinia, Italy. 1882.

FOR JEAN CARREL, it all started with a pyramid. This wasn't the sort he'd read about people going crazy for a thousand miles away in the desert sands, though.

This pyramid was certainly not constructed by Pharaohs, or anything of that sort. This pyramid was the work of a force much larger — the careful, merciless, hands of mother nature herself.

Carrel stepped from the door of the house in which his family lived and took two paces in the biting morning cold. Frost crunched beneath his shoes. He took a moment to feel the condition of his feet. They felt good, well rested, and ready.

No, Carrel thought to himself, this was no pyramid like those children read about in books. This was something far more grand and far more imposing. With that thought, Carrel turned towards the fourteen-thousand-foot-high pile of rock and ice which reared up a few miles away. The

Matterhorn — the pyramid of stone which crowned the Alps, and with that, half of Europe.

"Are you sure we should do this?" said Lewis Antoine, striding up beside his friend and lifelong climbing partner. Antoine passed Carrel a mug of freshly brewed coffee, the smell intoxicating.

Both men sipped at their drinks and gazed up at the challenge ahead. The sun had just risen somewhere behind the monolithic angular peak, igniting the ridge with jarring sunbeams shooting out into the crystal sky.

Carrel turned and considered his friend. "Of course, this may be our only chance for the record."

Almost twenty years ago, when Carrel had just been a boy, a team, including several men from the village, had been the first in the modern era to reach the Matterhorn's peak. Many before had tried, and several of those brave men, had not returned. Those who did return, did so dejectedly, glaring at the peak which hung over their village day and night, as a constant reminder of their failure.

"If you're sure," Antoine said, taking another sip of the quickly cooling coffee. "You know I would follow you to the ends of the earth, and probably beyond if that's where our adventure led."

"The record we are going for today is something quite different," Carrel said, running his fingers through his beard. "We are to summit the Matterhorn in the winter. No one has done that before, for good reason. We have two challenges ahead. The mountain is one, and the weather is the other."

The men stood and watched the mountain together for several long seconds, the haze of their breath mingling in the glacial breeze.

Many thousand feet above, a long strip of cloud swirled towards the peak, as though pulled by an invisible hand.

"You see," Carrel said, pointing at the cloud as though it was performing on his command. "The wind up there has a mind of its own."

Antoine placed a hand on his friend's shoulder. "You're not getting rid of me. We do this together, whether you like it or not."

The men locked eyes for a long moment and Carrel nodded. "Then let's go. We've a long way to climb today and fair weather waits for no man."

The men were in good spirits as they walked from the village. Word had spread that through stupidity or madness, Carrel and Antoine intended to summit the mountain during the winter. Many residents endured the cold to watch the pair leave, standing at their doors and waving or rushing forth with best wishes and gifts. The men thankfully received and tucked away a selection of small gifts — a quart of whisky to keep off the cold, several cuts of cured ham and some dried fruit.

After two hours Carrel stopped and gazed up and the wall of rock and ice that now towered above them.

The sky had changed too. What was once a dome of benevolent blue, was now a circling mass of cloud.

"This is it," Antoine said, as they set off scrambling up over rocks. "No turning back now. We are going to the top."

"If nature intends it," Carrel kindly corrected his friend. "The way to think about a mountain is this... it is not something to be conquered, because man can never overcome nature." Carrel paused his dialogue and scrambled up an outcrop with the speed and agility of an ape.

It took Antoine two minutes to traverse the same section which his friend had scaled in just a few seconds.

When Carrel spoke again, he was not even out of breath. He leaned back, eyeing the peak.

"You must approach a mountain the way a baby approaches its mother." He slung his pack around and pulled out a parcel of cured meat wrapped in cloth. He passed one slice to his friend and took one himself. "You must approach a mountain knowing that you are powerless against it. You will crawl useless and blubbering into nature's lap, hoping for food."

The men assessed the mountain a moment longer, chewing their meat. After a sip of water, Carrel slung his pack over his shoulders again and set off.

Several hours passed in much the same way. Carrel would scale a section of the incline with incredible ease and then chew on something until Antoine approached.

Just after midday, the men paused and stared at the village far beneath them which was now only visible by its twinkling lights. The weather was not on their side, and cloud filled much of the valley.

"It's not dense enough to worry about, yet," Carrel said, as Antoine huffed his way passed. Antoine had taken to not stopping when his friend waited, he would plod forward at his slow and steady pace.

"We push on as far as we can," Carrel said, pointing towards a forty-five-degree band of snow which filled the gap between the cliffs. "Every footstep is a victory," Carrel shouted, quickly overtaking his friend, his spiked shoes easily digging through the powder. The rope which ran between the two men, should either of them fall, snaked in the leading man's wake.

Antoine followed, placing each foot carefully in the prints made by his friend. Then, all at once, a shroud of silence fell across the mountain.

Antoine paused, listening. The sound of his beating heart seemed to be the only noise on the mountainside.

Carrel, now forty feet up ahead, didn't even slow.

Antoine pushed on, trying to forget the eerie silence. Every step he fell behind would be one to catch up later, after all.

He took several steps forward. Still, the only sound was the crunch of his shoes in the snow, the deep rumble of his breathing, and the distant thump of his heart.

Then, it felt as though a giant fist crashed into the ground. A colossal boom roared up and then down the mountainside. The powdery snow shook from side to side, feeling no more solid than water. A thousand explosions roared at once, or at least that's what it felt like.

Antoine cried out and stumbled forward into the snow. He extended his hands just in time to arrest his fall but sank into the powder up to his elbows. Glancing up just in time, he saw his friend stumble or throw himself headlong into the snow.

Then cloud, or snow, or ice, or even the hands of mother nature herself closed in around Antoine. He glanced frantically around, but whatever it was now blocked his vision of everything in front, to the sides, and behind.

"Carrel, where are you?" Antoine shouted, but his voice couldn't to cut through the curtain that surrounded him. Each breath roared in his ears like a howling wind.

He whipped one way and then the other, trying to see something, trying to work out what was going on, but all he saw was grey.

Antoine climbed slowly back to his feet and stood crouched forward.

The shaking came again, this time causing the mountain beneath him to quiver like a feather in the wind. The vibrations continued, getting more savage and violent as the Earth let out its pent-up energy.

Antoine steadied himself. He gazed back toward the village, but swirling mist now cloaked their homes.

Antoine turned back around just in time to see a boulder plummet down the mountain, cutting a groove through the snow just three feet to his right. Then another plunged to the left.

Antoine sunk further into his crouch, his body coiled and ready to react. He focused all his senses on the wall of mist ahead, should anything fall towards him. His muscles strained, ready to launch. The white-out gave up no clues. Distorted shapes moved and swirled beyond the curtain.

Then the wind started again, wailing, and whipping up around the mountain ridges.

Antoine closed his eyes to slits to keep the snow away.

Then he felt the rope tied around his waist go taut. Carrel was pulling him onwards.

"Carrel, is that you!" Antoine shouted through the cloud. He heard nothing but the whirling mist and the distant skittering of rocks. Shouting up here was like screaming into a pillow — the snow and mist just absorbed sound, sucking it in to nothing.

Antoine climbed to his feet and, still searching for oncoming danger, pushed his way forward.

"Did you see that?" Carrel roared, appearing just a foot from Antoine's left. "An earthquake! A big one too. Just incredible!"

Antoine glanced at his friend to check the other man hadn't taken a knock to the head. Experiencing an earthquake halfway up a mountain at a dangerous time of year, certainly wasn't his idea of incredible.

"I... I don't..." Antoine stuttered, his voice instantly lost in the gale.

"We're going to have to wait it out," Carrel said, pointing forward. "There's a rock face around twenty feet through the cloud there. We can hole up beside the rock and sit it out. Conditions like this won't last long."

Still twittering on about how exciting the earthquake was, Carrel led them through the cloud. Within two minutes, the wall of rock loomed high in front of them.

With no more quakes shaking the ground, Antoine felt the pit of his stomach solidify and his feet steady. He put his back against the rock wall and sucked in a deep breath. Slowly, the world around him stopped spinning as panic receded. It felt good to be still.

"Now what is that," Carrel said, pointing along the mountain.

"What? I don't see anything," Antoine said, reluctantly leaning forward and peering in the direction his friend had indicated.

A silver tongue of ice hung beyond the cliff face just a few feet away. In the mist and confusion, Antoine hadn't noticed it.

"That glacier," Carrel said, now almost bouncing with excitement. "It's split. The earthquake must have broken it in two. We'll use the hollow to shelter for the next few hours. That'll be perfect."

It sounded far from perfect for Antoine, but before he could offer a reaction, Carrel stomped off towards the glacier and disappeared through a two-foot-wide crack in the ice.

Afraid to be left behind again, Antoine climbed to his feet and staggered after his friend. At the mouth of the opening, he paused and gazed upwards. The great shimmering block of ice towered over him, its surface a translucent silver. The gap through which Carrel had disappeared was little more than the width of his shoulders. Two sheets of rock-hard ice loomed either side like the jaws of some great beast. The thought of climbing in there made Antoine's stomach churn.

"Are you sure this is a good idea?" Antoine shouted, cupping his hands around his mouth. "What if there's another quake and we can't get out again?"

The wind slicing through his skin was Antoine's only answer. The cold slashed in through his coat and a shiver agitated his bones.

Carrel was right, Antoine thought, they couldn't spend the night out on the side of the mountain. They would need to find shelter, and soon.

Antoine steeled himself and slipped into the fissure. Inside the glacier, the world felt completely different. Although the cold continued to gnaw at his exposed skin, the wind instantly abated. The sound changed, too. Outside, the wind had howled and screamed. Just three feet inside the glacier, it was little more than a murmur.

Antoine slipped off his backpack, allowing him to move more easily, and slipped further into the glacier.

Somewhere ahead, a light flared and glimmered. Antoine pushed towards the glow.

"Look at this place," Carrel said, holding up a small oil lamp. They'd stepped into a cavern right inside the glacier. The light from Carrel's lamp danced across the icy walls in an ethereal tapestry of blue and white.

"Never in my life," Antoine muttered, inhaling. The whole cavern, which extended as far as he could see, glittered, and sparkled as though the walls were embedded with a million diamonds.

Carrel glanced back at his friend, his eyes wild with excitement. Ice crystals twinkled from his beard.

"We're probably the first people to see this," Carrel said, stepping further into the cavern.

A groaning noise reverberated from the surrounding ice. Antoine froze in mid stride, suddenly afraid the gap behind them would close, sealing them inside forever. A fine coating of crystalline dust floated down through the cavern.

"It's the glacier adapting to the new shape of the surrounding mountain," Carrel said. Now inside, his voice boomed confidently from the walls. "We'll be fine. Don't worry."

Antoine took a moment to calm his pounding heart. The ambience of the cavern was disorienting, as were the blended sensations of awe, danger, and fear.

Carrel wandered on, exploring with the nonchalance of a child in a sweet shop.

Another creak reverberated through the cavern, this time sounding as though it were some distance away.

"It's like it's alive," Carrel said, tenderly touching one of the ice walls.

After another twenty feet, the cavern widened further, allowing the pair to stand side by side.

"These patterns are incredible," Antoine said, his worry finally melting into wonder. He pointed up at the roof, which was now formed with the patterns caused by thousands of years of shifting pressure.

Carrel swung the light in a wide arc from right to left. Suddenly, it illuminated something inside one of the cavern's ice walls. Something solid.

Carrel stopped abruptly and then swept the lamp backward inch by inch.

"What's that?" Carrel hissed, pointing with his free hand

at the object. He raised the lantern higher with the other, bringing the full beam to bear on the thing.

Both men stepped forward and recognized what it was at the same moment.

Antoine's muscles locked solid. His breath caught in his throat. He pointed at the thing, dumbstruck.

Carrel mumbled something, but for once his mouth couldn't form the words either.

Both men stared for long seconds, saying nothing.

As though checking they weren't in a private dream world, the men glanced at each other and then back at the wall.

Antoine shook his head slowly as the truth became plain to see. Encased within the ice, just a few feet away, was a woman. She was positioned vertically, frozen inside the solid wall of ice. Her hands hung out at her sides, her wrists slender and her fingers splayed. Her position, frozen several feet above the cavern's floor, gave the illusion that she was peering down at the interlopers.

Shaking now from shock rather than cold, Antoine took another step forward and stared up at the woman's face. She was young and her eyes were closed. She looked peaceful, as though she had merely fallen asleep in that position. Tendrils of hair floated around her face like a crown and her skin reflected the light in a pearlescent, creamy white. She was dressed in woven animal hides, with bone jewelry at her neck and wrists.

She was clearly dead. Both men could see that. But preserved in this icy cavern, life could have just left her lips hours ago.

"Mon Dieu," Carrel whispered, his breath turning instantly to vapor in the icy air. "My God."

1

The British Museum, London. April 8th, 1912.

MARCUS NETTLEBY LEANED back in his chair and scrutinized the papers and maps which were scattered across the deck in front of him. One large black-and-white photo showed a human figure. The woman, whose origins were presently unknown, had been found inside a glacier almost thirty years ago. The find had caused something of an international stir, with museums and universities all over the world proposing different theories. Of course, being technically found in Italy, she was at first carted to one of the prestigious Italian universities who promised to solve the mystery in mere minutes. When they couldn't, with years already passing, she was moved on somewhere else, and somewhere else again.

Finally, decades later, she had arrived in London for Nettleby and his team to have a go at solving the mystery of the *Lady of Leone*. The name was the work of a creative member of the press, who had coined it after the mountain ridge on which she was discovered.

Fortunately, some care had been taken to embalm and preserve the body, which was the best specimen of an early human the scientific community had ever seen. It was uncanny really.

Nettleby glanced at the mahogany clock, mounted on the far wall. Seconds ticked away as though reminding Nettleby that he wasn't getting any closer to a breakthrough.

Made by John Bennet and Company in London, the clock was one of Nettleby's most prized possessions. The clock's loud ticking was the only noise in the office, although Nettleby was so used to the sound that he no longer heard it.

Nettleby closed his eyes. The problem was, despite all the work Nettleby and his team had put in, they were no closer to understanding how the woman ended up several thousand feet away from the nearest known civilization with bare feet and no sign of any climbing equipment.

Nettleby shook his head and then returned his attention to the map, which marked the location of her discovery. For the last few months, Nettleby had been comparing the map with all the known civilizations in that region over the last few thousand years. It was long and tiresome work, which so far had revealed little.

Nettleby scowled, took off his eyeglasses, and pinched the bridge of his nose. He huffed out a breath. Whilst Nettleby often considered the work he did to be like a police detective, he honestly believed that his job was even more challenging. He was not just hunting for a metaphorical needle in a haystack, but trying to search through a haystack which existed centuries or even millennia ago. Even so, Nettleby was expected to peel back the ravages of time and produce the answers people felt they deserved. Now, more than ever before, the pressure was on.

Nettleby closed his eyes slowly and inhaled. His office, deep within the bowels of the British Museum, smelled the same no matter whether it was day or night, summer or winter. It was a mixture of books and tobacco smoke — the former caused by the overburdened shelves which covered every wall in the small office, and the latter a result of his constant smoking. He glanced down at the pipe which sat in the palm of his left hand, a string of smoke twisting towards the yellowed ceiling.

A sharp tapping at the door drew Nettleby's attention back to the present.

"Come in," Nettleby muttered. He cleared his throat and then shouted. "Come in!"

The door swung open, and a young woman stepped through. Nettleby recognized her immediately as his assistant.

"What is it, Miss Thompson?" Nettleby said, more sharply than he intended. His gaze rose to meet hers and Nettleby noticed the woman wore the look of a frightened animal, her eyes wild and her limbs a moment away from an instinctive escape.

"Sir, I apologize for the intrusion," Miss Thompson said, her voice just a whisper. "There are some men here to see you. They haven't got a scheduled appointment, but they are rather insistent. They say it's of the utmost importance they see you now."

Nettleby sighed and glanced down at the desk. His eyes locked on the *Lady of Leone* once more, but didn't linger. Sometimes the living needed his time, as well as the dead.

Nettleby met his assistant's gaze and his expression thawed. The pressure he was under was no fault of hers. Nor was it the fault of the people who wanted to speak with him.

Nettleby would see them now, get rid of them as quickly as possible, then get back to work.

"I suppose you'd better show them in," he said, folding the papers and sliding them to one side. A clean desk presents an ordered mind, or something like that, Nettleby reminded himself.

"Of course, sir... thank you... thank you," Miss Thompson murmured, visibly sighing with relief. She turned and scurried from the room, the door banging closed behind her.

Nettleby scanned the shelves of books for a moment. His personal library contained books he used for reference and those he'd authored himself.

His notoriety as a researcher and as a curator of the British Museum meant it wasn't unusual that people wanted to see him. They usually arrived, wanting him to examine some artifact or other which they'd unearthed while tending the garden. Many of Nettleby's visitors watched with the excitement of a gambler, as though the museum was crying out to buy any piece of rock that *'sort of looked a bit like an ancient creature'* in the mind of an imaginative child. Most of Nettleby's visitors, unfortunately, were sorely disappointed when they learned their journey to London had been wasted.

Expecting such a visit now, Nettleby withdrew a hipflask from his jacket pocket and took a greedy sip. Rather than the hard liquor some men kept in a flask at their breast, Nettleby preferred an excellent claret. The choice wasn't traditional, but it kept the chill off all the same.

Nettleby had only just slid the flask out of sight when the door swung open, and two figures entered. If Miss Thompson was at the meek end of the spectrum, then these men were at the opposite. Just their presence brought a tension to the office to which Nettleby was quite unaccustomed.

Their attire was curious too, both wore well-tailored suits that were too fine to be anything but custom-made. The younger of the two wore a crimson silk tie, and the older wore a black bow tie. The men removed their bowler hats, placed them beneath their arms, and then turned towards Nettleby.

"Mr. Nettleby, thank you for seeing us," the older man said, his tone suggesting he was anything but thankful. In fact, Nettleby sensed these men took no pleasure in the conversation that was about to take place. They were here for professional reasons and thought of Nettleby as their inferior. Even so, the men conformed to courtesy and held their hands out for Nettleby to shake.

"How can I help you, gentlemen?" Nettleby rose into a half stand, shook one hand, then the next, then settled back into his chair.

"I'm Harrison Pike, and this here's my associate, Robert Mallory," the older man said.

Nettleby nodded in greeting as he recognized Pike spoke like an American. That was hardly surprising. London was full of Americans and several of them had a lot of money to spend.

Pike and Mallory took the seats in front of Nettleby's desk without waiting for an invitation to do so.

"I hope you'll forgive us if we get straight to the point," Pike said, pulling a leather document holder from his briefcase. "I'm afraid we're here to tell you that your time is up."

"I'm sorry, I..." Nettleby began to say but Pike placed the document folder on Nettleby's desk and swung it open.

"We're here because our employer has acquired the *Lady of Leone.*" Mallory's tone was even more officious than his senior's. "We intend to transfer her to the United States next week."

"That's just not possible," Nettleby said, his hands closing into fists. "My team and I have been working night and day trying to understand the *Lady of Leone*..."

"Well, you can thank us for taking something off your to do list then, so to speak," Pike said.

"There has to be some mistake," Nettleby said, his eyes now searching the document although not really focusing on anything.

"I'm afraid not," Pike said, pointing towards several signatures at the bottom of the document. "As you can see, all the legal formalities have been fulfilled. This order comes directly from your government."

"We've only come to inform you personally as a professional courtesy," Mallory replied, his voice bordering on disdain.

Nettleby leaned forward to scrutinize the signatures, a knot tightening in his stomach. They appeared to be authentic, one of them even bearing the Department of Antiquities official seal.

Nettleby huffed and leaned back in his chair. "I must say, this is highly irregular and upsetting. The *Lady of Leone* is one of the most important discoveries of the last few decades. This is a loss not just for us, but for British academia at large."

"We understand that, Mr. Nettleby," Mallory said. "But sometimes things are just a matter of business."

"A matter of business?" Nettleby roared, a sour taste bubbling into his mouth. He poked hard at the table. "Gentlemen, this is a place of science and history, not a market."

"And yet, transactions occur," Pike said, closing the document folder and removing it from the table.

Both men stood and replaced their hats. Pike led them towards the door and then turned back to the curator.

"There is one more thing you need to know." He locked eyes with Nettleby.

A shiver moved up Nettleby's spine one inch at a time. Although not a superstitious man, Nettleby got the feeling he wouldn't like what Pike was about to say, one bit.

"You are to transport *The Lady of Leone* to our contact in New York. Your return passage is booked and paid for, sailing next week."

Nettleby's eyebrows inched together, and his mouth curved at the edges.

"You're going to like it," Mallory muttered. "First-class, on the brand-new White Star Line. We've really extended the budget for your safety and comfort."

Pike's gaze locked on Nettleby for a long moment. When the American finally spoke, his voice was little more than a grumble. "She's called *The Titanic*."

2

Southampton, England. April 10th, 1912.

As the British Museum's Rolls Royce slipped its way through the bustling streets of Southampton, Nettleby couldn't help but feel a growing sense of disquiet. He leaned back into the leather seat and dabbed at his forehead with a handkerchief.

Twenty feet ahead, his eyes remained locked on a truck which was hauling the *Lady of Leone*, in a specially constructed temperature-controlled crate, towards the docks and onwards to the United States. Currently obscured beneath a large tarpaulin on the truck's flatbed, the object didn't look like the most important historical find of the century. Of course, Nettleby knew it was. Nettleby knew that with every inch the truck rolled on, the *Lady of Leone* was slipping through his fingers.

Scowling, Nettleby thought back through what he knew about the deal. The trade had been signed off by the Minister of Antiquities, but Nettleby had no idea why. During the intervening days, the curator had tried to arrange a meeting with the minister, but the statesman was conveniently traveling somewhere up north and wouldn't return until after Nettleby's departure.

Nettleby frowned. It felt like a setup with him stuck in the of it. Whatever backroom dealing had occurred for the *Lady of Leone* to be sold like a hunk of precious metal, he didn't like it one bit.

The Rolls Royce slowed to a crawl. Hearing voices, Nettleby glanced out through the windows. A group of children paused their game of football to eye the gleaming car. Ahead, the truck slowed further and then creaked around a row of houses, the Rolls Royce following a few feet behind.

Nettleby peered again through the windshield. This time, he gazed beyond the truck and unconsciously drew a breath. Beyond the squat houses and dockyard buildings, *The Titanic* rose like a metallic mountain range.

Although Nettleby wasn't often impressed by the creations of modern man, *The Titanic* was a remarkable machine. Blocking out the sun for several hundred feet in both directions, the ship became taller and taller the closer they got.

The small convoy moved even more slowly now as traffic and pedestrians filled the streets. Dockworkers hustled back and forth, pulling carts, boxes, and supplies for the ship. Empty trucks shuddered the other way, their loads already in the ship's stores.

Street vendors half-heartedly peddled their wares. Today they were more interested in the strange metal beast moored nearby than eking a few pence from passing travelers.

Eventually the truck sighed to a stop, the driver letting the pressure out of its steam engine, and the Rolls Royce murmured into silence behind.

Nettleby got out and, momentarily distracted from his malaise, craned his neck upwards to gaze at *Titanic's* great bow.

Above them, cranes swung heavy cargo this way and that, their engines groaning. The combined smells of salt, machine oil, and coal laced the air.

Nettleby turned and watched a group of dockworkers in oil-stained overalls and flat caps surround the truck.

The men passed Nettleby without acknowledgement and scrambled on to the flatbed. The men quickly secured the crate to an overhead crane and the foreman turned and signaled up to the crane operator. With a deep mechanical groan, the chains pulled taut, and then the crate rose.

Nettleby watched the process, reading the words painted on the crate's exterior.

The British Museum. Fragile.

Nettleby hoped the heavyweight steel crate which had been designed especially to protect the *Lady of Leone* during the voyage, was enough. The hermetically sealed box would keep humidity and temperature at a constant level, as well as to prevent her suffering bumps and bangs during transportation. Right now, Nettleby reminded himself, it was the best they could do.

He slipped a hand into his jacket pocket and was reassured to feel the key. He was the only person who held the key to the crate, and he had special permission from *The Titanic's* captain to check on the crate as often as he saw fit. That was something, at least.

The crate hovered over the truck for a few moments before swinging further into the sky. As the crate dangled in mid-air, Nettleby grumbled again. The *Lady of Leone* was so much more than an artifact. She was a piece of human history, a sacred relic that needed to be treated with the utmost care.

Finally, the crate cleared the railing high above and disappeared into the hold. The crane operator sounded a horn, signaling the cargo was safely aboard, and Nettleby felt a miniscule sense of relief.

Nettleby shook his head, then drew out his ticket. He glanced down at *The White Star Line* logo glimmering at the top of the paper. As an ear-splitting cry sounded from *The Titanic's* whistles, Nettleby headed off toward the passenger ramp.

3

Leavenworth, Washington State. Present day.

DOCTOR ROBERT HUNTER glanced up at the clock on the wall of his clinic. The big hand struggled its way towards the zenith, marking well over an hour since his normal retreat up the mountain road towards home. Tonight, though, it would be several hours until Doctor Hunter got home.

With the same careful attention to detail that he had shown over his thirty years in medicine, Doctor Hunter finished the notes he was working on and slid the document into his briefcase. He clicked the lid of his pen into place and then slid it into a jacket pocket.

Doctor Hunter climbed to his feet and yet again ignored the dull aching pain in his knees. He knew that he needed to move more. Long, sedentary days in the clinic took their toll. But with his patients needing him, Doctor Hunter didn't have a choice. His time here was not just work, this was his calling.

After a few years in the Army Medical Corps at the start of his career, Doctor Hunter loved his work in Leavenworth.

Although he often joked that his patients worked him harder than the Army, Hunter wouldn't change a thing. His patients appreciated him too, over the years bestowing various accolades and awards on the doctor who always seemed embarrassed to receive them.

Crossing the room, Hunter glanced at a pair of certificates in gilded frames. One was a commendation from the mayor on behalf of the townspeople, and the other was a letter of thanks from the State Senator. The State Senator who, on this very evening, Hunter would stand alongside.

"I trust you're ready for your hour of fame?" came a friendly voice as Hunter stepped into the waiting room.

Momentarily startled, Doctor Hunter froze mid-stride. He whipped around to see the receptionist still ensconced behind her desk.

"Angela, you know things like this make me very uncomfortable," Hunter said. "I'd much rather get on with my work in peace without all these public interferences. Anyway, what are you still doing here? You should have been home over an hour ago."

Angela glanced at the doctor and then returned her gaze to the computer screen. "Mrs. Maggoty is having trouble again and needs to see you urgently," Angela said. "You didn't have any availability until next week. I know she should go into a care home really, but the longer we can keep her comfortable at home, the better."

Doctor Hunter slipped on his coat and then crossed to the reception desk.

"I told her you'd call first thing in the morning. You drive past her place, anyway. I'm halfway through shuffling around your other appointments to accommodate it." Angela picked up the phone with one hand while working the mouse with the other.

"Angela, you're an angel," Hunter said. "I don't know what I would do without you."

"Just playing my part." Angela's fingers dialed a number as though automated. "Got a couple more calls to make, then I'm out of here. You get going, don't want to keep the senator waiting."

Hunter waved thanks and strode towards the door.

"Oh, one more thing." Angela wrapped her hand around the telephone mouthpiece as she spoke. "I'll be watching your moment of fame from the back of the auditorium." Then, without missing a beat, she leaped straight into a conversation with the person on the line.

Doctor Hunter smiled nervously and pushed through the door. An icy wind whipping at his coat, Hunter stepped out into Leavenworth's small marketplace. Right in the center of town, his clinic occupied one of the original Bavarian-inspired buildings for which the town was famous.

Now, with winter taking root, ice hung from the wide eaves and snow collected on the roof.

"It's going to be a cold one," Hunter muttered as a flurry of snowflakes swirled around him. Hunter pulled his coat tight and set off down the sidewalk.

Fortunately, the town's theater and the venue for tonight's event, was just a hundred yards away. Still, the short distance was enough for a dusting of frost and ice to cling to Hunter's overcoat.

He pushed through the theater's double doors and into the warm foyer. Letting the door swish closed behind him, Hunter scanned the grand foyer. His eyes roamed from the glinting chandelier, and then to the brass decorations and ornate paintings which covered every inch of the walls. Hunter couldn't help but smile. To him, this theater resonated with memories of another time. Walking through those doors, Hunter could picture the men and women who founded their small mountain community.

"No entry until seven," came a gruff voice from somewhere nearby.

Hunter had been so preoccupied enjoying the warmth of the foyer that he hadn't noticed the burly man stalking towards him.

The man wore a suit which barely contained his muscle-bound chest. Hunter gazed up at the man, which was some feat considering the doctor was three inches over six feet tall.

"I'm not a guest," Hunter said, more meekly than he'd intended. "Senator Van Wick has asked me to attend."

The man snarled, resembling a pig devouring its lunch. Rather cruelly, Hunter decided the overall effect made the man appear as though he were auditioning for the leading role in the amateur dramatic society's retelling of Animal Farm. A couple of clip-on ears and he'd be away.

"It's Thorne," the man barked, poking at a radio system attached to one of his ears. "Got a man here who claims to have been invited by the senator."

"I'd rather go home," Hunter mumbled, turning to glance back through the door.

"You're to see the senator in his dressing room," Thorne said, pointing a thick finger towards the back of the foyer. "Follow me."

"Don't trouble yourself," Hunter said, setting off across the carpet. "I know my way around this place."

Hunter found the dressing room in minutes and knocked on the door. The door flew open almost buckling the hinges before Hunter had the chance to lower his hand.

"Doctor Hunter, thank you so much for coming!" Senator Van Wick roared, beaming his world-famous thousand-watt smile. "It's important to me that you are here, today of all days."

The senator reached out and pumped Hunter's hand as though he thought it might produce oil.

"It's my pleasure," Hunter said, trying not to wince as the bones in his wrist rattled together like the strings of a honky-tonk piano. "And senator, please call me Robert."

"Only if you call me Everett," the senator said, pretty much dragging Hunter into the room by the hand.

An ex-sportsman, the senator had kept in good shape since taking office. This evening, his lithe figure moved beneath a perfectly tailored suit.

"Agreed." Hunter appraised the other man with a doctor's gaze and noticed that he had lost weight since their last meeting. Everett Van Wick's square jaw now appeared more chiseled than ever before. His teeth shone like the grille of a Mustang and were almost as wide.

"Would you like a drink, doctor? I mean, Robert." Everett turned the smile on Doctor Hunter.

"Why not," Hunter said. "My day's work is done."

"You surely work far too hard," Everett said, pouring a healthy measure of scotch into two glasses. "You're one of this country's unsung heroes, do you know that?" Everett held out the glass and Hunter accepted it gratefully.

"I get compensated well for my work," Hunter said. "How is it I can help you this evening, senator?" Hunter asked, sipping the scotch.

"You know what politics is about?" the senator said, ignoring Hunter's question.

Hunter chided himself for thinking he could steer a conversation with the senator. Everett Van Wick was an expert on talking about the things he wanted to, at the time that suited him.

"I'll tell you," Van Wick said, pointing a finger at the doctor. "Politics is about connection. A lot of my peers would do well to remember that. That's why, this year, I will travel tirelessly across our great state meeting..."

Hunter dropped into a chair in the corner and settled in for the explanation. He would no doubt learn the reason he was summoned when the Everett was ready to tell him, and not a moment before.

Almost an hour later, Hunter, still none the wiser, stood at the side of the stage along with several other notable people from the town. He greeted the mayor, the chairman of the Rotary Club, and the principal from the local high school.

"You are to stand at the back of the stage during the senator's speech," explained a woman holding a clipboard and wearing a large headset. "Right there." She pointed at four cross-marks on the floor and detailed the order in which the group should stand.

Peering out onto the stage, Hunter noticed the stars and stripes covering almost every inch.

"Please applaud and smile," the woman instructed, as though directing a troop of actors. She checked her watch. "This is an important night for the senator and your town. Places everyone! Curtain up in three minutes!" She clapped her hands several times before disappearing somewhere backstage.

Sure enough, three minutes later, the curtains swung open to reveal the auditorium full of people. Red, white, and blue bunting spanned the auditorium. Standing on his cross-mark, Hunter scanned the crowd. With the dazzling stage lights, he could only see the first three rows, but recognized several people gawking excitedly at the stage.

"Ladies and Gentlemen," the deep voice of an

announcer boomed through the sound system. "Please welcome Senator Everett Van Wick!"

The crowd cheered. The sound of several hundred hands clapping rang through the room.

Hunter and the other local representatives applauded too.

A camera panned across the crowd, while another focused on the stage. Whatever the senator had planned, it was going live across the country.

Senator Van Wick strode onto the stage and the cheering increased.

Some audience members were so excited they leaped to their feet and hollered at the top of their lungs.

The senator waved at the crowd and smiled, his super white teeth glinting beneath the powerful stage lights. Van Wick made several laps of the stage waving and shouting thanks to each section of the audience, then he made his way up to the lectern in the center of the stage.

"Thank you, Leavenworth!" Everett Van Wick said, his voice projecting crisp and deep through the powerful speakers. "What a tremendous honor it is to stand before you today."

The applause intensified, accompanied by cheers and whistles.

Not knowing what else to do, and feeling incredibly out of place, Hunter applauded too. He really hoped not to see himself on the television later, clapping like one of those wind-up monkeys.

But the senator was still not done. He turned this way and that, making sure each part of the audience was dazzled by his grin. Finally, he held up a hand for silence and the audience quickly obeyed.

"I stand here today, not just as your senator but as a

fellow citizen who believes in the power of democracy. Democracy is the lifeblood of our civilization. It means that every person in this country has a chance to shape our future. That is something which has always been incredibly important to me and my family." Everett Van Wick glanced down at his hands on the lectern and remained silent for a moment. Not a single person in the crowd made a sound.

"As such, it is with great honor and humility that I announce my candidacy for the presidency of the United States of America!"

Thunderous applause hammered through the small theater. The crowd's energy rose another notch or two. The applause lasted almost a minute before Everett Van Wick raised his hand to silence the crowd.

"Thank you! Thank you, all!" He turned his head from side to side like a searchlight. "This decision has not come lightly. It results from careful consideration, countless conversations with family, friends, and constituents, and a burning desire to serve this great nation in the highest capacity."

The senator paused and then glanced at Hunter and the others standing beside him.

"Our country stands at a crossroads, facing challenges that demand bold leadership, unwavering principles, and a deep commitment to the American people." His voice took on a deep and serious tone now. "We need a leader who will restore trust, foster unity, and tackle the pressing issues that affect us all."

The crowd sat silently, enraptured by Senator Van Wick's words.

"The time has come to bridge the divides that separate us, to put aside partisan politics and work together for the common good." The senator's fist crashed down against the lectern. "We must rebuild our economy, provide quality education for all, ensure affordable healthcare, combat climate change, and protect the very fabric of our democracy."

Applause erupted again. Hunter applauded too, squinting in the light.

"Together, we can rewrite history," Senator Van Wick said, pointing out at the crowd. "We can, and we will, forge a future where every American has an equal opportunity to succeed, regardless of their background. Together, we can overcome adversity, heal our wounds, and reaffirm the American Dream for generations to come!"

Squinting out at the auditorium, Hunter saw a figure moving in the shadows. At first, he thought it was one of the camera crew, who shuffled around getting shots of the senator and the enraptured crowd, but it wasn't. The figure strode alone and purposefully from the back of the auditorium to the front.

The crowd's applause swelled to a crescendo. People took to their feet, clapping and cheering.

"I invite every one of you to join me on this journey. Together, we will shape a brighter tomorrow, a stronger America."

The figure continued striding towards the stage, pushing through the crowd. The only person not applauding, the figure's hands were tucked out of sight.

Then, watching the figure step into the glow from the stage lights, the blood in Hunter's veins turned as cold as mountain snow.

"Let us restore the ideals upon which this great nation was founded..." Everett continued, still totally fixated on the crowd.

As Hunter watched, the figure in the front row lifted a gun and aimed it squarely at the senator.

The senator continued talking, unaware of the threat so close by.

Hunter shouted, but his voice was lost in the clamor.

The gun roared once, twice, three times, maybe more. The sound cut through auditorium like an icy wind. Then, cheers of joy and excitement merged, almost seamlessly, into cries of fear.

4

The Titanic, Mid-Atlantic. April 15th, 1912.

Marcus Nettleby didn't hear the impact, but he felt it. Lying half asleep in his first-class cabin, he woke with a jolt as the ship lurched from side to side. He fumbled around in the darkness, found his eyeglasses and then the light switch. Nearby something crashed to the floor.

Nettleby mumbled and then blinked several times.

Finally, his eyes came into focus, and he pushed himself upright on the super-soft mattress. Nettleby looked around the room which had been his home for the last five days. The highly polished mahogany furniture shone in the light cast from beneath an ornate lampshade.

Nettleby forced himself to sit up a little straighter. His head swam, most likely from the several cocktails he'd consumed the previous evening. Nettleby had decided, as the ship steamed out of Southampton a few days ago, that since he was being forced to go on this trip, he might as well make the best of it.

Glancing down at the floor, he noticed a tea tray lying beside the remains of two china cups. Although the cups were smashed into several pieces, Nettleby could see the 'White Star Line' logo, proudly displayed like a coat of arms.

"Funny," he muttered. "I didn't feel a storm. I'll get that cleaned up in the morning." With that, he switched off the light, turned over in the bed and let the hazy feeling of the alcohol in his bloodstream wash him back into oblivion.

What felt like two minutes later, Nettleby was awake again. This time he sat bolt upright. His eyes jolted open as though someone had placed an explosive device beneath each lid. An alarm sounded through the ship, and he felt the reverberations of movement through the superstructure.

"What's going on now?" Nettleby murmured. He staggered out of bed and dressed in the same clothes he'd been wearing the day before.

Opening the door, bleary-eyed and a little unsteady on his feet, Nettleby stepped out into the corridor. The occupants of the cabin next door were already out of their room and making their way towards the deck.

Nettleby grabbed the arm of a steward who was rushing the opposite way down the passage.

"What's going on?" Nettleby said, positioning himself in the steward's path. "What's all this racket in the middle of the night?"

"We've had the order to abandon ship, sir," the steward said, his complexion almost as pale as the *Lady of Leone*. "Please get the lifejacket from your cabin and report to the main deck." The steward scuttled down the passage before Nettleby could ask another question.

Nettleby swayed forward and backward, the steward's words resonating in his ears like a death knell.

"But... but... I thought that was impossible," Nettleby said to himself, barely able to take a breath.

Then a new panic seized him and all at once Nettleby felt his mind focus and his balance return.

"The *Lady of Leone*," he said, startling a couple who shuffled past already in their lifejackets. "I can't leave her here, she must..." Nettleby's voice caught in his throat. He scrabbled around in his jacket, finally removing the key — the only key which unlocked the case in which the *Lady of Leone* was ensconced.

Not wasting another moment, Nettleby charged down the passage leaving the door of his cabin open. He took the stairs two at a time and pushed out on to the deck. Cold whipped around him, instantly causing his face to flush and making him wish he'd brought his overcoat. The deck, which for the last few days had been a stately promenade, now was a scene of panic. The ship, which had always seemed as indomitable as the streets of London, now tilted a few degrees to the bow.

A series of shouts boomed from the side of the vessel as a lifeboat was lowered into the water. The lights strung between the funnels flickered, eliciting a cry from the passengers.

Nettleby charged on, ignoring the line for the next lifeboat. Almost slipping on the wet deck, he narrowly avoided crashing into a distraught woman, clutching her children close by, all pale with terror.

Reaching the center of the ship, Nettleby passed a string quartet. Instead of rushing to save their own lives, the men were playing as calmly and perfectly as they had every night of the voyage so far. The melody, when juxtaposed with the panicked cries of desperate passengers, and rumbles of the doomed ship, sounded strangely haunting.

Nettleby flung open the doors for the central staircase and ran through. Inside, the grand central staircase curved its way up towards the restaurants and down towards the staterooms and then deeper towards the hold. Without a break in his stride, sweat now pouring forth despite the cold, Nettleby headed down. Taking three steps with each stride, he pushed passed a group of people hustling the other way, their gaze hard with fear.

Nettleby's eyes had the same deer in the headlights appearance, although for very different reasons.

"Move out of the..." he roared at three sobbing women who shuffled along in their bulky lifejackets.

Nettleby didn't get to finish his sentence as at that moment, the ship lurched to one side causing the grand chandelier which hung in the stairwell to slam against the balustrade. Breaking crystal tinkled and chimed before ribbons of razor-sharp glass flew like confetti at a wedding.

The ship lurched back the other way, righting itself. The chandelier swung again. This time the movement was too much, and the grand light fixture came free from its mountings. The light flickered and died and then the whole assembly of crystal and steel fell towards the staircase bottom.

"Get out of the way," Nettleby roared, his pulse now hammering like the engines of the stricken liner.

A moment later, the sound of half a ton of crystal glass slamming against the floor — part jingle, part roar, part crunch — resounded through the ship.

Nettleby peered nervously across the balustrade. The chandelier lay in ruins several floors below, its hanging crystal jewels returned to their origins as nothing more than grains. People watched, frozen in shock. Fortunately, no one had been crushed beneath the fixture.

Nettleby hurried on, again forcing himself further into the ship's ruptured guts. He pushed past another group of people, shuffling their way out of a stateroom. Nettleby glanced at the abandoned luxury inside the room. Photographs, paintings, and expensive clothes lay strewn everywhere — all forgotten in the occupants' mad dash for safety. Even the wealthiest people knew that when it came down to life and death, physical things didn't matter at all.

Nettleby charged on. He reached the end of the stateroom corridor, threw open a door and clanged down a metal staircase. After descending three levels, he unbolted a steel door and stepped into a narrow corridor of third-class cabins.

Nettleby paused, shocked to see twenty, thirty, maybe even fifty people waiting in the corridor beside their doors. Each had a lifejacket tied tightly around them and were listening for news through the ship's speaker system.

With a welling anger, Nettleby realized exactly what was going on. The ship's crew were keeping these people locked down here until all first-class passengers were on board the lifeboats.

"Get out of here!" Nettleby roared, holding open the door which he noticed could only be opened from the outside. He pointed up the staircase and shouted directions to the main deck. Then, pushing against the crowd, Nettleby hurried on.

At the end of the passage, Nettleby glanced over his shoulder as the last of the passengers ran upstairs.

"Good luck," he whispered, already realizing how scant their chances of survival were.

Nettleby turned back to the door at the end of the third-class corridor. Having memorized the route on his first day aboard, he knew he was getting close. In fact, he had checked on his cargo twice a day during the voyage.

He pushed through the door and into another stairwell, this one only big enough for the steep stairs to zigzag their way between the decks. Here in the belly of the ship, stairwells and corridors were constructed from white-painted steel, the mahogany and brass being reserved for the upper decks.

Like the cry of a waking giant, a rumble passed through the hull. Nettleby stopped and clung on to the balustrade.

The ship lurched forward, stumbling like a drunk man on icy streets of winter London. For a heartbeat, Nettleby thought about London, his home city. In his mind's eye, he pictured the gleaming streets and bustling markets. He saw the Thames slipping her way towards the estuary, topped by steamboats and barges, all fighting against the tide.

He stayed in the memory for a long moment, remembering fondly those days when he would leave his office at the British Museum and amble down to the river. That was the perfect place to clear his head and think.

Then Nettleby thought about the *Lady of Leone*. If he'd known how much trouble she'd cause, perhaps he would have thrown her in that river to begin with.

"Maybe she's cursed after all," the curator whispered. He released his grip on the balustrade and descended again. There had been strange talk about such things in the places she'd been examined first. Strange goings on and unexplained accidents.

"Nonsense," Nettleby hissed as the lurching ship dragged him from his thoughts. He stumbled to the left and crashed into the wall. He held on for a few moments, his heart climbing its way into his throat.

The lights flickered off, plunging the stairwell into the deepest darkness Nettleby had ever experienced. The complete absence of light made him realize he must already be beneath the waterline. Nettleby's breath made the sound of a speeding steam train. For a fleeting moment, Nettleby wondered whether he would ever see the surface again.

5

Leavenworth, Washington State. Present Day.

AFTER HIS TIME in the Medical Corps, Hunter knew a gunshot when he heard one and reacted instantly. As the shots boomed over the uproar of the auditorium, Doctor Hunter ran towards the senator.

Everett Van Wick staggered backward, his expression a mix of fear, pain, and confusion. He clutched his hands to the side of his stomach. Blood blossomed across his suit.

The crowd leaped to its feet in a state of panic, and surged toward the exits, inhibiting the progress of the security personnel trying to force their way towards the stage.

The two security guards on the stage stepped forward with guns raised and fired at the shooter.

Hunter glanced at the shooter. He saw the young man clearly as several bullets tore through his body. One bullet ripped through the guy's forehead, assassination style, and he fell, lifeless to the floor.

Hunter raced towards the senator.

Everett dropped to his knees and gazed up at the ceiling, his eyes bulging.

Hunter reached the fallen senator. He pulled away the senator's jacket to examine the wound. Blood soaked through his shirt.

Screams and the pounding of frightened feet boomed through the theater. The crowd was still in panic mode, despite the shooter having been savagely neutralized.

"Move back," Hunter shouted, signaling for people to give him the space he needed. "Give me some room."

People parted, creating a small circle around the senator.

Hunter pulled a handkerchief from his pocket and pressed it firmly against the wound. The fabric was instantly blood-soaked.

"I'm going to need a cloth, something bigger than this."

The stage manager reacted first, running to one of the dressing rooms to fetch a towel.

Hunter grabbed the towel and swapped it for his handkerchief. Instinctively, Hunter slipped the now blood-soaked cloth back inside his pocket.

"Bring me the first aid kit," he shouted at the stage manager. "Is there a defibrillator here? We might need it."

Without a word, her clipboard and headset now abandoned somewhere, the stage manager rushed off.

Hunter glanced up to see two of the senator's security team standing over him. One of them was the pig-like thug who had challenged Hunter's entry to the theater.

"Don't just stand there," Hunter roared. "Call the medics. The senator has sustained a serious injury."

A gurgling noise came from Everett's lips.

"Sir, I need you to stay conscious," Hunter said, assessing crumpled figure of the man who, just minutes ago, had entranced several hundred people. "I'm going to help you as best I can, but I need you to stay with me, okay?"

Everett Van Wick nodded.

Hunter beckoned the big security guy over. "Thorne, that's your name, isn't it?"

The guy nodded and lumbered to Hunter's side.

"We need to control the bleeding! Apply pressure here with the towel." Hunter moved his hand aside and the hulking bodyguard knelt.

"Where is that ambulance?" Hunter roared. "We don't have time for this!"

No longer having to apply pressure to the wound, Hunter assessed the situation. He noticed the entry wound just below the Everett's ribcage. Time was running out for this man.

Everett's eyes fluttered and then closed.

"Sir, you must try to stay awake. It's very important you stay awake," Hunter said.

The stage manager re-appeared with a first aid kit the size of a shoebox. Hunter tore it open and rummaged through the contents. There were a few gauze pads, latex gloves, band aids printed with pictures of cartoon characters, and a cleaning solution. "What am I supposed to do with this?" Hunter hissed, throwing the box to one side.

Hunter head a distant hiss from Thorne's in-ear comms device.

"Emergency crew is ten minutes out," Thorne said, with the urgency someone might use to order a pizza. "There was a traffic accident on the mountain on the other side of town. Now with the weather, they're struggling to get back."

Now it was Hunter's time to pale. His gaze moved from Thorne's piggish eyes to Everett Van Wick's almost lifeless body. Hunter knew for certain that without proper medical care, Everett would be dead before ten minutes was out. Hunter glanced around, his mind on overdrive. He had to save the senator. He had to do it now.

"There's no time to wait for the medics," Hunter said, his voice more confident than he felt. "We need to get the senator to my clinic. It's one minute from the theater. I have the equipment to treat him there."

"No. Protocol says we wait for the medical team," Thorne said, indicating that another man should take over applying pressure to the wound.

Thorne stood and stepped towards Hunter. "You've done your best, doctor. I'm in charge. We wait."

Hunter stood to his full height, which was about level with Thorne's chin.

"I'll say this again, just in case you didn't understand it," Hunter shouted at Thorne, his voice filling the whole auditorium. "If we wait ten minutes, this man will be dead. He needs medical attention now."

"That isn't protocol," Thorne said, as though reading from a script. "We wait for the medics."

Hunter stepped closer to Thorne and stood on the balls of his feet so that he was yelling in the guy's weirdly shaped ear. "I'll say this once more, and once more only, the senator will be dead in ten minutes. The only way to save him is to get him to my clinic *now*."

Other than Hunter's voice, the theater was silent. Countless eyes watched Thorne to see if he would disagree.

Hunter heard the tiniest hiss come from Thorne in-ear comms. Thorne snarled, the expression making him appear even more hoggish than usual.

"Fine," Thorne snorted. "But we will stay with you the entire time."

Thorne commanded two men to stay in the theater.

Thorne and three others would go with Hunter and the senator.

"The stage door will be the best route," Hunter said, crouching down beside Everett. Hunter turned to the man holding the towel against the wound. "I'll take over here now. You help with the lift."

Hunter took the towel. Everett's blood flow had slowed almost completely. A bad feeling rose in Hunter's stomach. His chance of survival was thin at best.

Thorne and three other men surrounded Everett and lifted him with ease. Hunter took over applying pressure to the wound. Together they carried the injured man out through the theater's side door. The small brigade carried Everett Van Wick down the sidewalk and stopped outside Hunter's clinic.

"Press here," Hunter commanded one man, as he fished out his key and unlocked the door. He led the team into the clinic and instructed them to lay Everett on the bed.

"Keep pressure on that wound," Hunter shouted, replacing the towel with a gauze pad. Hunter rushed around the room, collecting the necessary supplies.

He passed a pair of round-ended scissors to one man. "Cut away the senator's clothing. I need to see the wound."

Hunter ran to the fridge at the far side of the clinic. "He's lost a lot of blood, I'm going to do an emergency transfusion. Do you know what blood type he is?"

"No transfusions," Thorne said, stepping alongside Hunter.

Hunter narrowed his eyes, trying to assess whether Thorne was actually serious.

"This is not the time to be messing around," Hunter said. "The senator has lost several pints of blood. Do I need to explain to you why blood is important?"

"The senator is stronger than you think," Thorne snarled. "Just patch him up."

"No," Hunter said, crouching and grabbing a pouch of blood from the refrigerator. "If I don't do this, he will die."

Hunter stood up, the pouch of blood in his hands.

Thorne stepped in between Hunter and the senator. "I'm in charge here. No transfusions."

"This is no time for your schoolboy games." Anger bubbled his Hunter's veins. "Grow up and get out of my way. I have a life to save."

Thorne grabbed the pouch of blood from Hunter's hands with enough force to knock the doctor off his feet. Hunter crashed against the cabinet behind him.

Thorne threw the pouch against the wall. The pouch burst, spraying blood all over the wall and floor.

"No transfusions," Thorne roared, his small eyes riveting into Hunter's. "Patch him up and we get out of here."

Hunter took a deep breath. Anger and shock reeled through his body. He calmed himself and accepted that whether he liked it or not, there was no way he could perform a transfusion without this idiot's agreement.

"Fine," Hunter snarled. "But you are severely limiting his chances of survival."

Hunter stepped up to the senator and assessed his vitals. He still had a pulse, although it was incredibly weak.

Hunter washed his hands and then put on a pair of sterile gloves. He gathered the equipment he needed and placed it on a tray beside the patient. When he was ready, he instructed the man who had been applying pressure to the wound to stand back.

Thorne stood two paces away, watching Hunter's every move.

Using forceps, Hunter explored the wound. As he had

initially thought, the bullet had struck Everett's stomach, about an inch below the rib cage. Fortunately, it didn't appear to have ruptured any internal organs or bones.

Hunter used tweezers to remove the bullet, then threaded a needle and closed the wound. His hands moved steadily, not indicating for a moment the frustration he felt, or the situation's high pressure.

Stitch by stitch and minute by minute, the wound closed. Finally, Hunter tied off the last knot and re-checked the senator's vitals.

The man was alive, just.

The door crashed open, and the emergency medics barged into the room.

"About time," Thorne sneered, quickly briefing the medics on the situation.

One of the medic's examined Hunter's work. "Good work doctor," she said. "You might well have saved the senator's life."

6

The Titanic, Mid-Atlantic. April 15th, 1912.

As quickly as they'd died, the lights came back on.

Nettleby blinked. Colors danced across his vision.

A scream echoed up the stairwell, followed by footsteps below him.

Nettleby continued his descent, passing a man coming the other way. The man carried a small black suitcase, not dissimilar to Nettleby's own. The suitcase had been jammed shut in such a hurry that clothes trailed from the seam. The man scurried up the stairs two at a time, his clanging footsteps quickly fading into the noise of the grumbling ship.

Nettleby finally reached the floor he required. He swung open the bulkhead door and stepped through. Then, he froze. His shoes slipped across the floor and then ground completely to a halt.

A chill moved up Nettleby's spine, freezing each vertebra before moving on to the next.

At first, Nettleby wasn't sure he was seeing correctly. He shook his head and squinted.

What his eyes were telling him just seemed so bizarre. He blinked hard, as though the movement would somehow change reality. It didn't. The vision remained unaffected.

Moving like an eyeless monster, a finger of seawater slipped beneath a door at the end of the passage. The water moved with a serpentine gait, as though licking, tasting, and feeling its way out into the passage.

Nettleby watched the liquid slither with a menacing, almost absurd tranquility, in his direction. The liquid glimmered in the flickering lights, as though it was mercury rather than water.

Nettleby forced himself forwards. His Italian-made leather shoes splashed through the water. His feet instantly felt like blocks of ice in the unfathomable cold. He approached the door at the end of the passageway and eyed the *'no admittance'* sign.

For the time it took one of *Titanic's* great engines to complete a revolution, Nettleby considered what he was doing. He wondered whether he should just turn around and head to the lifeboats. That way, there was a chance, albeit a slim one, that he could get out of here alive.

Once again, he thought about his important cargo. *The Lady of Leone.* If she went down, then so would he. He considered the ridiculousness of it all. Even if he got to her, there was no way he could get her to the top deck and on to a boat — not with thousands of the living fighting for a space.

Nettleby turned around. Running at least a hundred feet through the belly of the great ship, the passage rose behind him. The angle made it seem as though time and space had warped in on itself.

Nettleby turned back to the door. His nerves hardened.

He stepped up to the door and twisted the handle. Deep within the steel, the mechanism clunked.

Nettleby swung open the door and a foot high wave of water swept out into the passage. The wave swept over Nettleby's knees, forcing him to take a step backwards. Nettleby hadn't even considered the danger of water held back behind the closed door. That could have been a lot worse.

Nettleby suppressed a shiver and stepped over the threshold. He glanced around the cavernous hold. Boxes and crates, ranging from a couple of feet square to the size of cars, loomed above the water. Fortunately, the lights were still operational and bathed the space in a sepia-toned glow.

Nettleby splashed on, walking his practiced route by memory alone. The further he moved into the hold, the higher the water rose. As he approached the rear of the hold, water lapped across his stomach. Nettleby shivered uncontrollably now, his jaw chattering so hard he was in real danger of dislodging teeth.

He splashed forward a few more paces and saw his target. The steel crate with *British Museum* printed across the sides.

Nettleby waded forward, struggling against the flow of the water which now lapped around his stomach. He reached the crate and examined it closely. Fortunately, the crate's upper edge was still a few inches above the water. The crate's heavy construction had prevented it from floating around and it was still in good condition with no signs of damage.

Previously on the voyage, with no desire to upset the *Lady of Leone* any more than necessary, Nettleby had only checked the crate externally.

Now, though, he longed to see inside. Fortunately, the crate opened from the top, allowing the lady to be placed inside like a casket. Nettleby was confident that he could open the case and check the contents with no water spilling through.

He removed the key from his pocket, unlocked and removed the padlock. Then he curled his fingers around the edges of the lid and heaved. The lid didn't budge.

Another shudder moved through the ship's superstructure, followed by an earsplitting groan. For a second, Nettleby feared that pressure on the hull had reached such a point the whole vessel would split in two. The lights flickered but stayed on.

Nettleby heaved against the lid again, but the thing just wouldn't budge. Back in the museum, it was placed in position by a team of strong men. Now, the diminutive Nettleby was trying to open it alone.

Nettleby scowled but refused to be beaten. He glanced around for something to help pry open the lid. A Rolls Royce Silver Ghost sat on the other side of the hold, water already covering the wheels. For the briefest moment, Nettleby thought about the car's owner, fighting for their lives somewhere nearby.

Nettleby splashed across to the Silver Ghost and popped the trunk. Fortunately, the thing wasn't locked. The trunk was almost pitch-black inside, forcing Nettleby to search with his fingers. The water had yet to reach inside the trunk. At the back of the space, Nettleby's fingers struck something cold and metallic. He pulled the object forward. It was a small toolbox, still gleaming and new like the car.

Nettleby flipped open the lid and found a tire iron. The iron in hand, he splashed back across to the crate.

The water had risen another inch now, reaching Nettleby's chest.

"If I was six-feet tall, this wouldn't be a problem," Nettleby moaned, finding the whole thought strangely amusing. He half-swam, half-walked back toward his important cargo, pushing a pair of floating suitcases to one side.

Nettleby reached the crate and slotted the tire iron beneath the lid. Progress was made more difficult by the streaming water and the cold.

"Come on." Nettleby clenched his teeth to stop them from chattering. With an inordinate show of strength, he popped the lid. The breaking seal sounded like a champagne cork.

Three stacked crates at the far end of the hold toppled and splashed into the water.

Nettleby shuffled around to the next corner and repeated the process. For several minutes he moved around the crate, loosening the corners. Finally, using all the strength he could muster, Nettleby heaved the lid out of its position. He stopped pushing and checked the results. The lid had moved about one inch. Nettleby peered inside but couldn't see a thing.

"I'm afraid we won't make it to New York after all," Nettleby said soothingly.

The ship groaned once more, and the sound of water ingress increased.

Straining back against the crate, Nettleby managed to shift the lid another two inches. He pushed his arm through and swept aside the packing straw which lay on top of his cargo.

Then a realization hit him. He froze to the core.

"No way," he muttered, a strange wolfish grin lighting his face. "That just makes no sense."

But then, slowly at first, like the movement of the tilting ship, it made perfect sense.

"This is only delaying the inevitable." Nettleby set about resealing the crate and closing the padlock.

Then, all at once, the lights went out.

7

Dragontail Peak, Chelan County, Washington State. Present Day.

"Are you sure this is a good idea?" Eden shouted over the roar of the Eurocopter's rotors. Still a couple of miles away, the thick snow of Dragontail Peak shone through the window in the first light of the new day. A steep band of snow curved down the mountain, only broken by rocky outcrops, jutting out like broken teeth.

"Hit one of those, and you'd have more than broken teeth to worry about," Eden muttered to herself.

Nestled amongst the rugged beauty of Washington State, the mountain was both a challenge and a warning at the same time.

"It's a great idea," Athena said from beside her. "You've been ski-training for months now. You said yourself that even the double blacks were getting boring."

"I might have said that, but this is something else." Eden pointed a thumb at the mountain.

"It's not like you to be having second thoughts," Baxter said, laughing from the pilot's seat.

Eden grumbled a reply.

"You think you've been learning to ski so that you can have a fun weekend on the slopes?" Baxter said.

"Well, I thought that was part of it," Eden muttered.

The Eurocopter thundered over the icy waters of a lake and then banked high over a cluster of shivering pine trees. The rocky flank of Dragontail Peak filled the windshield now.

"But we need to be ready for anything," Baxter said, deftly working the chopper's controls. "Who knows, the next threat to The Council might involve a daring mountain escape. It's important that we're always prepared."

"Yes dad," Eden said, rolling her eyes. "Remind me why I signed up for this again?"

Athena smirked from the seat beside her.

"Reaching the drop off point in two minutes," Baxter said. "You know the drill?"

"Sure do. Make sure you're home by dusk and don't talk to strangers." Eden climbed from the seat and slid open the Eurocopter's side door. Fifty feet beneath the chopper's landing gear, jagged fingers of rock clawed through the puffy snow.

"Keep the comms active. Any issues, I'll be right there," Baxter said, slowing the chopper as they reached the top of a great tongue of snow and ice, which swept down the mountainside.

The chopper descended until they were hovering just a few feet above the snow. The craft's powerful down-draft whipped powder in great spirals seriously reducing the visibility.

"Don't hang around, or there'll be no snow left," Athena said.

Eden pulled on her ski goggles and then scrambled down until she was sitting one of the chopper's skids. Athena passed down her skis one by one and Eden clicked them into position.

"Remember, this is a training exercise," Baxter said, now just audible through the comms. "Although, of course, it's dangerous. Don't take any unnecessary risks."

Athena scrambled down beside Eden. The women shared a smirk.

"Who are you to be talking about unnecessary risks? You'll be nice and cozy in your chopper."

Athena grabbed her skis and deftly clipped them into place.

"What I mean is that we want you back in one piece!"

"Yes, dad!" Eden and Athena said in unison.

"You ready for this?" Athena said to Eden.

"Absolutely," Eden said. "Last one in the bar buys the drinks." Eden leaped from the chopper and out into the void.

She plummeted, the downdraft from the chopper and the spiraling snow whipping at her face. Then, the snow rose to meet her, slamming into the underside of her skis. Eden instinctively dropped into a crouch to absorb the fall. The shockwave from the impact moved up through her legs, providing a momentary reminder of how small she was against this giant lump of rock and ice. Sure, this was a training exercise, but things could go wrong at any point.

Athena thumped down into the snow a few feet away.

"Clear," Eden said into the comms. "See you at the bottom."

The pounding of the Eurocopter's rotors increased and

the great machine powered away, banking hard and then following the mountain's slope down.

As the powder settled around them, Eden scanned the rugged undulations of Washington State's famous mountain ridges. The sun had broken free of the peaks now and bathed the scene in a milky, rose-tinted half-light. Her breath fogged in the icy air.

"Beautiful, isn't it?" Athena said, sliding up beside Eden.

The sound of the chopper's engine faded into the silence. All Eden could hear was the murmur of the wind and the crunch of snow as she shifted from foot to foot.

"It really is," Eden agreed.

"Don't let that..."

"Catch you off guard," Eden interrupted, finishing the other woman's sentence. It was a phrase she'd heard Athena use many times in the past. It was a phrase that Eden knew to be correct. Nature was a powerful force, and respect had to be taken.

"Shall we?" Athena said, pointing a gloved hand down the slope.

"Absolutely." Eden stabbed her poles deep into the snow and shoved herself forward.

The skis slipped few inches before grinding to a stop. Eden dug the poles in again and pulled herself forward. The muscles in her arms and legs tingled with the exertion and her heart beat with the ferocity of a war drum. Again, the skis slipped forward a foot or two, before crunching to a stop.

Eden scowled, her steely gaze locked on the glimmering surface of a lake several hundred feet below. She pulled the poles free from the snow and leaned forward, further than before. She jabbed the poles deep into the snow, then she swung herself forward with all the force she could muster.

Her skis slid across the snow, but this time didn't stop. In fact, this time, the skis shot forward as though powered by a rocket.

Eden yanked the poles free from the snow and settled into a crouch. Having spent a lot of time on the slopes as a child, Eden had already been comfortable with most graded slopes. With excellent balance and a fearless streak, the younger Eden would frequently leave her father a quivering wreck as she bombed down black and double-black slopes with ease.

Now, with several months of intense training behind her, she was ready for a real challenge.

Eden accelerated hard, the mountainside blurring into a whirlwind of white. Ice bit against her face, tingling her skin, despite the gaiter she had pulled up to just beneath her goggles.

Up ahead the tongue of snow passed between two jagged columns of rock.

Eden swung into several tight turns, her skis biting into the snow. The movement lined her up with the narrow gap between the towering outcrops and slowed her descent. Colliding with either of those rocky shards would cause, at best, several broken bones.

Eden pulled one more turn and then zipped through the gap. The rocks shot past in less than a heartbeat. Eden glanced at one of them, its jagged wall just two feet from her body.

Back in the open, Eden pulled into another series of turns and took the moments they afforded her to check out the terrain ahead. The incline had reduced now as they approached the mountain's lower slopes. The snow was wide but undulating. Just to make things a little more difficult, icy trees poked out at all angles, some rising just a foot or two above the powder.

Plunging downwards, Eden prepared for the bumpy ride. She weathered the first few bumps with ease, using the undulations to leap totally free of the snow.

No sooner had the bumpy terrain begun, than it ended with a wide snow-covered plateau.

Eden stared ahead but couldn't see what lay beyond the untouched snow.

She knew what was coming next, though. The Dragon's Fang was a sheer cliff, jutting out over a sheer drop. Thoughts of the drop caused Eden's adrenaline to spike anew, her heart beat like the pounding of Baxter's helicopter blades. There were two ways to take the Dragon's Fang. Either you approached slowly and navigated the thin paths around the drop, or you took the drop straight on and fell through thirty clear feet of nothing before landing in the snow below.

"Slow down and head to the right. We'll take the paths from here." Athena's voice hissed in Eden's ear. She was so caught up in the descent's thrill that she'd almost forgotten about Athena making her way down the slope behind. Eden stole a glance over her shoulder and saw the other woman cutting a wide arc just forty feet away.

Eden turned back toward the precipice, two-hundred feet ahead. She angled her skis as though to slow down, then felt a bolt of adrenaline shudder through the body. She wasn't here to take things the easy way. The safe way wasn't how Eden Black did things. Not now, not ever.

"Start slowing now, Eden," Athena's voice came again. "We're almost there!"

Eden blocked out the noise and, her mind now made up, tucked herself into a compact position. Her acceleration was instantaneous, gravity tearing her down the untainted snow. The precipice drew closer and closer.

Athena's voice came again through Eden's headset, but Eden didn't hear the words.

Eden's eyes narrowed and her muscles tensed. She flew forward like a human missile. She reached the edge of the plateau and shot into the air. The snow dropped away beneath her feet. She flew for what felt like a long time; gravity, for once choosing to turn a blind eye.

Then gravity caught up, pulling her downwards. Eden refused to look down, keeping her eyes locked on a small cottage about half a mile away. She dropped into a crouch and prepared for the landing. Her skis hit the ground, and she absorbed the impact with her knees. A cloud of white powder billowed around her.

Buzzing from adrenaline and excitement, Eden sliced into an arc and slowed just in time to see Athena follow suit. The other woman shot from the cliff, a picture of grace and poise.

Athena thudded gently to the snow and slid to a stop beside Eden. Athena shook her head and pulled off her goggles. The pair locked eyes.

"I know, that was stupid," Eden said, before Athena had the chance to speak.

"Great fun, though," Athena said, glancing up at the slope, winding its way up the now distant peak. "Let's get back and get some breakfast."

Then another sound jarred up the slope. This wasn't the sound of skiers out enjoying themselves, or even the sound of the approaching helicopter. It was a sound that Eden and Athena knew well. All too well.

Gunshots.

8

The Van Wick Estate, Near Bellingham, Washington State.

Ludwig Van Wick worked the control of his electric wheelchair, humming through the grand rooms of the family's country estate. As usual, the house was dark. The curtains were drawn, and what illumination there was, came from heavily shaded lamps scattered here and there.

Van Wick turned into the main hall, which ran like a spine through the house. Humming across the wooden floors, he passed countless large paintings of the previous leaders of the Van Wick family. Each of the men gazed proudly across the hallway, as though stewarding the family from beyond the grave.

As he normally did when passing his forefathers, Van Wick slowed his chair and eyed the men. He reached the last picture and clicked back on the control, allowing the chair to stop completely. He turned and considered the painting. Johannes Van Wijk — who later Americanized the spelling of their name — was the first of the family to cross the North Atlantic and start their new life in America. Van Wick knew better than anyone how much they owed to the courage of Johannes Van Wijk.

In the painting, Johannes was represented as a powerful man, with piercing blue eyes and rugged features. His brown shoulder length hair was pulled back, and he wore 17th-century Dutch attire which included a high-collared white shirt, a deep blue velvet doublet with gold buttons, breeches, and a pair of tall leather boots.

He was every bit the Van Wick patriarch that his sons, grandsons, and great-grandson aspired to be.

Van Wick Senior, as he was known to his family, Ludwig to his business interests, sighed and thought about the day when he too would make it into the family's vast hall of fame. He had already appointed an artist who was going to paint him standing on his own two legs on top of a mountain — that's how he wanted to be remembered.

"Sir, Everett is asking for you," a voice cut through Ludwig Van Wick's day dream. He swung the chair around and saw one of the family's many assistants running towards him.

"What does he want now?" The old man snarled to himself.

"He wants to talk to you about something of great urgency," the assistant said, reaching Van Wick Senior.

"Fine," Van Wick said. He spun the wheelchair around and set off toward the family infirmary. Reaching the end of the corridor, a door swung open automatically, letting Van Wick Senior pass through without slowing his progress.

The bright lights in this room made the old man blink, his grey eyes watering as they constantly did.

Ludwig pulled back on the joystick and the wheelchair slowed. A strange contrast of past and present, Van Wick

Senior found the family infirmary to be strangely unsettling. The stark white walls in here stood in sharp contrast to the plush, dark woods of the rest of the mansion. Rows of steel cabinets lined the sides, their surfaces reflecting the glare of lights which were far too bright.

On one side of the room, a long counter held an array of modern medical equipment and computers.

In the center of the room sat a state-of-the-art medical bed, with various wires and tubes strung to a plethora of surrounding machines.

Ludwig Van Wick glanced at his son, Everett, who was sitting up on the bed, his powerful physique still visible beneath the white hospital gown.

Everett laid down the tablet computer on which he was working and smiled softly at his father.

Ignoring his son altogether, Van Wick Senior turned to a rakish grey-haired man who poked at one of the medical monitors at the side of the room.

"Doctor Vos, what's his condition?"

The man spun around and pushed his thick spectacles further up his nose. Doctor Vos had served as the Van Wick family physician for as long as anyone could remember. He had a mop of white hair, which always seemed to contrast his face's purple hue.

Doctor Vos took a deep breath, clearly collecting his thoughts before he addressed his demanding employer. When he spoke, his voice was little more than a whisper.

"Everett sustained a gunshot wound to his lower left abdomen. Fortunately, the bullet missed all the major organs and vital arteries. It caused some internal bleeding, which we have controlled." Vos thumbed his eyeglasses. "He lost a lot of blood and I have to tell you, if he hadn't received good medical attention at the scene, the outlook wouldn't be so... well... favorable."

Ludwig nodded, his face scrunched together in concentration. "How long will he be like this?" Van Wick pointed disdainfully at his son.

"He's on some strong antibiotics. The wound has been successfully treated and he's had a full scan to check no bullet fragments remain. With full rest and care, he should make a full recovery."

"That's not what I asked," Ludwig spat. "I know he will make a full recovery. I asked how long we should expect him to be like... like this." The father flicked a dismissing wrist towards his son.

"It's... it's hard to tell exactly," Doctor Vos said nervously. "As you know, the body is a complicated thing and it can't be rushed."

"It can't be rushed! Ha!" Ludwig Van Wick barked out a humorless laugh. "You're telling me everything needs to be on hold for his body to play ball? No way! We need him ready for the speech tomorrow."

Doctor Vos pushed his spectacles up his nose again and made a noise as though he were about to speak.

Van Wick gazed up at the other man and wondered why, with all the money they'd paid him over the years, he didn't get spectacles that actually fit.

"With all due respect, sir," Doctor Vos said, finally finding his tongue. "I don't consider that to be a good idea. Master Van Wick has just been through a major ordeal. He needs rest."

"Not possible." Ludwig crashed a fist down against the arm of his chair. "Think about the headlines. The world will be watching. Make sure it happens. Now, leave us."

Doctor Vos looked as though he were about to say something but then thought better of it. He bowed his head and ran from the room.

Ludwig Van Wick flicked the wheelchair's control and zipped over towards his son.

"You *will* be fine by tomorrow," he said.

Despite the pain in Everett's eyes, his chiseled jaw was set firm.

"You've got that look about you, hard, resilient." Ludwick Van Wick pointed at the intravenous lines which ran into his son's forearm, supplying him with a cocktail of drugs to aid his recovery. "You'll have to get off these drugs. But Doctor Vos can dose you up with something before the speech. You'll feel great."

"I don't feel great now," Everett said, his voice weak. "As Doctor Vos said, I am lucky. I would be dead if it wasn't for the work of Doctor Hunter."

Ludwig Van Wick pointed up at his son with a bent finger. "You know what people will think? They will think that you look like a hero. You'll wow the crowds on stage tomorrow. We are going to turn this assassination attempt into the biggest media frenzy of the twenty-first century." Ludwig nodded, impressed with his own idea.

"Sure. Some pain medication, and I think I'll be fine," Everett said, the confidence not making it to his voice. "But listen, I want a thank you to Doctor Hunter written into the speech, okay? It's important, without him, I wouldn't have made it."

"Ha! You want me to send him a bunch of flowers, maybe some chocolates too?" Disdain laced the older man's voice.

"Father, I'm serious. If it wasn't for him, we wouldn't even be having this conversation."

"I'm serious too. No such thing will happen. It's not

possible." Van Wick pulled his wheelchair backward. "The speech is already written. We will not waste one of your biggest campaign opportunities on some... some nobody."

"Father, you don't understand. Without him, I would have died. Without him, there would be no campaign, no speech, nothing."

Ludwig Van Wick inspected his son for a long second. "I wasn't going to tell you, but since you keep bringing it up, the doctor is going to have to be dealt with."

"What do you mean?" Everett hissed, the strength returning to his voice. "He is a hero. What are you talking about?"

The older man raised a twisted finger to silence his son. "First, remember who you are speaking to. I am your father, not some high school friend, have some respect. Second, he knows too much. He is a loose end. You are about to enter a presidential campaign, and we can have no loose ends."

Everett Van Wick's face became even paler than before. He lurched forward in the bed and tried to reach for his father, but Van Wick Senior slid out of the way.

Everett's face contorted with the pain of movement.

"He is a good man. He saved my life," Everett said again, his voice straining.

"And he will be remembered as a good man," his father replied, as though talking to a child. "He will be remembered as a good man who gave his all, and then was the victim of a tragic accident. Now you heard what Doctor Vos said. Get some rest."

With that, Ludwig Van Wick sped out of the room.

9

DOCTOR ROBERT HUNTER awoke with a start. He sucked in several quick breaths as his eyes registered where he was. He was in his bed, a thick bar of light streaming in through his curtains.

"What time is it?" he muttered out loud, rolling over and grabbing his phone from the nightstand. He squinted at the screen, colors dancing in front of his vision. Finally, his eyes focused.

"Seven am! Damn!" He scrambled out of bed, still wearing his shirt and underwear from the evening before.

He was scheduled to see a patient before his clinic opened today, and with the weather as unpredictable as it was, the journey into Leavenworth could sometimes take an hour.

Hunter rushed through to the bathroom and started the shower. Then he raced to the kitchen and powered up the coffee machine. Even if the coffee made him two minutes later, the thought of a day without his required stimulant made Hunter want to crawl back into bed. When the coffee machine was hissing studiously, Hunter ran back through to the bathroom, undressed, and stepped beneath the steaming water.

The water lashing across his tired muscles, Hunter thought about the events of the previous evening. After Everett Van Wick had been taken away by the medics, Thorne and one member of the security team remained behind to help Hunter clean up the clinic. Whilst Hunter had initially thought the gesture was one of kindness, it seemed the men were more focused on making sure nothing Hunter had used to treat the senator remained behind. They had bundled everything — the bloodied swabs, gauze, towels, latex gloves, bandages, and the tools Hunter had used, into a bag and taken it with them. It was strange behavior, sure, but Hunter had heard that people in power often behaved in ways that seemed curious to the rest of us.

Stepping out of the show, Hunter noticed his suit lay over a chair in the bathroom. He picked it up, turning each item around to check for damage or stains. There didn't appear to be any.

Then, Hunter realized that he had yet to hear whether the senator made it through the night. Personally, he was doubtful. The man had lost so much blood, that even with the patch-up job Hunter had done, survival was an outside chance.

If only Hunter had given him the transfusion, then it would be a different story entirely.

Hunter toweled down and dressed in a clean white shirt and then, to save time, pulled on the same suit as he'd worn the day before. While getting ready, Hunter resisted the urge to check the news. He was a local doctor first and foremost. The people who came to him day in day out, were his priority, not a senator whose life he may or may not have saved.

Hunter knew that a slight delay at the start of the day would mean him chasing his tail for hours. Plus, he would listen to the radio on the drive to Leavenworth. They would no doubt tell him about the politician's fate. This was probably the biggest thing to happen in Leavenworth since the arrival of the railroads.

Hunter swung a tie around his neck and charged out of the bedroom. In the kitchen, he switched off the coffee machine and grabbed a travel mug from a cupboard. He glanced out of the kitchen window and up at the sheer side of the mountain half a mile away. Even in that fleeting moment, the doctor appreciated the beauty of his home. He loved the way the snow glimmered on the slopes of the summit they called Dragontail Peak in an ever-changing natural kaleidoscope.

Hunter placed the travel mug on the counter and removed the coffee jug from the filter machine. In one movement, not wanting to waste a single moment, he swung around and tilted the jug to let the steaming coffee stream into the mug. Like Pavlov's dog, the smell of the fresh brew enlivened him instantly, preparing him for the day.

One moment the coffee was streaming in a thin shimmering ribbon into the mug, the next there was a pop, the sound of shattering glass, and Hunter felt the coffee scald his face. He looked down at his hands, not quite understanding what had happened. He was still holding the coffee jug's plastic handle, but the rest had shattered into shards of splintered glass and spilled liquid.

Then Hunter looked up. The window was a web of cracks. Cracks all disseminating around a single hole. A bullet hole.

Glass shattered as another bullet smashed through the window. Instinct kicked in and Hunter hit the deck. The bullet sizzled an inch above his head and buried itself in the wall.

With Hunter's nearest neighbor over two miles away, there was little chance anyone would hear the shots, and even less chance anyone would come to help. Hunter searched his pockets and realized that his phone was on the table in the hall, next to his keys, ready to go out the door.

Hunter instinctively remembered his time in the Medical Corps. That was a long time ago, a different lifetime, and Hunter thought he'd left gunfire behind. Even so, crouched on the kitchen floor, surrounded by shards of broken glass and steaming coffee, his training kicked in.

Staying low, Hunter turned towards the window. The shooter wouldn't yet know if the job was complete. The assailant would either wait for Hunter to move or not, or more likely, come in and finish the job.

Keeping out of sight, Hunter scuttled across the kitchen floor. He stretched for a block of knives on the counter at the far side of the kitchen, but they were just out of reach. He pulled his tie from around his neck and, holding both ends, swung the tie up and over the knife block. He pulled, and the block slid off the counter, crashing to the floor beside him.

Although the move had given him a weapon, it had also revealed his survival. Another bullet zipped through the kitchen and crunched into the tiles.

Hunter pulled out the largest knife and angled the blade so that he could see through the window in the highly polished steel. The area directly at the back of his house was clear for about fifty feet. Beyond that, densely packed pine trees provided the perfect hidden approach for an assailant.

With one hand, Hunter pulled the other knives from the wooden block and then threw it high. Watching in the blade's reflection, he saw a spark of light flare from the center of the tree line. The knife block splintered into three and crashed to the floor. The shooter was an excellent shot but had just given away his location.

For ten minutes, Hunter lay still, the knife held in position, watching the tree line. Although his assailant was a sharpshooter, Hunter had one thing many men didn't — patience. As a doctor, you had to realize that recovery takes time. No mad could rush the body's healing process, and trying to do often caused more damage.

Sure enough, finally, Hunter saw a figure stalk out of the tree line and pick his way towards the house.

Hunter scurried across to the door and stood up slowly. He positioned himself beside the door so the intruder wouldn't know he was there until it was too late. Hunter glanced down at the knife he held between whitening knuckles. The cold weight of the blade felt both terrifying and comforting.

His moment of preparation was shattered by the sound of the back door splintering open.

Hunter braced himself, waiting for the intruder to approach. He didn't have to wait long.

A hulking figure, all muscle and menace, crashed through the door and charged into the kitchen. Hunter noticed the man had left his long-range rifle amid the trees and approached the house with just a handgun, which he now held in a meaty fist. The man's Kevlar boots crunched across the broken glass. The assassin reached the center of the kitchen and paused. His head flicked left and then right.

Hunter launched himself at the intruder, intending to bring the knife to bear against the man's throat. Hunter didn't plan to kill him, just disarm him, and then call the police.

As Hunter swept the knife in a wide arc, the assassin took a step further into the kitchen. Hunter attempted to correct the swing but was out of line.

Making a split-second decision, he re-angled the knife towards the brute's bicep. The blade sliced through the thug's clothing and deep into the muscle.

The man yowled in pain and the gun slipped from his fingers. The gun crashed to the floor, the sound reverberating through the kitchen like a drum.

With surprising grace, the assassin stepped backward and then spun around to face Hunter.

Hunter froze, the bloodied knife now outstretched. Getting a good look at the assassin, Hunter felt as though he'd been punched in the guts.

A deadly silence settled over the kitchen.

"Senator Van Wick sends his thanks," Thorne said, taking a step forward. The brute placed one balled fist into the palm of the other hand. His knuckles crunched. "Don't worry. This won't take long."

10

Shortly after the first gunshot had rolled up the mountainside, another two followed.

Eden and Athena glanced at each other.

"That's a high-caliber weapon," Athena said, recognizing the sound.

Eden nodded and turned to face the only property in the area. The cottage was single-story and built in the Bavarian style, which was strangely common to this part of the Pacific Northwest. The house had wide eaves and white painted walls. A dusting of snow covered the roof. Set against the pine trees and mountain slopes, it was a postcard-perfect sort of place.

"Something's up," Eden said, pointing towards the house. "Shall we check it out?"

"Absolutely," Athena agreed, nodding.

Athena tapped the button on her comms devices and told Baxter they'd made it down the mountain and were now investigating rogue gunshots from a nearby home.

"It's probably someone doing target practice in the garden," Eden said. "We just want to make sure."

"Okay," Baxter said, uneasily. "I've touched down about a mile away. I can be there within two minutes if needed."

Using their ski poles to propel them down the gentle slope, Eden and Athena approached the house. On one side, the house was set on the shores of the turquoise lake Eden had seen during their descent. Ice covered the edges of the lake and water lapped in the center as though trying to break free.

On the other side, about fifty feet behind the house, a thick pine forest stood like an upturned brush.

Eden and Athena skied towards the narrow ribbon of snow which separated the house from the forest.

When they were approaching the edge of the forest, Eden saw movement within the trees. "In there," Eden hissed, forcing them out of sight.

A moment later, a large man rose from his prone position on the forest floor. He removed a gun from a holster on his hip and then stalked through the snow towards the house.

"That guy's massive." Athena watched the man-mountain pace towards the house.

Silence clung around the scene like a shroud.

"He's definitely not making a social call," Eden said.

Eden and Athena un-clicked their skis and tucked them beneath the branches of a fallen tree. Then, listening for any movement, they cut through the forest to the position from which the man had emerged.

"He's not delivering a parcel, that's for sure," Athena said, pointing at a sniper rifle which lay set up across a log.

Athena crouched down and examined the weapon. "That's a serious bit of kit. You certainly don't use it to ring the doorbell." Athena got into the sniper's position and peered through the optical scope. "Just as I thought, one window is blown out. No sign of life inside."

"You think he's already made the kill and is going to check his work?" Eden said.

Athena shuddered, a reaction which was not caused by the frozen soil on which she lay. "That's exactly what I think he's doing. This is a professional job."

"Baxter, can you find out who lives here?" Eden asked, using the comms system. She gave the location of the house.

"No problem. Give me a minute or two," Baxter replied.

"You stay here," Eden said, pointing down at the sniper. "I'm going to find out what's going on. Stay listening." Eden tapped the comms device and then set off at a sprint towards the house.

∽

"You," Robert Hunter said, pointing at Thorne.

Thorne nodded, and then coolly assessed the wound on his right arm. Even though the gash was oozing blood, and must have hurt a lot, Thorne showed no pain.

"What do you want with me... is this about the senator..." Hunter said. The doctor took a step backward and steadied his hand which still held the knife. "...I did all I could to save his life."

"Oh, the senator is alive," Thorne said. In a fraction of a second, he bent down and picked up the gun. "He needs a couple of days' bed rest. Before long, he'll be back to normal."

Hunter blinked several times as though the gesture would help him understand what was going on.

Thorne switched the gun to his uninjured arm and

pointed it directly at Hunter's chest. Although now using his non-dominant hand, the gun stayed level and true.

"But... then... I don't understand," Hunter stuttered. "Why are you here?"

Hunter's brain whirred into overdrive. He recognized Thorne was planning to immobilize him with a bullet to the chest, increasing his chances of a hit by striking the largest body mass. Then, once Hunter was down, Thorne would follow with another bullet through the forehead. It was a classic and effective strategy.

"You saw things you shouldn't have," Thorne said. "You're a loose end, and the Van Wicks don't allow loose ends."

In the silence, Hunter heard the radio device in Thorne's ear hiss. From across the room, Hunter couldn't hear the words, but the fact Thorne was communicating with others shook him to the core. That meant there were other men nearby. As slow as a winter sunset, Hunter's hopes of survival dwindled to nothing.

"Just finishing up here," Thorne said into the device. His lips seemed to curl around each word as though speaking was painful to him. "Bring the truck out front."

Thorne stepped forward and raised the gun another inch. "No more wasting time. The senator thanks you for your work." His finger curled around the trigger.

Robert Hunter stared at the gun's devilish eye, waiting for the shot.

He had treated enough bullet wounds to know what would happen when Thorne's finger reached the required pressure to fire the weapon. The bullet would discharge from the muzzle at a thousand feet per second and hit him square in the chest. On impact, there were several options. The force of the bullet would pass through his chest, perhaps breaking ribs, and most likely severing a vital organ or two. Hunter realized that pneumothorax was probably his most likely outcome — where air and blood seeps into the space between the lungs and chest, causing the lungs to collapse. The sensation is like drowning, Hunter had heard.

Hunter swallowed and took a deep breath. His eyes lost focus on the room. He tried to find calm and peace in the last moments of his life.

Thorne's finger closed around the trigger and pulled.

The sound of a gunshot filled the room.

Hunter held his breath, waiting for the pain to envelop him. He felt his heart beating as normal. Yet, there was no panic, and no pain.

After a long moment, Hunter opened his eyes.

Thorne took two staggering steps backward and slumped against a wall. Blood streamed from a hole in the side of his chest.

At that moment, a young woman burst into the kitchen.

"Doctor Hunter, you're going to have to come with me, right now."

11

THIRTY SECONDS EARLIER, Athena watched Eden stalk towards the house.

"Wait," Athena said. "That big fella is about to shoot a man in the kitchen. I've got a clean shot."

Eden pulled back behind the door so that she was out of sight from anyone inside.

The sound of several heavy-duty diesel engines grumbled from the road. "We're not alone," Eden hissed. "Baxter, got a name yet?"

"The house belongs to a guy called Robert Hunter. He's the doctor down the road in Leavenworth," Baxter replied. "Real pillar of the community sort of guy."

"That decides it then," Eden whispered. "Take the shot."

Athena didn't have to be told twice. The sniper barked, sending a cartridge punching through the glass and thwacking through the assassin's upper body.

"Clear. Hostile is down," Athena said.

"There'll be more." Eden rushed through the door and into the kitchen. The room was a scene of chaos. The man Eden and Athena had watched enter the house lay on the floor, gripping his chest. Blood splatter on the wall behind him suggested the bullet had gone straight through. Shattered glass twinkled in a rainbow of destruction across the floor.

In the center of the turmoil stood a man in his middle age. He was tall and lithe, his hair graying about the temples.

"Doctor Hunter?" Eden said, stepping towards the man.

Hunter spun around, his eyes as wide as a newborn child's.

"I have no time to explain, but we need to get you out of here now." Eden pointed towards the rear door. Eden grabbed Hunter by the arm and pulled him out into the snow.

The door at the front of the house smashed in and several men, all wearing tactical gear, swarmed in.

"What is going on?" Hunter roared.

"Honestly," Eden said. "I don't know. But we will find out!"

Crashing echoed through the house as Eden and Hunter pounded over the snow-covered lawn and towards the trees.

"We're going to need some cover," Eden said breathlessly.

"I've got you," Athena said, peering through the rifle's sight. "Hostiles moving through the house now."

Athena watched the first man pass like a shadow through the kitchen. His movements showed many years of military experience. He checked each corner of the room, assessing the scene for hostiles. The man glanced down at his fallen colleague, but just stepped over the body and appeared at the rear door.

"Get down," Athena roared.

Still twenty feet from the tree-cover, Eden flattened herself, dragging Hunter down too.

The man in the kitchen didn't have time to fire, as Athena shot him in the chest. It wasn't a perfect shot, but it would certainly be sore in the morning.

The man slumped backward, dropping his assault rifle.

"Move now," Athena barked. "It's clear, but it won't be for long."

Eden and Hunter leaped to their feet and closed the distance in what could well have been record-breaking speed. They tucked in behind a tree just as the next hostile opened fire. Bullets thundered into the tree trunks and up into the canopy. Firing an assault rifle over a long range had the unpredictability of rolling a die. The man leaped behind the door jamb the moment before Athena lined up a shot.

Eden and Hunter worked their way back through the forest and joined Athena at the first assassin's makeshift sniper's nest.

"Five men," Athena said. "One now with a bullet wound in his shoulder. Although he'll live, he won't be doing any pushups for a while."

Hunter glanced from Eden and then down at Athena. "Who... who are you? What's going on?"

"We were hoping you could answer that," Eden said. "If it wasn't for us, you'd be the one bleeding out on the kitchen floor."

Hunter paled until his skin was almost blue. Hunter shivered aggressively, his thin suit jacket was no match for the cold.

Eden glanced down at her own jacket, but Hunter was nearly a foot taller than Eden or Athena. Giving him one of theirs wouldn't help at all.

Another flurry of gunfire pounded into the surrounding trees.

"We're going to have to get out of here," Athena said, firing a shot into the kitchen. The round smashed into the kitchen wall like a sledgehammer, spraying plaster, and brick dust across the room. The internal walls of the old house were constructed in solid stone, meaning the round blew a six-inch crater in the plaster but didn't sail on through.

"On my way." Baxter's voice came through the comms system. "There's a small clearing on the far side of the trees. About half a mile from your position. I'll be there in two minutes."

"Understood," Eden said, turning back towards the trees. What was supposed to be an early morning training exercise, had turned into something much more dangerous.

As though in response to her thoughts, another flurry of lead pounded into the forest.

"Three shooters now," Athena said, panning the gun from side to side. "One in the kitchen, another on the far side of the building, and one on the roof."

"Lay down several shots, knock them back a bit, then we're out of here," Eden said.

"Negative." Athena sent another shot into the kitchen, missing the hostile by a fraction of an inch as he leaped out of sight. "As soon as I stop firing, they'll come after us."

"What other options do we have?" Eden asked, looking from the house, being torn to bits by gunfire, to Athena lying on the earth.

"I'll stay behind and lay down some covering fire so that you can both get out of here." Athena said. "Don't even think about arguing." Athena tilted the sniper back towards the guy hiding behind the roof's apex. "As soon as I stop firing, they'll come this way. Five skilled and well-equipped operatives could bring down a chopper that close to the ground."

"I hate to say it, but Athena's right," Baxter said.

"Fine," Eden said. "But as soon as we've got Hunter to safety, I'm coming back for you."

"Roger that," Athena said, sending a slug into the rooftop. "Go now." Athena glanced up at Eden, her face a mask of stoic concentration. She slid another round into the chamber. "See you soon!"

Eden nodded once, grabbed Hunter by the arm, and pulled the man through the trees.

Lying on the earth, Athena heard their footsteps pound away and then scanned the house once more. When Eden and Hunter were well out of sight, Athena unclipped the magazine and checked how many bullets remained. As Athena had suspected, there weren't many — two, plus the one in the chamber. Athena purposely hadn't checked the ammo while Eden was nearby. If Eden had known that the gun was running empty, Athena suspected she never would have taken Hunter to safety.

Athena clipped the magazine back in place and turned her attention back to the house. She watched the men, trying to read her opponent as much as possible. There were three shooters currently on point. That didn't mean there weren't more waiting behind.

As though on cue, the man at the side of the house leaned from his position and unleashed a flurry in Athena's direction. Athena stayed dead still. From that distance, his shots weren't accurate, and she didn't think he knew her exact location, either. Shots pinged and sizzled through the canopy above her, and a couple of bullets thwacked into tree trunks.

"In position," Baxter said through the comms.

Listening carefully, Athena heard the familiar patter of the Eurocopter's engines drifting through the forest. For a moment, she considered leaping to her feet and running for the chopper. She would probably make it to the chopper before the men reached her position, but whether the Eurocopter would make it out of range before the assassins unleashed a whole typhoon on the craft, she couldn't be sure. Athena remembered a time in Mexico, mere weeks ago when the chopper had come under fire by a band of arrogant thugs. Those men had no military training and were shooting at the chopper already airborne and moving at speed. A chopper on, or even near the ground, was a sitting duck.

The man beside the house leaned from his position and fired again. Peering down the scope, Athena got a visual on his arm, shoulder, and the side of his head. It was the best shot she'd had in a while. Her finger curved around the trigger as she made a micro adjustment to the rifle.

Then she paused. With three shots remaining, she couldn't afford to waste a single one. It was only a matter of time before the men pressed forward. Then she would make her move.

"We're aboard," Eden's voice came through the comms. "We'll get Hunter to safety, then we're coming back for you."

"All good here," Athena said. "Just lying around. Don't mind me."

In the distance, Athena heard the chopper's engine noise increase. She took a strange sort of comfort from the sound. It meant that Eden, Baxter, and the unfortunate Doctor Hunter were almost clear.

Then she heard a different sound — a whooshing, hissing blast that shattered the air. Athena knew instinctively what it was. Panic surged, at first riveting her to the spot, and then kicking her into action.

Her eye still clamped to the rifle's scope, Athena saw nothing. She pulled her head back and looked out at the scene with her naked eye.

Like a deadly firework, a rocket-propelled grenade streaked towards her. Athena saw the rocket's fiery trail as the deadly device hurtled in her direction. In that split second, time moved like cold molasses.

With a swift, agile motion, Athena rolled into a crawling position and then half crawled, half ran deeper into the forest. Her feet slipped uselessly across the forest's damp earth. At any moment, she expected to feel the white-hot distractive heat of the grenade. For what felt like an incredibly long time, nothing happened.

Then the explosion rocked the forest. The trees shook from the roots to the uppermost branches. Shockwaves swelled like ripples on a lake.

Athena stumbled, first on to her knees, and down into the dirt. She tasted blood and acid and earth in her mouth. She pushed her hands against her ears as the colossal boom — the size of a freight train hammering into a cliff — physically rocked her body. The deafening blast reverberated through her bones, drowning out all other sounds.

Then, all went silent.

12

Eden stared out at the forest as the Eurocopter lifted from the ground. The trees appeared to quiver beneath the chopper's rotors, as though something powerful and dangerous was coming their way. Deep in the pit of Eden's stomach, she felt a sense of unease grow. Athena was back there, facing an unknown force, alone.

As the chopper lifted above the level of the forest canopy, Eden saw the first flicker of the explosion.

A brilliant flash of light erupted, illuminating the trees like a strange, ghostly orb. The shockwave surged outwards, sending a fierce gust of wind tearing through the forest. Leaves and branches whipped in a chaotic frenzy. The force of the explosion ripped through the canopy, shaking the trees forward and then back. The wave of impact swept through the air, shaking the Eurocopter in its ascent.

Baxter wrestled with the controls, countering the force of the explosion a second before the chopper would have collided with the forest's thick canopy.

The explosion froze Eden in fear and shock. Then, it

shook her into action. Athena was down there, alone. Athena needed her help.

A tumultuous eruption of flames followed, licking hungrily. Tendrils of smoke and ash billowed up into the sky.

"I'm going down," Eden shouted. "We can't leave Athena."

Baxter replied, but Eden didn't hear a word of it. She threw open the Eurocopter's rear sliding door. With the door open, the downdraft and the rocking of the chopper threatened to throw Eden clear of the craft. She clung on to a pair of handles fitted to the ceiling. The smell of burning wood rushed into the craft.

Eden thumped the button to lower the chopper's winching mechanism.

The cable, attached to the fuselage above the cabin's sliding door, unwound. With no time to get into a harness, Eden leaped from the door and grabbed hold of the cable.

In the cockpit, Baxter struggled to keep the chopper level in the turbulent air.

Eden slid down the cable until she reached the end. The cable whipped from side to side, aggravated both by the downdraft and the force of the explosion.

The cable unfurled slowly, taking Eden down through the forest canopy. Eden removed one hand from the cable and covered her face as she dropped through the highest spikey pines. When she was through the canopy, Eden swung on the cable, then sprang into a tree.

"I'm clear," she said.

The pounding of the rotors intensified, and the cable slid up.

Eden scurried down the tree and then dropped the last

dozen feet towards the forest floor. Then she ran toward the explosion.

~

THE FIRST THING Athena heard in the explosion's aftermath, was a high-pitched ringing sound in her ears. It sounded like some cruel sound technician was holding a microphone next to a speaker, purely for their own sick enjoyment.

She tried to open her eyes, but they felt as though they had been welded shut by the heat of the explosion. Either that, or a thousand tons of dust had come to rest there.

A few moments later, the whining in her ears subsided, and other sensations returned. That was when Athena heard the voice. At first, she couldn't be sure where the voice was coming from. It sounded weirdly distant and close all at the same time. Then she felt hands pulling at her, urging her to move.

A moment later, the voice became clear.

"Athena, we've got to go. We need to move now!" Athena recognized the voice, too. It was Eden.

Athena opened her eyes and this time her work-shy eyelids obeyed. Colors twirled in front of her vision for a few moments until Eden came into focus.

"They're coming," Eden hissed. "We need to move."

The sounds of the explosion had died away and a creepy stillness hung about the forest. It reminded Athena of those unsettling moments in movies where everything goes quiet in preparation for a jump-scare.

Snowflakes drifted gently from the canopy, skipping in wide arcs before resting peacefully on the ground.

Eden pulled Athena up on to her feet and together they charged through the woodland. After a hundred feet, they dropped in behind a large tree and listened, their senses heightened, and their bodies primed for battle.

Somewhere close by, the crunch of boots on the forest floor signaled the location of their adversaries.

Eden figured the men would start running as soon as the explosion detonated. The men were now coming to either check the job was complete or finish it themselves. They were professionals.

Eden clenched her fists, preparing for conflict.

Athena shook the last ravages of confusion from her mind. Less than one minute after the explosion, she was as sharp as usual and ready to give someone hell.

The first assassin charged past their hidden position. Eden let him take two paces before leaping out into his shadow. She didn't let a moment more pass. In a blur of fists and elbows, she sent countless strikes into the guy's abdomen and neck.

Unprepared for the attack, the assassin tried to turn quickly. His legs continued running forward and then his boots slipped across the wet earth. The thug tried in vain to raise the gun towards his unseen assailant, but Eden was too quick. She pulled the gun away from him and used the butt to land a solid blow to the man's jaw. The telltale vibrations of a broken bone shook the rifle in Eden's grip.

The man howled and tried again to grope around for the weapon.

Without time to aim the firearm, Eden swung the rifle again. This time, the butt connected with the man's temple. He slumped to the ground, sleeping like a baby.

"Eden, move!" Athena roared, just as a barrage of scorching metal zipped in their direction.

Eden threw herself down behind the fallen thug. Bullets

flew just inches above her. One thudded into the motionless thug's guts, certain to finish the job Eden had started.

"Talk about honor amongst thieves," Eden said, swinging the rifle up and over the fallen man. She squeezed the trigger and countless rounds flew back towards their foe.

The hostiles leaped for cover, narrowly avoiding Eden's return fire.

Eden used the momentary lapse in their attention to run for cover behind a tree.

An arc of bullets raked across the forest floor and up the trunk.

The hostile stepped forward, closing in on Eden's position. Eden swung the gun around the trunk, but without time or opportunity to aim properly, the bullets thumped off into the forest. Eden was pinned down tight by the approaching man.

The hostile stepped forward again, his attention, and the snout of his rifle, focused on Eden. Stalking like the king of the jungle, the hostile closed in on Eden's position.

Eden stood as still as she could, even breathing lightly to reduce the rise and fall of her chest.

The hostile took another step forward, unknowingly drawing level with Athena's hiding position. It was the last mistake he'd ever make.

Athena charged from behind the tree, picking up a fallen branch. She swept the branch low, aiming to swipe the man's legs from beneath him. The assassin saw her approach and spun around just in time. He caught the branch in a gloved hand, shockwaves surely jarring his elbow.

Undistracted, Athena let go of the branch and swung a left hook into the man's neck.

He stumbled backward, taking two steps to recover his balance.

Athena rushed forward again with a flying kick to the ribs and knocked the breath from his lungs.

Hearing the commotion, Eden peered out from behind the tree. She tried to bring the gun to bear, but Athena and the assassin were locked so tightly in conflict that she couldn't get a clean shot. She scouted the woodland for more adversaries but couldn't see any.

Athena stepped back and then, with a hiss of exertion, sent a killer kick straight into the assassin's knee. His leg snapped, bending backward in the way a leg had no right to go. Before the hostile could even react, Athena sent another kick into his sternum, cracking ribs. The man slumped to the ground.

"Athena, get down. Two o'clock!" Eden yelled.

Another hostile, clearly attracted by the movement, materialized from between the trees.

The man took a step forward, shaking his head as though Athena was a naughty child. He lifted the rifle, leveling it at Athena.

Watching unseen from twenty feet away, Eden prepared to take the shot.

But when Athena leaped again into action, Eden knew the guy had just signed his own death warrant.

Athena lunged to the side. The hostile fired, but Athena was already clear. Athena shot forward and grabbed the barrel of the assault rifle. With little more than the flick of her wrist, Athena yanked the rifle from the man's grip and spun it through two complete rotations, pulling the strap tight around the man's neck and back.

Athena then tilted her head to the side and smiled up at the thug before squeezing the trigger. A thundering strafe of bullets hammered into the assassin's foot and ankle.

The man roared in pain and tried to push Athena away. Athena did the opposite and pulled him closer still, not allowing him to build up the force to strike her properly.

While the thug was still trying to work out what was going on, Athena stepped backwards, spun the rifle upwards and sent a single round through the man's chin and up into his brain.

Athena unclipped the weapon as the man fell. She ejected the spent magazine, jerked another the fallen assailants vest, and rammed it home.

"Not bad." Eden eyed the three neutralized hostiles. "Especially considering you were just lying about when I arrived."

"I hate to interrupt your pleasant walk in the woods," Baxter's urgent voice cut through the comms system. "Another truck has just arrived. At least ten men. You need to get out of there now."

Eden and Athena glanced at one another. Neutralizing three men was one thing, avoiding an assault from ten in a harsh environment like this was something else altogether.

Eden dug out her phone and pulled up a map of the area. "It doesn't look good," she said. "We've got mountains on two sides, the lake on the third, and them approaching from the fourth."

"I suppose a lift is out of the question?" Athena asked Baxter.

"That was a rocket-propelled grenade they used back there," Baxter's voice was even more icy and humorless than usual. "One of those could take down the copter from half a mile away. If you get across the mountains, I'll be able to help."

"Across the mountains!" Athena hissed, remembering their descent less than an hour ago. "That'll take us days!"

"Not necessi..." Baxter was cut off mid-sentence by another sound cutting through the forest.

It was the deep, two-toned, mournful cry of a train's whistle.

"What's that?" Eden said.

"Right on time as usual," Baxter replied. "That's your escape plan. The Amtrak Empire Builder from Chicago to Seattle. It slows to pass a bend less than a mile from your current..."

"But they're not just going to open the doors and let us on, are they?" Eden said, thinking about the modern trains she'd seen swishing up and down the tracks in the United States.

"No. But you don't like to do things the easy way, anyway, do you?" Baxter replied, the hint of a smile returning to his voice.

The train howled again, it's call cutting through the forest as clear and sharp as a ray of morning sun.

"You'd better get going," Baxter said. "You've got a..."

"Don't say it," Eden and Athena replied in unison.

"...train to catch," Baxter muttered before closing the connection.

13

Denzel Wetzel had been driving the Amtrak Empire Builder on the Chicago to Seattle route for as long as he could remember. Of course, he didn't drive the whole forty-six-hour journey, but worked in shifts with several other drivers who would leave and join the train at various stops along the way.

This part, though, as the train cut its way towards the Cascade mountains of Washington State, was his favorite.

Denzel listened in to the reassuring clickety-clack of the wheels against the tracks. After nearly fifty years on the rails, he knew the sound as well as his own heartbeat. He also found it reassuring that the sound would continue long after his stewardship of this great line, as it had begun long before he was born.

Denzel glanced down at the dials. At fifty miles per hour, The Empire Builder was far from the fastest train in the country, but Denzel liked that. There was something stately about the way the sleek silver cars slid through some of the nation's most dramatic countryside.

With everything on the locomotive's control panel

appearing as it should, Denzel turned his attention back to the landscape through the windshield. The train was taking a gentle curve around the steep foothills.

Through the windshield, the snow dusted forest unfolded like a tapestry. To the left, towering evergreens and leafless branches clawed at the sky, their shadows stretching across the tracks. To the right, the snow-covered slopes climbed steeply skyward, frozen streams cutting through the powder like veins.

The Empire Builder rounded the curve and the track straightened out. Ahead, he saw the barriers of the crossing swing downwards, blocking any vehicles. Beyond that, the track swung out of sight around one of the tightest bends in the region.

Denzel's gloved hand moved instinctively, adjusting the train's throttle. The engine's roar quietened to a murmur. He altered the throttle again, further reducing their speed.

As the train neared the crossing, Denzel tugged the whistle lever in the long-long-short-long pattern which came instinctively after all these years. The shrill blast pierced the forest and rolled up the mountainside.

A large bird, probably a Northern Goshawk, pounded from the treetops and wheeled down across the tracks, momentarily attracting Denzel's attention.

The Empire Builder rumbled across the empty crossing and started twisting around the curve.

Through the window, the forest scenery rushed by. The tall trees blurred in a smudge of greens and browns. Shadows danced across the snow-dusted ground as the train slid beneath the branches.

As the great train completed the corner, Denzel pushed forward on the throttle again. The engine roared and

Denzel felt the vibrations of steel against steel far beneath his feet.

∽

Two minutes earlier, Eden and Athena had peered around the trunk of a large fir tree and seen The Empire Builder's silver nose round the curve a few hundred feet away. Positioned at the curve central point, they could see the track in both directions. Across the line, the mountains posed as a visual reminder of how important getting on this train really was.

Eden turned and cast a glance amid the trees behind them. Although they hadn't seen or heard anything from their pursuers in several minutes, the men wouldn't be far behind.

She swung back to face the locomotive as the noise rose from a distant clattering to an all-out howl. The locomotive rumbled near, its powerful lights lancing through the shadows.

Eden and Athena ducked further out of sight. The ground beneath them shuddered with the chuntering wheels.

"How are we going to get on there?" Eden said, eyeing the locomotive. Although the machine was still two hundred feet away, it towered over them.

A shrill electronic sound cut through the forest. Eden whipped around to see the road crossing, one hundred feet away, warn of the approaching train.

"Baxter said it would slow for the corner," Athena muttered, her voice laced with doubt.

As Athena spoke, the brakes of the immense vehicle screeched like nails on a chalkboard.

"He was right," Eden said.

The train slowed into a crawl. The cars clacked together, their brakes working hard to slow the giant machine.

Eden and Athena ducked out of sight as the locomotive passed their position. Eden felt the mighty wheels churn against the tracks. She glanced around the tree and saw the driver through the windshield, tiny in comparison to the size of the train.

"How are we going to get up there?" Athena pointed at the double height silver cars which followed the locomotive.

Eden searched the side of the cars but could see no obvious way up. Each one was designed with no steps or hand holds. The train was just a wall of moving aluminum.

A report of gunfire hammered through the forest behind them. Although the sound was faint against the rumbling of the train, to Eden and Athena's trained ears it was as loud as an explosion. They instinctively flattened themselves into the ground. Shots streaked overhead, some burying themselves in the gravel, others sparkling from the tracks and the wheels.

Eden peered behind them. A shadowy figure moved through the trees some distance behind. Too close for an accurate shot, for now. Although Eden only saw one man, she knew for certain there would be more not far away.

"The locomotive at the back, look!" Athena said, pointing upwards.

Eden swung around as the engine at the rear end of the train rounded the curve. Then she saw what Athena was pointing at. The locomotive had a ladder leading up to the driver's door.

"That's our way up there," Eden shouted, already shuffling forward. "Move now."

Another strafe of gunfire sounded from somewhere

behind. The rounds whizzed overhead as Eden and Athena scurried from their crouched position. After a few paces, they straightened up and sprinted towards the rear locomotive.

The engine bellowed, sending a great plume of diesel smoke skyward. They approached the colossal wheels, each reverberating against the track with a relentless force.

"It's accelerating," Eden shouted over the noise.

The powerful, grinding noise shook the cartilage between Eden's joints.

Eden glanced back into the forest. Several highly trained killers were visible now, moving between the trees.

Athena ran forward and without a break in her step, leaped up and grabbed the ladder on the side of the locomotive. She hauled herself up hand over hand. She reached the driver's door and tried the handle.

Eden pulled herself up onto the ladder, just beneath Athena.

"It's locked," Athena shouted down, her voice almost lost against the roaring diesel engine. "It won't open."

Eden glanced towards the front of the train to see the first assassin break through the tree line. Black fatigues covered the man's muscular body, and he handled the rifle as though he was born with it in his hands. The man noticed Eden and Athena clinging on to the side of the locomotive, and his face contorted into an ugly snarl.

"Climb!" Eden shouted, her fingers weakening beneath the vibrating train. "We've got to get up on to the roof."

Athena tilted her head backward and studied the side of the train.

"Got it," she said, initially reaching out for the door handles. She lifted herself up to the sturdy window frames. Now just using the tip of her fingers, Athena dug into a row of protruding rivets as she pushed up with her legs.

Eden turned away from Athena and watched the thug taking aim. The train dragged them, inch by inch, closer to the assassin's position. All he had to do was wait until they were close enough to be picked off with a point-blank shot.

Athena groaned as the train's vibration worked her hands loose.

Both women looked closely at the side of the train, searching for a way to climb.

Athena removed each hand in turn and wiped away the sweat.

"The vents!" Eden shouted, suddenly seeing a solution.

Athena glanced up and saw what Eden was pointing at. A ventilation grill ran from the side of the door all the way up to the roof.

Athena reached out, extending her hand as far as she could. Her fingers whipped overhead, inches away from the grill.

"Come on," Athena muttered, her mouth set into a hard, determined line.

Eden's head whipped from the thug standing beside the tracks, less than one hundred feet away, to Athena just above her, reaching out for the grill.

"I'm going to jump," Athena shouted, pulling back like a coiling viper.

Before Eden had the chance to react, Athena threw herself forward. Her hands and feet left their holds as she half slid, half jumped along the side of the locomotive. He hands thrashed above her, scrabbling for the vent. Her left hand brushed across the aluminum, unable to get hold at this speed.

Eden watched, unable to tear her eyes from her flailing friend, her stomach in turmoil.

Athena slipped down towards the tracks, towards the wheels. Athena swung her other hand towards the vent and pushed her fingers through the bars. She gripped and stopped her fall.

The assassin, now just fifty feet away, took aim and prepared to fire.

Now with the handhold she needed, Athena scrambled upwards like a spider climbing a wall. Hand over hand, she reached the top and rolled on to the roof. All in the same slick move, Athena swung the rifle that had been concealed against her stomach during the climb.

She rolled over, took aim, and showered the assassin with hot lead. The man tried to fire, but two bullets found their home — one in his chest and the other, gaping like a third eye, in his forehead.

The man collapsed backward and tumbled down the bank beside the track.

Athena pushed the gun to her back and reached over the side of the locomotive.

Eden scrambled up the side of the door and leaped for Athena's outstretched hands. The women locked hands and Athena hauled Eden up. Eden rolled sideways on top of the locomotive, gasping for breath. She took several deep breaths of exhaust filled air and watched several more men appear from the trees.

14

ALMOST HALF A MILE AWAY, a man pulled himself up the side of the leading locomotive, arm over arm. Far beneath him, The Empire Builder's wheels ground against the rails with a rhythmic clatter.

The man kept his body flattened against the vibrating aluminum, conscious of the train driver working the controls just a few feet away. The man had considered bursting into the cab, all guns blazing but decided that for now it was better to keep the train moving. For once, he would move stealthily.

The train's whistle sounded as they rounded a curve. Deep within the vast machine's innards, the diesel engine, which powered the electric motors driving the axles, roared.

The man peered over his shoulder at the woodland where several of his subordinates lurked in the shadows.

The thought of his useless team made him scowl. This should have been a simple job — end the life of one small-town doctor, and if possible, make it appear to be an accident. Suicide maybe, or a house fire — both were disastrously common, particularly with people like the good doctor who kept a stressful profession. They could have decided that after the event, if his men had gotten their act together.

They could easily have ensured investigators concluded the doctor had been so tired he'd failed to notice a gas leak, or maybe the work had got to him, and he'd instigated the whole thing himself.

Either way, by now it should have been taken care of. Sorted out. And they should be well and truly out of here. In this game, short certainly was sweet. The longer you stayed around, the messier things became.

The man pulled himself up the final two feet by jamming his fingers into the vent and rolled on to the locomotive's roof.

The movement caused the gash in his chest to ache anew. He grunted and poked at the gauze beneath his shirt, which had been hurriedly placed over the wound. The gauze was still in place. That was good. Apparently, the wound had seemed much worse that it was.

In fact, with all the blood spewed around the kitchen, his subordinates were shocked to see him alive. He had told them to stop gawking and get the medical kit. The wound set with medical-grade glue and bandaged; the man known only as Thorne was back in the game and ready to strike.

～

EDEN AND ATHENA picked their way along the locomotive and sat on the roof of the final passenger car. Dramatic mountain slopes rose on both sides as the train snaked its way through a deep valley. Water as clear as crystal gushed over rocks in a stream to the side of the track and trees stretched up the lower slopes like sentinels, their tips quivering in a gentle breeze.

"That was too close," Eden said, trying to get comfortable.

"Yeah, you're telling me," Athena said, pulling the zipper on her coat right to the top. Now, with their body temperatures dropping after the intense chase through the forest, the cold bit against any exposed skin. "Why do you think those men wanted to kill Doctor Hunter?"

"I've no idea," Eden said, turning and locking eyes with Athena. "But I've got a feeling we're going to find out. This isn't over yet. Those men had some serious firepower."

Athena grinned.

"What?" Eden replied, eyes locking on her friend.

"Nothing," Athena muttered, snapping her mouth shut. Athena pulled her legs up towards her chest and wrapped her arms around them.

"You're grinning," Eden said, scrutinizing Athena. "Unless you find the attempted murder of an innocent man amusing, then something else has made you laugh."

"It's nothing... well..." Athena's voice trailed off.

"It's not nothing." Eden positioned herself beside Athena to hear better. "What's going on?"

"Well, the other day I was talking to Baxter and..."

"Oh, I see." Eden folded her arms. "You two were having a laugh at my expense. That's really nice of you. Tease the new girl."

"You're hardly the new girl anymore. You've been with us for months..."

"Don't change the subject," Eden retorted, pointing at Athena in mock seriousness. "What were you saying about me? Huh? You tell me now!"

Several hundred feet away, Thorne gazed along the roof of the train. The great locomotive, plus the string of double-decker Superliner cars, made an imposing serpent of steel, curving back through the forest for half-a-mile.

Thorne climbed to his feet and took a moment to find his balance. Then, treading carefully to avoid any pipework or machinery on the roof, he walked to the back of the locomotive and jumped across to the leading car. Thorne recognized the leading car as the sightseer lounge with its windows curving up across the roof. He walked carefully down the metal in the center of the roof, peering through the windows below. Fortunately, at this early hour, the car was empty.

At the end of the car, Thorne stopped and assessed the length of the train. The track beneath them had straightened out, giving Thorne a view of the whole train stretching before him like a giant walkway.

Thorne squinted. Early morning light reflected from the metal, obscuring his view. He cupped a hand above his eyes, pulled his sidearm from its holster and screwed a silencer into place. Even above the hungry rumble of the train, he didn't want to risk being heard. Finally, he checked the magazine. Satisfied everything was as it should be, Thorne tucked the gun away and started towards the two figures moving about on the roof of the train almost half a mile away.

"Alright, fine, I'll tell you," Athena said, holding up her hands. "But don't you go around causing issues with everyone? We've got enough going on without a load of bickering."

Eden shook her extended finger. "You guys are the ones who have been gossiping about who knows what. Now you need to tell me what the issue is, and then I'll decide whether it's worth going around causing problems about."

Athena huffed and shifted her gaze out to the forest.

"Right now," Eden said. "If you haven't got anything more pressing going on, that is."

"Okay fine," Athena said. "But don't tell Baxter I told you this."

"I will make no such promise," Eden said, her voice taking on the tones of the high and mighty.

"Baxter said that since he's known you, there's been more trouble in his life than ever before," Athena said, chuckling guiltily.

"Did he, now?" Eden said, raising an eyebrow. "That's probably because his life was really dull before he met me."

"Maybe that's it." Athena shrugged. "But you seem to attract a certain type of... how to put it nicely..."

Eden's other eyebrow raised to join its partner.

"Put it this way," Athena said, sighing. "There's never a dull moment when you're around."

"You agree with him!" Eden shouted, trying but failing to keep the grin from her face. "You think I'm some kind of troublemaker, just roaming around the world making issues for everyone?"

"I didn't say that!" Athena roared, her hands held up in surrender. "It's just, we're out for a ski, and you stumble across an assassination plot. I mean, is there anyone else on Planet Earth that sort of thing happens to?"

"I don't know," Eden said, sticking her bottom lip out in faux hurt. "Maybe the 'A Team'."

"They're a fictional TV series. You can't compare..."

"How. Dare. You!" Eden said, pronouncing each word as though it were its own sentence. "The 'A Team' is totally a documentary." Eden held up a finger to stop Athena interrupting. "Anyway. It's hardly my fault. These things happen, right?"

Athena opened her mouth to speak, but Eden got there first.

"Whatever you're about to say, pick those words carefully."

"It's totally your fault!" Athena's face broke into a smile.

Eden leaned over and pushed Athena on the shoulder. Athena dramatically sprawled across the roof of the locomotive.

At that exact moment, a single bullet streaked past, missing Athena by a hair's breadth. The bullet ricocheted from the roof with a spark and tore into the forest.

Smiles instantly melted from Eden and Athena's expressions.

They jumped to their feet and whipped around to face the shooter.

At the end of the car, just thirty feet away, a man took another step towards them. He walked along the roof of the train with apparent ease, effortlessly compensating for the movement.

Eden's eyes locked on the man. She recognized his snarling piggish expression, set on top of a neck which was probably wider than her hips. He was a tall man too, unnaturally tall, which was especially obvious now as he took another step towards them.

"It's you!" Eden roared, pointing up at the man. "This is the guy you shot in the kitchen," Eden said, glancing at Athena.

"Merely a flesh wound," the man shouted down the train. He touched the side of his chest. "It will take a lot more than that to put me out of action."

The man took another step forward, closing the gap between them.

"That was a lucky escape," the man said, raising a pistol. "You won't be so lucky this time…"

15

"Who are you?" Athena howled, taking a step backward.

Eden glanced around. They had a few more feet to retreat before reaching the locomotive. The rails shimmered a lethal distance below.

"I'm Thorne and now you're dead." The man's rubbery lips twisted into something of a grin.

Eden thought that he was probably the ugliest man she'd ever seen.

"Your parents really must have hated you, naming you that," Eden said, laughing out loud.

Thorne froze for a moment, his gaze becoming harder still.

Eden watched the change in the man's expression with interest. It seemed like she'd hit a nerve. There was something almost inhuman about the way he looked. His face didn't seem to show the usual range of expressions a person might use.

"I'm going to enjoy this." Thorne took a step closer. "Keep talking all you want. It's going to be the last thing you do."

Eden and Athena took another step backward. Eden glanced down and behind. The assault rifle lay abandoned on the roof a few feet back. Although Eden could reach it in a second or two, Thorne would fire first and probably wouldn't miss a second time. Eden regretted them not staying on guard.

Eden's brain whirred, searching for solutions. Beyond the rifle, Eden eyed the gap between the cars. She spotted the coupling system, a bundle of thick cables and pipes, and beyond that, the ice flecked tracks. She noticed all that in half a second and then concentrated on their foe.

The train, indifferent to the drama unfolding on its roof, swept into another curve.

"Why did you try to kill Doctor Hunter?" Athena shouted.

"I don't have time to explain." Thorne took another step forward and leveled the gun at Athena. "You'll wish you stayed out of another person's business."

"It's funny you should say that." Athena pointed at Thorne as though he'd just said something really intelligent. "I was telling her that one minute ago." Athena swung her finger around and pointed it at Eden.

"You should have listened to your friend," Thorne said, his gun moving from Athena to Eden.

"Yeah, but I disagree," Eden said. "Saving an innocent man *is* our business."

Beyond Thorne, the front of the train curved out of sight.

"We make it our business," Eden added, glancing at Athena, then down at the gap behind them. The women shared a microscopic nod, indicating they both understood.

"Killing you is our business now," Athena said.

Thorne clearly found the idea that two women would be

a threat to him amusing. He roared with laughter, tilting his rubbery lips up towards the sky.

Athena and Eden reacted at lightning speed. In a blink of an eye, they ducked, rolled backward, and disappeared down the gap between the cars. Athena grabbed the assault rifle on the way, swinging it over her shoulder. They slid down between the cars, using a pair of metal hand holds to slow their fall, and landed nimbly on the coupling mechanism.

Athena made sure there was a bullet in the chamber and leveled the gun at the roof.

Clearly frustrated at the delay in his plan, Thorne stomped towards them.

"This is so easy," Thorne roared, approaching the gap between the cars. "Like shooting ducks."

"Did he just call us...?" Eden whispered. "I thought this was a family show."

"Shooting ducks in a barrel," Thorne roared, stomping closer still.

"Does that answer your question?" Athena said, glancing at Eden.

"That's the worst mixed metaphor I've ever heard."

Thorne's footsteps thudded to a stop, and his face appeared between the cars. Looming over the edge, his bulk was a sizable silhouette against the bright blue sky.

"Can ducks do this?" Athena shouted, squeezing the trigger. A barrage of bullets hammered up through the gap. The sound of the rifle was almost deafening in the narrow space.

Thorne reacted in lightning speed, flipping out of sight.

Athena kept her finger on the trigger until the weapon clicked empty.

"That's some aggressive wildfowl." Eden scrambled up the rear wall of the car and peered over the edge.

Thorne was still on his feet, right at the edge of the car. His gun had fallen from his grasp and was teetering on the edge of the train's roof two feet away.

Using the handholds, Eden half sprung, half clambered up on to the roof.

Eden closed the distance in two giant leaps and slammed into the brute with the force of a juggernaut. Her hand clamped around Thorne's wrist a moment after his fingers closed around the gun.

Thorne pushed back against Eden's grip, raising the weapon towards her.

Eden shoved his arm to the right at the same time as Thorne fired the gun. A bullet sailed wide, finding a home amid the trees.

Eden swung onto her back foot and then pushed forward again.

Thorne fired again and again, hitting nothing.

Although Thorne was a giant, and clearly stronger than Eden, she was far quicker than him.

Eden jammed her feet into the ridges on the train's roof and pushed. Thorne teetered on the edge. He glanced at the wheels churning thunderously below.

"You're going over there," Athena said, lunging in to help. She swung a solid punch at Thorne's exposed side, aiming for where she imagined the injury to be. The brute grunted, his grip on the gun wavering.

Thorne tried again to bring the gun to bear on either of the women, but like a school of fish veering from a predator, the women twisted to safety. The gun popped, but the bullet skittered uselessly down the roof.

"Need shooting practice?" Eden said, twisting the gun down towards the roof.

Athena pushed Thorne further over the edge.

Finally, their efforts united, the pair felt the big man's center-of-gravity sway across the abyss.

Thorne reached for the roof with his free hand. His fingers slipped against the smooth aluminum, inches from a handhold. He grunted and groaned in frustration.

"No, you don't," Eden hissed from between clenched teeth.

Thorne eyed his other hand, which was closer to the roof but held the gun.

"Decision time!" Athena pushed the man harder, sending him a fraction of an inch further over the void.

"You're going to regret this," Thorne barked. He twisted violently and swung the gun out over the side of the train. The firearm spun several times and then disappeared into the forest.

With a grunt, Thorne lashed out with both hands. He shoved Athena backward and landed a solid blow on Eden's face. Eden sprawled backward, her face throbbing.

The train straightened up through a cutting. The sound of the engine reverberated from the rock walls which now surrounded the track.

"You'll wish you'd just kept going." Thorne rushed forward, launching at Eden.

His arm swept in a wide arc, aiming for her head.

"Try again," Eden said, bobbing just in time. The fist missed her skull by a hair's breadth. She countered with a swift jab to Thorne's midriff. The punch landed solidly, sending a jarring pain through Eden's arm as though she'd just whacked a brick wall.

Thorne grunted and shifted backward.

Thorne recovered quickly and sent a sledgehammer of a punch into Eden's stomach.

Eden sprawled backward, clanging hard to the roof.

The train roared onto a viaduct. The sudden shift in landscape transformed the scenery, replacing the tight confines of the ravine with a large valley. Far below the tracks, the glittering Wenatchee River carried the seasonal snow melt out towards the ocean.

"Long way down..." Athena said, lurching forward and attempting to shove Thorne from the train.

Thorne dodged Athena's onslaught and shoved back, sending Athena sprawling across the roof. Thorne stepped over her, his fists clenched and ready.

Eden jumped to her friend's defense, delivering a series of rapid punches.

"Eden, duck!" Athena shouted from a prone position on the roof.

Eden struck again, smashing at the man in any way she could.

"Not the time to bring up the duck thing," Eden said, landing another strike on Thorne's stomach.

"I'm not messing around! Get down!"

Ignoring Athena, Eden shoved a knee into Thorne's kidneys.

Eden felt an arm close around her shoulders. For a moment, she looked in confusion towards Thorne.

"I mean, get out of the way of that," Athena shouted directly into Eden's ear, pulling her down onto the roof.

Eden and Athena fell backward as the train rumbled onto the viaduct's central section. To compensate for the wider span here, thick steel girders crisscrossed the tracks, just a few feet above the train's roof.

Thorne turned around a moment too late. The first

girder slammed him in the face with a solid metallic clunk and the crack of breaking bones. The man was torn from the moving train, now just a limp, ragged figure.

Eden turned and watched the body fall down and down and down, landing somewhere in the ravine below.

"Let's hope that's his last stop," Eden said, collapsing flat against the roof as several more girders flashed overhead.

"I really wish you'd told him to sleep with the ducks," Athena murmured through gritted teeth.

"Dammit," Eden replied. "It's hard to keep track of these one-liners."

"Try better next time," Athena quipped.

"I really hope there won't be a next time." Eden shuffled to the edge of the car and peered down into the ravine. Although Thorne's body had to be somewhere beneath them, she couldn't see it.

16

The Balonia, Bell Harbor Marina, Seattle. Present Day.

THE MAN KNOWN as Helios glanced at his watch. They were already thirty minutes behind schedule and his patience was exhausted.

"I just think that we should be in control of this." A voice boomed from the office. Although the voice came from a wall mounted screen, the speaker's face was not shown. The members of The Council of Selene were anonymous, even from each other. "The Council was established to allow humankind to develop in an effective way, the widespread development of Artificial Intelligence poses a direct threat. We must act to bring it under control now."

Several other members of The Council muttered their agreement.

"Thank you, Uriel," Helios said, sighing silently. Each member of The Council was given a codename which was their only identification to other members. "And thank you all for attending this meeting. We all have a lot to consider. I propose we re-convene in two weeks' time when we've had time to..."

"We don't have time..." Uriel stated, their tone aggressive.

"My decision is that we will re-convene in two weeks' time," Helios repeated, his voice hard. "The Council has operated successfully for thousands of years because we have taken the time to consider things carefully. Thank you for your exhaustive presentation today, Uriel."

Uriel acknowledged Helios' authority with silence.

"Thank you all again, we will talk in two weeks." Helios pressed a button on the computer terminal the connection was cut.

He let two frustrated breaths leave his body and crossed to the doors at the rear of his office. Sliding the doors open, he padded out on to *The Balonia's* expansive rear deck.

In the fresh air, Helios began to decompress. With another deep breath he started to feel himself again.

Alexander Winslow had fulfilled the role of Helios within The Council of Selene for several decades. For the first two, he worked for The Council as well as continuing his duties as a world-famous archaeologist, and university professor. Those days were behind him now, but the work of The Council of Selene never seemed to end.

The Council of Selene had been responsible for carefully monitoring humankind's progress for thousands of years. No one quite new when The Council had been established, but it's mention in a set of tablets recently discovered from before The Great Flood, indicated that it was several thousand years at least. With the roles within The Council moving within families or social groups, the council members had continued their work ceaselessly that entire time.

All new technology, pharmaceuticals, and even film and TV programs needed approval by The Council before they made their way out into the world.

Of course, this wasn't all the work of Winslow and his team on board *The Balonia*. The Council of Selene controlled countless organizations from the bodies that awarded patients, to the company that classified films.

Alexander Winslow wandered to the railing and surveyed the skyscrapers of Seattle's skyline. Winslow glanced guiltily over his shoulder, then certain that he was alone, fished a packet of chamomile cigarettes from his pocket.

Change was in the air for The Council of Selene, though. For now, Winslow had instructed that the tablets which revealed The Council's existence should stay under wraps. With only a handful of people able to read the language in which they were written, this was an easy thing to do. In the future though, Winslow had decided, it would be time for Humankind to look after themselves.

With the cigarette lit, Winslow gazed upon the Olympic Mountains rising majestically in the distance. Although *The Balonia* had moored in Bell Harbor before, it had been several years, and Winslow had forgotten how breathtaking the view here could be. He spun a slow three-sixty and took it all in. To the East, the skyscrapers of Seattle. To the South, the majesty of Mount Rainier and the Cascade range. To the West, the snowcapped Olympic Mountains, and to the North, the myriad islands of Puget Sound. It was a view of contrasted the human and natural world. A view that reminded him that nature was so much more powerful, every time.

Winslow tapped on *The Balonia*'s railing and took a deep lung full of smoke.

For a moment, Winslow closed his eyes and let gratitude swell within him. He was thankful not only for their completion of several dangerous missions in recent months, but also because he was now able to spend more time with his daughter, Eden. Winslow knew that even though he was chairmen of a very powerful organization, his real legacy wasn't a thing, but a person. The ultimate expression of humanity, Winslow realized, was the ability to choose to do the things that inspired you and spend time with the people you loved. The legacy of time well spent was more important than anything else he could imagine.

Winslow exhaled and the image of his daughter swam into his mind's eye. Having worked side by side for several months, they were now closer than ever. Their connection also brought with it some feelings of guilt, which Winslow realized he'd been running from for several years.

Their previous mission had also reminded Winslow of the way Eden had come into his life. It hadn't been, as he'd told his daughter when she was young, as part of a short-lived marriage to a woman who had died far too young.

Now, Winslow knew, it was time the truth came out for good. It was time Eden knew that Alexander Winslow was her father in every way, but biologically.

Actually telling her, that was the problem. With the hive of activity that *The Balonia* was, spending time alone together was a challenge. In truth, Winslow had been trying to tell her for weeks with no luck.

Another sound cut through the gentle lapping of water against the hull and the cawing of sea birds. The sound grew, now slicing through the fluttering sails and the murmur of boat engines. Winslow recognized it as the patter of the Eurocopter's engines.

Winslow turned one way and then the other, eventually spotting the chopper powering up the coast from the south.

Suddenly, with a pang of guilt, he finished the cigarette, then padded inside and dropped the butt in the toilet. He sprayed himself to remove the smell of the smoke and strode back out on to the rear deck. The Eurocopter powered across the marina, banking as it decelerated and prepared to land on *The Balonia*'s specially designed rear deck.

Although *The Balonia*, at Winslow's request, occupied a section of the marina all to itself, the chopper's downdraft still sent the lines and flags of several boats into a whipping frenzy. The waters around *The Balonia* sloshed and churned into foam.

With the noise of the engines roaring in his ears, Winslow watched Baxter's expression of concentration as he lowered the chopper on to the deck. Winslow saw Eden in the co-pilot's seat beside him and felt his usual welling of pride.

The Eurocopter touched down, sending the slightest shudder through *The Balonia*'s newly reenforced hull. Baxter reached up and flicked several switches. The engines whined, and the rotors slowed.

Eden jumped from the front and slid open the rear door.

Winslow raised a hand in a wave. Eden waved back, and the pair locked eyes for a moment. Winslow knew the dangerous ordeal Eden and Athena had been through this morning. He also knew they wouldn't stop yet, not while an innocent man was in danger.

Watching the small group rush inside, Winslow thought again about The Council. The sooner people like Eden, Baxter and Athena got to choose their path, and the path of humanity, the better.

17

The Van Wick Estate, Near Bellingham, Washington State.

LUDWIG VAN WICK once again rolled his electric wheelchair into their private infirmary. Everett had vacated, been discharged, or whatever the doctor's term was, but now another man was propped up in the bed. This man was larger than Everett. From a distance it looked as though the bed contained a baby elephant, rather than a human.

"Ah, Thorne!" Van Wick Senior said.

Ludwig swung his chair around the room and eyed the battered, bruised, and motionless body. "He's alive?" Ludwig questioned.

Doctor Vos rushed around Thorne, connecting wires to a medical monitoring machine in the corner. The doctor spun around and then shoved his spectacles up his nose with his thumb.

"Miraculously, yes, he's alive. I don't understand how."

Van Wick Senior assessed Thorne for visible injuries. He was all in one piece, which was a good start.

Doctor Vos glanced at the patriarch. The doctor's mouth moved as though he was about to say something and then thought better of it.

"He's... He's... just come in, sir," Vos stuttered, finally. "He's been here just a couple of minutes. I've not even completed an initial observation. Your men dropped him off. He's been pretty badly injured, I'm afraid." Vos pressed some buttons on the medical monitor, causing the screen to light up and display a reading of the patient's heart rate. The machine hummed and then begun its the regular bleeping noise.

Ludwig Van Wick pressed his lips together so tightly that they disappeared into the folds of his face. After a few seconds, he opened his mouth and his face morphed in to a mask of rage. "What have they done to him?" Spittle flew from his mouth. "I will find them, and they will pay." His hands clenched together like bony balls.

"I,.. I don't know exactly," Vos said. "He was found beneath a train viaduct. The train line runs nearly one hundred feet above. The injuries are consistent for an impact on a hard surface. Luckily, he didn't land in the water."

Van Wick's anger burned out as quickly as it appeared and he grinned. His teeth poked out from between his lips. "Ha! They pushed him from a train. That's nothing. That's child's play. He'll be back in no time."

"With all due respect, Mr. Van Wick, I think you're underestimating the severity of Thorne's condition. I don't know the extent of his injuries yet, but he could have fractured vertebrae, broken bones, or internal organ damage."

Van Wick flicked the control of his wheelchair and swung around to face the doctor. "And yet, he's still alive," he said, his eyes burning.

"Yes, against all odds, he's still alive," Doctor Vos conceded.

Thorne groaned and then coughed several times.

"You see, he's even trying to tell you himself," Van Wick pointed at Thorne as though the man were little more than an object. "His body is designed to repair itself and will do so more quickly than you can imagine. Increase the level of nanobots in his system and give him two doses of the Xero+ serum."

"Two doses, sir?" Vos inhaled deeply. "I'm not sure that's a good idea. You are surely aware of the dangers? The Xero+ serum speeds up tissue growth. In a high concentration it could become uncontrollable and lead to internal complications, perhaps even growths on the skin."

"I don't care," Van Wick snarled, pointing at Thorne. "I want him back on his feet now!"

Vos pushed his eyeglasses up again and studied a patch on the floor. "But... But sir, there's more. The serum doesn't just affect the body, it can also interfere with neural... er... neural pathways. Mr. Thorne could suffer from changes in his personality, memory lapses, or hallucinations. I must strongly advise against this."

Ludwig Van Wick zipped forward in the chair and stared up at Vos. "Do as I tell you right now, or it'll be your own health you'll need to worry about."

Vos blinked, his eyes appearing huge behind the thick lenses. Finally, the doctor nodded, thumbed his eyeglasses up his nose, and retrieved a syringe with an extra-large barrel. He pushed the needle into a small vial containing the nanobots which were programmed to supercharge the body's natural repair functions and pulled back the plunger. When the nanobots were loaded into the barrel, Vos turned the syringe upright and pushed out any air and then loaded the Xero+ serum into the barrel too. Vos crossed towards the room and for a second stood motionless beside Thorne, as though waiting for Van Wick to change his mind.

"Get on with it. You're wasting time!" Van Wick shouted.

Doctor Vos swallowed, steadied his hands, and stepped towards the patient. Carefully, he slid the needle in through Thorne's thick and rubbery skin. When the needle was in place, he slowly pushed down on the plunger. After the injection was complete, Vos stepped back and watched the patient.

Silence hung across the room like a shroud.

Doctor Vos glanced from Van Wick to Thorne and back again, holding his breath.

The monitors tracking Thorne's vital signs beeped more rapidly, showing a flurry of activity.

A moment later, Thorne's expansive chest rose as though it were being manually inflated. Then it fell again as the man exhaled. A sheen of sweat formed across his skin, shimmering beneath the infirmary's bright lights. The color in his face turned from a ghostly white to a ruddy glow.

"Yes," Van Wick said, leaning forward excitedly in his chair. "I told you it would work. Ha!"

Thorne's eyelids fluttered, his fingers twitched, and he drew a sharp intake of breath.

"He is waking up!" Ludwig Van Wick said. "It's worked. It's worked!"

He zipped across the room and positioned his chair beside Thorne's bed. He adjusted a control, and the chair rose on a hydraulic lift. When the old man was looking down at Thorne's body, he tapped the control again and the chair stopped.

"I have to agree. The initial physical recovery seemed promising, but the effects are yet to manifest," Doctor Vos said. "We need to monitor him closely." He stepped up to one of the machines and tapped a few buttons.

"Yes, you do that," Van Wick said. "That's what I pay you for." He focused hard on Thorne's motionless body. His chest rose and fell, and he groaned with each exhale.

"Don't move just yet," Ludwig said softly. The old man reached out and touched the back of the giant bloodstained hand. "Your bones are yet to be fully healed, but the bots are at work, and they will soon have you back in one piece."

Thorne exhaled, although it sounded more like a groan. "What... where did they find me?" Thorne's voice sounded hoarse and labored. His lips were cracked and bloodied.

"Beside the railway viaduct," the doctor said.

"I remember," Thorne hissed. "I remember what happened."

Thorne's eyes, which a moment ago had been dull and lifeless, now glinted with a hint of cognizance. They darted around the room, and then finally settled on Ludwig Van Wick.

Van Wick leaned closer, studying the giant's face. "Welcome back," he whispered. "I knew you'd come back. Our work here is far from done. Now tell me what happened."

The machine bleeped wildly. Doctor Vos scurried towards it. "I really must insist that Mr. Thorne rests for a while. His body must repair itself, and for that, he needs rest."

Ludwig Van Wick held up a hand to silence the intrusion.

"Tell me who did this to you," Van Wick hissed.

Thorne grunted, and then a fire burned in his eyes. "The women who saved Hunter..."

18

"Let's start by going back over what happened this morning," Eden said, glancing at Doctor Hunter. Along with Winslow, Baxter, and Athena, they were gathered in Winslow's office, ready to discuss the morning's events. Although Eden and Athena appeared disheveled from their experience, they were pleased to be back on board *The Balonia*.

After a shower and a change of clothes, they were ready for answers.

"I... I... I'm not sure. I really can't make sense of it," the doctor stuttered.

Eden crossed to the window and peered out at the marina. The morning had turned into afternoon and a steady easterly wind pulled at the sails and rigging of the other boats.

Hunter sat in one of the leather chairs nursing a mug of coffee, which also contained a large measure of Winslow's best whisky. Introductions had already been made and Doctor Hunter had been checked over by one of *The*

Balonia's medical team. Except for the whisky, Hunter insisted that no medical treatment was necessary.

"Start with what you do know," Winslow said. "We can fill in the blanks later if necessary."

The doctor glanced up at the older man and nodded. "Okay. I was just getting ready to go to work. I was running late for an early morning appointment. I needed to see a patient before going to the clinic..."

Eden spun on her heel and was about to tell the doctor to get to the point, when a subtle shake of the head from her father froze her into silence. She clenched her jaw to stop words spilling forth and let the doctor continue.

"I was making coffee when the kitchen window shattered." Hunter's skin blanched into the color of a cadaver. "My army training kicked in and I dropped to the floor."

"When were you in the army?" Winslow asked. Of course, the crew already knew everything about Hunter's distinguished career as an army medic.

Eden suppressed another flurry of frustration. She knew that her father's method was to let the guy get comfortable before they addressed the big issues. It was effective, but frustratingly slow.

Hunter ran through some of the conflict and humanitarian situations in which he'd served, then downed the dregs of this coffee. The stresses of the morning seemed to line the man's face as clearly as the scars of battle.

Winslow strode across to the bottle of whisky which stood on his desk. He poured a double measure into a pair of crystal glasses and added ice. He placed one beside the doctor and took a sip from the other. "I wouldn't normally drink at this time of the day, but I have a rule that our guests won't drink alone."

Hunter smiled weakly. It was the first time he'd used such a facial expression.

"I think that's a great rule," Eden said, helping herself to a measure. "Plus, I've had a hell of a morning." She stretched out her aching muscles and then took a deep sip.

"Good point." Baxter helped himself to a measure. "Plus, we're English, and it's way past five pm there."

Eden thought about the conversation she'd had with Athena on top of the train and shot Baxter a frosty glance. "Excuse me." Eden raised an eyebrow. "You've just sat in the chopper all…"

"This morning…" Winslow said, interrupting his daughter. "…what do you remember?"

Hunter thought about it for a long moment. "For you to understand that I should tell you what happened last night."

Eden hoped that the doctor's memory had held up okay. She knew how stressful situations could impact someone's memory. She'd read about occasions when people didn't even know their name, let alone what had happened after a crisis.

"Last night, I was at the theater in Leavenworth where Senator Van Wick was shot," Hunter said, describing what had happened.

"I heard about that," Eden said. "It sounded awful. It's a miracle he survived."

"He did?" Hunter said, his eyes the shape of quarters.

"Yeah, that's what I heard. Let's have a look now." Eden sauntered over to the desk and pulled up the website of a local newspaper. The story about Everett Van Wick's shooting was on the front page.

"It sounds like he's recovering at home," Eden said, scrolling down the page. "There's even a photograph of him here." Eden displayed the photograph on the large screen. In the picture, Senator Van Wick was helped from the hospital and towards a waiting SUV.

"But... but... that's not possible..." Hunter shot up in his seat, almost spilling the whisky that was balancing precariously on the arm of the chair.

Eden and Winslow turned towards the doctor, who was now almost shaking with shock.

"Last night, I honestly didn't think he was going to survive. He had lost an incredible amount of blood. I thought he was a dead man, right there. His pulse was so weak. I could barely feel it. It's a miracle."

Eden and Winslow scowled at each other. Skeptical of so-called miracles they were starting to feel uneasy about this entire series of events.

"Then this morning, the guy who came to... The guy who tried to..." Hunter struggled to finish the sentence.

"The guy who shot at you this morning," Winslow said.

"Yes. He was one of the senator's security guards. I recognized him."

Everyone in the office shared a dumbfounded glance.

"You saved the senator's life, why would one of his security guards want to assassinate you?" Eden asked the question everyone was thinking.

"You should be treated as a hero," Athena said.

Winslow nodded, showing he had been thinking the same.

Hunter paled again at the mention of the assassination.

"I just... I just can't understand it either..." the doctor said, speaking in short, sharp bursts. "I've met Everett Van Wick several times at various events. There must just be some kind of confusion. He's not involved in things like..."

"Think back to last night," Winslow said, soft but firm.

"Was there anything else unusual about the time when you were treating the senator? Anything at all could be useful here."

Hunter stared blankly down at his hands, his mind spooling back through the hours. His gaze hardened with a realization. He sat up a little straighter.

"What is it?" Athena said, reading the doctor's change in posture.

Hunter cleared his throat. "That guy, Thorne, he was the one in charge last night, I think... he behaved like it, at least... throwing his weight around and telling everyone what to do."

Eden nodded. He was one of the nastiest guys she'd ever had the displeasure of meeting.

"It was strange, he stopped me from giving Everett a blood transfusion. I mean, he physically stopped me. He tore the packet of blood from my hands and threw it against a wall. Then, after Everett had been taken by the medics, he stayed around to make sure every drop of blood was removed from the clinic. They even took the swabs, my scrubs, and all the cleaning equipment. Everything."

"That's really weird," Athena said. "Did they say why?"

"No," Hunter said, looking at Athena as though noticing her for the first time. "Now that I think about it, at the time I didn't register how weird it was. Last night I was just focused on saving the senator's life and then I was so exhausted it didn't cross my mind."

"Famous people can be strange, especially politicians," Athena added.

"True, but that's a lot of effort for no reason," Baxter said.

"I'd say there's something they didn't want you to find out," Eden said, speaking before she really thought through what she was about to say.

"What secrets could possibly be contained in the senator's blood?" Hunter said, a sudden flame of fury burning inside him. "What could be serious enough to send someone to kill me?" He thumped a fist down on the arm of the chair. "What! I don't understand it!"

Shock moved through the doctor's body as though a thousand volts had just been fed into his ankles. He jerked upwards and knocked the glass of whisky from the arm of the chair.

The glass spun, splashing its golden contents across a rug, and then crashing into splinters on the floor.

As though acting purely with muscle memory, the doctor leaped from his chair. "I'm so sorry. I didn't mean to." He ran across to the spilled liquid.

"It's fine. Don't worry," Winslow said, his palms outstretched. "It really doesn't matter."

Hunter crouched down over the damp spot and dug a handkerchief from his jacket. Still clearly acting on instinct, the doctor balled up the handkerchief and was about to dab at the spilled liquid.

"Stop," Winslow roared, noticing what the doctor was about to do.

Hunter, his face a mask of confusion, turned to Winslow.

"The handkerchief," Winslow said, pointing at the stained bit of fabric in the doctor's clenched fist. "What happened to your handkerchief?"

Doctor Hunter studied the object as though he'd never seen it before. All thoughts of the spilled whisky now dissipated, he stood and unfurled the fabric. The previously white square of cotton was stained blood red.

"Is that stained with Everett Van Wick's blood?" Winslow said, pointing at the handkerchief.

Hunter nodded. "In the chaos, I must have slipped it away. Out of habit."

Eden crossed to the desk and dug a plastic evidence bag from a drawer. She opened the bag and Hunter dropped the handkerchief inside.

"I suggest we find out what it was Mr. Thorne didn't want you to see," Eden said.

19

Seattle, Washington. Present day.

The atmosphere in Seattle's Climate Pledge Arena was electric. Red, white, and blue streamers ran from one side of the vast space to the other, and the stage was draped from top to bottom in the stars and stripes.

For the twenty thousand people who crammed into the arena's mix of seating and standing, this was the making of history. They had, for the last twenty-four hours, been glued to their screens as their beloved senator, Everett Van Wick, declared his intention to run for office, and then was gunned down mere moments later.

Each person had, logically, thought his address would be canceled. But, when the senator made the sort of recovery that bordered on the miraculous, their excitement built into a fevered frenzy. Now, crammed into the area, they waved flags, hollered, and clapped with a previously unknown passion.

With airport-style security in place, many of the attendees had arrived several hours early just to be sure they were in place for the main event. Performances by music stars and rousing speeches by dignitaries had already set the tone, and now the crowd was ready for the main event.

The lighting dipped and as though controlled by a single mind, the crowd hushed into a murmuring silence. An ocean of smart phones rose as people tried to capture on video the miraculous moment that was about to occur. Thousands of people held their breath in anticipation of the man who had fallen into the jaws of death and survived.

For a long moment, nothing happened.

Then, the announcer boomed through the arena's sound system, powered only by renewable energy. The voice was so bass-heavy, it sounded as though it was rumbling up from the earth itself.

"Ladies and Gentlemen," the announcer began, before thanking the staff of the arena and a few local dignitaries. "It is my pleasure, to introduce to you, the next President of our great country, Senator Everett Van Wick."

The crowd erupted into madness, whooping, and hollering at the top of its lungs. A few thousand more smart phones and cameras appeared, flickering and strobing in up-stretched hands.

Clearly a man of drama, Everett waited until the cheering reached its peak, then limped on to the stage.

Helped on one side by a member of his security detail, the senator was clearly in pain. His face was pale, and walking was clearly uncomfortable. As ever, he was impeccably dressed in a tailored, grey suit.

His less than ebullient entrance didn't dampen the crowd. They roared ever louder, twenty-thousand throats creating the sort of noise that was normally associated with hurricanes.

Ten feet from the lectern, Everett Van Wick held up a

hand. The security guard stopped. The senator whispered behind a cupped hand and the man stepped back.

Then the senator, his face half pain, but half determination, limped on. Everett Van Wick's point was clearly made — this is for anyone who doubts my ability to succeed in adversity.

A thousand tears rolled down a thousand cheeks as a sense of pride moved through the auditorium.

After a dozen clearly uncomfortable steps, Senator Van Wick reached the lectern. He took a moment to steady himself and then raised a hand. As though cast under a spell, the crowd hushed into silence.

Van Wick smiled. Then, already every bit the statesman his electorate wanted him to be, he spoke.

"You know, there was a moment..." the senator checked his watch dramatically. "...when I didn't think I'd make it here."

The crowd roared in laughter at the understatement.

"But you know what?" Van Wick continued, waiting for the laughter to subside, his voice steady despite the flicker of pain in his smile. "Not making it here was never an option. Never an option!"

A wave of applause swept the arena.

"Yes, let me be honest." Everett Van Wick's voice dipped into a husky whisper, giving each of the listeners the illusion that he was talking just to them.

"The events of the last few days were unforeseen. They have proved a struggle. But I can assure you this, this will not be the last struggle I face on the road ahead." His voice boomed now, as strong, and deep as ever. "And I can tell you, it will not be the struggle that defines me. It will not be the struggle that defines us." The senator gestured to the crowd, sweeping his hand from left to right.

"You know as well as I do, as citizens of our great nation, we are not defined by the obstacles we face, but how we rise to meet them. How we persist despite them."

The crowd howled in agreement, lapping up every word.

"Let us look to the men and women who built our nation. They did not do so by shying away from challenge and danger. They did so by rising to the challenge, by putting danger in its place and saying out loud, one and all, 'we will not be stopped.' Repeat it with me, 'we will not be stopped.'"

And everyone did. From the security guards standing at the door, to the staff manning the café, to a pair of homeless men, listening at the door.

The senator paused and surveyed the audience.

Another wave of applause, this time stronger, thundered through the arena. People stood, tears streaming down their faces, their roars filling the stadium.

"We stand up," the senator said, the pain in his voice growing more obvious now. "We stand together, and we push forward. I want to make it very clear to everyone in this arena, and everyone watching at home, or anyone — God forbid, who should want to get in our way — I am standing. I am pushing forward. I will not back down."

The audience exploded, standing up, their cheers reverberating across the stadium.

"What I said in Leavenworth still stands. I will run for president. And if I must limp my way into the Oval Office, then so be it." Everett grinned, then rested a tender hand on the side of his abdomen where the bullet had seared through his flesh. "That's what this country needs: dedication, resilience, and a leader who won't back down. A leader who will stand strong in the face of adversity, and who will never stop fighting for you."

As the applause finally subsided, Van Wick spoke again, his voice quieter now, yet no less passionate.

"Tonight, I stand here, not as a man who nearly died, but as a man who lived. As a man who has been reminded of just how precious life is, and just how important it is to fight for what you believe in."

As he said these words, a renewed sense of determination etched on his face, the crowd erupted in a deafening applause that seemed to shake the very foundations of the arena. Van Wick raised his hand in gratitude, his eyes shining with resolve and sincerity.

"Thank you, God bless, and let us change the lives of every man, woman, and child in our wonderful country. Goodnight."

Everett Van Wick lifted his hand in a wave. He paused for a long moment, then spun around and staggered down from the podium. Two of his security detail rushed forward and helped him across the stage.

At the side of the stage, the senator paused, turned back towards the crowd, and waved. His million-dollar smile beamed as bright as ever, straight down the lens of a camera positioned at the front of the stage.

The camera operator hungrily snapped away. It was the picture that would cover the front page of every newspaper across the country in just a few hours' time.

∼

BACKSTAGE, Everett slipped out of his jacket and collapsed into a chair. The façade that he'd worn on stage was no more. His face was now a tense mask of pain. He squeezed his eyes shut and waited for the next batch of painkillers to kick in.

Doctor Vos, the Van Wick's private physician got immediately to work. Vos attached an IV drip to Everett's arm and then checked the dressing.

"How's it looking?" came another voice, followed by the whirr of electric motors.

Everett opened his eyes and saw his father roll into the room on his electric wheelchair.

"It's healing well. The pain should also recede," Doctor Vos said, pushing his eyeglasses up his nose.

Ludwig Van Wick slid up close to his son, examining the dressing with the care of a doctor. "Good. Leave us." Ludwig Van Wick snapped his gnarled fingers.

Doctor Vos nodded, gathered up his things and hurried from the room.

"You'll be fine in a few days. You did a good job tonight, considering."

"I'm glad you think so," the younger Van Wick said. "Why didn't you have us announce the candidacy here? It would have been so much more impactful, and no chance of this..." Everett glanced towards his wound and winced.

Ludwig Van Wick looked at his son. "Announcing it here is what people would *expect* you to do. This campaign is all about the unexpected."

"If you say so," Everett muttered, his jaw set in a grimace of pain.

"But it was a good speech today, you had them there," Ludwig said, clearly focused on something else. "You're winning hearts and minds and that's what we need."

"I had the writers keep it simple today. Less is more, I think," Everett said.

"Yes. You'll have plenty of time to speak later. In fact, in the weeks to come, every news broadcast will include your voice. For now, less is certainly more."

The younger Van Wick smiled. The powerful drugs coursed through his system, dulling the pain.

"This is just so frustrating," the younger said, glancing down at the wound. "There is so much more I need to be doing."

"We may be powerful, but there is no man alive who can control everything," the older replied. "Things will happen that get in the way of our plans, and we will use them to our advantage." He screwed his slender, age-spotted fingers into a fist.

"With words like that, maybe you should have written the speech," Everett said, his voice soft under the effects of the drugs.

Ludwig Van Wick scowled, clearly unused to his son's attempt at humor. His eyes flicked around the room.

"Any news on the doctor?" Everett said.

Ludwig Van Wick's pale and wrinkled face drew together into a scowl. "That doctor is causing us many problems. He seems to have been able to evade our team at every turn."

A smile flickered across Everett's face, disappearing before his father noticed it. "What? How is that possible? He's just a doctor?"

"He seems to have fallen under the protection of some rather well-connected people." A string of drool hung from the older man's lips. He inhaled sharply, and it slithered back into his mouth. "It's all very unfortunate for us. In fact, it couldn't have gone much worse."

"Who could be more well connected than..." Everett sounded woozy now as the painkillers completed their work.

"Don't you worry about that," Van Wick Senior snapped, pointing a finger at his son. "They shall be dealt with. I have a team searching for him as we speak." He squinted until his eyes were barely visible in his wrinkled face.

"Listen, father. Don't you think we could just leave the doctor?" Everett said. "His quick work saved my life while the medical team was still trying to get through the snow. I've met him several times in the past, he's a good man. Ex-military. We can trust..."

"You have no idea who we can trust," Ludwig Van Wick roared, his papery skin flushing red. "You may trust him now, but what about in the future? What about when you are elected? Doctor Hunter is a loose end, and we did not get where we are today, leaving loose ends untied."

"I... I..." Everett Van Wick tried to speak but was interrupted again by his father.

"You never should have gone into a public place without the medical team in situ." Van Wick Senior pointed at his son's injury.

"If... if I'd waited, then the event would not have happened," Everett said. "The medics were over an hour late..."

"You gave some low life the opportunity to use you as target practice and now we're in this mess. In the future, you do what I say, and you wait." Ludwig Van Wick descended into a fit of coughing. He dug a handkerchief from the folds of his jacket and hacked into it for almost a minute.

When the coughing had subsided, Van Wick the younger spoke again. "I think we should leave the doctor be. He's a nobody. He'll go back to his small-town practice, and we will never hear from him again."

"Impossible," the older man snapped. His voice was just a hoarse grumble coming from somewhere deep within his chest.

A beeping sound issued from a tablet computer attached

to the wheelchair. The old man tapped at the screen, then his eyes shone like burning coals.

"That's interesting," he mused.

"What?"

"The Doctor has been traced to a yacht moored in Bell Harbor Marina. Our problem should be resolved within the hour."

20

"What do you make of all this?" Eden said, pacing into Winslow's office an hour later.

Winslow looked up from the book he was reading and smiled at his daughter. He placed a bookmark between the pages, closed the book and placed it on a side table.

Eden crossed towards the sofa on which her father was lounging. Opening directly onto his private cabin, the office became more of a living area during the evening. Winslow would often invite members of the team to join him on the comfortable sofas for drinks and lengthy conversations.

"What do I make of what?" Winslow said, stretching out.

Eden noticed that her father had showered and was wearing comfy sweatpants and a thick jumper. His bare toes curled into the rug at his feet.

"This situation that we've unexpectedly got mixed up it. Do you really think the Van Wick family would try to have Doctor Hunter killed? What secrets could he possibly know?" Eden sank into the sofa beside her father.

The lighting in the office had changed too. During in the

day, bright ceiling lights made the room feel like a work space, now shaded lamps gave it a cozy atmosphere.

"There really is no knowing," Winslow replied, sighing. "I fear this rabbit hole is going to go a lot deeper than any of us can imagine."

Eden kicked off her shoes and pulled her legs up on the sofa beneath her. She turned to face her father and the pair locked eyes.

Eden felt a momentary and unusual welling of contentment. Sitting on the sofa with her father felt like such a simple thing, but the battle to get here had been long and arduous.

Eden stretched in the way a relaxing cat might and then rested her hand on her father's arm.

"Can I ask you something?" Eden said, breaking the silence.

"Of course, my dear, anything you want."

"Do you think I was wrong to get involved in saving Doctor Hunter? Should we just have left him?"

Winslow pulled a deep, thoughtful breath.

"But then Hunter would be dead. He's a good man, you said so yourself." Winslow spoke as though the problem was merely hypothetical, not something they were currently living through. Eden loved the way he examined problems from the outside in the way a mechanic might assess a faulty engine.

"Yes, and I know it sounds awful, but now I think I've put us all in danger."

"I see," Winslow said, sounding out the words carefully. "That is tricky..."

Eden half closed one eye in fond frustration. Her father never gave a direct answer in conversations like this. He would ask questions to let her figure out what was right or wrong.

"And don't say that we'll just have to stay one step ahead," Eden said, pointing at Winslow. "That might work today, but we can't always be one step ahead. One day our latest enemy will catch up and then we'll be in trouble."

Winslow's face lightened. "Well, if you're going to think about it like that, then one day we're all going to die, anyway. Our good fortune is only delaying the inevitable for some length of time."

Eden folded her arms and pouted.

"Look, it's all a matter of perspective," Winslow said. "Yes, choosing to help Doctor Hunter has put us in danger..." Winslow stopped talking for a moment, clearly thinking carefully about what to say next. "You know one of my favorite proverbs — it's Greek, I think — although who first penned it, I can't tell you."

"Go on," Eden said, arms still folded tightly.

"A society grows great when old men plant trees whose shade they know they shall never sit under."

"Meaning what?" Eden said, her arms loosening around her chest.

"Look at it this way. You sit under a tree and enjoy its shade, yet you were not the person to plant it. You are part of that tree's surrounding, but not its originator. Doctor Hunter is not your problem, but yet, if we seek guidance from this proverb, then he is part of your solution."

"Now you've lost me," Eden said.

Winslow leaned forward, his hands resting on his knees. "It means that we are part of something bigger than ourselves. We are just here for a moment in the history of the world, but during that time, we have a choice..."

"I think I get it," Eden said, her arms falling into her lap.

"You're saying that we should help Doctor Hunter because that's the right thing to do? That's our legacy, in a way."

"I'm not saying that, but if that's your interpretation, then great," Winslow said.

Eden almost laughed out loud. "I'm not sure if that's really..."

"All I'm saying is that there's a reason you were in that place at that time. Maybe part of that reason was to help a good man out of a difficult situation," Winslow said.

"So, I did the right thing? Even though it's endangered the people I love?"

This time, Winslow just smiled softly.

"I know that's what you want me to say," Winslow said. "Yes, I think you did the right thing. If someone is in trouble, and if we are in a position to help them, then we must."

The pair shared a moment of silence.

Eden gazed at the water through the darkened glass and a smile lit her face.

"I'm glad you've said that. Sometimes I just need reassurance. I'm not used to this..." Eden's voice dried up in her throat.

"Go on," her father said.

Eden swung around to look at her father. "All those years I was on my own, without you, without this." She held her hands up to indicate their surroundings.

"But I" Winslow began, but Eden silenced him with a finger.

"I know you're sorry, and I know it couldn't have happened any other way. Believe me, I do. But my point is, I just got used to not having people around. There was no one to help me, but also there was no one to worry about. If I got in danger, then it was only my neck on the line."

"And now you feel as though you're responsible for us?" Winslow said.

"More than that," Eden said, staring deep into her father's eyes. "Now I feel as though couldn't be without you." Emotion welled and Eden shifted her eyes down in an attempt to hide it.

Alexander Winslow leaned forward and hugged his daughter. "That's good, because you don't need to be without us."

"Maybe one day I will, and if we keep antagonizing crazy people that day won't be far away," Eden said. "Or if *I* keep antagonizing crazy and violent people."

Winslow straightened his arms and looked and his daughter. "Do not live in fear, you hear me. You must do what you know to be right, and if that puts us in danger then that's the way it must be."

Eden nodded and wiped her face with her sleeves. "One more thing. Please change your cleaning products, I think I'm allergic to something in this office," she grumbled. "It's made my eyes water."

Father and daughter shared a laugh.

"Actually, I'm glad you came by because there's something I want to talk to you about," Winslow steeled his nerves.

"Sure," Eden looked at her father and then saw something twinkling on the floor a few feet away. "What's that?"

"It's something I've wanted to discuss with you for a while, actually, but just haven't found the…"

"No, sorry, I mean, what's that on the floor? There's something sparkling on the carpet over there." Eden moved her head from side to side, trying to see the blinking light again. "I think it's a bit of that glass Doctor Hunter smashed earlier. You don't want to cut your feet."

Winslow sighed. "Sure, let's sort that first if it's going to distract you." He got out of the chair and crossed the room. "Where did you see it?"

Eden gave directions and Winslow sunk to his hands and knees. He tried to spot the shard of glass, but couldn't see anything on the patterned rug. He crawled forward a foot and then yowled in pain.

"I think you've found it," Eden said, grabbing a handful of tissues from the desk.

Winslow sat up on his haunches and peered down at the sliver of glass which had dug itself into his palm.

"Told you," Eden said. "You wouldn't want to get that in your foot in the middle of the night. You could be laid up for days."

"Yes, boss," Winslow groaned. "Sort it out for me, then." He held his hand out and Eden used one tissue to pluck out the shard and then held the other tissue against the tiny gash. Within a few seconds, the bleeding subsided.

"All better," Eden said, as though talking to a child. "What was it you wanted to tell me?"

At that moment, someone knocked at the door. Then without waiting for a reply, the door swung open and Baxter hurried in.

"There's something you should see." He turned on the office's large video screen.

"I think it'll have to wait for another time," Winslow said, giving Eden the warm smile she had noticed he was using more and more recently. "It's nothing urgent at all."

Winslow climbed to his feet and crossed to see what Baxter wanted to show him.

Eden gazed down at the tissue in her hands, spots of her father's blood staining the paper, and was suddenly struck by an idea. She glanced from the tissue to her father, and then back at the tissue.

21

Michael Nattrass checked his Casio for the fifth time in the last ten minutes, then turned his attention back to the small television in the corner of the Bell Harbor Marina Security Office. If one mindless game show hadn't just finished and another begun, he would have thought the old watch was on the blink. As it was, his mind settled on the only plausible explanation: that good-for-nothing-lay-about who was supposed to relieve him at midnight was late, again. Michael felt a flame of anger roar up inside him. He should be cruising his way home already, perhaps passing by a takeout joint to avoid concocting something from the scraps left in the refrigerator.

The guy who was supposed to come on at midnight had only started a week ago. He was fresh out of college, by the looks of it. Still not used to the demands of the real world.

People like that didn't exist when he was a young man, Michael mused, rubbing his stomach. Back in those days there were not enough jobs to go around, so you had no choice but to shape up. Any sign of missing shifts or turning up late and you'd be out on the streets before you could say *'union representative.'*

"It's just a damned shame," Michael said, knowing full well what the protocol was. He would have to wait another hour, and then if the lay-about still didn't turn up, he could report the absence to central, and they'd send a replacement. Either way, it meant Michael was here for another two hours at least.

Michael stared morosely at the small television on which an excitable game-show host was unveiling the star prize — a car which had been out of production for at least two decades.

"And they don't even have cable," Michael said, thinking of all the good shows he could watch if he was at home. He started hunting around for the remote control.

"Where is that..." Michael pushed a stack of papers to the side. "Why they keep playing these re-runs, I have no idea. Surely someone can invent something new? I've a good mind to do it myself," Michael said, as though the television might answer him.

Talking to yourself was a curse of working alone for hours on end. In fact, Michael thought, it was probably one of the few ways to stave off the madness. He searched the desk for the remote control, his chair creaking with his weight shifting from side to side.

"Where is that damned thing?" He picked up a clip board which detailed the vehicles that had arrived during the last ten hours. There had been a few deliveries and boat owners returning or leaving either in taxis or executive cars. Nothing out of the ordinary. Nothing at all exciting. Nothing exciting ever happened here.

Still at a loss as to where the remote control had gone,

Michael shoved his chair backward and checked the stained carpet.

"Ah, there you are!" He spied the control right under the desk.

In a motion which was devoid of all grace, Michael scrambled under the deck and retrieved the control. He straightened up, cracking at least five vertebrae in the process, and then slumped into the chair.

"Let's see what else we've got on here." He stabbed at the control with a force that suggested it was responsible for the channel's dated content. The television popped, and the screen went black.

"No, that's not what I..." Michael glanced at the security console to his left and froze. The screens of the console had blanked too.

Michael was suddenly alert. The protocol stated that any trouble should be called in immediately. He wondered whether a power outage was a sign of trouble.

Protocol also stated that if in doubt, backup should be called. There was no harm in calling the team and having to send them away again for a false alarm. Except for the fact he'd look like an idiot when they came down here, sirens howling only to find him sitting in the dark.

Michael grumbled and his eyebrows inched together in thought.

His mind made up and his nerves steeled, Michael's hand slid across the desk towards the handheld radio, which was his constant lifeline to central control.

Michael's hand reached the radio and his fingers closed around the device. He lifted the radio to his mouth and took a breath, ready to give his report.

A jacketed hollow point bullet, moving at one-thousand

feet per-second, stopped a single word from leaving Michael's lips.

The first shot struck Michael in the chest, throwing him forward into the desk. His arms slumped to his sides and the radio clattered to the floor.

A man stepped from the shadows at the back of the security office. He raised a silenced handgun and fired another two shots into Michael's back. Blood gushed out across the stained carpet.

The figure stepped up behind Michael's slumped body and disconnected the camera system from the back-up power device which continued to record even if the power failed. Then, just to make sure, he severed the connection to the network too. The cameras mounted around the marina were now nothing more than decoration.

"Security office is clear," the figure said into a hidden comms device. "Ready."

The figure strode out of the office, crossed to the water's edge and lit a cigarette. To a disinterested observer he would just look like the security guard smoking a cigarette in the middle of the shift.

After a minute or two he heard the gentle sound of splashing water. A small boat materialized from the darkness. Completely black, the craft was almost invisible and powered by two men with paddles, almost silent too.

The boat drew alongside, and a man climbed on to the quay. The men with the paddles stayed in the boat.

As soon as the man was clear, the boat slipped away, melting immediately back into the night.

The man flicked his cigarette into the water and the pair slunk into the shadows. With the power out, the marina was swathed in darkness. A few of the yachts still glowed across the water. These craft had onboard batteries and power generation systems that would keep them going for weeks — it was unlikely anyone aboard had even noticed the power outage. If they had, it would take them hours to report it.

The other vessels were now just blocks of shadow against Seattle's skyline.

Dressed in black fatigues and using night vision technology, the assailants moved silently across the marina. The gentle lapping of the water and the distant hum of traffic was the perfect cover for their discreet footsteps. The jarring cry of a lone seagull cut through the ambient noise as it pounded overhead.

The figures moved to the end of the first quay and then turned towards the far corner of the marina where only one yacht stood. This vessel, one of the largest and grandest in the marina, sat isolated from the others by almost one hundred feet.

The figure in front moved towards the vessel with the calculated precision of a seasoned hunter. His gloved hand gestured a silent command and the two men split up, ready to complete the next part of their task.

The leader moved up to the side of their target vessel. The craft was a thing of beauty, its sheer white flank reared up over forty feet above the quay.

The other man slipped into the water behind the craft and swam along its starboard side. Reaching the hull, he pulled out a series of small, magnetic charges, and set about fixing them to the hull where he knew the ship's fuel tanks to be. The strategy was not only the destruction of the vessel, but the elimination of anyone on board. With several thousand gallons of fuel igniting in a fraction of a second, the chance of any survivors was minimal.

Their plan here was assured destruction while drawing

as little attention to themselves as possible. If they'd just wanted to destroy the craft, a couple of rocket-propelled grenades could have done the job in a fraction of the time.

The task now complete, the man hauled himself back out of the water.

The leader's gaze swept the marina once more, again making sure their presence had raised no alarms. Satisfied that everything was in place, he nodded, and the two men moved away from the vessel.

Reaching a safe distance, the man removed a detonator from his pocket. With his face still a mask of icy calm, he pressed the button.

The result was immediate and cataclysmic.

The charges detonated in perfect sequence. Although muffled by the water, the boom of the explosion rippled through the night.

A towering column of water spewed skyward. The yacht disintegrated into a fiery spectacle. Flames sparked a thousand times more in the surrounding water. The shockwave rolled in all directions, shaking the docked boats, triggering alarms, causing lights in the nearby buildings to flicker. A deluge of debris followed, hissing, sizzling, and pounding down into the water.

The two men slipped back into the water and waited a full five minutes to see if any survivors emerged from the burning yacht. Satisfied there were no survivors, the men merged back into the inky water and swam toward their extraction point.

22

The Balonia, North Pacific Ocean.

"There she goes," Baxter said, captivated by the explosion on the screen. Flames roared up, instantly engulfing the craft, and licking hundreds of feet into the clear night sky. When the explosion died down, Baxter turned to Winslow. "How did you know they wouldn't be able to tell the difference between that yacht and *The Balonia*?"

Winslow rocked back on his heels. "Both craft are the same size and shape, both were made by the same manufacturer, and that one was where ours was supposed to be. Once inside, you'd be able to tell the difference, but I didn't think they would look that closely."

"If it looks like a duck and sounds like a duck..." Athena quipped.

"I wish you'd stop talking about ducks," Eden said, shooting Athena a side eye.

"Only goosing around." Athena attempted to elbow Eden in the ribs. Eden swished out of the way just in time.

"That sounds just about right," Winslow said, ignoring

the girl's friendly hostility. "Obviously, we had to do the switch last night when no one was around to notice. We also set up our own camera system and had an agent placed in the security office. He's going to have a couple of bruises where the body armor caught the bullets, but that saved the regular guy's life."

"You've thought of everything," Eden said, captivated by the fire on the screen.

A fireboat roared on to the screen, red lights strobing. The surrounding boats bobbed back and forth in the wake of the emergency craft. Once in position, a firefighter on the helm aimed a powerful water jet into the yacht's charred remains.

"That must be less than three minutes," Athena said, glancing at the timestamp at the top of the screen. "They got there quickly."

"We've got connections with emergency services all around the world," Winslow replied, his arms folded. "They were waiting just outside the marina."

"Useful people to know," Eden said, unconsciously mirroring her father's stance.

"What about the person who owns it? They'll be really upset in the morning," Athena said.

"Sheikh Hassan Al-Mansouri and his entire crew are back in the Middle East right now," Winslow said.

"That's still a big hunk of cash going to the bottom of the marina," Athena said, as the fire crew on the screen got a handle on the flames.

Winslow's smile widened. "I have it on good information that he already has a new one in construction. It will be ready in a few months. I wouldn't feel too sorry for him."

Eden spun from the screen to the glass door which led

out to *The Balonia*'s rear deck. Doctor Hunter stood against the railing, staring morosely out at the ocean.

"If we're talking about feeling sorry for someone..." Eden said, pointing at the doctor. With the glass door closed, she knew he wouldn't be able to hear their conversation.

"Tell me about it," Athena said. "Just over twenty-four-hours ago, he was a normal small-town doctor living in a cute little house. Now his house has been shot to bits, and he's on the run from a group of relentless mercenaries, in the middle of the Pacific with a bunch of people he doesn't know."

"And you thought I attracted trouble," Eden said, throwing at ice glance in Baxter's direction.

Baxter was too busy reading something on the computer to even notice the gesture.

"But all that aside, I hate people like that," Eden moaned. "You can't just go around killing people when it suits you." She cracked her knuckles as a response to the anger which simmered in her gut.

"How long do you think this will put them off?" Athena asked Winslow, pointing at the burning wreckage on the screen.

"Well, we've certainly got the upper hand now, but I don't think it'll last more than twenty-four hours," Winslow said.

"Let's assume we've got no more than twelve." Eden turned away from the screen and faced the assembled crew. "Remember the last time we underestimated someone?"

The crew exchanged an uncomfortable glance. They all remembered the last time they'd underestimated someone too well. In fact, they'd invited the man aboard *The Balonia* thinking he was a powerless victim when in fact he had been the mastermind behind the whole operation. It was a whole daisy chain of failures that almost cost them the ship and countless lives.

Winslow cleared his throat. "You're quite right. When it's reported that no one died in the blast, the Van Wicks will figure out that they've been had. We've got a head start and we need to use every second."

"I think it's fine, what happened last time was all Beaumont's fault," Athena said. "He's not here now, so..."

"Athena, you know we don't attribute blame here. But yes, he certainly had some egg on his face," Winslow said, cruelly.

"Where are they now, anyway?" Eden asked, talking about Richard Beaumont and his reconnected teen sweetheart Vittoria DeLuca.

"Helping to investigate a newly discovered Buddhist Stupa in the Maldives," Winslow said. "It potentially dates back a couple of millennia, they think, as the structure is believed to be from the era when the Maldives practiced Buddhism, before converting to Islam in the 12th century. It's quite a remarkable find, especially considering the Maldives' propensity for rising sea levels and changing landscapes."

"Some people have all the luck," Athena said.

"That's just typical," Eden said. "They pair slip off to investigate something in a place known for white sandy beaches, crystal clear water..."

"...and unlimited cocktails," Athena said.

Eden raised her voice a touch to talk over Athena "...and leave us to deal with a crack team of ruthless assassins who will stop at nothing until..."

Eden saw her father's grimace and her voice dried up in

her throat. Athena's expression mirrored Winslow's. Eden turned around slowly.

Hunter stood at the door behind her, having slid open the glass without Eden hearing. The man looked, pale, dejected and downright scared.

"I'm sorry," Eden murmured, her words sounding hollow. "You're safe now, that's the..."

"We've got the time advantage, so let's put it to good use," Winslow said, clapping his hands, and turning to face Baxter who had been silently tapping away at the computer throughout the conversation. "What do we know about the Van Wick family so far?"

"Quite a lot, unsurprisingly," Baxter said, minimizing the video of the burning ship and loading their one-of-a-kind research system. The system not only had access to public information, but private records, university research, and all the published works in existence. Using the system, they were able to trawl every electronic document on the planet.

"The Van Wicks are an incredibly wealthy and reclusive family who have a known lineage of several hundred years," Baxter read from the screen. With a couple of taps on the keyboard, he brought up the Van Wick's family tree.

"Look at that," Eden said, pointing at the screen. "I think I've heard of about half of those people."

"Yes, they have family ties to all sorts of people in America and Europe. Politicians, business leaders and sports stars, musicians, you name it," Baxter flicked to through pictures of oil paintings showing stern looking men. "But it's these guys we're particularly interested in, the Van Wick ancestors."

"This is crazy," Athena said. "And for all these years I've been thinking that Game of Thrones was fictional!"

"But that just means they're a well-connected family,"

Eden said, tapping her chin. "That just doesn't explain why there's a crew of blood-thirsty mercenaries..."

"Let's just stop taking about the mercenaries," Winslow said, softly. He turned towards Hunter. "Eden has a very *dramatic* turn of phrase."

"Sorry, I didn't mean to..." Eden glanced at Doctor Hunter who had paled even further.

The computer beeped, indicating the receipt of a message through their secure email system.

"It's the results on the sample of the senator's blood we sent over to the lab," Baxter said, quickly opening the email.

Everyone in the office turned to face Baxter as he opened the report. So eager to read the report, Baxter forgot to display it on the large screen for everyone else to read too.

"Oh wow," Baxter mumbled, placing his hands over his face.

Winslow, Eden, Athena, and Doctor Hunter turned to Baxter.

So engrossed in the report, Baxter didn't even notice.

"That's... I don't quite..." he muttered again. "That's really interesting," he whispered.

"WHAT!" everyone else shouted, startling Baxter.

Baxter realized what he'd done. He clicked a couple of keys and the report appeared on the screen. The team gathered around and read in enraptured silence.

23

The Van Wick Estate, Near Bellingham, Washington State.

"Eden Black," Ludwig Van Wick uttered to himself. "I bet you're sorry you meddled in someone else's business this time. Ha!" The laugh at the end of the sentence was more of a snort and caused a string to trickle from the old man's nose. He dug a handkerchief from his pocket and dabbed at his face.

Van Wick Senior was in his study on the mansion's second floor. Positioned by the window, he could see the night-cloaked grounds of the estate spread out before him. Decades of experiments on himself had weakened Ludwig Van Wick's skin, meaning bright sunlight caused him searing pain. The night time, Ludwig thought, was the closest he ever got to a normal existence.

"Now with that little problem out of the way, the real fun can begin."

Ludwig Van Wick tapped the wheelchair control and slid towards his desk. The size of a family car and constructed from mahogany, the desk was the room's centerpiece.

The only light came from a green shaded brass lamp on the corner of the desk, and the fire which flickered in the grate. The room was silent save for the faint ticking of an antique grandfather clock.

Bookshelves packed with leather-bound volumes lined two sides of the room, and a large window filled the third. The fourth wall contained two things which Ludwig Van Wick held dear — a massive oil painting of the family patriarch, Johannes Van Wijk, and the head of a rhino.

The painting was like the one in the hallway below, except here Johannes was pictured on the bow of a ship staring out at the horizon as though welcoming in the future. The rhino, Ludwig Van Wick had shot himself during a trip to South Africa as a guest of then Prime Minister Balthazar Vorster. Van Wick remembered the trip fondly. The two men had spoken extensively in their native Dutch and enjoyed time on Vorster's various ranches. They had shot the rhino from the back of Vorster's Jeep, while her calf looked on. Ludwig remembered the young rhino's expression as though it were still right in front of his eyes.

Van Wick shook his head slowly as the corners of his eyes turned up into something of a smile. Those were good times. Simpler times. Forcing himself to concentrate, Van Wick flicked through the papers stacked on his desk. The weight of the upcoming campaign was enormous, and so were the stakes.

The private line on his desk phone lit up, interrupting Van Wick's thoughts. Only a few people knew the number to that phone, which meant the call was of grave importance. He reached across the desk and tapped the answer button.

"Yes," Van Wick said.

"Mr. Van Wick." The voice on the phone sounded nervous. "I'm afraid I have some bad news. We've just got a report from our man on the salvage crew down at the Bell Marina…

Van Wick's eyebrows rose.

"Sir… the thing is… it's quite complicated. It was supposed to be simple, of course it was, but what with it being in the middle of the night, without the ability to use lights…"

The voice stammered and Van Wick could practically hear the caller wringing his hands.

"Get to the point dammit." Van Wick crumpled a report between his fingers.

"The problem is. The ship we targeted wasn't the right one. Our intelligence was flawed. The crew of *The Balonia* must have switched places before we arrived at the Marina. As I say, the odds were against us with the darkness and everything…"

"What exactly are you telling me?"

The caller drew a breath. "*The Balonia*. It's still out there."

24

The Balonia, somewhere in the North Pacific.

"To be honest with you, I've absolutely no idea what this means," Eden said, stepping back from the screen and glancing around the room.

"I am so glad you said that," Athena said. "I was feeling like the class dunce."

"It's a report on the blood sample we recovered from Everett Van Wick," Winslow said.

"I know that," Eden said with her hands on her hips. "But what does it show us?"

"Urrrm." Winslow rubbed a hand across his face. "That he... umm... that the blood on that handkerchief was..." Winslow stood in silence for almost three seconds and then shook his head. "No, I've got to be honest. It makes no sense to me either."

Eden laughed out loud. "The great Alexander Winslow, leader of one of the most powerful organizations in the world, speaks a dozen languages, knows more about anything than anyone I've ever met and..."

"There is no shame in admitting you don't know something," Winslow said defensively. "And I only know ten languages, some have multiple dialects."

Eden glared at the information on the screen, as though it was defeating her. "Well, your ten languages are no help here..."

"This report says... although I can hardly believe it myself... Everett Van Wick's blood is Xero+."

Coming from behind them, the voice caught everyone by surprise. They all whipped around to see Doctor Hunter step towards the screen. The doctor removed a pair of spectacles from his jacket and carefully put them on.

Eden had been so focused on trying to work out the report herself, she'd forgotten there was an actual doctor in their midst.

"Okay," Eden said. "Now we're a class full of dunces."

Hunter stepped up to the screen and ran his finger across the information. For what felt like an ice age the doctor murmured sentence fragments to himself and shook his head. "...just incredible... I thought this... It can't be..."

Snapping from his trance, Doctor Hunter whipped around to face the others. "Do any of you understand what this means?"

Everyone shook their heads.

"Well, isn't that just lucky I'm here?" Doctor Hunter's voice took on the tone of a lecturer. He turned from his audience back to the screen. "It just so happens when I first left the army, I planned to go into hematology... that's the study of blood," Hunter said, quickly answering the question before anyone asked it.

"I spent almost two years studying the subject, but the lab time was just too much." The doctor removed his eyeglasses. "All that artificial light.... All that working on screens... It just wasn't what I went into medicine for."

Eden's finger beat an impatient pattern against her arm. She knew her father would be giving her his *'be patient'* look, but she refused to turn around and see it.

"I wanted to work with *people*," Hunter continued. "I went into medicine to help people directly, not spend all that time analyzing digits on the screen. So, I made the hard decision to turn my back on that specialty."

Eden's impatience grew, it felt as though she was holding her breath underwater.

"I did what I had to do, I handed in my notice. My professor asked me to reconsider, but of course I couldn't, by then my mind was made up. I packed my bags and the next week saw the practice up for sale in Leavenworth and..."

"What about the report?" Eden burst out, gasping for air.

The doctor turned to Eden. His manner suggested that he'd completely forgotten the point of the conversation.

"Yes, the report. Well, every person's blood is different, but generally they fit into groups which comprise certain proteins and antibodies. The primary system we use to classify the blood is called the ABO system," the doctor continued, warming to his theme, "...and within that there are four types, A, B, AB and O."

"Right, sorry if this is obvious," Athena said, concentrating hard, "but how can you tell what blood type a person is?"

"It's not obvious at all." Hunter pointed at Athena with his eyeglasses. He answered the question using a lot of language Eden didn't understand. Eden tried to focus on the doctor as the terms rushed into her brain and then dissolved somewhere between all the other stuff she knew.

For a moment, it reminded her of being at school and why she'd hated every minute.

"That's called the Rh factor and is another protein on the red blood cells," Hunter said, as though concluding. "If you have it, you're Rh-positive, and if you don't, you're Rh-negative."

"Okay," Eden said slowly. "But what does that have to do with Everett Van Wick?"

"Well, it's essential to..." The doctor suddenly paled, and the next word died on his lips. He swallowed, and the room was suddenly silent. "That makes sense now. Everett Van Wick's security guy..."

"Thorne?" Eden offered.

"Yes. He was very adamant that I couldn't give the senator a transfusion." The doctor turned, looking at each of the assembled people in turn. "That makes perfect sense now. It's as clear as day!"

"it is?" Eden said.

"In order to give the Everett a transfusion, I'd have had to know his blood type. In that situation, I wouldn't have had time to perform a test, so I would have given him blood type 'O', which is the most universal."

"But not for people with this Xero+ type?" Eden said.

"Exactly." The doctor pointed at Eden. "There's no knowing how an actual Xero+ patient would react to a regular blood type."

"I have a question," Athena said, raising her hand as though she were in a classroom.

"Hold on a second," Eden interjected, talking over Athena. "Am I right in thinking the Xero+ blood could be what makes the Van Wicks so good at everything they do?"

"Without proper study, I wouldn't be able to give a definitive answer. It certainly wouldn't be statistically relevant. Mutations in the blood can cause all sorts of things. Some mutations can be neutral, having no impact on the organism. Others can be harmful, causing genetic disorders or health conditions. On the other hand, certain mutations can cause beneficial traits that offer advantages..."

"But, just here, amongst friends, do you think it's possible?" Eden pushed, interrupting before Hunter lost her with all his science jargon again.

"Yes. I do," Hunter said simply. "In fact, it's more than just a hunch. We worked on a Xero+ blood sample back at the university. It contained very intriguing properties, including indications the patient had an incredibly robust immune system and increased stamina and physical endurance."

"Hold up a minute," Winslow said, breaking his usual cool countenance. "You told us you'd never seen a person with this blood type before."

Hunter spun around to face Winslow. "That's right. No living person. In fact, before five minutes ago, I would have bet my life on the fact the last person with Xero+ died over five thousand years ago."

No one answered for a second, then Eden asked what was on everybody's lips. "Then how were you able to test the blood?"

"By using the only place Xero+ has ever been detected. A tiny sample which has been in a German laboratory for over one-hundred years."

"And where did *that* come from?" Eden asked, trying to keep the frustration from her voice.

Hunter turned towards Baxter, who was sitting behind the computer. "Can you run an internet search for me, please," Hunter waited for Baxter to nod before continuing. "Please search for the *Lady of Leone*."

Baxter's hands flashed across the keys and in less than ten seconds, an image filled the screen.

Hunter's voice took on the grandeur of a showman. "Ladies and gentlemen, I give you the only human known to possess the Xero+ blood... that was until about ten minutes ago."

Winslow, Baxter, Athena, and Eden gasped all at once. Then they all stepped forward to get a closer look at the blurry picture on the screen.

Registering what she saw, Eden stepped back again. Her face was a mask of disgust.

"Woah, woah, woah," Eden said, making the basketball *'time out,'* gesture with her hands. "I think we all need a bit of a reality check here. This just can't be..."

"I remember reading about this." Winslow interrupted his daughter and examined the picture with amazement. "This beautiful woman caused quite the stir. No one knew quite what to do with her back then."

Eden tried to look away from the haunting image but found it weirdly compelling. The picture was more like a murder victim than a scientific discovery, she thought.

"That's right," Hunter said, pointing at the screen with the arm of his spectacles. "She was one of those finds that had the historical and the science communities competing for her attention."

"I can imagine," Winslow said.

"Stunning," Eden said, sarcastically.

"Amazing," Athena said. "What is it exactly that I'm looking at?"

"This is the *Lady of Leone*, or at least that's what she became known as. Named after the Leone Ridge in the Alps, which is where she was found," Hunter said.

"If my memory serves, she was frozen solid inside a glacier," Winslow explained, clearly pleased to be back on familiar ground. "The story goes, in 1882 a pair of climbers were trapped at high altitude in a storm and sought refuge in a cave which led right inside a glacier. Of course, they weren't to know that no one had ever seen the cave before."

Hunter took over the story. "Fortunately, they had the sense to contact people who knew what they were doing before digging her out. Somehow the poor lady had been frozen so quickly that she was almost perfectly preserved..."

"...What was so ground-breaking though, was that the state of preservation allowed scientists to extract samples of tissue! Real undecayed tissue!" Winslow's eyes blazed with excitement.

"Imagine what we could do if we had that now!" Hunter said, bouncing off Winslow's excitement. "With a thorough DNA analysis, we could learn more about the origin of our species." Hunter counted the points with his fingers. "We could study the population's health. Using gut microbiota, we could find out what they ate. It would be like a snapshot of their life..."

"We could even find the genetic markers to trace to their current ancestry, linking them to modern populations around the world," Winslow said.

"Or clone them like in Jurassic Park and create a land of the living mummies!" Athena said, grinning widely.

"Spielberg has a lot to answer for," Winslow said, shaking his head.

"James Cameron more likely," Hunter said.

Silence hung throughout the room for a moment.

Hunter sighed when no one picked up on his comment.

"Hold on a sec." Eden turned to the doctor. "You said, imagine what we could do *if* we had that now?"

Winslow and the doctor exchanged a glance.

"Yes," Winslow said. "After nearly three decades of being pushed around Europe, it was decided that the *Lady of Leone* should be brought to the United States."

"That's right. Of course, the few samples that had already been taken were kept in Europe, but they were nothing more than microscopic," Hunter said. "The lady herself was packed up, incredibly carefully from what I've read, in a specially designed climate-controlled crate which really was cutting edge back then."

"Where is she then?" Eden said.

"You've got to remember, at this time, blood testing was still in its infancy, and the world's greatest experts were here in the United States," Hunter continued. "It was a dangerous move, but probably…"

Eden held up a hand to silence Hunter. "My brain is going to overload with all this science talk…"

"Me too," Athena interjected.

"Let's keep it simple," Eden said. "We will find out where the *Lady of Leone* is now. We will go there using any means necessary, and run the tests…" Eden stopped talking as she saw Hunter shaking his head.

"I'm afraid it's really not that simple," Hunter said.

"How did I know you were going to say that?" Athena said.

Winslow gazed dejectedly at the floor. For a few seconds no one said anything.

"Well, what happened?" Eden said, shrugging.

"The *Lady of Leone* never made it across the ocean," Hunter said, shaking his head. The grief on his face was plain to see.

"After a lot of political wrangling, and several days of careful transportation from London to Southampton, The

Lady of Leone's special crate was finally loaded into the cargo hold of the brand-new White Star Ocean liner."

A silence settled across the office.

"James Cameron," Eden mumbled, finally picking up on Hunter's comment a minute before.

"They set sail from Southampton on April 10th, 1912," Winslow said.

The ghostly image peered out from the screen, as though taunting the living from beyond the grave.

"*The Titanic*," Eden said, her voice little more than a whisper. "The *Lady of Leone* was on board *The Titanic.*"

"The *Lady of Leone* is *still* on board *The Titanic*," Winslow corrected her.

25

The Van Wick Estate, Near Bellingham, Washington State.

Ludwig Van Wick heard the door to his study open and close. Footsteps padded across the wooden floor and then on to the large Persian rug. The approaching person stopped and stood awkwardly in silence for a few seconds.

His chair facing out towards the window, Van Wick didn't see who had entered, but he didn't need to. Although his body wasn't how he would like it to be, there was nothing wrong with his ears. His mind was sharp too. Ludwig would recognize Doctor Vos's shuffling gait anywhere.

Ludwig let another second or two pass. An owl hooted from somewhere on the estate. Eventually, he turned to face his visitor.

Doctor Vos stood in the middle of the room, the white lab coat dangling around his ankles.

Ludwig smirked. In all the years Doctor Vos had worked

with the Van Wicks, Ludwig didn't think he'd ever seen the doctor not wearing his lab coat.

Doctor Vos thumbed his glasses up his nose and inhaled in the way a dog might before dinner. "You asked to see me, sir?"

"That's right doctor, thank you for coming so quickly." Van Wick slid his wheelchair towards the doctor. With no personal use for chairs, Ludwig didn't have any in his office. That meant whoever was visiting him had to stand, often shuffling awkwardly from foot to foot. Ludwig Van Wick was pleased to see Doctor Vos do exactly that, like a child needing to use the toilet.

"Things have taken a rather unexpected turn," Ludwig said, stopping his chair a few feet away from the doctor. "Unfortunately, a loose end has not been tied up as effectively as I would have liked it to be."

"I'm sorry to hear that sir," Vos said, followed by another snuffle and then a thumb of the spectacles.

"To cut to the point, as we're both busy men, I need Thorne ready for deployment."

The doctor blinked several times. "When sir?" Vos said, finally.

"Tonight. In fact, within the next hour."

The doctor stood stationary for a long moment. His mouth opened and closed. "Sir, I don't think you are aware of the severity of the injuries Thorne has sustained. Any normal person would have been dead in an..."

"He's not a normal person though, is he?" Van Wick roared, spittle flying from his lips. "You have made sure, over the last twenty years, that he is a long way from normal."

Doctor Vos Adam's apple bobbed. "Sir, Thorne has fractures in multiple vertebrae, a broken tibia, and a punctured lung. The nano bots are working to speed up the repair, but it's still very early."

"Increase the dose and have him here in one hour," Van Wick said, his face a squirming ball of rage.

"I really must implore you, sir," Vos raised both palms. His tongue moved along his lips one way and then back the other. "We've already pushed the dosage of the nanobots and the Xero+ serum beyond any levels that we've tested before and..."

"Any negative effects so far?"

"Some swelling of the skin. It's too early to say if there will be anything more serious..."

Van Wick held up a hand to silence the doctor. "Doctor Vos, please pass me that silver box over there." He extended a hand towards the fireplace. Embers smoldered in the grate.

Vos thumbed his glasses up his nose and crossed obediently to the fireplace. He picked up the box, walked back across the room and held it out towards the older man.

"No, you open it," Ludwig said, sliding his chair backwards.

Without question, Vos did what he was told, his hands shaking more than usual. Vos peered inside and gasped. Two black scorpions raised their tails.

"Doctor Vos," Ludwig said, his tone glacial, "these are Saharan Deathstalkers. Their venom, as you might know, is particularly potent. A sting can be... excruciatingly painful, and often fatal."

Vos paled, his eyes darting between the scorpions and Van Wick.

"You can shut the lid if you want."

Vos didn't waste a second slamming the box closed.

Van Wick leaned forwards. "Wouldn't it be terrible if one

of these beauties was to find its way into your bed tonight, or one of your shoes, or even that lab coat you never take off?"

Vos nodded frantically.

"You make sure Thorne is here in one hour. Do you understand?"

Vos nodded again, placed the box on Van Wick's desk, and ran full pelt from the room.

∽

Fifty-six minutes later, the door swung open, and Thorne's long shadow swept into the room.

"Ah good, you're here," Ludwig said, turning to face the giant man.

Thorne stepped into the room, his footsteps shaking the floorboards. The door swung closed behind him. Thorne crossed the room and stepped into the light cast by the lamp. As the glow enveloped him, Van Wick Senior noticed that Thorne's once angular features were now bloated and misshapen. His skin which was once the color and texture of marble, was now blotched and sagging.

"We have a problem." Van Wick tapped document on the desk. "A serious problem, and I know you're the man to deal with it."

"How can I help you, sir?" Thorne said, his voice little more than a deep grumble.

Van Wick pointed up at the giant man. "Now that is exactly what I wanted to hear. It's such a shame more people don't have your attitude." Ludwig slid behind his desk and looked closely at an image on a computer screen.

"It appears those women who tried to stop your assassination of Doctor Hunter, are a little more than keen off-piste skiers."

"That was my failing, sir," Thorne replied. "You tell me where they are and I'll put that right, immediately."

Van Wick tilted his head in appreciation at the other man's comments and then spoke uninterrupted for several minutes.

Thorne stood, listening in silence.

"Questions?" Van Wick asked when he had finished his explanation.

"Just one sir," Thorne replied.

Ludwig felt a fission of frustration. Thorne had been trained to hear an explanation once and then act. He didn't need repetition, encouragement, or niceties. Maybe Vos was right, maybe the serum was having a cognitive effect.

"Yes."

"When do we depart?"

Van Wick's lips split into a sneer. Thorne was right. That was one thing he'd yet to say.

"If my calculations are correct, you should be able to catch up with them if we move now. Take a team, ten of the best. The chopper leaves in twenty minutes."

"Consider it done," Thorne said, without question. Thorne turned, crossed the room, and swung open the door. A square of light shone into the office from the hallway.

"One more thing," Ludwig Van Wick said.

Thorne paused and turned towards the older man.

Van Wick almost recoiled now seeing the man's face in brighter light. Swollen patches of red and purple blotches spread unevenly across his cheeks and forehead, reminiscent of the burns one might get from radiation exposure. His eyes, once sharp, now had a cloudy, almost milky appearance, and they bulged slightly as if under pressure.

"Make it slow and painful," Van Wick said.

Thorne simply nodded and stepped out through the door.

26

The North Atlantic. Two days later.

EDEN STOOD at the deck of the *Njord Fadir*, admiring the sunset. Although the surrounding ocean, glittering beneath the sinking sun, was similar to what she'd seen many times from the decks of *The Balonia*, the two ships couldn't be more different.

Owned and operated by a Norwegian company which specialized in accessing the bottom of the world's deepest oceans, the *Njord Fadir* was a hulking block of steel which didn't so much slip through the waves, as force the waves into submission beneath her rugged hull.

Eden thought back over the last few days which had brought them to this lonely corner of the Atlantic Ocean. When they'd realized the key to the Van Wick's shady success might be in the hold of the world's most famous shipwreck, the team had sprung into action. First, they'd searched for a ship that would do the job. Fortunately, the *Njord Fadir* had been laying cables two hundred miles away. Using a bit of influence and a wad of cash, Winslow persuaded the crew to agree to a slight detour and a few days away from their current task.

It always surprised, and disgusted Eden, how easily things came together when someone like her father with cash and influence was asking. For a moment, she remembered the days when she used to work alone. Back then, getting help from anyone was a struggle, even if she offered to pay for it.

Next there was the matter of transport. They'd taken the Eurocopter back to Seattle and then an off the books private jet to Halifax, Canada.

Eden glanced at the Knighthawk helicopter which had picked them up from Halifax and brought them here. Constructed above the ship's superstructure, the helipad soared fifty feet above the decks. Now tethered in place in case of high winds or rough seas, the Knighthawk looked like a nesting bird of prey, scrutinizing the decks below for its next meal.

Eden turned back to face the ocean and felt the ten-thousand horsepower hydro propulsion engine slip into a lower register.

And finally, they'd had to deal with Doctor Hunter. Much to the doctor's frustration, it was unanimously agreed that it was too dangerous for him to come on the expedition. In the end, Winslow had arranged for a contact to put him up in London.

"We're nearing the site," Winslow said, padding across the deck and joining Eden on the railing. Like Eden, he wore one of the insulated orange jackets which were a uniform aboard the ship. The north Atlantic wind sliced through anything else as though it were a thin piece of cotton.

"Any word from Hunter?" Eden said, watching the water churned white by the propellers.

"He's arrived at the safe house in London," Winslow said, the wind blowing his hair backward like a tattered flag.

"There's no way the Van Wicks can trace him? They're very well-connected people."

"Not possible. He used fake identification all the way. Nothing to trace him there at all."

"And the safe house is secure?"

"Oh yes. Penthouse apartment overlooking Hyde Park, guarded by one of the best private security firms in the world. No one gets in or out unless they're supposed to."

"Good," Eden said, reassured. "Things like that worry me."

"I know," Winslow said. "They worry me too."

"It's like the people who lost their lives in this place." Eden narrowed her eyes against the wind. "They trusted people to get them across the ocean safely, and those people in power failed. I would have hoped that in over one hundred years things were different but wealthy people like the Van Wicks still use their power for evil things."

Eden's voice trailed off in the wind. She felt a chill slide its way inside the regulation issue thermal jacket.

"You're right, and that's why we do what we do," Winslow said.

"To leave the world a fairer place than we found it."

The pair stood in silence for a moment.

"It's awful to think that this view was the last thing all those people saw," Winslow said, narrowing his eyes to slits.

For another few seconds, neither of them spoke.

"I can't help but think about what that must have been like," Eden said, her voice barely audible over the wind and the distant murmur of the ship's engine. "Those people got on board thinking it would take them to a new life, to something better."

Winslow nodded. "We trust people in positions of power every day — our governments, the people who treat our water, or those who drive our buses."

Eden eyed her father. "And this is what happens when power is abused. Thousands of people lost their lives right here." Eden turned back to the ocean surrounding them on all sides. "Left in one of the world's most hostile places."

Eden imagined for a moment what it must have been like that night.

"Imagine the terror," Winslow said, clearly thinking the same thing. "All because a group of men thought they could build something more powerful than nature."

"The classic human hamartia," Eden said. "I have no spur to prick the sides of my intent, but only vaulting ambition, which o'erleaps itself and falls on the other."

"Ahh, The Scottish Play," Winslow said, glancing at his daughter. "I see those expensive schools taught you something."

"Mostly how to climb over walls and avoid doing what I was told."

"That's an important lesson too," Winslow smiled. Secretly it made him proud that his daughter railed against any school he tried to place her in. He knew from long years of experience, that happiness and success was more about standing out than fitting in. In the end, he'd removed Eden from school, and they'd traveled together, her learning on the way.

"But this is a reminder to us," Eden said, pointing down at the concrete-colored water. "We need to keep doing the right thing, even if it may be difficult."

"Absolutely," Winslow said. "We still have judgment

here, that we but teach bloody instructions, which, being taught, return to plague the inventor..."

"Stop it now," Eden said. "I know you love Mac..."

"The Scottish Play," Winslow interrupted. "You know it's bad luck to issue his name."

"You... thespian," Eden grumbled. She knew Shakespeare's Macbeth, or the Scottish Play more than most. Several years ago, while still at school she'd uncovered a stash of gold coins which the playwright had hidden in order to avoid the overbearing new taxations brought in by King James the first. Unbeknown to anyone at the time, the only clues to the location of the stash were hidden amid riddles in the play. Eden loved the irony of Shakespeare having the play performed for the king, essentially telling him the location of the hoard without the royal ever knowing it.

Winslow cleared his throat and again thought about what it was he wanted to tell his daughter.

"As I said the other day, there's something I've been meaning to discuss with you." He tried to keep his voice steady, although inside his heart beat furiously.

"Sure, I'm all ears," Eden said, turning to face her father. In her mind's eye she pictured the blood-stained tissue and wondered if her theory was correct. Either way, she would find out soon enough.

Winslow coughed again and kept his eyes fixed on the horizon. When he spoke, his voice was much weaker than before. "It's about..."

A squawk issued from the radios attached to both Eden and Winslow's belts. "We've reached the dive site," a Norwegian accented voice came down the line. "Crew briefing in two minutes."

Winslow closed his eyes for a moment.

"Go on," Eden said, her heart fluttering now.

Winslow shook his head. "There's no time. We'll do it later." He drew a breath of the saline air and turned to face his daughter.

"We'd better go inside," Eden said, turning away from the railing.

"Tomorrow, and tomorrow, and tomorrow…" Winslow boomed, shouting through the North Atlantic wind. "Creeps in this petty pace from day to day…"

He turned around to see Eden pass through the door and inside the boat.

27

The interior of the *Njord Fadir* bustled with energy. As Eden climbed the steel staircase towards the canteen which doubled as a conference room, she passed various members of the crew rushing the other way.

She pushed in through the door and glanced around. The gloom was punctuated by the soft glow from the computer screens, casting long, dancing shadows around the deck.

Baxter stood with two of Fadir's crewmen examining something on one of the computer screens. Since they'd arrived on the ship, Baxter had been learning how to operate the submersible.

Eden was pleased to learn that he needed all this training. Baxter frequently made the loft claim that he could control any machine ever built. This, as far as Eden was concerned, proved otherwise.

Athena pored over a map stretched out on the table in the center of the space.

Eden stepped up to the central table and noticed there were in fact two documents spread end to end. One was a map of the ocean floor, and the other was a schematic of the submersible which would allow them to access such depths.

"Impressive thing," Eden said, pointing at the craft.

"Yeah, I'm pretty happy to stay on the surface, though," Athena said. "It might have all that state-of-the-art technology, but..." Athena grinned in a way that said more than words ever could.

Athena's gesture conjured up all sorts of images in Eden's mind, from the deep ocean's crushing pressure, to being swept away by undersea currents, or even the unlikely event of mechanical failure so far beneath the waves.

"Yeah, I hear that," Eden said, a bolt of fear moving up her spine. "But it's no more dangerous than some of the other stupid things we've done."

Athena smirked. Whilst Eden was right, she was clearly using humor to cover her fear.

The door behind them swung open and Winslow stepped in. He slid out of his thick orange coat and hung it on a hook by the door.

"Good, everyone is accounted for," boomed a Norwegian accented voice from the far side of the room. Erik Gustavsson, the ship's chief engineer turned from the screens and scrutinized each of the room's occupants for a long moment. Eden froze as the Norwegian's ice-blue eyes locked with hers.

The Norwegian broke off the stare, then turned back to his computer. Gustavsson thumbed a key and a light in the center of the room flickered. Then, as though by magic, a holographic representation of *The Titanic* shimmered into existence above the table.

Eden gasped, surprised by the quality of the image. She stepped in closely and examined the ocean liner. The ship sat half buried in the silt of the ocean bottom but was still clearly recognizable with her multitude of promenade decks and rows of portholes.

"This is one of the latest 3D scans of the wreck," Gustavvson said. "Taken by a team just a few months ago."

Gustavsson tapped another key, and the ship began to rotate.

"She's down there, two and a half miles straight below," Gustavsson pointed a thumb towards the floor. "She's at some serious depth. 12,500 feet to be precise. I'm sure you know, but it ain't... how you Brits put it... A walk in the park?" For a moment, he mimicked a British accent, causing a few uneasy chuckles among the Norwegians present. "We're talking about a dangerous dive here," Gustavsson pressed on. "People have lost their lives in much lesser depths."

"The submersible is capable and tested at that depth, right?" Eden said.

The icicle eyes swiveled in Eden's direction. Gustavsson held Eden's gaze for a long moment before answering.

"Look, the *Njord Havspeil*, the submersible we will be using for this dive, has been to that depth many times. She's proven herself. But what many who come out here forget, or just don't understand, is that this isn't some controlled environment. This is the wild, unpredictable ocean. She's got a temper, and she'll change her mind quicker than Olsen's girlfriend." Gustavsson pointed at a chuckling man at the back of the room with a beefy finger. The room lightened with laughter.

"Olsen doesn't even have a girlfriend!" another man teased.

"That's my point," Gustavsson retorted instantly, causing even louder laughter, including from Eden.

"But, jokes aside. Down there, it's one of the world's

fiercest oceans. Conditions can shift in a second." With a swift motion, Gustavsson snapped his fingers, the echoing sound punctuated his stark warning.

Eden's anxiety cranked up to the next level. It felt like a family of bugs were setting up camp in her stomach. She shared a glance with Baxter who would join her on the mission. He too looked grave.

Winslow stepped up to the spectral display and traced the contours of the sunken ship.

"According to the original manifest, the *Lady of Leone* is in the hold on D deck. That's in the ship's bow section." Winslow indicated the area with his finger. "When she sank, *The Titanic* descended at an angle. Inside, you'll have debris and sections of the ship's superstructure in the way. You'll be facing a maze of collapsed bulkheads, mangled compartments, and fallen debris."

Eden swallowed, the bugs in her stomach now felt like they'd had babies. Lots of babies.

"Let's get one thing straight." Gustavsson's intense gaze first met Eden's and then shifted to Baxter's. "You might not be able to get what you're looking for. It just might not be possible. An' I tell you this now, the only heroes on this ship are dead ones. If things get sticky, you get topside pronto. If you're trapped below, there's no cavalry coming for ya."

Gustavsson pressed a button, and the hologram changed to an image of the submersible craft.

"Meet the *Njord Havspeil*." Gustavsson's voice held a note of pride. "She's the tiniest craft to attempt a descent on *The Titanic*, making you folks the first to glimpse the great ship's insides since that fateful night." He gestured towards the hydraulic arms protruding from the submersible's front. "Once you're inside the wreck, if you can get inside, one of you will handle the craft's movement, while the other manages these arms. It's gonna be a snug fit, I won't lie. And like Winslow pointed out, we're not entirely sure about the obstacles you'll encounter on your way to the cargo hold, or if it's even doable."

"Say we find her," Eden said, stepping up to the hologram. "How do we get her out again?"

"From what Mr. Winslow's documents show," Gustavsson began with a squinted gaze, "what you're after is sealed inside a steel crate. Those hydraulic arms," he pointed towards the submersible, "are what you'll use to free that crate from any rubbish or mess down there." He then motioned to a mechanism affixed to the submersible's underbelly. "Once you've got it free, this winch here will pull the crate up to the *Njord Havspeil's* underside. The winch is sturdy enough to handle nearly a ton."

"One more thing worth noting," Winslow said, stepping towards the glowing holograph. "We're not treasure hunters, and this is not a smash-and-grab operation. Be aware that everything down there is a historical relic. It's a graveyard. A mass graveyard. Countless people lost their lives here, and we must proceed with utmost caution and respect."

A moment of eerie silence settled over the room.

"That's the good news over with." Gustavsson clapped his hands. Gustavsson pressed a key, and the image of the submersible disappeared. A picture of a weather map faded on to a screen.

"The unfortunate part," Gustavsson grumbled, glancing at a weather chart on the wall, "is that our weather folk have spotted a storm brewing, and it's heading straight for us."

"How long have we got?" Winslow asked.

Gustavsson turned and poked at the map. "At best, 24-hours, at worst, I'd say 10."

"Could we wait for it to pass?" Eden said.

Gustavsson scratched his thick beard, contemplating. "We could wait it out, sure. But the dicey bit is the timing. Over the past year, the gods have only given us five days good enough to dive to that depth. This part of the North Atlantic is a fickle beast."

Eden swallowed, but it felt like a tribe of insects had now spawned another whole family.

Gustavsson's brows furrowed, accentuating the age lines on his forehead. "Descending is one thing, searching is another, and coming back up yet another. It all takes time." He glanced at his watch. "If the *Njord Havspeil* is still under when the storm arrives, we've got problems."

"Surely the storm won't affect us two miles under the water?" Eden said. The moment she asked, she wished she hadn't.

Gustavsson swung around and the icicle eyes drilled into Eden's.

"I'm not sure who jumped overboard to make you an expert?" Gustavsson said.

Several of the Norwegians laughed nervously.

"I'll humor you since we're trying to get off on the right foot here. The problem isn't while you're under the water. The problem is trying to pull a ten-ton submersible out of the ocean in thirty-foot-high waves. It would be like trying to dive with a wrecking ball. I will not put my crew or my ship in danger. If the storm hits and you're still down there. You stay submerged until it passes.".

The room fell silent, each person absorbing the daunting reality of the mission.

"We go now," Eden said, her voice hard. "Sure, it's getting dark, but that won't make any difference two miles down, right?"

Everyone around the room looked at her.

Eden turned and locked eyes with Gustavsson. For the first time, she felt an edge of respect in the Norwegian's icy gaze.

Gustavsson nodded once. "Prepare the *Njord Havspeil*. We launch in one hour."

"We've got an appointment with a ghost," Eden said, locking eyes with Baxter.

28

FLOOD LIGHTS BATHED the *Njord Fadir's* back deck as crew members prepared for the dive. The last forty-minutes had passed in a whirlwind, as the crew readied their systems and reminded Eden and Baxter of everything they needed to know.

"It'll be cold down there," Gustavsson said. "In order to save space and energy, the submersible only has a minimal heating system. Just enough to keep the machines operational." Eden and Baxter slipped into the thick thermal coats, as well as wearing several warming layers underneath too.

"Bringing her out!" Gustavsson roared.

Eden turned and saw a large door swing open, exposing a cavernous storage compartment in the ship's superstructure.

"Moving!" a crew member shouted, followed by the whine of electric motors.

A second later, the submersible slid out onto the rear deck. Although Gustavsson had said the craft was small, Eden hadn't realized it would be quite that small.

The *Njord Havspeil* was about ten feet long and six feet wide. Thrusters positioned on each corner would allow the craft to move whilst under the water. The craft's dominant features, however, were the two powerful hydraulic arms, which made it look like a metallic lobster.

The *Njord Havspeil* stopped in the center of the deck. Gustavsson and his crew leaped into action, checking again through all the craft's systems. One of the crew placed a ladder against the craft, climbed on to the top, and unbolted the hatch.

Eden focused beyond the submersible and out at the ocean. She focused on why this was so much more than recovering a relic from an old shipwreck. This was about justice.

"Ready to embark," Gustavsson roared from beside the submersible.

"Good luck," Winslow said, locking eyes with his daughter. "And be careful. I want you back."

Father and daughter merged into a hug.

"I'll be back before you know it," Eden said. "What's twelve-thousand feet below the ocean anyway, right?"

Winslow smiled weakly, his stomach churning like the storm that was closing in on their position.

Eden and Baxter crossed the deck and inspected the submersible. Eden stepped forward and peered through one of the portholes. Fitted with super thick glass, they distorted the view of the space inside. Soon, that glass would be the only thing protecting them from the lethal force of the ocean's depths.

Baxter scurried up the ladder and dropped in through the hatch. Eden watched him settle into a seat through the porthole. Once Baxter was in place, Eden scaled the ladder and climbed on top of the submersible. She stepped up to the hatch and peered inside. The first thing she noticed was the smell. She crinkled her nose, attempting to stop the smell taking root.

"Did the cleaner fall overboard?" Eden said, turning to Gustavsson.

The Norwegian snarled, and the lines on his weathered face deepened. Maybe the guy had been at sea so long he didn't have any sense of smell left.

"I can't decide if it's closer to damp washing or gone off food." Eden stepped close again and prepared for the stench.

Gustavsson scowled and pointed at Eden. "Maybe on your posh yacht you have time for this sort of thing, not out here. This is a hard place for hard people, not air freshener." The Norwegian pressed his lips together in a gesture that clearly showed disgust.

Eden raised her eyebrows like a scolded child and slipped inside.

"It really stinks, doesn't it?" Eden whispered in Baxter's ear.

Baxter nodded once and then grinned.

"Good, I'm glad it's not just me." Eden glanced around. The inside of the submersible was just big enough for Eden and Baxter to sit side by side. Eden tried extending her arms forward, but the screens got in the way when her elbow was at forty-five degrees. She extended her arms upwards and found the same. It was cramped to the extreme.

"All this technology, you'd think they could just run the seat covers through the wash or something?" Eden slipped on the headset and heard distant radio static.

Baxter's grin expanded further.

"At least leave the hatch open for half an hour and get some fresh air in."

This time, Baxter actually giggled.

Eden turned her attention to the controls. A series of switches and levers allowed both people to control different functions of the craft.

Gustavsson clanged up the ladder and peered in, his head framed by the hatch. "I'm sorry, it's not the Ritz. Shall I get one of the crew to fetch some potpourri?"

"No thanks. I think we're used to it now," Eden replied sweetly.

"Good. Well, good luck to you. She's a difficult ocean to navigate, but I think you'll be just fine. Check in every few minutes." With that, Gustavsson disappeared from the hatch.

"Wait, wait!" Eden said, looking around frantically.

Gustavsson reappeared. "Yes?"

"How will we know if something's gone wrong?"

Gustavsson smiled, causing the wrinkles around his eyes to deepen even more than usual. "Don't worry. You won't know something's gone wrong until it's too late. We have a saying out here, you don't hear the crack that kills you. Good sailing!" With that, Gustavsson disappeared. A loud thump echoed through the submersible as Gustavsson threw the hatch closed and bolted it in position. The bolts ground tight, reminding Eden that there was no way out now until they returned to the ship.

"That's reassuring," Eden glanced at Baxter, who was systematically going through the controls. "Do you think that guy should write motivational speeches?"

"Maybe he could get a job with Senator Van Wick," Baxter quipped in reply.

Eden laughed out loud and then elbowed Baxter in the ribs. "I think that's the funniest thing you've ever said."

The pair went silent for a minute while they familiarized themselves with the various controls and dials.

"Do you know what you're doing?" Eden said, watching Baxter count off a row of switches. She was glad that she just had to operate the hydraulic arms using a pair of small joysticks.

"It's just like flying the chopper." Baxter moved the controls.

"You reckon you could fly that underwater?" Eden replied.

"I could fly anything, anywhere," Baxter said, deadpan.

"That's why you needed all that training?" Eden teased.

The pair sunk into silence for a few moments.

Another clunk reverberated through the submersible as it was hooked on to the crane.

"Is this the craziest thing we've done so far?" Eden asked, when she thought the silence had gone far enough.

"That depends on whether it works," Baxter said. "So far, we've been lucky."

"Yeah," Eden said, her focus through the tiny porthole. "So far we have."

Then, the submersible moved.

Eden gripped on to the seat and kept her eyes fixed on the ship through the small porthole. The window gave a strange fisheye-like view of the deck. Eden stared at her father. Although Winslow was looking up at the submersible, Eden couldn't be sure he saw her through the thick glass.

The submersible inched upwards, swinging left to right on its cable. Then, the crane operator swung the boom around, hanging the submersible out over the water.

Eden peered down at the rolling waves and imagined

the shipwreck, thousands of feet below. She already felt a chill shudder its ugly way through her senses.

The sound of the crane changed, and the submersible sunk down towards the waves.

Eden stared back at the *Njord Fadir*, instinctively finding her father standing amid the assembled people. He stood motionless, watching them.

Eden locked eyes with him until they sunk out of view. It appeared as though he was looking back at her, although Eden still couldn't be totally sure.

The submersible thumped into the water, sending a shudder up through the fuselage. Water splashed up and over the portholes, blurring Eden's vision. It felt as though the submersible was trying to float on top of the waves before the weights strapped to its underside pulled them down.

Eden felt the submersible pull against the cable in a swell.

"All systems operational?" came a voice through their headsets. Eden recognized Gustavsson's Norwegian burr.

Eden glanced at Baxter, who was once again systematically checking the dials and switches. Eden had been so caught up in the drama of the dive, she'd forgotten all the essential checks they were supposed to be doing.

"Thrusters operational. No leaks through the hatch," Baxter said, before reading the oxygen and co2 levels inside the submersible.

Eden peered out through the porthole and watched the team of divers converge on the submersible. The divers were there to make sure the craft launched and returned to the ship safely. Eden had a new appreciation for them, diving in open waters like this was dangerous. This was not their fight, and yet here they were, taking part in it. She remembered the discussion she'd had with her father two nights before.

"A society grows great when old men plant trees whose shade they know they shall never sit under," she whispered to herself.

Eden noticed one diver was smaller and leaner than the others. The diver swam up to the porthole and brought their face in close to the glass. Eden recognized Athena's smile and remembered that she'd offered to join the dive team. Athena then formed a circle with her thumb and forefinger while extending the other three fingers, giving Eden the "okay" sign — a universal diving gesture which meant everything was alright.

Eden mimicked the gesture. Then the women shared a smile.

Athena pushed away from the glass and faded into the coal-colored waves.

"You are good to go," Gustavsson said. "Releasing in three, two, one..."

A clunk moved through the submersible's body. For a heartbeat, the craft hung still in the waves and then began to sink. The sloshing noise which had pounded against the hull now quietened, then the grunt and grumble of the *Njord Fadir* faded too. In less than a minute, Eden and Baxter heard nothing but the gentle hum of the submersible's systems and saw nothing more than water passing the portholes.

29

Alexander Winslow crossed to the railing and watched the submersible drop beneath the waves. For a few moments, the lights on the top of the craft were visible, then they too disappeared. He took a deep breath and sent up a silent prayer for Eden and Baxter's safe return.

A heavy hand thumped against Winslow's back, almost knocking the wind from him. He slumped against the railing, the metal cutting into his ribs.

"They'll be fine," Gustavsson said, sidling up beside Winslow and leaning on the railing. "It's not as dangerous as you might think down there." He pointed down at the waves.

"It's not a walk in the park, as you said," Winslow replied.

The Norwegian barked with laughter. "I thought you'd like that. Heard that on one of those American shows! Na, the sad thing is that it's safer down there than walking down the street in some places. That's the mad world we live in." The Norwegian dug a packet of cigarettes from his pocket, stuck one between his lips, and lit up.

He offered one to Winslow, but Winslow shook his head.

"True," Winslow said quietly, eyes still focused on the water.

"Hold on, what's that?" Gustavsson said, suddenly alert. "That noise, listen."

Winslow listened closely but heard nothing. He glanced at the Norwegian, whose eyes flared.

Whatever the noise was, it was clear Gustavsson didn't like it.

Gustavsson grabbed the cigarette from between his lips and dropped it to the floor. He crushed it out beneath the toe of his boot and then snagged the radio from his belt.

Winslow strained his ears. Sure enough, a throaty growl cut through the rumble of the *Njord Fadir's* on-board systems and the slapping waves on the hull. Winslow listened for another second and recognized it as the engine of an aircraft.

"Bridge, bridge, come in," Gustavsson barked into the radio. "I can hear an aircraft approaching." Gustavsson held the radio to his ear until a reply hissed down the line.

"Airplane coming this way," Gustavsson said. "How close?"

Winslow couldn't hear the reply, but from the expression on Gustavsson's face, knew that it wasn't good news.

Both men scanned the skies in silence for a few seconds.

"Isn't that normal?" Winslow asked, still scanning the skies. "Surely this is a busy flight path."

"Not just two thousand feet above the ocean," Gustavsson said. "And they're approaching us down-wind so that we wouldn't hear them coming."

The pair scanned the sky in silence for almost a minute.

"There she is," Gustavsson said, pointing into the sky. "The low cloud has been keeping her out of sight. If I'm not mistaken, that's a Lockheed L-100, the civilian version of the military C-130."

Winslow squinted, trying to make out the silhouette of the aircraft. The blinking lights pierced through the low cloud layer intermittently. "That's a big aircraft for such low altitude."

"It's not the size I'm worried about," Gustavsson said, narrowing his eyes. "It's the intention. Civilian planes have no business being this low over open waters, especially not this far from land."

The engine noise from the incoming plane grew as the Lockheed powered overhead, its four turboprop engines leaving ghostly trails through the sky.

"What are they doing out here?" Winslow grumbled, the worry in his stomach already telling him the answer.

"I guess we're going to find out soon," Gustavsson said, pointing up at the plane as numerous paratroopers stepped out.

Winslow cursed under his breath. All this time, he'd thought they were one step ahead. Now they were vulnerable, with nowhere to run. Again, he thought of Eden and Baxter so far beneath the waves. Winslow felt the breath leave his body and fear engulfed his chest.

"What do we do? Do you have weapons on board?" Winslow said, his mind suddenly spinning with options.

"We're a research vessel, not military. We have a few handguns, but they're locked away below decks. They're too far away to help us right now."

Gustavsson drew out and lit up another cigarette, the image of calm.

"What do you mean they're too far away?" Panic laced Winslow's voice.

"They're several flights of stairs away from here. By the

time we got back, these guys will have taken the ship, if that's their intention."

The paratroopers swung in an arc down towards the *Njord Fadir*. The Lockheed's rumbling engines faded.

"But... but... we've got to do something?" Winslow stuttered.

One by one, the paratroopers traced a line towards the *Njord Fadir's* rear deck.

"I suggest we see what they want," Gustavsson said. "Then we'll decide what to do."

Winslow's worry turned into nausea as the first man touched down. He was quickly pursued by the second and third. Each executed a perfect landing, unclipped the chute and then swung a short-nosed rifle into position. The men formed a line from one side of the ship to the other.

Winslow watched the final man thump down behind the line. Towering over all the other men, he was probably one of the biggest people Winslow had ever seen. The man landed with an unusual grace for someone his size, then unclipped the chute all in one slick move. The big man stepped towards Winslow and Gustavsson.

Winslow glanced anxiously towards Gustavsson.

The Norwegian pulled the final drag from his cigarette, dropped it to the floor, and then took a step towards the intruders.

"This here's my ship," he shouted over the wind. "I suggest you tell me what you're doing or turn around and get back off."

The giant man stepped between his comrades and strode towards Gustavsson. Like the others, he had a rifle slung around his shoulder, although he made no move to use it.

The man stepped into the beam of the *Njord Fadir's*

floodlights and Winslow got a good look at his face. His skin was scarred and bubbled with an enormous growth on his left cheek. It looked as though he'd been badly burned or exposed to something radioactive.

"It's not possible," Winslow said, gasping. "How is this man alive?" He recalled, line by line, Eden's description of Thorne from their fight on the train, although she hadn't mentioned the facial disfigurements.

"I'm here to represent the interests of the Van Wick family," Thorne shouted. He pointed towards the empty cradle on which the submersible usually sat. "I believe you're heading to the wreck to retrieve something that belongs to us."

"I have no idea who you are or what you think we're doing." Gustavsson took a step forwards. Standing at his full height, the burley Norwegian was still at least a foot shorter than the intruder. "We're laying cables. Don't know anything about a wreck."

In one smooth move, Thorne slammed his fist into Gustavsson's stomach. The Norwegian doubled up, coughing and retching.

With one hand, Thorne grabbed Gustavsson by the throat and lifted him from the deck. "If you lie to me again, I'll snap your neck and throw you overboard. No one lays cables in the presence of Alexander Winslow." Thorne pointed at Winslow. Thorne dropped Gustavsson to the floor, then turned to Winslow. His swollen face twisted into a grin. "I believe I've had the pleasure of meeting your daughter. What a special person she is. This time, the pleasure will be all mine."

To Gustavsson's credit, he climbed straight back to his feet and stood as though nothing had happened.

Thorne pointed up at the ship's superstructure. "Let's go

inside and wait for those brave submariners to return. You lead, captain." Thorne's eyes bored into Gustavsson, challenging him to disagree.

Gustavsson turned and marched inside the *Njord Fadir*.

30

Over twelve thousand feet below, Eden peered through the porthole. The descent had taken just over an hour. With little to see through the submersible's windows, it had seemed like a lot longer. A few times, curious and increasingly unusual creatures swam towards them, attracted by the submersible's lights. Realizing the submersible offered no food, the creatures always turned back. Eden supposed that with such a vast and empty ocean to search, these creatures didn't want to waste time on the whimsies of humankind.

About halfway down, Eden and Baxter pulled on hats and fingerless gloves. The journey was also punctuated by the frequent statistics they sent back to the ship above, including read outs of their position and machine operations.

"We'll reach the bottom in about two minutes," Baxter said, checking a dial. "We're about two hundred feet starboard of the wreck, give or take for sea currents."

Baxter clicked a switch, and the submersible released several hundred ounces of tiny steel balls. This slowed the submersible's descent to little more than a gentle downwards drift.

Baxter deftly moved the controls, and suddenly the submersible hummed to life. They were no longer just drifting downwards, but now moving purposefully through the ocean depths.

"See that bank of switches above your head," Baxter said, nodding upwards towards the switches. "Turn them all on."

Eden reached up and flicked the switches on, one after another.

The bright lights mounted around the submersible blazed, flooding the sea bed with light. Eden inhaled sharply and then leaned forward towards the porthole. About twenty feet below them, flat and shapeless, lay the ocean floor. Even with the lights burning, visibility was no more than thirty feet. Eden peered upwards, somewhere in the direction of the *Njord Fadir,* riding on the waves over two miles above them.

Baxter checked a screen and then adjusted the controls. The submersible spun in the water and then slid forward.

"Wait, stop," Eden said, almost shouting. Above them, right in the area where their lights faded to nothing, Eden thought she saw movement. A shape slipped through the lights almost directly above them.

Baxter flicked the thrusters into reverse, and the submersible stopped.

"I'm sure I saw something," Eden said, pointing upwards. "There's something moving up there."

Baxter flicked the controls again and tilted them backward, allowing them an undisturbed view of the ocean behind.

Eden gazed into the featureless water. There was nothing there.

"Probably an eel or something," Baxter said. With a flick of the control lever, he righted the submersible and set them off towards the world's most famous shipwreck.

"There's more life than you think down here."

"Really? Do you think they've got a Burger King? I'm starved."

Baxter tutted a humorless laugh and slowly increased their speed.

"Or maybe there really are ghosts down here," Eden said to herself, feeling ridiculous for the thought.

"No, it's just an octopus, or a trick of the light or something," Baxter said. "You'll see."

Learning about *The Titanic* and her ill-fated maiden voyage as a child, Eden had always been fascinated by the drama and tragedy of the event. How such a vessel — the most technologically advanced of her day — could fall foul of the natural world in such a spectacular way, was not only a warning to humankind but, Eden thought, a reminder of our place as mere residents of the planet.

"All we can do is approach the natural world in the same way a baby does its mother," Eden had once heard an old mountaineer tell her somewhere in the Swiss alps. "We crawl into nature's lap and look up at it through eyes that hardly understand the world. If we think our place is anything more, then we're fooling ourselves, because nature has given us all this, and in a second, nature can take it all away again."

The sonar pinged, dragging Eden back to the present.

"We've got something," Baxter hissed, a hint of anticipation breaking his usual calm demeanor. "It's big, and it's close."

Eden shook the memory from her thoughts and leaned in towards the sonar display. The screen revealed an enormous mass lying on the ocean bed less than one hundred feet ahead. Although the object was distorted in places, its shape was unmistakable.

Eden peered through the porthole. Illuminated by the submersible's spotlights, the ocean floor was desolate but strangely, hauntingly beautiful.

"She's close," Eden whispered, a shiver running down her spine.

Then, with all the drama and tragedy Eden had imagined, something miraculous happened. Through the murky water, as though appearing from the actual mists of time, the gargantuan outline of the shipwreck took form. At first, she was just an apparition against the water, her monumental hull rearing from the ocean floor. Then, as the submersible crawled forward at a frustrating speed, it became clear what they saw.

Baxter tweaked the controls, and the submersible rose through the water until they were level with the great ship's upper deck.

The Titanic lay there in all her glory, as though frozen in time.

Eden inhaled her hands covering her mouth. The sight was awe-inspiring and eerie. It was as though the ocean had taken the ship that night and frozen her in space and time.

First, materializing from the gloom, as though dragged through the mists of time, the ship's iconic bow appeared. Rusticles hung from the railings and decks, making it look as though she was melting into the ocean, drifting back into the seabed one particle at a time.

Eden's heart worked its way up into throat.

Baxter worked the controls and the submersible rose.

Eden shook herself into focus and powered up the high-definition cameras, mounted on the hydraulic arms. They slipped close to the bow and Eden saw something on the screen.

"Look at that," Eden said, pointing at the ghostly image. She looked through the porthole and could see the same thing, albeit more faintly, just with her eyes.

"The name, Titanic, it's still there," Eden whispered, unable to turn her eyes away from the enduring letters which had been painted on the bow all those years ago.

"It's as though some force wants her to be remembered," Baxter said, softly.

Eden agreed. Although time and saltwater had gone to work on the rest of the vessel, the name endured.

In her mind's eye, Eden pictured the once glossy black and white livery she'd seen in so many photos and films. Now the ship was a spectrum of greens, blues, and other earthy tones — painted in the colors of the deep.

Baxter pulled back on the controls, and the submersible climbed up and over the bow. Eden and Baxter, their eyes pinned to the portholes, were both stunned into silence.

Staying in close to the structure, they slid a few feet above *The Titanic*'s once grand decks. Eden peered down and pictured the activity that would have once taken place there. She thought about deck chairs, lifeboats, and the elegant fittings which were now lost to the ocean.

"Look at that," Eden said, pointing out an area of the deck where colonies of coral had colored the iron with splashes of bright orange and pink.

Baxter pulled back on the controls, and the submersible stopped.

"There," Baxter said, pointing down at the foredeck. "That's the main cargo hatch for the forward decks."

Eden pressed her forehead against the glass and squinted. Beneath the rust and an entire colony of anemones, she could just about make out a large hatch.

"The last time that hatch was opened was in Southampton Docks over one hundred years ago." Eden pointed one of the high-definition cameras at the rust which had fused the iron in place. "How do you suppose we open it now?"

Baxter pointed at a crane standing sentry beside the hatch, a hook hanging from its rust encrusted wire. "What are the chances that still works?"

Baxter inched the submersible forward. A school of fish darted from one of the B Deck windows, their scales flashing silver and blue in the submersible's beams.

Eden watched the fish shimmy off into the ocean, then picked up the control for the submersible's robotic arms. The control had a small yoke which moved the arm, and buttons that opened and closed the hydraulic fingers. Eden pushed forward on the yoke and one of the arms stretched out towards the crane.

Baxter goaded gently on his control and the submersible stirred forward a foot.

Eden worked the claw into position and then pushed the button. The claw shot closed, gripping the old hook tightly.

Baxter put the thrusters in reverse and the submersible moved backward, tugging on the one-hundred-year-old chain. The chain drew taut, and the submersible snapped to a stop. Baxter gently pulled backward on the controls, increasing the power of the thrusters. Nothing happened. Baxter increased power on the thrusters, sending them into a frenzied whine. Through the port hole, Eden could see the water currents raking at the old deck.

All at once, the chain ground, cracked, and then gave

way. Now untethered, the submersible shot backwards, dragging the chain with it.

Baxter worked quickly with the controls, trying to angle the thrusters in the opposite direction to stop their motion.

A deafening thud reverberated through the submersible's hull as it collided with the foremast.

The breath leapt from Eden's lungs. She closed her eyes tight, expecting thousands of tons of highly pressured water to bombard the submersible obliterating them and the craft in milliseconds. The clang reverberated through the hull several times and then died out.

Eden opened one eye, followed by the other. They and the submersible were still intact.

Eden and Baxter glanced at each other, clearly both thinking the same thing. Eden looked up towards the surface and seriously thought about calling the whole thing off.

"You don't hear the sound that kills you," Baxter said, his voice softer than Eden had ever heard it.

Eden drew a deep breath and felt her heart slow to its normal speed.

Baxter worked the controls, pulling them away from the mast, and turning around. They'd collided with a jagged spike on which ship's forward mast had once stood.

"Luckily we didn't hit that," Eden said, pointing at the sharp edge a few feet above them.

Baxter agreed. "At least we got the chain." He pointed at the chain gripped tightly in the robotic claw.

"Let's just get on with this," Eden said, uncharacteristically seriously. Eden worked the controls and pulled the chain towards them.

Baxter tilted the submersible, and they sunk down towards the hatch doors.

"There, look," he said, pointing to a large iron ring on the top of the door.

Working together, Eden and Baxter attached the hook to the large ring.

"Now all we need to do is fire that thing up," Eden said, pointing towards the crane.

"I'm not sure that will work," Baxter said, angling the controls so that the submersible zipped over to the crane.

As they approached the old crane, Eden pushed hard on the controls, sending the robotic arm into a swing. The arm struck the crane, sending a shudder through the old steel bars and high-tech aluminum appendage. The crane wobbled for several seconds, upsetting an eel, who darted towards one of the B deck windows.

"We've loosened it up a bit," Eden said. "This thing is only held together with rust."

"Just like that old truck of yours," Baxter quipped, referencing the RV in which Eden used to live.

"That's a classic machine," Eden said, scowling. "If you can just concentrate for a moment, we'll try this again. Full power on my count." Eden swung around on the controls and grasped the old crane with the strong hydraulic claw. "Go now."

Baxter pushed the thrusters into full power. The submersible rocked the crane on its rusting supports. Iron crunched and split near the crane's base, sending reverberations through the water.

"It's going!" Eden said. "More power!"

Baxter swung the submersible to the left, and then engaged full power. This time, they caught the old crane off balance. After a hundred years of rust and rot, the old metal crumbled under the weight, teetering over the edge of the ship. With a continued whine of effort from the submersible's powerful thrusters, the crane broke free from the position the men at the Harland and Wolff shipyard had riveted it all those years ago.

The crane lurched forward and fell freely down the side of the ship. Eden reacted quickly, opening the jaws, so the submersible wasn't dragged down too. The pockmarked lump of iron tumbled down the side of the ship, pulling the chain with it.

"Move now," Eden said. "Get out of the way."

Baxter tore back on the controls just in time as the chain whipped from side to side like an injured snake. The chain pulled tight against the heavy hatch.

Eden shot forward in her seat, watching the movement play out as though in slow motion.

The chain stayed taut for what felt like a long time. Then the hatch moved. Slowly at first, it groaned upwards, reopening the hold doors after their century of slumber. When the hatch reached halfway, it snapped backwards with its own weight and thumped against the deck. Shockwaves ricocheted down the length of the hull, sending silt and debris high into the water.

"That's exactly how I thought it would work," Eden said, grinning. "Now let's get down there and find this lady."

31

With their visibility now reduced further, Baxter inched them forwards until they were just above the hatch. He angled the thrusters carefully and lowered the submersible beneath the decks of the great ship.

"We're the first people to come inside since that night," Eden whispered with the reverence of talking in a cemetery.

They drifted down into the hold, Baxter paying close attention to their position against the jagged, rusting iron which surrounded them on all sides.

One crash was more than enough, Eden thought, looking at the severed ends of steel beams which had punched their way into the shaft. The beams bristled as though destined to snag the submersible, either piercing its hull or trapping it here for eternity. Eden wasn't sure which option was worse.

For what seemed like an age, they crept down and down with just sheer iron walls on all sides. Despite the cold, sweat ran down Baxter's forehead as he worked the controls with more focus than ever before.

Although Eden knew it was impossible, the ocean

seemed to get even more silent now they were inside. She remembered her father's words, reminding them that the wreck was a mass grave and should be treated as such. Not only did Eden now feel the pressure of the water against the hull, but the ghostly pressure of the diseased.

"We're passing the third-class berths on one side and then, believe it or not, we'll pass the squash court," Eden said, checking their location on their 3D schematic of the ship. "Then we'll reach the cargo area. We're almost there."

"Twenty feet to the bottom of the shaft," Baxter said, glancing at a screen.

A minute later, they emerged from beneath the wall of iron. The submersible's lights lanced out into a cavernous space.

Baxter studied the tangled webs of detritus strewn across the hold and carefully considered their way forwards. Having decided, he adjusted the submersible's controls, and they rose across the debris, avoiding the roof by a few feet.

"It's going to be tight," Eden said. "What if the *Lady of Leone* is buried under all of this?"

"Then we go back empty-handed," Baxter replied, concentrating hard.

"All of this for nothing," Eden muttered. "No way."

Baxter dexterously worked the controls, maneuvering the submersible around several piles of debris.

Using the large video screens and the porthole, Eden searched for anything that could resemble the crate from the British Museum. Using one of the high-powered cameras, Eden zoomed in on an object which sparkled on the far side of the hold.

"Look at that," Eden said, pointing at the screen.

Baxter glanced at the screen but still couldn't clearly make out the object. He flicked the controls and drew them closer to the object. When they got within a dozen feet, Baxter saw what it was clear as day. A Rolls Royce sat half-buried in the silt. The front half of the car pointed upwards, as though it was sinking into a bog. The silver lady still stood proudly, albeit now slightly discolored, on the hood.

Eden used the camera mounted on one of the maneuverable arms to take a series of photographs.

"Hey, look at that," Baxter said, swinging the sub around to study a collection of bottles piled a few feet away.

Eden moved the arm up close and took a few more pictures. "It's whisky, I think, judging by the shape of the bottles."

"I expect they were originally in wooden crates, although they've long since disintegrated," Baxter said.

Eden glanced at Baxter, a twinkle in her eye as she worked the arms into position and picked up a bottle. Miraculously, the thing was still in one piece, although a thick layer of silt covered the glass.

Eden wiggled the control, and the arm shook the bottle, sending a cloud of filth floating off in all directions. She then drew the bottle close to the porthole.

"Dewar's White Label," Eden said, successfully reading the indentations on the bottle. "I wonder what it tastes like."

"Put it down and let's get what we came for," Baxter said, his jaw tense. "We're wasting time and lowering visibility."

"Fine," Eden grumbled. "Wow, look at that!" Eden pointed at a colorful fish which floated out from between two smashed up crates. It had fierce spikes which danced in the current.

While Baxter was distracted with the fish, Eden pressed a couple of buttons and placed the whisky in one of the submersible's specimen compartments.

After the fish had flounced out of sight, Baxter carefully

maneuvered them to the rear of the cargo hold. Strips of metal, which would probably once have been part of wooden cases, lay piled up in the corner. As they drew near, Eden glimpsed something deep within the junk.

"Stop, there," she said, pointing at the debris.

"This better not be just something you like the look of," Baxter said, exasperated. "We're not here on a shopping trip."

"Just because I'm a girl you think I'm always thinking about shopping," Eden quipped. "It's not true..."

"I didn't say that, it's just..."

"Wait!" Eden interrupted. "Look at that."

Eden focused the camera on a crate in the far corner of the hold. The crate was in superb shape considering the destruction which surrounded it.

"There's some writing on it, there." Eden worked the controls, trying to get the camera angle right. Her breath caught in her throat with anticipation.

Baxter shimmied the submersible to the side and suddenly the writing on the crate came into view.

Baxter let out a sigh and leaned back in his seat. His hands dropped into his lap.

"The British Museum," Eden said, reading the writing which was now clearly visible on the side of the crate. "I think we've found our lady."

32

"Damn it, why can't we see what they're doing down there," Thorne said, pacing around the control room.

Gustavsson and Winslow sat in the operators' chairs in front of the computer monitors. The rest of the *Njord Fadir's* crew were assembled at the back of the room, watched over carefully by Thorne's gun toting thugs.

"It's not as simple as a video call," Gustavsson grumbled. "Sending radio signals through that much water is problematic."

"Did I ask for your opinion?" Thorne said, jabbing the Norwegian in the back with his weapon.

Winslow silently urged Gustavsson to stop winding the guy up, for fear they both might end up floating in the drink.

"Try the radio again," Thorne snarled.

"Sure, anything you say boss." Gustavsson picked up the radio transmitter with a hand the size of a bear's paw. "*Njord Havspeil*, come in *Njord Havspeil*. Do you copy?"

Everyone in the room listened intently. Most people

turned to watch Gustavsson, the pressure of the situation infectious.

The only people who remained focused on their task were Thorne's men, closely watching the prisoners.

For a few seconds, the room was completely silent.

A bolt of static came through the radio and then the silence returned.

"They may be inside the wreck. That can cause havoc with the radio signals too," Gustavsson said.

"Try again," Thorne barked. "I want to know the moment they've got the artifact."

"*Njord Havspeil*, come in *Njord Havspeil*. Do you copy?" Gustavsson said.

Silence returned.

A minute later, the radio squawked, and Eden's voice boomed through the room. "Come in *Njord Fadir* this is *Njord Havspeil*..." the radio cut out into a bolt of static.

Excitement moved through the room like a wave.

Thorne spun around on his heels and marched back to the desk. The *Njord Fadir's* crew who had been lounging at the back of the room suddenly stood up straight. Even the men tasked with guarding the prisoners cast a glance over their shoulders.

"Again, again!" Thorne roared.

"Great to hear your voice *Njord Havspeil*," Gustavsson bellowed. "Didn't catch that. Please repeat."

"This is *Njord Havspeil*," came Eden's voice, even clearer this time. "We have located the artifact and will head up soon."

Gustavsson glanced up at Thorne, who was standing right above him. "Understood, *Njord Havspeil*. Notify when on ascent and we will prepare for immediate exfiltration. Over."

Thorne grabbed the radio from Gustavsson's hands and placed it a few feet away.

"Well, gentlemen, I don't think we will trouble you for much longer."

33

Over twelve thousand feet below the surface, Eden tapped the button on her headset and closed the radio connection.

"That was strange," Eden said, thinking about her brief interaction with the Norwegian captain.

"What's that?" Baxter asked.

A pair of eels slithered through the hold. They paused and examined the submersible for a few seconds with obsidian-colored eyes, before sliding back into the gloom.

"That was Gustavsson on the radio, right?" Eden said.

"I think so," Baxter replied. "He's the guy in charge. It sounded like him, anyway."

"It just wasn't..." Eden tapped a finger against her chin. "He's just normally so formal. The guy usually sounds like he's eaten the navy handbook for breakfast."

Baxter scowled and then checked the instruments again. "He's probably just relieved to hear from us before the weather closes in. Trying to get this thing out of a choppy sea must be a nightmare."

"True." Eden shrugged, trying to shake off the uneasy

feeling smoldering in the pit of her stomach. Something aboard the *Njord Fadir* was wrong. "How do we get this thing out of here then?" Eden said, peering at the crate wedged in the corner of the hold.

Baxter worked the controls and the submersible shuffled over towards the crate. Fortunately, the area around the crate was clear.

It took Eden a few minutes with the mechanical arms to remove a few strips of thin metal which were on top of the crate. Once the top was clear, Baxter moved them directly above the crate.

Using the winch and the hydraulic arms together, Eden hooked the crate on to the base of the submersible. When it was all attached, Baxter heaved back on the thrusters. The thrusters whirred and groaned, kicking silt up in all directions. The submersible strained, pulling the cables taut. After a few seconds of hard labor, the silt released the crate.

Cautious after their earlier collision, Baxter carefully controlled the thrusters to keep the submersible level. The winches strained, pulling the crate in close to the submersible's stomach.

Eden angled out of the hydraulic arms so that they could see the crate positioned beneath the submersible.

"Now we've just got to get out of here with this thing attached," Eden said.

Focused on searching for and then attaching the crate, Eden had almost forgotten about their precarious position so deep beneath the ocean.

In an effort to improve their buoyancy, Baxter released a load of lead ballast from the submersible's tanks. "That means we shouldn't have to use the thrusters to stay afloat," He explained.

Baxter reduced the thrusters' power, the submersible didn't move. He released another load of ballast and dialed the power back even further. Eventually he got the buoyancy correct and the submersible floated with the power on low.

Without the strong currents caused by the submersible's thrusters, the visibility started to improve. Within a few minutes, they could see enough to picking their way back towards the shaft.

As Baxter started to them forwards, Eden moved the arms so that they could use the cameras to see the submersible's top side, and the base of the crate.

Baxter shuffled them forward, working the controls carefully to avoid the undulating piles of silt and detritus.

It took them almost half an hour to pick their way slowly back towards the shaft, Eden constantly reporting on the clearance both above and below the craft.

They slipped into the shaft after painstakingly working their way past a steel beam which had fallen at an angle, reducing their clearance to just a few inches either side of the craft.

Inside the shaft both Eden and Baxter breathed a sigh of relief — the first of many.

"Straight up from here." Eden drew the hydraulic arms in close to the craft.

"You make it sound easy," Baxter said. He spun the submersible around and then carefully angled the thrusters to take them straight up.

"We've done the hard bit," Eden said.

"The hardest bit so far," Baxter replied.

Baxter increased the power and the submersible, slowly at first, rose through the shaft.

Twenty minutes later they emerged on to the deck.

A burst of static came through the radio, followed by Gustavsson's voice. "*Njord Havspeil*, please report."

"We've got the crate and we're out of the wreck," Eden said.

Gustavsson acknowledged the information in the strange formal manner which Eden was struggling to connect with the man she knew.

Although Baxter and herself were the ones in real danger down here, Eden couldn't help but worry about her father and Athena on the ship above. Something up there wasn't right, she could feel it.

Eden looked out at the ghostly wreck, lying dormant in the dark. Once again, she was amazed by the sheer size of the liner. From the foredeck, the promenades led away, merging into the gloom. There was something eerie, but almost sublime about the craft.

Baxter kept the thrusters on, allowing them to climb slowly away from the hulk.

Eden gazed out through porthole as the remains of the great liner were there one moment, and then gone, dematerialized into the gloom, the next.

When they were a safe distance from the ship, Baxter released the rest of the ballast at the submersible rose of its own accord.

~

ALMOST AN HOUR LATER, the submersible broke the surface. With only the uppermost edge of the submersible standing clear of the dark water, Eden and Baxter couldn't see anything through the portholes. The on-board instruments told them that the *Njord Fadir* was one hundred feet away.

The choppy sea Gustavsson had warned them about was eerily calm.

Baxter used the thrusters to pull them alongside the ship. Once they were in position, he turned the thrusters off. A sudden silence fell over the craft, punctuated only by the lapping of waves against the hull.

Eden tapped the button on her headset. "We're topside and ready for collection," she said.

"Good to hear you," came Gustavsson's voice. Again, to Eden, it just didn't seem right. The worry she'd felt miles beneath the ocean bubbled up again.

"We'll get the divers out to you now. Hold tight," Gustavsson said. The line went dead.

A few minutes later, the sound of an outboard motor rumbled through the water. The small boat appeared on their instruments. The motor died and a series of splashes rung through the craft as the divers rolled backward into the ocean.

Lowered into the ocean by a crane, the submersible needed a team of divers to release and attach the cable, and to make sure everything was working as it should in those first few seconds.

A diver appeared in the submersible's porthole. Eden recognized the man as one of the ship's crew. However, she was surprised not to see Athena, who had insisted on being part of the dive team which released the sub a few hours ago. The burning rock of worry in Eden's stomach grew to something a lot more sinister.

Then the diver made a hand gesture. Eden knew the gesture all too well. With his hand flat, fingers together, he moved his hand from side to side — the universal distress signal. Danger was nearby.

"There's something wrong," Eden said, her voice barely a whisper.

Baxter nodded. He had seen the gesture, too. He reached for his belt and unclipped the handgun he'd stashed there before the dive. Eden had come prepared too and pulled her weapon from the compartment beneath her seat. Eden and Baxter locked eyes for a moment, communicating silently.

A clunk boomed through the submersible's hull as it was hooked on to the crane.

"Rising," came a stony voice through the radio. The vibration of the straining crane worked its way down the reinforced steel cable as the submersible rose.

Eden's vision cleared as water ran from the glass. She peered up toward the *Njord Fadir's* deck. Lights blazed, sending angular shadows into the surrounding ocean.

Every inch the submersible rose, the sense of unease gnawed further into Eden's stomach.

Eden glanced at Baxter. His features were set in an unreadable expression, brow furrowed, eyes focused on whatever was about to appear through the inch-thick glass.

The familiar sight of the ship's deck loomed into view, illuminated by bright floodlights.

Eden found the view oddly comforting and terrifying at the same time.

Eden noticed several people standing around the cradle into which the submersible would soon be lowered.

The crew stepped forward and steadied the submersible as it swung over the deck. The crane operator kept the submersible hanging over the deck as the team unhooked the crate.

Eden's fear grew as she noticed numerous figures keeping to the shadows at the deck's periphery. From inside the sub, the figures around the outside were mere silhouettes. Unless Eden was very much mistaken, she hadn't known there were that many people aboard the *Njord Fadir*. Then Eden noticed something that sent a spear of ice through her heart. The men were armed.

Eden reached over and snapped a switch above her head. The submersible's lights blazed, affording Eden a full view of the assembled crowd.

The men reeled backward for a moment, dazzled, and surprised by the invasion of light.

One of the men stepped forward, unperturbed by the light.

Staring at the man, It took Eden a moment to recognize him. His face was now weirdly swollen and distorted. When Eden did recognize him, she gasped and physically jolted back in her seat.

"That man." Eden pointed at a giant man standing front and center. "It can't be possible. It's just not possible."

Eden's mind raced. Nothing made sense.

"What?" Baxter said, looking from the man to Eden.

"That's Thorne. We killed him two days ago."

The crane whined and lowered the submersible into its cradle, sending a clunk through the hull. No one moved. Eden and Baxter stared out. Thorne and his men gawked in through the glass as though admiring a strange creature in the aquarium.

Thorne's rubbery lips twisted into a grin, then he lifted a radio to his face. The radio inside the submersible buzzed and then Thorne's sickening voice came through loud and clear.

"Welcome aboard, Ms. Black."

34

Eden reacted in a heartbeat. She slid her weapon from beneath her seat and leveled it through the glass at Thorne. Her hand already in place, she curved her finger across the trigger and slowly added pressure.

"No!" Baxter shouted, pushing the gun downwards. "You shoot in here and that bullet will bounce around, cutting us to shreds."

Eden lowered the gun. Of course, Baxter was right.

Watching the whole interaction, Thorne tilted his head backward and roared with laughter.

"Firing a bullet through inch-thick glass. Even the great Eden Black couldn't do that." Thorne's mocking voice came through the radio.

Eden peered up at the hatch above them. The thing was locked from the outside with six large bolts. Without someone releasing them from the outside, they were stuck.

Eden glanced down at the crate which contained the *Lady of Leone*. The crate was just visible, sitting on the deck in front of the submersible.

Eden's stomach roiled in anger. They'd risked their lives

to recover that thing, and now it was going to go to the very people they wanted to keep it away from. Eden's knuckles turned white as she squeezed the armrests of her chair.

Thorne stared at the crate. He lifted the radio to his lips. "Thank you for bringing this up for me. I really appreciate it. In case you're wondering where your father is." Thorne beckoned to someone out of Eden's eyeline.

A thug marched on to the deck, forcing Alexander Winslow with him.

Eden looked at her father, her anger flaring. Although her father looked uncomfortable, he was currently unharmed.

"If you hurt him in anyway," Eden shouted down the radio, "I will personally make sure it's the last thing you do."

Thorne tilted his head back and laughed again. "Now, now, that isn't very nice."

Thorne signaled to another man, who levelled his gun at Winslow's chest.

"Just try me," Eden snarled, her blood bubbling.

"You've already tried to kill me, and I'm still here," Thorne said, tapping his chest. "For now, your father will live. For how long, remains to be seen."

Father and daughter locked eyes. Eden saw power in her father's gaze. Although right now he was the prisoner of these thugs, the fight was far from over. Eden calmed down and forced herself to think tactically.

Thorne clicked his fingers and the thug dragged Winslow away.

Eden watched the men, her mind spinning. The problem was, at that moment, their options were painfully limited.

They were held powerful inside a secure bullet proof box, just feet away from their foe.

"A secure bullet proof box," Eden said to herself.

She glanced at the submersible's two hydraulic arms which stretched out in front of the craft. An idea formed in her mind.

"We're in a secure bullet proof box!" Eden shouted.

Baxter glanced at her as though she'd lost the plot.

"All we need to do, is get them to shoot at us!" Without wasting a moment to explain, Eden grabbed the controls and swung the arms into use.

"Hold on!" Eden yanked the control sticks, the motors whirring through the hull.

"You control one arm, I'll take the other," Eden commanded. The motors whined and then purred as the systems came to life. "I'm going for Thorne, you keep the men away from the crate."

A grin lit Baxter's face as he too came to the same realization. "A bullet proof box. Genius."

The super-strong yet lightweight system was designed for use under high pressure, so here on the surface it moved with great speed.

Baxter swung the arm to the left, catching two of men who were heading towards the crate off guard. With an ominous crunch, and a thwack which reverberated through the body of the craft, the strike sent the men sprawling across the deck. One of them fell hard against a barrier and would have windmilled into the ocean if he hadn't grabbed the railing at the last moment.

Baxter doubled back with the control to take another man who was now charging forward. He swept the arm to the right and smashed the guy in the shoulder. The man flew sideways and landed unceremoniously on his backside. Suffering from nothing but a bruised ego, the thug swung his weapon towards Baxter and Eden. Less than fifteen feet away, Baxter saw the man's expression as he squeezed the trigger.

For a painful moment, Baxter feared the craft wouldn't hold and they would be shot like the proverbial fish in a barrel. The man kept his finger locked on the trigger, sending a long burst of gunfire into the front of the submersible.

Baxter held his breath. Eden scowled with expectation.

But, the Norwegian engineers had done a sound job. The bullets smashed into the front of the submersible, punching dents in the surface like the strikes of a woodpecker, and then ricocheted backwards in a great arc, spraying the bullets across the deck. One bullet hit the shooter in the leg, and another zipped a quarter of an inch above his head, no doubt scorching his skin.

Clearly one step ahead of his crew, Thorne flattened himself against the deck and roared at the men not to shoot. It was too late. Two more men opened fire on the submersible, doing nothing but adding to the chaos of bullets pinging around the deck. One of the stray rounds found a home in one guy's chest, while another smashed through a man's cheek.

The first man roared with pain and gripped his leg where blood was now visibly pumping out on to the deck. He glanced around with mad eyes, as though he didn't understand where the bullets had come from.

From inside the submersible, the commotion sounded like little more than a distant series of pops and thuds.

Controlling the second hydraulic arm, Eden focused in on her quarry. Thorne lay against the deck, less than six feet away from the submersible. Flattening himself to stay out of the path of anymore bullets, he shouted madly at his men.

From inside the submersible, his voice was inaudible, giving the scene a strange comic quality.

Eden worked the controls, and the arm snaked towards him. Thorne was so busy berating his men for effectively shooting themselves that he didn't notice the robotic appendage coming his way. Eden positioned the arm an inch above his ankle and then closed the powerful jaws.

Confusion and horror swept across Thorne's face as he realized what was happening. Eden pulled him backward across the deck. For a moment, the man tried to claw his way forward, but he was no match for the powerful machine. Eden took control of the other arm and positioned the pincers around Thorne's neck. Thorne tried to get his fingers inside the grips but was too slow.

Working the controls carefully, Eden lifted Thorne from the deck and moved him in close to the porthole.

"Let us out of here or I'll push this button," Eden said into the radio. She tweaked the controls, and the jaws tightened. "This will snap your spine like a twig."

Thorne scrabbled around, trying to worm his way free but was getting nowhere. His swollen face turned even redder than before.

"Tell someone to undo the hatch, now," Eden said.

Thorne shouted something. From inside, Eden couldn't work out what he was saying but he seemed to be calling for help.

She tapped the control and Thorne howled again. The muscles on his arms and shoulders stood out like anvils. Thorne's face turned from red to deep purple.

A moment later, two of Thorne's men appeared on the deck. They dragged another man with them. The man's clothes were bloodstained. From inside the submersible, Eden couldn't see whether the man was alive or dead. A shudder of fear jolted through her as she thought they were dragging her father out again.

Thorne shouted at the men. They spun their prisoner around and pushed him towards the submersible.

Gustavsson. The tough Norwegian had already sustained quite a beating but was not through yet. Although the man was gruff, Eden had respected his knowledge. Despite the tough situation Gustavsson was in, Eden breathed a sigh of relief that so far, her father was still safe and well.

Thorne's men surrounded Gustavsson. They leveled their guns at him. Words were shouted, although Eden couldn't understand them.

Gustavsson shook his head adamantly, staring hard at his captors.

"Any idea what they want with him?" Eden asked.

"I don't think it's going to be good," Baxter replied.

"Stop messing around," Eden snarled into the radio, turning her attention back to Thorne still dangling from the claw. "You have ten seconds to have us out of here or I'll snap your spine. Ten..."

Thorne shouted again, more aggressively this time.

"Maybe they're actually doing it," Baxter said. "Maybe they need Gustavsson to open the hatch."

"I'm not so sure," Eden said. "Thorne's as slimy as they come." Counting down the next few numbers into the radio, Eden felt Baxter's words boost her confidence.

Then she felt all that confidence drain away.

One of Thorne's men shot Gustavsson in the leg. Blood sprayed out across the deck. Gustavsson howled with pain and gripped his leg. No matter how tough you were, that was bound to hurt.

Thorne's man shouted at Gustavsson again. The Norwegian's face twisted between pain and anger. Finally, he nodded and then shouted something in reply.

Two guards bent down, scooped Gustavsson up and led him towards the rear of the submersible.

"Three seconds," Eden said. "Get this hatch open."

Clunking noises reverberated from the rear of the sub. Eden knew that it wasn't the noise of them opening the hatch.

"Two..." Eden was halfway through speaking when the hydraulic arms dropped to the floor. Thorne's giant body slammed to the deck. The powerless hydraulic arm laid across him like a dead snake. Thorne lay still for a moment, then pulled the jaws from his neck. He stood up kicking the once powerful arms to the side as though they weighed nothing. He ran a hand across his neck, sucked in a deep breath and then scowled up and Eden and Baxter.

"They've cut the hydraulics," Baxter said, pointing down at a pool of liquid which seeped out of the sub.

"Damn it," Eden grumbled.

The instruments inside the sub went dark. Where lights had once flashed, there was just gloom. The screens which gave an increased view of the outside strobed for a moment and then clicked off.

"Now they've cut the power," Baxter said, stating the obvious.

Then it got a lot worse still. One of Thorne's men walked across the deck carrying a pair of gas cannisters. Eden recognized the cannisters as those the engineers had shown them earlier.

"That's the main oxygen tank, and the back-up supply," Baxter said, in little more than a whisper.

Thorne held the cannister as though it were a trophy in

a competition. He looked hard at Eden and Baxter, then dropped the cannister to the ground.

Thorne beckoned his men back out in front of the submersible. They dragged Gustavsson with them. Thorne withdrew his gun and aimed it at Gustavsson's head. Thorne eyed Eden and Baxter, his swollen lips parted. Then he shook his head and pointed up towards the chopper. Thorne's guards dragged Gustavsson, who was still alive for now, up towards the helipad.

With a backwards glance at the stricken submersible, Thorne followed them away.

Eden watched them go and then turned to Baxter. "I swear that guy gets uglier every time I see him."

35

Dawn was on the approaching, rolling her colors across the sky, as Eden saw the rotors of the helicopter power up. Eden and Baxter sat in near silence, aware that everything they said or did was reducing the amount of oxygen inside the submersible.

Eden peered through the porthole and saw two of Thorne's thugs force the Norwegian crew into the chopper. Then another pair of thugs appeared, surrounding her father and Gustavsson. Winslow helped the bulky Norwegian stagger towards the chopper.

A moment before boarding, Winslow stopped and glanced back at the *Njord Havspeil* marooned on the deck below. One of the thugs nudged Winslow in the back, earning himself a snarl from Gustavsson.

Seeing her father sent a bolt of determination through Eden's body.

Winslow looked at the submersible for a long moment, then conceded to the thug's command, and climbed inside the chopper.

"Can they take everyone on board that chopper, as well as and the *Lady of Leone*?" Eden said, her mind desperate for some good news.

"That's an MH-60S Knighthawk," Baxter said, as though stating the obvious. "Capable of transporting 13 people, plus the pilot and co-pilot in its current configuration. If they strap the crate beneath somehow, then it's possible."

"Fifteen in total," Eden said, thinking out loud. "That means..." she worked out the number of the Norwegian crew she knew were alive, including Gustavsson and her father, plus Thorne and his men. The answer struck her like a blow to the guts. "That's 15," Eden said, her voice was so quiet she wasn't sure whether she'd actually said it out loud.

Baxter nodded and gazed down at his hands.

"So, there's no one on board this ship?" Eden said.

"I don't know for sure," Baxter replied. "But it's possible that they all left on that chopper."

The pair sat in silence for almost a minute.

"But this is a big ship. It can't just be left to drift. Someone will find us, right?"

"Yes, but there's no telling how long that'll take. It could be weeks, or even months, depending on the weather and the currents."

Then the distant sound of the chopper increased as the engines reached their full thrust.

Eden peered through the porthole again and saw Thorne fastening something beneath the chopper. Once he was satisfied that the object was fastened securely, the brute climbed inside and closed the door.

"How much oxygen do we have?" Eden said, glancing at Baxter.

Baxter leaned over and checked the oxygen monitor

which thankfully wasn't connected to the submersible's power supply. "It's hard to say exactly, as it depends how much we use." He ran through some calculations. "At an estimate, we will be comfortable for around fifteen minutes."

"What do you mean comfortable?" Eden asked.

Baxter turned to look at her, his expression grave. "I mean, after that we will start to experience the effects of oxygen deprivation. Suffocation could come quickly, or take a while, there's no knowing."

Eden felt her heart skip a beat. She felt the thump-thump-thump of the chopper's rotors vibrating through the submersible's cradle as the machine prepared to depart. She looked through the porthole and saw The Knighthawk rise like a giant bird of prey, the crate containing the *Lady of Leone* swinging from the helicopter's underside.

For a moment, the chopper hovered over the ship before it tilted forward and accelerated away.

Eden watched helicopter and its stolen cargo until they became distant specks against the morning sky, and then disappeared altogether.

Eden and Baxter sat in a deafening silence, only punctuated by the groaning of the ship.

"I can't sit in silence," Eden said as though she'd been keeping the words in for hours. "What do we do now? There must be something we can do to help?"

Baxter took a deep breath, then turned towards Eden. "We wait," he said, his tone eerily calm.

"Wait! You're the great Captain Baxter, and the best idea you've got is for us to just sit here," Eden slapped her knees. "If you're not going to try, I will." Eden reached up to the hatch. For a moment she wondered whether someone had surreptitiously opened it for them. She pressed against the metal, but the hatch stayed firmly closed.

"I really think you should stay still," Baxter said. "Not only is your movement using up valuable oxygen, but it's also annoying."

Eden moved her hands around the rest of the tiny interior for no reason now other than because Baxter had told her not to. When she knew the activity was fruitless and had run out of things to press or poke, she slumped in her seat.

Baxter studied the oxygen meter and ran through the calculations again. "Seven or eight minutes," he said.

"It's going to be really annoying if you keep saying that," Eden said.

"Less annoying that you leaping around," Baxter replied.

"You've always found me annoying, haven't you?" Eden said, her eyes drilling into Baxter's

Baxter opened his mouth and then paused, clearly picking his words carefully.

"Do you remember when we first met. Who was that guy you were working with?" Eden said.

"Archibald Godspeed," Baxter groaned.

"What an idiot," Eden said. "What did you think of me then?"

"I might as well be honest," Baxter said, glancing at his hands.

Eden prepared herself for the verbal slap around the face which Baxter was about to deliver. She planned several barbed replies.

"I thought you were wonderful."

For several moments no one said anything.

"You... what?" Eden stuttered.

"I remember the first time Mr. Godspeed had us pick

you up. Remember how you spoke to him? You really put him in his place. That guy had been mistreating people his whole life, and you were one of the few people to tell him where to go."

"I remember that," Eden said, the memory warming her heart. "He really was a nasty son of a..." Another memory flashed into Eden's mind. She swung around and punched Baxter on the arm.

"Hey! What was that for?" Baxter said. "You're supposed to be saving oxygen by keeping still."

"That's for locking me in that hotel room, do you remember?"

Baxter nodded. "The problem was, I wanted to tell you everything. I wanted to tell you that your father was still alive, that I wasn't working for Godspeed, but I couldn't. I didn't trust myself to be around you."

"Sounds like rubbish. You just didn't want to hang out with me." Eden crossed her arms and made a childlike upset face.

"Oh, I did, so much," Baxter swung around to face Eden now. "That was the problem. See, I'm not very good at this..."

"Slowly suffocating to death?" Eden interrupted.

"No. Talking about what I think and feel. It's just alien to me."

Eden felt a strange feeling move through her.

"Then you let me think you were dead!" Eden roared, pushing Baxter on the shoulder again.

He held his hands up in surrender. "Again, not my fault. It was all part of a bigger plan. Remember, you weren't officially part of The Council at that time."

Eden grumbled an agreement and slumped back in to her seat.

They both watched the sky, which was now shimmering with the morning hues of peach and lavender. The calm water mirrored the sky, creating a vast canvas of color which seemed to stretch on forever.

Baxter glanced at the oxygen meter, although tried to hide the gesture from Eden.

"Okay, tell me how much is left," Eden said, reluctantly.

"Three or four minutes, I think."

The pair sat in silence for what felt to Eden like a really long time.

"What do you mean, you're not very good at talking about your feelings?" Eden said, thinking back to what Baxter had just said.

Baxter shrugged, his eyes still fixed on the oxygen meter. "I guess I've just never had to. All the conversations I have are about operational things. And then you came along."

Again, the feeling welled in Eden's stomach. This time, though, it wasn't fear or pain, but something else.

"I came along to frustrate you more than you've ever been frustrated before? I bet you don't learn about people like me in training."

"Absolutely not," Baxter said, his eyes still fixed on the small digital display. "One minute," Baxter added morosely.

"What, you don't learn about people like me in training, or I frustrate you more than you've ever known?"

"In all honesty," Baxter said. "Both."

Then a sound cut through the interior of the submersible like an arctic wind. Not understanding what the sound was, not truly believing that it wasn't a figment of their imaginations, Eden and Baxter locked eyes.

Ready to discount it as a delusion of hope, Eden sighed.

Then another clang resounded through the submersible's hull. This one was louder. To Eden, it sounded as though someone had dropped a metal beam against the side of the craft.

Then came the distant *clunk clunk* of footsteps on the rungs of the ladder.

"Someone's put a ladder against the side, they're climbing up!" Eden's words tumbled out like water from behind a broken dam. She watched the hatch, her eyes almost bulging with hope.

"And by the way," Eden said, looking at Baxter. "You're wonderful too."

The tension in Baxter's rugged face softened.

The sound of a tool being inserted into the bolts which sealed the hatch shut soon followed.

Eden and Baxter listened in painful silence as metal scraped against metal.

Eden's heart thumped wildly in her chest. A mix of hope and terror warred within her.

Eden placed her hands against the hatch, ready to help whoever was releasing them heave the door open.

"Wait," Baxter said, placing his hand on Eden's forearm. "We don't know who that is. What if it's one of Thorne's men staying behind to finish the job?"

With a screech and then a crack, the unseen person released the first of four bolts.

With Baxter's words still hanging, the sound had a threatening ring to it.

The person above them changed position and started working on the next bolt. It sounded like they were using vice grips or some other improvised tool to twist out the bolts. A few times the tool came loose and jarred against the hull, ringing through the metal like a badly tuned bell.

Eden scowled. Although she hadn't considered that their

liberator may not have good intentions, she realized that Baxter was right.

Eden grabbed her weapon from the floor.

"We have to be ready for anything," Eden said, her voice determined, her grip on her weapon tightening. "We can't take any chances."

Baxter nodded, his eyes fixed on the hatch, his body coiled like a spring, ready to react.

Eden held the weapon against her chest, feeling the thump of her heart through the metal.

With a whine of protest, the second bolt came loose. Their liberator pulled the bolt from the hole and then dropped it, it skittering down the side of the craft and bashing against the deck. The person relocated themselves to the next bolt and began working on that one.

"Who could it be?" Eden asked, her mind moving at light-speed through the various options as she saw them.

"We saw Thorne and his men get into the chopper," Baxter said. "It looked like his whole crew were on getting on board."

The bolt groaned and moaned against its threads. Then, with a screech the third bolt was released. One bolt remained, securing the hatch in place.

One bolt between Eden and Baxter and freedom. And one bolt between them and whoever was up there.

Once again, the person repositioned themselves above the fourth bolt and got to work.

"I've got a bad feeling about this," Eden said, holding the gun at her chest. In the confines of the submersible, she couldn't extend her arms to hold the weapon. For a second, she thought about the noise should one of them discharge their weapons inside — it would be deafening.

Another shriek came from the hatch. It sounded as

though, typically in Eden's experience, the last bolt was the most difficult.

Eden eyed the hatch and remembered Gustavsson's explanation of the pressure the small piece of metal would come under during the dive. He explained how it had to be bolted in place from the outside to ensure that nothing came loose while the submersible was underwater. With an incongruous grin, he pointed out that even the smallest break in the seal would crush the submersible in seconds. Eden remembered, as the last bolt neared freedom, how she had found the explanation less than reassuring.

Finally, with what seemed like the speed of a tectonic plate, the bolt shuddered out of its housing. The person above dropped the bolt. It bounced down the side of the submersible and crashed on to the deck. Whoever was up there positioned themselves to open the heavy hatch.

Eden and Baxter readied their weapons. In a few moments, they would know whether they faced friend or foe.

The hatch creaked and groaned as it was pulled from above. The seal popped like the sound of a jar being opened. Fresh air rushed inside.

Eden took two deep and delicious breaths and then felt suddenly lightheaded. She steadied herself on the armrests, forcing herself to focus.

The hatch creaked up another inch, revealing a crescent of peach-colored sky. A shadow darkened the opening as whoever was up there changed position.

Eden and Baxter extended their weapons further, both unblinking, both ready for whatever the next few moments held.

The hatch swung to the shape of a half moon and then

gravity took over the work. The hatch fell hard against the side of the craft, ringing loudly.

To open the hatch, their liberator had clearly moved to the other side. Slowly, a silhouette passed across the aperture.

Without realizing she was doing it, Eden held her breath.

36

EDEN KEPT her eyes locked on submersible's hatch as the figure moved closer. Muscles tensed and ready, Eden held the gun and prepared to fire. The noise of the shot inside the submersible's tiny cabin would be deafening. If the mystery person was one of Thorne's men kept behind to finish the job, Eden would shoot without hesitation.

The figure clunked around the submersible and then a face appeared in the opening. The eyes filled with concern and determination, it was a face Eden and Baxter knew so well.

"Thanks for the great welcome," Athena said, looking at Eden and Baxter both pointing their weapons up at her. "The ordeal I've been through today, and this is how you greet me?"

Eden suddenly felt weak, the gun dropped to her side and all the tension drained from her body. She glanced at Baxter, the look in his eyes told her that he was feeling the same.

"I have no idea what you've been doing, but it absolutely

stinks in here." Athena reached inside and helped Eden out through the submersible's hatch and then down the ladder.

"We're so glad to see you," Eden said, stretching her arms and drew a deep breath. Although exhausted and still terrified for her father, she was alive and that felt great. Eden reached out and held the side of the submersible as a wave of dizziness passed through her.

Athena helped Baxter out through the hatch and down the ladder. He stretched and yawned.

Eden and Baxter glanced at each other and then merged into an impromptu hug.

"Hold on a second," Athena said, pointing down inside the submersible. "You didn't like... make out, did you? You know, thinking you you're both going to die, you thought you might as well?"

Eden looked up at Athena, then glanced at Baxter.

"It would explain that smell," Athena said, clambering down the ladder. "All those hormones. Yuck."

"No... certainly not... of course..." Baxter stuttered awkwardly, turning from deathly pale to a shade of beetroot red.

"Shhh," Eden said, placing her finger against Baxter's lips. "What happened on the sub, stays on the sub, you know that." With a wink, she turned and walked away.

"At least that got some color in your face," Athena said, nudging Baxter with her elbow.

Athena flashed Baxter a smirk, and then the two women walked inside.

Ten minutes later, Eden and Baxter were changed, cleaned up, and already halfway through a mug of coffee.

"Oh my gosh, this tastes so good," Eden said, enjoying the smell, the feeling of the steam on her face, and the taste of the coffee. She turned towards Athena. "How come you're still here? We saw Thorne force everyone into the chopper."

"Not everyone," Athena paused to sip from her cup. "As you saw I was part of the diving crew that dropped you in the ocean. When I re-surfaced, I saw a plane approaching low overhead. I knew it had to be bad news."

"What..." Baxter stopped his question mid why through and shrugged.

"A Lockheed L100, if you must know," Athena said. "I only know that because we've used them for various deployments in the past."

Eden coaxed Athena on with a hand gesture.

"I asked one of the other divers to drop a rope over the side and stayed in the water," Athena said. "I was down there for nearly an hour, then climbed up and hid under a tarp on the deck. I don't think I've ever been that cold in my life."

"I'm so glad you did." Eden placed her hand on top of Athena's. Maybe it was the exhaustion, or the near-death suffocation inside the sub, but Eden's emotions welled like a tropical storm. "Thank you."

"Don't mention it," Athena said. "I had a feeling they had something nasty planned, but leaving you trapped in there was just cruel."

"We've still got a problem." Baxter struggled to his feet and studied the map on a large computer screen. "We're alone on this ship, with no way to get off."

Eden turned towards the window. Although it was still morning, patchy grey clouds scudded across the horizon.

Baxter clicked through to a weather report. "At least we've had some luck, the storm took a turn about two hundred miles to the south."

Eden nodded gravely, thinking about how much worse things could be if the storm had caught up with them.

"Actually, things are unusually calm for the next few hours, at least."

"Check out Mr. Positive over there," Athena said, pointing at Baxter. "It's not like you to be all sunshine and rainbows. Whatever you did in the sub, do it again, regularly."

"Nothing happened!" Baxter said, whipping around to face the women who were smirking together. He scowled and turned back towards the computer. "Stop messing about and find a way off this ship before our luck changes."

"Ahh there we are, the same old grumpy Baxter returns," Athena said.

"And we wouldn't want you any other way," Eden added. "And you're right, things are pretty bleak right now. That immortal madman has my father and the *Lady of Leone*."

"See Baxter, now you've brought the mood down." Athena turned to Eden. "Yes, I saw that guy, Thorne. How's that even possible? Last time we saw him, he was chewing on a bridge."

"I have no idea." Eden rubbed her hands together. "I have no idea how he could have survived that. It had spinal fracture written all over it."

"Maybe he's just lucky," Baxter grunted.

"Wait a minute," Athena said, her finger raised. "Do you think it's got something to do with this Xero+ stuff? Do you reckon he's the result of some strange medical testing, like that rat with an ear on its back?"

"The Vacanti mouse," Baxter said.

"Whatever type of mouse it was, it's cruel if you ask me," Athena said. "What's the point of having an extra ear, anyway? Of all the things you could do with science, and that's what you come up..."

"Anyway," Eden interjected, trying to pull the conversation back on course. "What if Thorne is the human equivalent of that? This Xero+ thing has been used to make him super strong."

"What if you're just wrong?" Baxter said, raising an eyebrow. "How do you know it's actually the same guy?"

"Because I can't close my eyes without having visions of that ugly hulk trying to push me off a speeding train," Eden said.

"It was a pretty memorable morning," Athena added.

"Why are you trying to kill my dreams here, anyway?" Eden said.

"I'm not. I'm just saying jumping to conclusions that the Van Wicks have a high-tech lab in which they're running experiments on people to create immortal soldiers is a bit of a jump in logic, don't you think?" Baxter said.

"He's got a point," Athena said, pointing at Baxter. "Although, I do hate to admit it."

"Alright then, brain box. What do you think?" Eden retorted.

Baxter surrendered, holding up his hands. "I have no idea. But one thing I know for absolute certain, is all this chatting is not getting us off this ship any quicker."

"The man's got another point," Athena said. "Do you think he can get three in a row?"

"Agreed," Eden said.

"Maybe he's just thinking with his head now, rather than his..." Athena smirked.

"Stop right there," Baxter said, this time not flushing so red. "Hold on a minute, you know there is one person who could help us..." Baxter glanced from Eden to Athena.

Silence filled the room for a beat or two.

Eden narrowed her eyes and then realized who Baxter was talking about. "No, no, no. Absolutely not. We need a professional..."

Eden eyed Athena for support but got none.

"What we need," Baxter corrected, "Is someone who's experienced at flying in all conditions, with a proven track record, perhaps someone who was in the US Air Force..."

"Three good points in a row," Athena said. "I hate to admit it, but the guy's just got a strike."

"But there must be other people who fit the bill?" Eden whined.

Athena sprung towards Eden, her eyes shining like shillings. "You're jealous!"

"What could I possibly be jealous of?" Eden quipped back. "It's just when these two are together they..."

"Don't give you any attention," Athena said, folding her arms.

Eden felt the sting of the comment, meaning it was probably partly true. "Alright, fine," she muttered reluctantly. "But if they start banging on about planes, captain this captain that, then I'm staying here."

"The problem is, how can we get a message out to her?" Athena said, tapping her chin. "Hey, golden boy, since you're on a roll, do you think we can re-configure the *Njord Fadir's* onboard communication system to get in touch with her?"

"I can do better than that." Baxter climbed to his feet and crossed to the computer terminal.

"Ah, I bet he's going to reprogram the satellite uplink to bypass standard channels," Eden said. Both women followed Baxter with their eyes.

"Maybe." Baxter opened his kit bag and rummaged around inside.

"Good idea. If we can tap into one of the backup communication satellites, we might be able to send a direct signal," Athena said.

"Just make sure it's secure," Eden said, frowning. "We don't know who else might be listening."

"Don't worry," Baxter said, still rummaging. "This is an expert task, but I know what I'm doing." Finding what he needed, his face brightened. He removed a smart phone from the bag.

"Ahh, good thinking," Athena said. "We can reconfigure the encryption protocols and bypass the network to establish our own connection."

"We could." Baxter tapped on the screen. "Or we could just use Facetime."

The women raised their eyebrows in unison.

"You're where?" Nora Byrd's southern accent boomed from the phone in record time.

"She was probably sitting next to the phone waiting for his call," Eden hissed in Athena's ear.

Baxter swung the phone around so they could all see the screen. Athena smiled and Eden faked it.

On the screen, Nora Byrd grinned widely. Her trademark beehive of jet-black hair was pinned on top of her head. The camera panned around to show an aircraft behind her, with one of its engine bays open.

Baxter gave their current location using a load of complicated numbers.

"What are you doing out there?" Byrd asked. "That's the middle of the North Atlantic."

"We've..." Athena started, but Byrd interrupted.

"Hold on one tick. That's just a few miles north of *The Titanic* wreck. You've not been..." Byrd said, almost shouting.

"Afraid so," Eden said, keen to just get on with things. "And we've run into some trouble."

Byrd let out a laugh. "That old Mr. Trouble just seems to follow you around."

For the next few minutes, Baxter and Byrd spoke in a series of words which Eden and Athena barely understood.

"Okay, I think I can help you. As luck would have it, I'm up in New York helping an old friend with a restoration project."

Bird pointed at the plane behind them.

"That's a Mustang," Baxter said, squinting into the phone. "If I'm not mistaken, the P-51D model." Baxter said.

"Told you," Eden groaned. "Hold my drink while I throw myself overboard."

"She sure is," Byrd crowed lovingly. "She's got a bit of engine trouble, but we will have her up in the skies before long."

"I'm not getting on that," Eden grunted from the other side of the room.

Byrd roared with laughter. "No, you certainly wouldn't want to, unless you're going to fly her yourself. She's a single-seat fighter, see."

Eden blushed — having not intended Byrd to hear.

"What are you suggesting?" Baxter said.

"Don't you worry about that," Byrd replied, every bit the coquettish vintage pin-up she embodied the style of. "Be on deck in say… eight hours' time… and you'll find out."

37

Eight long hours later, Baxter, Eden and Athena stood on the rear deck of the *Njord Fadir*. The trio had spent the day trying to rest and recuperate as much as possible. Eden had attempted to sleep, but with the Njord Fadir eerily quiet and worries of her father plaguing her mind, it hadn't worked. Predicting that whatever happened next would need every ounce of her strength, she cursed herself for wasting the time.

"She better turn up," Eden groaned, her teeth chattering despite the thickly insulated coat. She searched the horizon for movement. The sun was now beginning its descent, casting a glittering path in the water. Painted with shades of orange, pink, and gold, the colors seemed to stretch on forever, merging with the sea at some distant, unseen point.

"Nora Byrd wouldn't miss a party like this," Baxter said. "This is the stuff she lives for."

"Let's hope you're right," Athena said, her shoulders hunched against the cold. "I tell you, though, this is certainly not my sort of party."

"Too right, the parties I go to have more than microwave

food," Eden said. Having eaten three dishes in the last few hours which claimed to be different things but tasted exactly the same.

"Beaumont told me you used to live on that stuff when you lived in the truck," Athena teased.

"Do you gossip about me to the entire team, or is it just Baxter and Beaumont?" Eden threw a side eye in the direction of her friends. "It is true that after single-handedly rescuing Beaumont from Lulu King and her hardmen, I gave him some food from a packet. If I hadn't been so busy saving him, I'd have splashed out on a lobster for sure."

"You wouldn't know what to do with a lobster," Athena said, giggling.

"Now, that I take offence at," Eden said. "I'm a good cook when I want to be."

"Yeah, cooking up trouble," Baxter said under his breath.

Eden threw him a glare.

Athena giggled but didn't reply. The three sunk into silence, staring out at the horizon. With a stroke of luck, the weather had continued to be uncharacteristically calm, allowing the *Njord Fadir* to sit unhindered, even with no one in control.

"I'm glad we didn't see any icebergs," Athena muttered, her teeth chattering. "That would be a rubbish end to the story."

"I know. We run into enough trouble on our own, without nature having a go." Eden glanced over her shoulder. On the deck behind them, the battered submersible sat in a pool of its own hydraulic fluids. Stains of blood and oil also covered the deck.

"I don't think we'll get our damage deposit back on the *Njord Havspeil*," Eden said.

"There isn't a rental company in the world that would do business with you," Athena quipped in response.

Eden swiveled her gaze back across the ocean. Even looking at the submersible's wreckage made her uncomfortable.

The deep rumble of an engine rose above the lapping waves. Eden heard it first and stood up straighter, craning to hear the noise.

"You hear that?" she whispered, scanning the horizon for anything approaching.

Baxter and Athena nodded, both scanning the waves.

Baxter's ears perked up, and he nodded, his gaze narrowing. "Sounds like a plane."

"There!" Athena shouted, one hand shielding her eyes and the other outstretched. "There it is!"

Squinting at the sky, Eden saw a speck on the horizon. For several minutes, no one spoke. The speck grew bigger and bigger, forming slowly into the shape of an aircraft.

Finally, the SkyTrain sliced through a bank of thinning clouds and came into view.

"That's Nora's SkyTrain, alright," Baxter said, pointing excitedly at the craft.

Nora Byrd had used her lovingly restored Dakota Skytrain to help Eden, Baxter, and Athena out of a tough situation a few weeks before. Although far from a plane enthusiast, Eden had to admit the vintage craft was a thing of beauty — although she would never admit it to Nora Byrd.

Now, watching the aluminum fuselage glimmering golden in the setting sun, Eden felt a sense of relief that Byrd was here to help, mixed with a sense of embarrassment that they were relying on her again so soon.

"Okay, but that plane is traveling pretty fast, and it's all the way up there," Eden said, pointing into the sky. "How's that going to help us?"

The distinctive whine of the SkyTrain's twin propellers rose into a howl.

"Did you pack that thing?" Athena said, making a motion as though she were climbing a rope.

"The Skyhook," Eden teased. "I didn't pack mine, but maybe Captain Baxter did."

Baxter shook his head. "Don't worry, Nora will have a plan. She always has a plan."

"Don't worry, Nora's got a plan," Eden mouthed silently to Athena, eliciting a giggle.

The SkyTrain disappeared behind a bank of clouds for a few seconds. When it reappeared, it was almost overhead. Eden glimpsed the craft's brushed-aluminum up close now, glittering even more brightly in the evening sunlight.

"She's put amphibious floats on!" Baxter shouted, pointing up at the plane. "Look!"

Eden cupped a hand over her eyes and saw the SkyTrain's aluminum belly. Two long floats had been attached to the craft's stomach in place of its wheels.

The SkyTrain tilted from side to side — the pilot's version of a greeting — then banked into a wide arc around the *Njord Fadir*. The Skytrain completed a full circuit of the *Njord Fadir,* reducing altitude all the way.

Baxter gawked, his eyes riveted to the machine as though it were giving him a private show. The craft touched down in the water a few hundred feet away. It bounced twice and then turned towards the ship.

"I'll get the boat," Baxter said, pointing towards the small boat tied to the side of the *Njord Fadir*.

The SkyTrain's Twin Wasp engines chugged and then cut out. Byrd let the aircraft's motion carry it forwards, finally sliding to a stop about fifty feet from the *Njord Fadir's* vast flank.

Baxter shimmied down the ladder and started up the outboard motor. Athena and Eden followed, jumping down the last few rungs into the boat and taking a seat. Baxter took the controls, and they sped across the open water to the Skytrain. Nora Byrd swung open the door as they approached.

"And what a lovely evening it is," Byrd said, following the statement with a laugh. "Good to see you, Captain," she said, using Baxter's official title from his previous life in the Royal Air Force.

"Good to see you," Baxter replied.

"It seems like quite a situation you've got yourself in here," Byrd said, placing her hands on her hips and taking in the size of the *Njord Fadir* for the first time.

Eden rolled her eyes, and summoning incredible power, prevented herself from pointing out that they were all skilled in making statements of the obvious.

"That's true," Athena said, more sweetly than Eden could ever have managed. "We need to get out of here."

Byrd grinned, her eyes glinting.

"Gentlemen," Byrd turned behind her, talking to someone else inside the airplane. A group of men appeared at the door.

"Who's this?" Eden asked, peering in at the group.

"What, we can't just leave this beauty floating out here, can we?" Byrd pointed up at the *Njord Fadir*. "They'll have it in New York in a couple of days' time."

"You thought of everything," Athena said, genuinely impressed.

Eden, Athena, and Baxter changed places with the crew.

"Don't worry, there's not a ship on the seas that those men can't navigate," Byrd said.

"Sorry about the mess on the back deck," Eden said. "Things got a bit out of hand."

"Darlin' knowing you like I do, I ain't got a shred of doubt that's true."

Baxter passed out a few large duffel bags, and the men set off towards the *Njord Fadir*.

"I thought of a few options to get you out of here, but since the weather was playing ball, I thought these would be best." She pointed down at the floats. "You're on a tight deadline I expect."

"Yes, we are," Eden said.

"Then we'd better get moving." Byrd slipped through the cabin and dropped into the well-worn pilot's seat. "If you wouldn't mind joining me, Captain," she said, tapping the copilot's chair.

Eden thought the gesture was suggestive but was far too tired to comment.

Baxter walked to the cockpit, clearly trying not to appear excited.

"Make yourself comfortable back there," Byrd shouted over her shoulder. "We'll be back before you know it."

Byrd reached up and clicked several switches. The engines roared back to life, drowning out all other sounds. A soft vibration coursed through the plane's frame.

"Hold on tight. This might get a little bumpy."

Eden and Athena positioned themselves in the cabin beside one of the small windows. As the SkyTrain turned into the wind and started bouncing across the waves, Eden glanced out at the *Njord Fadir*.

In that moment, she once again thought of all the souls who had lost their lives on the wreck so far beneath the waves. She remembered the ghostly ship, emerging from the ocean bed, and the untold treasures still waiting in her holds.

As the SkyTrain leaped, bumbling like a drunk up into the air, Eden stared one more time at the unremarkable section of ocean on which the *Njord Fadir* bobbed.

Eden wasn't certain about much in life, but one thing she now knew for sure: whatever was left in *The Titanic's* hold, she wouldn't be going down to get it.

38

The Van Wick Estate, Near Bellingham, Washington State.

Ludwig Van Wick turned when he heard the knock at the door. This time, he was eager to hear the news.

"Come in!" he shouted, as loud as his moth-eaten lungs would allow. They felt moth eaten, although that wasn't the term Doctor Vos had used.

The door swung open, and a man stepped through. With the curtains tightly closed, the office was gloomy. It took him several moments to realize the man wasn't Thorne.

The man was slimmer, although still above average in height. Ludwig Van Wick assessed the man to be in his late fifties or early sixties, with well-trimmed grey hair. The man appeared crumpled, as though he'd just spent several hours cooped up in an aircraft — although this Van Wick knew for certain was the case.

Thorne's bulky shape filled the door behind the man.

The man paced to the center of the room, appraised the

space in the manner a prospective house buyer might, and then turned towards his host.

Van Wick worked the control and slid his wheelchair out from behind his desk.

"I know you," Ludwig said, although still unable to conjure up a name. He wondered whether he too should increase his dosage of Xero+ to keep his brain firing on all cylinders.

"This is Alexander Winslow," Thorne said, closing the door and stepping up behind the stranger.

Van Wick Senior glanced at Thorne for the first time. The bulges beneath his skin had swelled over the last few hours. The one on his jawline looked like a grapefruit was ripening beneath his skin.

Van Wick Senior turned back towards Winslow. "Ah, Mr. Winslow, yes, I knew I recognized you from somewhere. I'm sorry to drag you out here like this, but I am very particular about our property."

Winslow turned and locked eyes with Van Wick for the first time. "I'm certain you can't claim ownership of a relic which has been on the ocean floor for over one-hundred years," Winslow said, his voice edged with disdain.

"Ha!" Van Wick spat out a laugh. His head wobbled as though it might fall from his neck at any moment. "I don't think you want to talk about the intricacies surrounding the law of possession. Let's not get off on the wrong foot now. What do you think of our ancestral home?"

Winslow glanced around the office again. "Very nice. I once had an office a little like this, at my home in Brighton." He stepped towards the window and pulled aside the curtains. Through the glass, several gardeners worked in a grand and expansive estate. Beyond the garden, lush forest climbed up towards snow-capped mountains. Winslow had to concede that the view was something to behold.

Ludwig Van Wick placed a hand over his eyes, then slid his chair back behind his desk in an attempt to get away from the light.

"I liked that office," Winslow said softly. "That was until it was burned down by people who were little better than common thieves."

Winslow spun around and noticed the effect the light was having on his host. He let the curtain drop back into its closed position but made a mental note of the old man's reaction, should it be useful later.

"I'm sure you're a busy man, Mr. Van Wick. Let's cut the niceties and just get down to what you want from me." Winslow scanned the room for a chair. Seeing none, he stayed right where he was.

"I respect your candor, Mr. Winslow," Van Wick said, reversing his chair back behind the desk. "Yes, it is always good to be frank in business, I believe. You see your daughter, Miss Black... As an aside, it's funny that she rejected your name, isn't it? You must be very disappointed that the Winslow legacy will not continue."

"I think you misunderstand the meaning of legacy, Mr. Van Wick," Winslow said, his eyes boring into the other. "Legacy is not about having your name in lights. It's about leaving our world in a better than we found it."

Van Wick roared in what sounded like a genuine fit of laughter. He slapped the desk with surprising energy, causing a pair of glass paperweights to bounce. "Cute idea, Mr. Winslow. Very cute indeed. Did you read that on a postcard?"

Winslow didn't answer. "Get to the point."

"Absolutely, well, your daughter got involved with something she shouldn't have." Van Wick rubbed his fingers together as though trying to conjure up the word he was seeking. "A transaction of mine, you see..."

"A merciless killing," Winslow said, his tone level.

The two men locked eyes again and Winslow noticed how tired the other man appeared. Van Wick's eyes were red, and the skin beneath them hung as though it were too big for his skull.

"Again, that's a matter of perspective," Van Wick said. "Thorne here was tying up a loose end for me when your daughter got in the middle and made a right mess of it all."

Thorne grunted at the mention of his name.

Winslow sensed the man a few paces behind him.

"You were trying to kill Doctor Hunter," Winslow said.

Van Wick Senior sighed as though everything were a bit too much for him to deal with. "Yes, we were, but there you go again using all that dramatic language. Do you think it's possible for a family like mine to be among the world's wealthiest for generations without an issue or two?"

Winslow didn't reply.

"Let me simplify things for you, as I can see you're overthinking this," Van Wick said, rubbing a hand across his face. "Thorne here had a job to do, and the wonderful Miss Black impeded that job. We had no problem with you, your daughter, or your little organization before that. But now we have a problem because Thorne gets a genuine sense of completion when he finishes a task. Isn't that right, Thorne?"

"Yes, sir," the giant man said as quickly as if this was a well-practiced routine.

"That sense of satisfaction is what he lives for. Isn't that right, Thorne?"

"Yes, sir."

"And now, by getting in the way, you've robbed Thorne of that feeling. That's the problem in really simple terms."

"My sympathies," Winslow said staring hard at the old man.

"Thorne tried appealing to your daughter's better nature. He explained to her, using the language he knows best, that she really shouldn't get in the way. How does she respond?"

"She threw me from a moving train, sir," Thorne said.

"You head-butted a bridge from what I understand," Winslow said.

Thorne took an angry step forward, his hand drew back to strike Winslow.

"Now, now, Thorne. It's not time for that, yet," Ludwig said.

Thorne grumbled and returned to his position like a scolded dog being reprimanded.

"What I'm telling you, is that this can all be made right. You tell me where Doctor Hunter is so Thorne can finish the job, and everything can go back to normal."

Winslow glanced at the giant two paces behind him.

"There are no other options," Van Wick said. "You've seen what's out that window. There isn't a person within twenty miles who isn't loyal to me."

Winslow grumbled, tapping his chin to make it look as though he was thinking. "In that case, it seems like a good deal," Winslow said. "I'll tell you when you've returned the *Lady of Leone,* and my daughter is home safe and well."

Van Wick turned to Thorne. The big man nodded his head almost imperceptibly.

"Ahh, well that's the bad news. First, the *Lady of Leone* was ours to begin with. I even have the purchase documentation from 1912." Ludwig Van Wick steepled his fingers and locked eyes with Winslow. "As for your daughter, I'm afraid she's already dead."

39

The Van Wick Estate, Near Bellingham, Washington State.

"Disneyland's got nothing on this place," Eden said from her vantage point high in one of the ancient cedar trees which lined the estate.

Holding on to the tree with one hand, pressing the binoculars to her eyes with the other, Eden felt more alert than ever. After the bouncy cross-continental flight on Byrd's Skytrain, they had borrowed a Sprinter van, prepared with all the gear they needed, and headed up into the mountains towards the Van Wick Estate.

Pushing together a few crates, topped with a deflated life raft, Eden had managed a few hours of fitful sleep while on the plane. Now, she felt fired up and ready for action.

"Their security is tighter than Disneyland too," Baxter's voice came though the comms. Stationed in the back of the Sprinter van half a mile out, he was researching the mansion's security system.

Eden traced the serpentine driveway which snaked its

way from the gate to the house. Swinging the binoculars in a circular motion, she counted the patrolling guards as they made their way around the grounds.

"That's what we expected," Eden said. "There are separate teams protecting the house and the perimeter wall. They're heavily armed too, and some have guard dogs."

She gazed beyond the house and up at the mountains which flanked the property on the other side. The natural surroundings were not only a stunning backdrop for the mansion, but provided the privacy and security for which the family were famed. The dense woodland on one side and mountains on the other, would put off all but the most persistent visitors.

Watching a guard cross the well-manicured lawn, a German Shepherd pulling at its lead with its nose down in the grass, Eden wondered whether this was finally a step too far. But, Eden also knew they had no choice. Her father was in there, not to mention the *Lady of Leone*.

Eden pulled the binoculars from her eyes and squinted at the house. Sundown was still an hour away, but flood lights had already snapped on around the parameter wall. The house itself was swathed in gloom. That was probably the way the Van Wicks liked it, Eden thought. Keeping the lights off stopped people noticing the depraved stuff they got up to.

Stashing the binoculars away, Eden scurried down the tree. She dropped the final few feet and landed in a crouch. She set off at a jog and was back at the Sprinter van within a few minutes. Sporting the National Forest Association's logo, the vehicle didn't appear out of place parked at the side of the road.

Eden glanced around. Satisfied no one was nearby, she opened the door and stepped inside. It was dark inside the van, the only light emitting from two large computer screens mounted on the van's wall.

Eden shuffled up beside Athena on a bench seat fitted along one side of the van. Baxter sat on a swivel chair, working at a computer.

"Don't get me wrong, all this technology is great, but nothing beats actually seeing the place with a pair of these." Eden held up the binoculars.

"You're getting old," Athena said. "Soon we won't have to go out at all. We'll do everything from behind the computer keyboard."

"Let's hope not." Eden snapped on an overhead light and rolled out a schematic of the mansion which they'd found in an archive. There was no guarantee it was correct, but it was something to go on at least.

"The priority is my father," Eden said, worry pressing against her chest. "After we've got him safe, we will attempt to recover the *Lady of Leone* too."

"Agreed," Baxter said, scrolling through some infrared images on the screen.

"Do we have any idea where he's being held?" Eden said, checking the plan for entrances and exits.

"Not exactly," Baxter said. "I took these infrared pictures with the drone while you were having fun climbing trees."

"Hilarious," Eden said.

"The images show the greatest concentration of people in a room at the rear of the house on the second floor." Baxter scrolled from one image to the next. As Baxter had suggested, most of the house was blue, implying that it was unoccupied. One room at the rear of the house, however, glowed red.

"Have you got a closeup of that area?" Eden said, pointing at the room.

"We will get one just before we're good to go," Athena said, pulling the drone from its protective case and switching over the battery.

"Great," Eden said. "If it's still like that, then we know where to start looking."

"That's if we can even get across the wall," Athena said.

Baxter nodded. "It's not going to be easy."

"Every security system has a weak point, right?" Eden said.

"Absolutely, but they don't exactly advertise the weak points," Baxter said. "The Van Wicks are one of America's, no, the world's, richest families. They've got a very sophisticated system with cameras on the perimeter wall, which is twelve feet high and topped with razor wire. It's also patrolled by a team of men with dogs..."

"Vicious looking dogs," Athena said, gravely.

"Vicious looking dogs," Eden agreed, nodding. "Okay, so the wall is a difficult one. What if we go in through the front gate?"

Baxter and Athena glanced at Eden like she was nuts.

"There's one gate. It's also twelve feet high, made from steel, and guarded twenty-four hours a day by two guards, and watched over by several cameras," Baxter said. "We go in there and within ninety seconds, we will be in the crosshairs of every guard on the estate."

"Absolutely. *We* don't go in there, but someone else does." Eden tapped one of the house's rear doors on the schematic.

"A distraction," Athena said.

"Exactly. Bring up a map of the estate." Eden pointed at the screen and Baxter flicked across to the map. "Athena and I will get ready by the wall over here. We'll have to take out that camera, but I expect it'll be several minutes before someone comes to check on that. We cut away the razor wire, get everything set up. Then, as soon as the gate's breached and everyone charges that way, we can scramble across and be among those trees before anyone notices." She pointed at a pair of trees surrounded by ornate bushes about fifty feet from the wall.

"That would provide good cover," Athena said. "It's about a hundred feet from the house there and mostly in darkness."

Eden nodded in agreement.

"Okay, but who's going to be stupid enough to take on the guards at the front gate?" Baxter asked. He glanced at Eden who was now grinning. "You know, it really worries me when you smile like that."

40

It took them just half an hour to find what they needed using the drone, and then another hour to set it up. By the time they were ready to go, the sky was pitch black.

"I'm in position," Baxter said, from the driver's seat of a twenty-year-old Chevrolet Suburban. He turned the ignition. The powerful V8 engine coughed and then rumbled. Breaking into and starting the SUV had been easier than he'd expected by following Eden's instructions. What would come next — that was the challenge.

"All good down here. We'll shoot out the camera on your word," Eden replied.

"Roger that." Baxter peered out through the mud-streaked windshield. "Let's hope this works."

"Come on," Eden's voice sounded mocking now. "It's hardly the most stupid thing we've done."

"That's true," Baxter said, his voice cracking in his dry throat. "But we really don't set the bar very high."

Baxter clicked the Chevy into the drive and started off down the road. For half a mile, the road wound its way down the hillside. Just using the dim parking lights, Baxter navigated this part of the road slowly. Approaching the final corner, a gnawing unease twisted in his gut. He rubbed a hand across his stubbled chin.

He rounded the corner and applied the brake. The Chevy slowed with an ear-splitting screech. From here it was a straight run for about half a mile towards the gate.

Baxter figured the approach road was probably designed purposefully to give the guards an unobstructed view of whatever was coming their way. On this occasion, it also gave Baxter an unexpected advantage.

"In position," Baxter said, peering through the gloom. At the bottom of the road, he could just make out the brightly lit gate with two guards lounging off to one side. "Cut the camera in thirty seconds."

"Roger that." Eden's reply came almost immediately.

Baxter took a deep breath. He flexed his fingers and then gripped the steering wheel. Every muscle in his body tensed in preparation for the rapid sequence of events that were about to unfold. The clock inside the truck ticked, each second an eternity.

Athena's voice burst into his ear. "Camera's down. Go, Baxter!"

Wasting no time, Baxter hit the gas. The engine roared to life, and the vehicle shot forward. The wind whipped through the open windows, drowning out all other sounds. The engine howled as Baxter pushed harder on the gas. The truck tore up the road, leaving streaks of rubber on the asphalt.

Baxter cupped his hand above his eyes to see through the bright security lights.

The Chevy bore down on the mansion's entrance, like a lion on the cusp of making a catch.

Baxter watched as the guards shot to attention, drawing

their weapons. They shouted, although Baxter couldn't hear them above the roaring engine. At first, they scrambled in front of the gate, forming a barrier between the speeding truck and the Van Wick estate. When the Chevy didn't stop, they raised their weapons and fired at the truck. Bullets thwacked into the Chevy's grille, and the windshield spider webbed. The vehicle didn't stop.

Baxter watched it all as though in a dream. His heart pounded like the valves of the engine.

At the last moment, the guards decided that being the filling in a sandwich between a two-ton truck and a thick steel gate was a bad idea. As though reacting on the flick of a switch, they both sprinted out of the way.

Speeding at well past seventy, the Chevy was beyond the point of no return. Twenty feet in front of the gate, the vehicle hit a bump in the road. It reared up, tires completely leaving the asphalt for a second or more. Then it crashed back down to the road and tore up the remaining distance. The grille glinted against the floodlights and then another sound reverberated through the night. The raw, metallic screech of the gate's ornate bars bending, warping, and snapping under the force of the vehicle's front end. One gate was torn from the supporting pillar, sending chunks of masonry flying in all directions. The other gate twisted back on itself and slammed into the wall.

The Chevy bounded to the left, but the angle was too much. The Chevy teetered on two tires and then flopped down on its side. Glass shattered, and metal buckled.

Just as the reverberations of the impact died out, the wail of gunfire and pounding bullets hammered through the night. The guards at the gate sprinted towards the vehicle, shouting into their radios as they went.

The first guard dropped to his knee and fired on the

vehicle, shattering the windshield and further denting the metal.

The engine, pushed beyond its limits in the sprint toward the gates, let out a shrill wail and then hissed into silence. Fuel and oil sprayed out all over the grass. A cloud of steam and smoke burst from the shattered radiator, merging with the dust and debris thrown into the air by the crash.

Two more guards ran around from the far side of the perimeter fence and four from the house itself. Seeing the vehicle, they paused, and raised their guns.

The first guard scurried around the Chevy, two of his colleagues close behind. He reached the windshield and shoved the muzzle of his gun in through the broken glass. Then he reeled back in shock. He lifted the radio to his lips and sent out a message.

The driver's seat was empty.

Three hundred feet up the road, Baxter poked his head out from behind a clump of bushes. Through the binoculars he watched the guards surround the vehicle. The men shouted at each other, their guns raised and quivering.

Baxter whistled and then glanced down at the small remote control system he'd used to steer the vehicle. The simple addition of a length of wood on the gas had kept it powering forwards.

Once again, the audacity and simplicity of Eden's plan had worked.

"We're in," Baxter said, touching the comms device in his ear. "I'll say once, and only once, I'm impressed. Now, are you ready for the fireworks?"

"Fire away, captain," came Eden's smug response.

Baxter drew out another small remote control and jabbed the button. Three hundred feet away, a small explosive charge ruptured the Chevy's fuel line. Gas spewed out, igniting with sparks from the mangled engine. Flames boomed and roared, consuming the front of the Chevy, and flashing out for several feet on all sides. Thick, black smoke spiraled upwards, blocking out some of the floodlights.

Three men ran across the lawn ablaze. From where Baxter stood, they moved like the dancing flames of candles. The reality, Baxter knew, was a lot more horrific than that. Other men ran to help them, one fetching a fire extinguisher from the gate office. Baxter hoped the chaos wasn't a warning of what was still to come.

41

ON HEARING THE COLLISION, Eden and Athena leaped into action. They had already taken out the camera, cut away the razor wire, and fastened a rope in position to help them scale the wall.

Eden reached the top of the wall first and checked the grounds on the other side. A pair of guards rushed toward the commotion, guns at the ready. Eden waited until the guards were out of sight, then swung her leg over the wall and dropped down the other side. She landed on a gravel path which ran along the inside of the wall. In less than a second, she was up and sprinting toward the bushes they'd seen on the plan.

Eden crawled in behind the bushes, keeping as close to the ground as possible. Athena joined her a moment later. The women waited, poised to run or fight for a few seconds. When it was clear that no one had seen them and no one was heading their way, Eden parted the thick leaves of the bush and they both peered through. The thick foliage and the gloom that hung around this part of the garden had so far concealed their movements.

Two hundred feet away the Chevy lay on its side, wheels still spinning.

The guards were getting close now, stalking towards the vehicle.

The explosion roared from the Chevy. The noise rolled up the hillside and back down again. In a micro-second, the Chevy became a blazing fireball, flames licking as high as the nearby trees.

"Ouch," Eden uttered, watching the burning security guys throw themselves onto the grass and roll about frantically.

"Sucks to be them," Athena said, cruelly.

"I hope they're getting paid well," Eden said, before turning towards the house. "No time to waste. Let's get out of here."

Eden led them out of the bush and then across an open stretch of lawn. She ran hard, her feet sinking into the grass. The blaze from the Chevy made their shadows dance like the tribal festivities of generations past. Fortunately, nobody was looking their way.

Eden approached the wall of the mansion's west side and stopped.

Immediately sensing something was wrong, Athena froze just an inch behind.

"Two guards," Eden hissed. "Fifty feet away. Just around there." She pointed around the corner.

"I bet they're heading this way?" Athena said.

Eden nodded.

"Typical that. Why are the bad guys always heading towards us?"

Eden shrugged. "I'm just surprised someone has done their job properly and not gone into full panic mode when the party arrived." She pointed towards the burning truck.

"These guys deserve a raise," Athena said.

The women shuffled in close to the building and then glanced around the corner. As Eden had said, two guards moved their way, flashlights swinging from side to side.

"They're not in a rush," Athena said.

"Non-lethal force if possible." Eden touched the holstered knife at her ankle but didn't draw it out.

"If possible," Athena added.

Eden crouched down and grabbed a rock from the flower bed.

"What are you going to do with that?" Athena said.

"I was going to put it in their boot so it's really painful to walk," Eden said, deadpan.

Athena nodded as though it was a great idea, and then narrowed her eyes.

Eden leaned out from the side of the building and hurled the rock at a brass statue of Neptune riding a seahorse set amid a fountain twenty feet away. The rock hit home, clanging against Neptune's chest and banging several times on the seahorse as it fell.

"Much better idea," Athena murmured.

The guards stopped walking and the flashlight beams immediately swung towards the statue. The men murmured something inaudible and then strode toward the statue.

As the men stepped out beyond the corner of the building, Eden and Athena followed with cat-like grace.

When they were a few feet behind the guards, Eden and Athena leaped forwards. Neither man even saw the attack coming as Eden and Athena knocked them into unconsciousness.

Eden and Athena caught the men and laid them silently on the grass. The beams of the guards' flashlights shining off at random angles was the only sign anything was off.

The women soon saw to that, snatching up the lights and clicking them off.

"Quickly, check their pockets." Athena glanced back towards the fire to ensure no reinforcements were on their way.

Eden and Athena patted the men down, relieving them of their wallets, some loose change, and a pair of swipe cards.

"I'm not robbing him," Eden said, dropping the wallet and money beside the prone man.

"Ohh, but this guy's got a Dunkin' Donuts loyalty card," Athena said, flicking through the wallet. "Only joking." Athena dropped the guy's stuff on the grass beside him.

Both women slid the swipe cards into their pockets and paced to the back of the house. Carefully and keeping to the shadows as much as possible, they slipped along the rear wall. The commotion had subsided now, and eerie calm hung over the estate.

Their plan to get in had worked, but now with people returning to their positions, there was no knowing how long they could stay undetected. Once someone realized that two of their security men were missing, or they woke up and realized what had happened, alarms would start screaming and lights would blaze. For now, Eden and Athena planned to make the most of the silence.

Eden picked up the pace, cutting between the wall of the building and a series of small trees which definitely weren't native to this part of the world. Beyond the trees, the estate's sprawling grounds ran down a gentle slope.

Eden reached the corner and peered around to the rear of the property. A large terrace spanned most of the width of the house with a pool set into the center. A blue plastic cover had been rolled over the water, but the underwater lights were still on. Eden could see wisps of heat dancing through the air above the water.

Beyond the terrace, pathways crisscrossed beds of carefully manicured shrubs. Eden scanned the area again, looking for anything they could hide behind if anyone rounded the corner.

"Once we're out there, we're totally exposed," Eden whispered.

Athena leaned around the corner too and nodded her agreement.

"Gotta do it, though," Athena said. "No point hanging around."

With Eden still in the front, the women crept towards the pool. Taking the first few steps, Eden took a moment to focus in on her senses.

Eden pointed forward. They climbed the three steps up to the terrace. Sun loungers and other leisure furniture squatted in the gloom, seeming absurd in such a hostile situation.

Using the wall as their guide, Eden and Athena picked their way across the terrace. Stepping over a coiled garden hose, Eden thought about using the flashlight to help them navigate the terrace. They would get there quicker with the light, but switching the thing on would be like painting targets on their backs.

Just as they reached the side of the pool, about halfway between the corner and the door through which they'd planned to enter the house, Eden froze. A sound drifted over the pool's covered surface.

Eden glanced over her shoulder. Athena had stopped and dropped into a crouch — clearly, she'd heard the same thing.

The noise came again. A voice. Two voices. They weren't just figments of Eden's imagination.

"Did you hear about the explosion?" one voice said.

Boots thudded on the pathway.

"Yeah, heard it was an old car. Brakes probably snapped or something," the other man replied nonchalantly.

"Two of the guys pretty burned up though. Bad luck, that."

The beams of two flashlights swept around the corner, and then the men appeared.

Eden scanned the terrace, searching one more time for a place to hide. Other than the furniture, behind which they would be spotted in a moment, the rear of the house was a featureless brick wall. Eden looked back the way they'd come. The edge of the terrace was at least thirty feet away. Too far to dash in time.

Eden gulped while her eyes completed another circuit of the terrace. Even though she tried to control it, her hand quivered slightly as she signaled to Athena. It was the only option.

Athena nodded and stepped to the edge of the pool. Silently and without causing more than a ripple, Athena pulled back the pool's cover and slipped into the water beneath. Eden followed.

Un-surprisingly, the water was warm, no doubt kept that way as a show of opulence rather than a desire to swim. Eden took a deep breath and sunk beneath the water, letting the cover return to its previous position.

"Hey, what was that?" Came a distant male voice. Footsteps thudded loud and heavy across the terrace. A beam of light appeared on the pool cover, sweeping one way and then the other.

The men were standing directly above where Eden and Athena crouched, their backs pressed against the wall of the pool.

The breath in Eden's lungs turned sour. If the slightest breath should escape, she knew that the bubbles would be noticed in a moment.

"You're hearing things," a man said. "Maybe that old car has spooked you."

Both men stood still for a moment longer. The flashlight beams completed another circuit of the pool.

Forcing herself not to exhale, Eden placed her hands over her mouth. The air in her lungs burned like boiling water.

"I'm sure I heard something," the guard said. "Something moving. Should we call it in?"

"There's nothing there now, though, is there?" the other man said mockingly. "You want to call it in, do it, but you'll look like an idiot."

Finally, the beams of light swept away.

"Probably just a raccoon or something."

The guards lingered for a few more heart-stopping seconds.

"Damned animals." Their footsteps thudded off, away from the pool.

Eden surfaced, taking in deep and relieving breaths. Careful to make as little noise as possible, Eden slipped out of the pool. Athena followed, water dripping from her clothes.

"There, look," Athena hissed, pointing across the terrace. There was a door twenty feet further along the rear wall. A red light on an electric locking system blinked beside the door.

Eden made her way quickly across to the door and slid out the card she'd removed from the guard a few minutes before. She swiped the card through the locking system. The light turned from red to green.

"We're in," Eden said, pulling open the door.

42

Eden stepped into the gloom and clicked her flashlight onto its lowest setting. The finger of light swept through the cavernous hallway, flickering from the marble floors and wooden paneled walls. Eden glanced down at the water pooling around her ankles and hoped no one would notice.

Athena slipped in through the door behind her and then let it close. The automatic lock clicked back into the place and a new level of silence descended. Other than the distant humming of the ventilation system, stillness hung like a physical cloud.

"These guys don't look happy to see us," Eden said, sweeping the beam of her flashlight across the portraits. She stepped up close to one of them and read the small brass sign which was tacked beneath each frame.

"Johannes Van Wijk," Eden whispered. "He sounds like a big deal."

"No wonder he's miserable, with a name like Johannes," Athena said, sweeping her flashlight down the wide hallway which ran the whole way through the house. "This place is massive. Where do we even start looking?" Athena panned the beam of her flashlight from one door to the next.

The comms device in Eden's ear hissed. She almost jumped at the noise, the line having been silent for so long she'd almost forgotten about it.

"Where are you?" Baxter said, his voice coming through so loudly it sounded otherworldly in the silent mansion.

Eden pressed the button and whispered a reply. "No need to shout! You took your time. Did you stop for coffee on the way or something?"

"No... I..."

Eden smirked at Baxter's stuttered reply. With all the time they'd been working together, she'd have thought he'd got used to her teasing... but clearly not.

"We've just got inside the house. This place is massive. Fancy telling us where to go?"

"I put the drone up a few minutes ago. Hold on." The sound of Baxter typing furiously came down the line.

Athena signaled them on, passing two gilded chairs with green velvet cushions. After about fifty feet, the corridor opened to the left, exposing a wide marble staircase.

Eden snapped off her light just in case there was someone on the upper floors who might notice it. Light radiated from one of the upstairs rooms, causing the large crystal chandelier hanging in the stairwell to sparkle and glimmer.

"Same as before, weirdly," Baxter said. "There are three heat signatures in that room at the back. The rest of the building is empty. If your father is there, he's being held by two men on the second floor."

"Just two men guarding?" Eden said, her gaze hardening towards the staircase. "That feels off to me."

"And where's our elusive host?" Athena said. "I was looking forward to meeting the world-renowned Ludwig Van Wick."

"Is his name really Ludwig?" Eden said.

"That's what Wikipedia says."

"No wonder he doesn't go out much." Eden became suddenly thoughtful. "But, isn't it weird that there's only two men guarding dad? Where are the rest of them?"

"Maybe it's just our lucky day," Athena said, shrugging.

"There's no such thing," Eden replied.

Confident the powerful infrared camera on the drone had registered no people nearby, Eden and Athena switched on their flashlights again, but kept them on the lowest setting. They reached the bottom of the grand curving staircase and peered upwards.

More portraits of long-dead family members eyed the intruders suspiciously.

"It must be sad to have all this space but no friends to invite over," Athena said.

Eden went first, taking the stairs slowly. Halfway up the first flight she paused and listened for anyone approaching from above. Satisfied that all was silent, she continued upwards.

On the first-floor landing, they passed a display case filled with antique weapons. The swords, daggers, and ornate guns inside had been polished to a sheen.

"This stuff looks like it hasn't been touched since the Civil War," Athena said, leaning in close to a long sword with a shining blade.

"I expect it could still do some damage," Eden said, noticing how the blade gleamed in the light beam. "That's certainly not a toy."

She padded silently to a nearby door and peered through. Shelves covered every inch of the walls, lined with leather-bound volumes, globes, and manuscripts.

"I bet there are some secrets in here," Eden said, her light sweeping the shelves.

"Not secrets for us this time," Athena replied, moving on towards the next staircase.

"Down the hallway, third room on your right," Baxter said as they approached the second floor. Eden felt reassured that he was following their progress using the drone's high powered infrared camera.

Eden tapped the mic to send the signal that she'd understood but wasn't in a position to talk.

At the top of the staircase, they paused and looked around. A broad landing ran in both directions, with various closed doors lining each side.

"Turn left and head towards the end of the passage," Baxter said, his tone now hushed with tension.

Eden made a gesture, and the pair started down the passage. Grand archways curved from one side to the other with various sculptures and busts on pedestals.

Eden glanced up at a large renaissance-era landscape on the wall. A man wearing a funny hat stood next to a black and white spotted cow. There was a windmill in the background.

Eden turned away from the painting and glanced into a statue's stone eyes. The man looked as though he was wearing a toga and reminded Eden of some of the ancient Greek artifacts she'd worked with over the years. Knowing the resources available to the Van Wicks, Eden suspected this piece should be in a museum.

"The next door," Baxter said, his voice hushed with tension too, despite sitting safety on the outside of the wall.

Eden and Athena slowed their pace, placing each foot carefully to avoid any creaking floorboards. They reached the door Baxter had suggested and leaned in. Eden listened closely and silently counted out fifteen seconds.

At first there was silence, and then she heard something. The faint murmur of voices drifted through. An unfamiliar high-pitched voice spoke first. Eden didn't recognize the speaker and couldn't hear what they were saying through the door.

Eden remembered that the heat signatures inside could come from anyone. The people inside could just be some of the Van Wick's security detail skiving off work.

Then another voice spoke, and all of Eden's doubts disappeared. The voice rang out loud and clear, like a church bell on a Sunday morning. Eden would recognize her father's voice anywhere.

"I think you misunderstand the meaning of legacy, Mr. Van Wick," Eden's father said. "Legacy is not about having your name in lights. It's about leaving our world in a better than we found it."

Eden and Athena locked eyes, both instantly knowing what the other was thinking. They both took a deep breath and focused their minds on the challenge ahead. As usual, the odds were stacked against them, but, as usual, they had the element of surprise on their side.

Both women exploded into action.

Eden moved first, pushing her shoulder against the door. For a second, she wondered whether it would be locked. Fortunately, it wasn't. She shoved the door as hard as she could and then dove out of sight. The heavy oak door slammed back against the inside wall. The echoing thump sounded like an explosion in the silent house. The noise had the desired effect. The guards swung around to face the door, guns at the ready.

Eden was already out of sight, crouching behind the wall. As she'd expected, the guards were on edge and fired immediately. A burst of semi-automatic gunfire howled down the corridor, leaving a perforation of puncture marks in the plaster. Dust and strips of shredded oak rained down on the crouching women.

On either side of the door, Eden and Athena glanced at each other, each checking the other for injuries. Both relieved to see the other had avoided the flying bullets, they slid out their weapons and rose gently to their feet.

"We've got you pinned down. You're trapped," a guard said.

Eden grinned both at the guard's comment and the fact she hadn't heard them call for backup yet. That was another point that often worked in Eden and Athena's favor — burly male guards would often underestimate them. And that underestimation, was the last mistake of their lives.

"Yes, yes, you have," Eden said, weakly. They would have some fun with this.

Athena played along, her voice coming out shaky and fearful. "What do you want from us?"

The guards stayed silent for a moment. Eden imagined them exchanging smug smiles, congratulating themselves for such bravery.

"Drop your weapons, step out, and we might just let you live," the more vocal of the pair said, sneering.

Eden took a deep breath, making her voice quiver with fear. "We're coming out. Just please, don't shoot."

The sound of a fresh magazine clicking home told Eden all she needed to know about the guards' intentions.

Eden glanced at Athena and took a step forward. Both

knew what the other was thinking, having practiced the tactic many times in training.

"We'll slide our guns through now," Eden said, unclipping something from her belt.

"Do it slowly," came the barked reply.

Eden rolled a small flashbang across the floor toward the voices. It stopped a foot from the nearest guard.

Three, two, Eden counted the numbers down on her fingers and then they both placed their hands over their ears and closed their eyes. A super-bright light flashed. An explosion roared, shaking the paintings against their fixtures.

The flashbang device was designed to cause very little damage, but the burning light and howling noise was enough to disorientate anyone not expecting it.

As soon as the light died out, Eden and Athena leaped to their feet and charged through the door.

Once inside, they both assessed the scene. The guards cowered at either side of the room. The men had moved away from the device and turned their backs to the door. Eden glanced across the large room. Another shape lay slumped on the floor on the far side of the room. Having heard his voice, Eden assumed it must be her father. It wasn't time to worry about him yet, though. Not until the danger was neutralized.

Eden charged for the guard on the right, and Athena went for the other.

As Eden neared, the dazed guard turned and attempted to raise his weapon at her. Eden saw the move coming and countered it by ducking to the side and then swinging up from the guard's right side. She gripped the weapon and yanked it down towards the floor just as the man fired. The gun roared several times and bullets hammered into the floor, several slicing straight through the guard's foot.

The guard howled, and his grip on the weapon weakened. Eden tore the gun from his grasp, turned it around and slammed the butt into the side of his head. The man crumpled sideways like a rag doll. His hands windmilled, trying to regain his balance, but a swift kick to the back of his knees sent him to the ground. To finish things off, Eden sent the man into unconsciousness with another strike on the side of the head.

On the other side of the room, Athena delivered her own brand of justice. Although momentarily blinded, the guard swung a wild punch in her direction. Athena ducked beneath it and, with a swift upward movement, drove the heel of her hand into the base of the man's nose. Blood sprayed, and the guard staggered backward, clutching his shattered face. Without hesitation, Athena swung a roundhouse kick, cracking the guard in the temple. He crumpled to the floor, unconscious.

"Two touches, not bad," Athena said, brushing her hands together and glancing across at Eden.

It was only then the pair heard Baxter's panicked voice in the comms system.

"Something's not right!" Baxter said, his voice distorted from shouting. "I don't know what's happened. People just appeared. Loads of them... eight, maybe ten... Eden, Athena... can you hear me?"

The flush which had swept across Eden's face with the exertion immediately drained. She glanced at the door and saw the distant light of the several flashlights coming their way.

She turned back and rushed towards her father. Halfway across the room, she froze. Sure, there was a figure lying on the floor, but it wasn't Alexander Winslow. This figure was bigger. Much bigger.

Eden pulled out her flashlight and clicked it on. She reeled back with shock when she saw the ugly, swollen, brutish face. Thorne's rubbery lips were twisted into something of a grin, although the result looked more like a snarl.

"Very impressive," Thorne said. "Showing off time is over."

"But... but... I heard my father through the door," Eden replied.

Thorne tapped a tablet computer which Eden hadn't even noticed he was holding.

"You're going to regret this!" Alexander Winslow's voice came from a speaker somewhere in the room.

"The oldest trick in the book," Athena grumbled, glancing at the floor.

Footsteps echoed from the hallway behind them as the flashlight beams neared.

"I don't need to tell you that my men have their guns aimed at your backs," Thorne said, climbing to his feet. "Nor do I need to tell you they'll be happy to see you dead after that trick with the truck earlier."

He strode over to Eden and peered directly into her eyes.

Revulsion bubbled in Eden's stomach as the bulbous and swollen face drew close to hers. Her muscles tensed as she resisted the urge to attack him right there and then. From just inches away, she could smell his sour breath and another weird chemical smell.

Thorne pulled the gun from the holster on Eden's hip, then removed both her knives. He dropped them in a pile and then did the same to Athena's.

When both women were disarmed, the great brute reached out and plucked the comms devices from their ears.

He looked at the two tiny devices in his palm as though they were the work of an alien race. He clenched his fist so tight the muscles on his forearm stood out like the cables on the Golden Gate Bridge. When he opened his hand, the devices were little more than a mess of plastic and wires.

"Time to go," Thorne roared, signaling for his men to surround Eden and Athena. "There's someone you need to meet."

43

WITH SEVERAL GUNS pointed at her back, all held by men itching to score a kill and impress their boss, Eden knew there was no need for restraints.

Thorne directed the posse out into the corridor, which was now scarred with the wounds of the firefight, and back towards the staircase. Halfway along the passage, he commanded them to stop.

Eden glanced at the staircase about twenty feet away. She wondered whether she could barge through the men and make a run for it. Athena squeezed Eden's hand and issued a tiny shake of the head. Running now would achieve nothing more than a back full of lead.

Eden turned back towards Thorne. Now at the front of the group, Thorne stepped towards a large painting on the wall to the left. It was the one with the man and the spotty cow Eden had seen a few minutes before, or maybe it wasn't, but it just looked the same. There were cows and windmills in lots of the paintings.

The painting was so large that it covered the wall from the ceiling to the floor. The painting reminded Eden of how simple her life used to be when she lived in her RV, all alone in the English countryside. Although she still put herself in harm's way to recover stolen artifacts, she didn't have people she needed to rescue. Then she thought about her father, still at risk somewhere nearby. Then she thought about Athena, and Baxter, and the rest of the team, who were quickly becoming the best friends she'd ever had.

"Oh, is this the art appreciation tour?" Athena said, clapping her hands.

"I hope so!" Eden mocked in reply. "I can't wait to visit the gift shop."

"Shut up, both of you," Thorne snarled, stepping toward the painting. He reached around the gilded frame and flicked a hidden switch. A motor whirred and then, moving on hidden rails, the painting slid to one side.

"Wow, could you guys get any more stereotypical?" Eden moaned, her voice oozing with sarcasm.

Despite the derision, Eden cursed herself. Whatever was behind the moving painting was probably how the men had sneaked up behind them without being seen on the infrared image.

The gun-toting thug behind Eden jabbed her in the ribs.

"Look, we're just excited about the secret passage tour, that's all," Eden said.

"It's not every day you get to tour the house of actual lunatics," Athena agreed.

Thorne turned around and growled at the women.

"Alright, so maybe you're not a lunatic," Eden said. "But you really should get that face examined by a medical professional. It looks painful." Although Eden was aiming for a rise out of the giant man, she was telling the truth. Thorne's face seemed to swell and distort more with each passing minute.

The painting slid to the side revealing an old elevator with a birdcage door. With the elevator car on one of the other floors, they all gazed directly into the shaft.

Thorne thumbed the button beside the elevator and somewhere above them the winding gear hummed. With the grinding of steel on steel the elevator car rose, filling the corridor with light from a pair of florescent tubes.

Thorne swept open the door and beckoned them inside. The men at the rear shoved Eden and Athena in and blocked them at the back of the elevator car.

Eden leaned forward and glimpsed the elevator's control panel. They were currently on one of the upper floors, with several more below them.

"Up or down?" Eden said conversationally.

Without a word, Thorne swept the door closed and pressed a button. The elevator shuddered and then descended.

"Ahh, down for ladies' underwear," Athena said.

The men stared forward as though in a trance.

"Tough crowd," Athena groaned. "Luckily we're here all week."

Eden turned to look at the guard beside her. No older than she was, he had close cropped hair, and like his comrades, stared morosely at Thorne.

The elevator juddered slowly downwards, passing the floor below without stopping.

"What do you say we get out of here and grab something to eat?" Eden said to the guard in a half whisper. "You know anywhere good around here? There must be somewhere a girl can go to unwind."

The man said nothing, and Eden sighed.

They passed another shuttered door which meant they

were now going beneath ground level. To prove Eden's assumption, the temperature dropped several degrees.

For what felt like minutes, they shuddered down the featureless shaft. Bare concrete walls surrounded the elevator car on all sides. Whatever structure they were heading towards, it was not just a basement built directly beneath the mansion, but some kind of bunker far beneath the earth. With almost infinite resources, there was no knowing what secretive lair the Van Wick family could have down here.

Finally, the elevator trembled to a stop. The rumbling of the winding gear stopped, and the door unlocked. Peering between the assembled guards and out through the bars, Eden saw a concrete corridor leading away from the shaft.

Thorne swept open the door and stepped out. The guards herded Eden and Athena out behind.

To Eden, the place looked like one of those bunkers people built in the sixties when they thought the world was going to end in nuclear hellfire. She supposed this place probably was exactly that. She suspected the Van Wicks were exactly the sort of suspicious and egotistical people that would use their finances to create something to ensure the survival of their family, rather than invest in a better world for all.

"Beautiful place you've got here," Eden said looking around. "Is this where you bring all your guests?"

Thorne lumbered on in silence.

Fifty feet along the corridor, they reached a steel door. Thorne hammered several times on the door with a fist the color and size of a sledgehammer. A metal flap slid open, and a pair of eyes appraised them from the other side. Eden thought the system looked like a prison but set up in the other way — to stop people from getting in rather than out.

The eyes grew to the width of a caricature and then disappeared. A series of locks clanged and eventually the door squealed open.

Thorne was first in, followed by two of his guards. The other guards shoved Eden and Athena through and then came in themselves. Once they were all inside, the door swung shut and sealed them against the outside world with a resounding clunk.

Eden quickly jostled to get a good view of the room they'd stepped into. First, she was curious to know where they were. Second, she wanted to find something to level the playing field.

From what Eden could see, they were in a large, brightly lit chamber. In the center of the room, large steel tables contained all sorts of scientific equipment. Men sporting the classic white coat "Scientist Look" moved around the tables with such focus that it didn't seem like they'd noticed the new arrivals at all.

Then Eden looked beyond the tables. Surrounding them on all sides, lined up against the walls like a macabre army, stood giant glass tubes filled with greenish liquid. Eden glanced from side to side and realized there were at least thirty of the giant vials, each glowing a strange green hue. At first, Eden thought the tubes must have been for the storage of chemicals, then she saw something inside.

Bile clawed its way up her throat, threatening to make her puke right there on the floor.

In the liquid, floating as though suspended in some grotesque dance, was a figure. A human figure.

Eden looked from tube to tube, her nausea growing with the power of a tropical storm. The figures were all in different positions, some facing forward with their pale and flaking faces pressed against the glass, others were turned the other way, looking ghostly in the viscous liquid.

Although the forms were all clearly human, with arms and legs and pale skin, some had horrific deformities — bloated heads, mis-sized limbs or features that made them look more animal than human. Each figure was naked apart from a tiny pair of trunks which covered so little it was barely worth bothering with.

Eden's eyes rested on Thorne, still at the front of the group, and suddenly things made sense.

She glanced back at the tubes again and saw, just like the paintings in the grand hallways above, each tube was labeled with a small plaque.

The realization when it struck her, turned her stomach to jelly — this was the Van Wick family. They had been preserved in this weird dungeon for scientists to study, analyzing what went well and what could be improved for the family's next generation.

"The guests of honor, so glad you could join us." A weak voice drifted through the lab's hubbub. "You're just in time to witness our breakthrough."

44

"Bring our guests up to see me." The voice commanded. "Don't waste time, we have much to do."

It took Eden several moments to work out where the voice was coming from. She stared into the gloom and saw a small man ensconced in a high-tech electric wheelchair on the far side of the chamber.

"I'm pleased you're here. You've come just in time for the main event," the man said. Although the man's voice was weak and strangely nasal, he still sounded authoritative.

"I'm not going anywhere until you tell me where my father is," Eden shouted across the chamber.

The man's face contorted into a strange expression which Eden thought was probably supposed to be a smile. "There will be time for that. First, we have more pressing issues to deal with."

One of the guards jabbed Eden in the back to get her moving. Forgetting they were currently hopelessly outnumbered, Eden's reflexes kicked in. Using the momentum from the guard's nudge, she twisted around, grabbing his arm, and used her other arm to drive a sharp elbow into his gut.

The guard gasped, his grip on the weapon loosening. Eden locked her fingers behind the guy's head, then slammed her knee into his face. In a blink, she had his gun in her hand and him on the floor, her foot pressing against his throat.

The other guards surrounded her quickly and raised their weapons. A click issued from several of the weapons, indicating they were ready to fire.

"Stop that," the wheelchair-bound man hissed. "You must not shoot in the chamber. There is far too much to be damaged around here."

"You take me to my father, or there will be a lot of shooting." Eden turned and assessed the guards surrounding her on all sides. She knew their positions were all for show, anyway. They were surrounding her in such a way that one shot from any of them would not only kill her but take down the guard behind her too. These guys had spent too long watching TV shows and not enough time on actual training.

Athena placed a hand on Eden's forearm, communicating silently that for now they had to let the lunatics run the asylum. Begrudgingly, Eden dropped the gun and then just for fun delivered another hard kick to the man on the floor. She took some sick enjoyment from the sound of a rib cracking beneath her boot.

"Touch me again and see what happens," Eden said, turning to stare at each of the men.

The group shuffled towards the rear of the chamber. While they walked, Eden thought through the leader's instruction for the men not to shoot in the chamber. She looked at the surrounding guards — without their weapons they were as soft as clay. Maybe that was the equalizer she'd hoped for. Except for Thorne — he was a special battle all on his own.

They reached the rear of the chamber, and Thorne stopped. He nodded respectfully towards the man in the wheelchair. This was clearly the leader of this sick operation and the patriarch of the Van Wick family.

Using a small control on the chair's arm, the man maneuvered himself towards Eden and Athena.

"It's a pleasure to meet you," he said, soothingly. "I am Ludwig Van Wick, people call me Van Wick Senior."

"That figures," Eden said.

Eden smirked and Athena giggled. They were both working hard not let the stress of the situation show. They knew from experience that half the battle with people like this, was not giving them the power to make you scared.

"Welcome to our ancestral home," the older man continued. "You've already met one of my sons." Van Wick gestured towards Thorne. "And I believe the other is known to you too, Senator Everett Van Wick."

Eden looked in confusion from Thorne to Van Wick and then thought about the charismatic senator they'd seen on the screen a few hours ago.

Van Wick watched Eden's confusion with the amusement of a crocodile eyeing a drinking gazelle. He finally barked out a laugh.

"I see our family dynamic has confused you. That, I suppose, I can understand. As you may have assessed by our forefathers here, we don't abide by normal genetic rules." The old man swept an arm towards the tubes containing the deformed cadavers.

"It really is impressive," Athena said, shaking off the shock more quickly than Eden had.

Van Wick looked up at Athena and smiled. A string of drool hung from his small pink lips.

"Why, thank you. This is many generations of work," Van Wick said.

"It is really impressive because I've seen some disgusting things in my life, but this is truly the most revolting," Athena said, dispassionately.

Ludwig Van Wick inhaled sharply, and the string of drool whipped back inside his mouth. His pale eyes half closed, and his face pinched as though he was trying to eat something unpleasant.

"In this laboratory we have been carrying out cutting edge genealogical research for over one-hundred years. The world should thank us for our..."

"It looks like it's going really well," Eden said, looking from Van Wick, to Thorne, and then on to the lifeless figures floating in the green goo.

"Maybe you should have tried something less gross. I hear painting by numbers is a thing for adults now," Athena said.

"Or pottery," Eden said. "I'm sure there are several great pottery classes around here."

Instead of reacting with anger as Eden and Athena had expected, the patriarch just smiled as though he were watching the behavior of lab rats.

"Tell me, are you familiar with the story of Frankenstein?" Van Wick asked, his tone level.

Eden pouted. Of all the scenarios she'd expected to play out, a literary discussion was not one of them.

"Yes, I read it at school. A long time ago," Eden said, folding her arms.

"I was more of a Harry Potter fan," Athena said.

"Interesting. Well, you see, even the stories of Harry

Potter needed a good monster to get things going. Without a monster, there would be no story." Van Wick tapped at his chin with a twisted finger.

"Right... I'm not sure how this relates to me kicking you in the face and then getting out of here with my father," Eden said, looking around the chamber.

"Let me tell you this," Van Wick continued. "There has been a lot of talk over the last one-hundred-and-fifty years about who the monster in the Frankenstein story really is. Is it the creator?" Van Wick pointed at himself. "Or is it the monster?" He pointed at Thorne.

"Profound statement incoming," Eden said, rolling her eyes.

"I've always the monster is something else entirely." Ludwig Van Wick was not being put off. "The real monster is society, and their need to create monsters for themselves. Neither Frankenstein, nor his creation were monstrous until the rest of the world made them so."

"If it looks like a duck and quacks like a duck," Eden mumbled.

"Then it could be a goose?" Athena said, earnestly. Athena pointed at Thorne. "On a serious note, though, all this scientific messing about explains how this guy has survived everything we've thrown at him."

"Yes, he's something of an anomaly," Van Wick pointed at his so-called son, as though he were nothing more than an experimental specimen. "We're pleased with the results, if only we could..."

"Make him not look like an actual pig?" Eden interrupted.

Thorne seemed totally unaffected, or perhaps hadn't realized they were talking about him.

"Yes, his appearance is unfortunate, he also has lost

several cognitive abilities, including empathy." Van Wick's lips curled in frustration. "That makes him an excellent soldier, but not much else. Speaking of which, I think it's time he had another dose. Doctor Vos!"

A man wearing a lab coat and thick eyeglasses showed Thorne over to a bench and connected him to an IV drip. Thorne sat quietly during the process, as though he were under some kind of remote control.

"You talk about this like you're choosing a sandwich filling," Athena said, her eyes riveted on Van Wick.

"Ha! Yes, I suppose I do," Van Wick said, sounding manically joyful. "But think about the power of designing a person for their strengths? Think about the wonder of that. We could remove the tendencies to get diseases, produce a human who really is capable of everything possible."

Eden looked down at Van Wick's twisted body within the wheelchair.

"Of course, as with all scientific developments, there are those who must pay the price. And, we have done that for generations." He pointed at a figure in one of the tubes.

"This is the stuff of nightmares," Eden muttered.

"To the untrained eye, perhaps. But to me, it's an evolution, a testament to the perseverance and ambition of the Van Wick family."

"You call this evolution?" Eden gestured to the bodies. "These people... were they even given a choice?"

"Choice?" Van Wick's laugh was hollow. "In our quest for perfection, for power, choice is a luxury. Each one of these individuals," he paused, glancing affectionately at the tubes, "was a step forward, a sacrifice for the greater good of the Van Wick legacy."

"Sacrifice? You've turned them into monsters!"

Van Wick's gaze hardened. "Monsters? No. They're

martyrs. Through them, we learned, improved, and grew stronger. Every misstep brought us closer to our goal. And now, we are on the cusp of greatness."

Eden took a step towards the patriarch, her muscles rippling, struggling not to batter the old man for his messed-up ideas. "All I see is a madman playing God, messing around to create his own twisted vision."

Ludwig Van Wick smiled coldly. "You think too small, my dear. While you've been running around being the hero, the Van Wicks have been shaping the future. This," he gestured around the chamber, "is but a glimpse of what's to come."

A creepy silence settled over the chamber. The scientists continued moving around, completing their work in wordless concentration.

Eden's eyes darted from the macabre display of bodies in tubes back to the Van Wick patriarch. "All of this... for what? What could possibly justify such horrors?"

Ludwig Van Wick took a deep breath, clearly preparing himself for an exposition. "Ah, the age-old question of 'why?' It's quite simple, Miss Black. The Van Wick line has always sought power, dominance, and above all, longevity."

Eden frowned, trying to make sense of his words. "Longevity? You're talking about immortality?"

"In a manner of speaking," Van Wick nodded slowly. "I'm not really talking about living forever in the individualistic way our modern world is obsessed with. When I talk about it, I'm talking about the survival and improvement of the Van Wick family line."

"And that's why you wanted the *Lady of Leone*, so that you could poke around with her and see if there were any bits you liked?" Eden said. Even as Eden said the words, she knew there was something that didn't match up. She was still missing something or had something the wrong way around. Something big.

Now Van Wick really did roar with laughter. He tilted his head backward and sent a cloud of spittle high into the air above his flaking scalp.

Thorne, who was listening from the chair a few feet away grumbled out a laugh which sounded like distant thunder.

"Oh Ms. Black," Van Wick said, finally recovering from his private joke. "Again, you are so far away from the truth."

"Humor us," Athena said.

"Of course, of course. Sometimes I forget that normal humans, like yourselves, were not born with the incredible intelligence I've enjoyed all these years." Ludwig Van Wick pointed at one of the tubes behind them. "My great-grandfather, Cornelius Van Wick, who was responsible for some of the biggest leaps in our research, heard about the *Lady of Leone* shortly after she was discovered. Using all his influence, he was able to work with her over in Europe for almost two years. When he was done, and only when he was done, he handed her over to the British Museum, to put in a glass case for tourists to gawk at."

Eden stared hard at the old man, her thoughts a maelstrom.

"But that doesn't make sense. If your great-grandfather had already got what he wanted from the *Lady of Leone,* then why did he need to have her shipped to the United States?" Athena got to the question first.

Now, Van Wick turned deadly serious. All expression dropped from his face.

Suddenly an idea slapped Eden around the face so hard it felt as though the strike had come from Thorne. She inhaled slowly, her jaw hanging slack. For once without speaking first, Eden ran through the idea again. No wonder the events hadn't made sense until now, they'd been looking at the whole thing the wrong way around.

"You didn't, did you?" Eden said. Although she spoke barely above a whisper, her words sounded like gunfire through the chamber.

Clearly realizing the same, Athena stood rigid with shock.

"You didn't put the *Lady of Leone,* on board *The Titanic* for her to come to the United States." Eden spoke slowly now, all color drained from her face. "You put her on *The Titanic* so that she would be lost forever."

Ludwig Van Wick now grinned even wider than ever before. "Miss Black, I am very impressed," he said as though delivering a sermon. "Yes, that is true. We couldn't ever risk anyone finding out what my grandfather had done, incorporating the Ancient's genes with our own. Because the *Lady of Leone* was such a public specimen, we couldn't just add her to our collection. She had to be lost, somehow lost for all time."

"Wait a second. Just wind this back one tiny bit." Athena made a rotating gesture with her finger. "Your great-grandfather is responsible for sinking *The Titanic*?"

Van Wick leaned back in his wheelchair. Light from the nearby tubes reflected from his skin, making him appear even more monstrous. He was clearly reveling in Eden and Athena's shocked expressions.

"Yes," he said, a cruel glint in his eye. "My great-grandfather understood some sacrifices were necessary for the greater good, for our family's legacy. He had the ship fitted with explosives on the bow, and at the right moment…"

"It didn't hit an iceberg?" Athena said.

"Is that so hard to believe?" Van Wick said, his voice

hardening. "You must remember that electric light was primitive, and *The Titanic* was moving through the ocean at quite a speed, while most people were asleep."

Eden took a step forward, aghast. "But over 1,500 people died. You're saying he killed them just to hide a secret?"

Van Wick nodded, his expression unyielding. "Miss Black, in our world, legacy and power are paramount. Those lives, while tragic, were a price worth paying to ensure our family's secret remained intact. A secret that gave our family unimaginable power and privilege."

Athena's eyes darted around the room, taking in the grotesque tubes filled with deformed figures. "All of this, the *Lady of Leone, The Titanic,* these... experiments," she gestured around, "it's all about power for you, isn't it?"

Van Wick laughed, a dry, raspy sound that echoed eerily in the underground chamber. "Power is everything. And my family has always been willing to do whatever it takes to maintain it."

Eden clenched her fists. "You are monsters," she spat, her voice dripping with revulsion.

"Perhaps," Van Wick said, his grin undiminished. "But in this world, it's the monsters who rule." Van Wick glanced at the screen of the tablet computer attached to his wheelchair. "Enough talk, now it's time to add one more martyr to our number."

45

Van Wick snapped his fingers and four of the lab workers walked off into the gloom at the back of the chamber.

"Thanks to you, though, it seems the *Lady of Leone* was destined to be in our collection after all." Ludwig Van Wick swept an arm toward the tubes. "One-hundred years is nothing in the lifetime of a family like ours."

The men re-appeared half a minute later, pushing the crate which Eden and Baxter had rescued from *The Titanic*, strapped on a trolley. Reaching the center of the platform, the men stopped and applied the trolley's brakes. They detached the straps so the lid could be removed.

Even in the dim light of the chamber Eden could read the words stenciled on the crate's side — *British Museum, Fragile.*

Van Wick slid his wheelchair to the side of the crate, his eyes alight with anticipation.

"It doesn't look like much, does it?" he pointed at the discolored steel. "It is always a miracle when something wonderful emerges from something so plain. Much like our family, rising to the fame and fortune we have from..."

Eden yawned and stretched.

Van Wick stopped talking. "You're right, this is no time for words." He reached out, his fingers, distorted from decades of experiments, and caressed the surface of the crate.

"This is a time for action. We have waited so long for this moment that we must not delay."

Eden, Athena, and the others in the room watched the old man with rapt attention.

"You know, I'm actually glad this has happened," Van Wick murmured. He turned away from the crate and locked eyes with Eden. "It was meant to be. Of course, my great-grandfather took all he needed from her over one-hundred years ago, so we don't *need* the body here. But, I feel as though she deserves a place here, among the other wonderful members of our family." Van Wick again motioned up towards his long-dead forefathers.

"I wish you'd stop doing that, I'm trying to forget about those corpses looking down at us," Eden's stomach bubbled with disgust. Again, all she got from Van Wick Senior was the ghost of a smile.

"Now, she can come home," Van Wick bellowed, pointing at a glass tube at the end of the row. Eden noticed no corpse floating in the liquid inside that tube.

"Open this," Van Wick said, pointing at the crate.

One of the lab workers who had pushed the crate into position stepped forward with a battery-operated angle grinder. He fired the machine up and cut the chain, which was threaded through various rings around the steel crate. When the chain was cut, he pulled it out and dumped it on the floor.

The rest of the men stepped forwards and pulled at the handles on the top, but the lid stayed fixed in its position.

They tried again, the force lifting the crate from the trolley.

"How did you find these idiots?" Athena said, her eyebrows raised.

"Why don't you give them a shot of common-sense serum or something?" Eden quipped.

"Get a pry bar," Van Wick groaned, showing the first signs of frustration.

One man wandered off towards the back of the chamber.

"I've got a joke for you," Eden said. "How does a narcissist change a light bulb?"

"I don't know," Athena said, when it was clear no one else was going to answer. "How does a narcissist change a light bulb?"

"They just hold it still and let the world revolve around them," Eden said.

Van Wick Senior groaned. Although the noise was probably caused by the frustration of the delay, Eden liked the idea that she'd finally started getting to him.

After banging around in the gloom for a while, the man returned carrying a large pry bar.

"Quickly!" Van Wick snarled, causing the man to jog back to the crate.

The men turned their attention back to the crate. One man angled the pry bar beneath the lid and pushed down on it. The crate groaned but continued to resist giving up its secrets. The man tried again, this time calling another to help. The men leaned their combined weight against the bar while another two held the crate in place.

The metal groaned for a long second and then the pry bar slipped an inch, sending the men tumbling into a heap on the floor. To add injury to embarrassment, the pry bar then came loose and crashed down on top of the men, cracking one of them on the back of the head.

"Why is this so difficult!" Van Wick hissed, his anger clearly growing. "Thorne, sort this out!"

Thorne, who had been sitting quietly while whatever cocktail of drugs they were feeding him went into his system, suddenly looked up. The giant man nodded and climbed to his feet.

"Wait, wait!" Shouted the doctor who had hooked him up to the IV a few minutes before.

"What is it Vos? We can't have any more delays," Ludwig Van Wick snarled.

"Thorne is in the middle of a dose," Doctor Vos said, pausing to push his eyeglasses up his nose. "We can't stop mid-way. It could have disastrous effects."

"Fine." Van Wick closed his eyes in thought. "Sit down, Thorne. We will use the crane." He pointed towards the ceiling.

One man retrieved a control unit, and a motor whined somewhere far above them.

"Stupid men and heavy machinery. What could possibly go wrong?" Eden glanced up to see a large metal hook swing overhead. The system ran on rails mounted high on the walls of the chamber, like those used in factories.

The guard lowered the hook until it was about three feet above the crate. Then he placed the control on a table and crossed toward the crate. The men set about fastening the lid to the hook and then strapped the crate to several hooks set into the chamber's floor.

"We will get you out of there in no time," Van Wick whispered, stroking the side of the crate again. "You're more than an artifact... you're one of the family."

"Maybe we should leave you two alone for some private

time," Eden tried to look away but was riveted by the creepy sight. She was also intrigued at what might be inside.

"That is weird," Athena agreed. "However, there are some subtle clues in the room around us that the person we're dealing with isn't totally normal. Stroking a box is certainly not the worst of his symptoms."

"True," Eden said.

The would-be crane operator returned to the control.

"We really shouldn't let him do this," Athena whispered, stepping closer to Eden.

Eden nodded, her gut tightening. "I have a very bad feeling about this."

"Ready, sir?" The crane operator said.

"Open her up, now!" Van Wick roared. "It is time for my beauty to come home."

The man worked the controls, and the straps pulled tight. The crate lifted from the trolley and then pulled against the cables shackling it to the floor. The crane's engine whined and groaned.

"More power!" Van Wick shouted, shaking a finger in the direction of the crate.

The operator poked at the control, increasing the crane's power. The engine now howled and the smell of burning plastic wafted through the chamber. The cables vibrated as the motors fought against the crate.

Then, just as Eden thought the system was likely to fall on top of them, a metallic screech reverberated through the chamber.

"Yes!" Van Wick screamed. "It's opening. She's here!"

The crane howled, and metal scraped. Then, with the sound of breaking a seal, like an old jar being opened, the two halves separated.

The crate slumped back against the trolley and the steel lid rose. The smell of musty air filled the chamber.

"It smells like whatever you did in that sub," Athena said, poking Eden in the ribs.

The crane operator worked the controls with surprising care. When the lid was about two feet above the crate, Van Wick issued the order to stop.

Dust, undisturbed for over one-hundred years, billowed upwards.

"It's dry?" Athena said, clearly expecting the crate to have taken on water during its time at the bottom of the ocean.

"These guys knew a thing or two about making stuff watertight," Eden replied, also impressed.

Eden glanced around. Everyone was so focused on the crate and its contents that they could probably just slip away to find her father, but then they wouldn't get to see the *Lady of Leone*.

Eden knew exactly what her father would do, so stayed put for now.

Playing with his wheelchair's control, Ludwig Van Wick drew as close to the crate as he could. He worked another control, and the chair rose on a set of hydraulics. Reaching the top of the crate, Van Wick shut off the hydraulics and peered inside.

Eden didn't think it was possible for the man to get any paler, but she was wrong. Van Wick's skin became ivory white, crosshatched by veins throbbing in anger.

"Pass me a flashlight," he snarled.

A guard passed a flashlight across, and Van Wick leaned further inside.

"But... it can't be..." Van Wick whispered, his voice broken. "It's not possible."

Eden and Athena shared a glance in both excitement and amusement.

Van Wick's breathing became erratic. He held on to the side of the crate for support.

"Sir, what do you see?"

"Nothing," Van Wick snarled. "It's empty."

Eden and Athena stood, riveted to the spot, watching the scene play out.

"She's not there!" Van Wick roared now, sitting up straight, spittle flying from his lips. "The *Lady of Leone* is not there! The crate is empty!"

A few of the men rushed across and peered inside themselves. One pushed his head into the box as though the ancient corpse might just have slipped out of sight.

Another man reached a hand inside and started feeling around the base of the crate. When he drew the hand out it was covered in a fine dust. He clutched something between his fingers.

"The *Lady of Leone* isn't there, but this is." In his hand, the scientist held a small glass ball.

"Give me that," Van Wick snapped, taking the ball.

The room, once filled with anticipation, now echoed with the sounds of confusion and disbelief.

For the first time Ludwig Van Wick looked defeated. "How? How could this be? All of this for... for a marble?"

A stunned silence settled over the chamber as the gravity of the revelation became clear.

Eden grinned. The marble was a clue. She knew that once they got out of here, her father would know exactly where it led.

46

Ludwig Van Wick scowled and shook his head. He turned to look at Eden and Athena.

Eden tried to stop smiling but didn't achieve it quickly enough.

"You've done this! This is your fault!" Van Wick bellowed, pointing his mangled fingers at Eden. "You will pay for what you've done. Bring out the prisoner."

Now the smile vanished from Eden's face like smoke in the breeze.

Four of the guards moved in to surround Eden and Athena while the lab workers strode to the back of the chamber. Thirty seconds later they returned pushing one of the giant glass tubes.

Eden stood riveted to the spot. She stared wide eyed at the approaching tube. Bile worked its way up her throat. Her heart hammered, reverberating in her ears as though she had her face against a drum.

It wasn't the tube itself that Eden was looking at, but what was inside. Her father.

For one horrible, sickening moment, Eden thought her father was in the same condition as the floating bodies in the other tubes. Then she noticed he was standing of his own accord, very much alive and fully dressed, although clearly not enjoying the ride.

"Move them into position," roared Van Wick, gesticulating wildly.

Eden watched the patriarch's papery skin flush blood red. His jaw muscles twitched as though his anger was at boiling point and ready to explode.

Eden's muscles rippled, ready for action.

The men shoved the tube further forward. The weight of the glass, her father's bodyweight, and the top-heavy nature of the object was making it difficult to move.

Winslow placed his hands on the sides of the tube in an effort to remain upright.

Eden glanced around and noticed that the guards surrounding her were also watching the tube being inched into position.

The lab workers finally bumped the tube into position and then stepped back.

Eden took her chance and shoved the guards standing in front of her, hard. Both stumbled forwards. One crashed into a metal table, sending a glass beaker crashing to the floor. The other caught his balance and aimed his rifle at Eden. Remembering he'd been banned from shooting in the chamber, the guard let go of the weapon and swung a fist at Eden.

Eden ducked out of the way easily, shuffling to the left. Her first instinct was to run for her father and try to free him from his glass prison, but first she needed to get past the guards.

As the nearest guard made a grab for her, Eden skipped backwards and then bolted towards a computer console filled with various buttons and switches. With no idea what any of them did, Eden poked numerous buttons. Nothing appeared to happen at first, then the tubes bubbled more furiously, sending the cadavers into what looked like a horrible tribal dance.

"Get her, get her!" Van Wick screamed, his voice reaching a pitch which could have seen him perform in opera houses around the world.

As two of the guards neared, Eden ran on, easily outpacing the men.

Several scientists, who had until now diligently continued with their twisted work, looked towards the melee.

"Don't just stand there!" Van Wick roared, his body twitching with rage. "Stop her before she does any damage."

The scientists put down the tubes of liquid they were working on and shuffled around to place themselves in Eden's path.

Eden ran on hard, ducking out the way of the first white coated man who tried to get in her way. The man swung his arms, clearly knowing no better technique than to catch her in a bear-like hug. He was evidently more used to dealing with the dead than the living, Eden thought, skirting him with ease.

The next scientist ran at Eden, trapping her between two long steel tables. Eden hopped up on to the table and slid along the steel, sending tubes and bottles of liquids spilling everywhere.

The next scientist was better placed and lunged towards her. Eden skipped past the man and then swung her elbow hard into his gut. The man crumpled, gasping for breath.

Eden turned just in time to see another one coming at her from the back. With a swift motion, Eden stamped hard on his foot and head-butted him squarely in the nose. He reeled back, clutching his face, blood pouring between his fingers.

For Eden, who trained daily for conflict, taking these guys down was child's play.

Eden ran towards a set of steel shelves laden with delicate-looking equipment and vials. She barged into the shelves and sent the whole array crashing down. Glass shattered, complex machinery sparked, and strange colored chemicals mixed, hissing and smoking across the floor. Every piece of equipment she laid her hands on was thrown, broken, or smashed to the ground.

Another scientist stepped out in front of Eden. He was a large, bearded man with thick arms. Eden didn't hesitate to smash the heel of her hand into his nose and then follow through with a kick to the groin. The man doubled over, wincing and panting, blood staining his white jacket.

Just as she was about to send a bone-shattering elbow into the guy's back, Eden felt a strong-arm snaking around her neck. The very moment she felt it, the arm tensed and pulled Eden back against a chest which felt as though it was made from concrete.

"Enough," Thorne roared, holding Eden still with ease. Suddenly, with Eden incapacitated, a silence fell over the chamber.

Eden tensed and tried to move, but against the inhuman strength of Van Wick's monster, her efforts were futile.

Thorne dragged Eden back across the chamber and stood her beside Athena.

Van Wick peered up at Eden, his eyes like an eagle's.

"Impressive," he coughed out, "but ultimately futile."

Van Wick turned back towards the lab workers still assembled around the tube containing Winslow. "There will be no more delays. Move our new subject into position."

Eden stood still and felt Thorne's grip weaken somewhat. She took a deep and angry breath as the giant tube was finally barged into position alongside the others, right next to the tube that had been set up for the *Lady of Leone*.

Satisfied the tube had been correctly placed, Van Wick turned towards Eden and Athena, his face split into a devilish grin.

"I have, for many years, admired your father's work. But I never expected to have him as part of my collection," Van Wick said. "Don't worry, we will look after him. We will study him, and he in turn will make the Van Wick family stronger. He will live on within us."

Eden glanced up at her father. She wasn't sure whether he could hear the crazed man's words from inside the tube. If he could, he was doing a great job at appearing stoic.

Van Wick touched his lips as though suddenly realizing something. "Then, once you have watched your father's embalming, we will do the same to you." Van Wick turned towards one scientist who had developed a limp after his run-in with Eden. "Start the process."

The scientist stepped across to the computer terminal and tapped at the keys. A machine somewhere in the chamber hummed.

Eden glanced up and saw a hopper sliding into position above her father's tube.

Once the hopper was in position, the scientist pressed another key, and a stream of green liquid ran into the tube. At first, the liquid hit Winslow on the back of the neck. He wiggled sideways, and the goo fell directly around his ankles. He stood calmly as the goo flowed, meaning it clearly wasn't hot or painful. Eden breathed a momentary sigh of relief — they still had time.

"This is going to be very interesting," Van Wick hissed manically. "We don't usually begin the embalming process until the subject is dead. I've never tried it on a live one before."

47

"That's my father you're talking about," Eden snarled. She struggled forward, but Thorne kept his grip firm. "You can't do that to him."

Van Wick toyed with the controls of his chair and spun around to face Eden. "Ms. Black, for an intelligent person you're taking a long time to understand this. I can do whatever I want."

"Not true," Eden growled, fighting against Thorne's iron grip.

Silently watching Eden and Van Wick in their heated exchange, Athena took a step backward out of the eyeline of the assembled guards.

In the last few minutes, Eden had caused so much chaos and Athena had stood so still, that she doubted people even noticed her movements now. It was a funny quirk of the human mind, Athena knew, that if you did something slowly and quietly hardly anyone noticed. For example, picking up the remote control to the overhead crane whilst Eden was on the rampage.

Eden noticed Athena's movement in her peripheral

vision. Although she didn't know what her friend was up to, Eden took the cue to keep Van Wick's attention elsewhere.

"You know, I've been thinking about what you said about Frankenstein. I think you might have something there," Eden said.

Athena removed the remote control from beneath her shirt and pressed the forward button, then the backwards button. High above them, the crane's motor whirred.

Athena worried the sound may be heard, but it was drowned amid the noise of scientists trying to clear up their smashed experiments.

"The creature was shunned, and feared, and attacked, not because of his actions, but because of the way he looked," Van Wick said, his voice a bitter murmur.

Out of the corner of her eye, Athena noticed the liquid pass Winslow's waist. They would need to get him out of there soon before the liquid filled the tube completely.

"Yes, that's true. But he went on to kill people after that, right?" Eden said. "He made the choice to murder."

Athena concentrated on controlling the crane, swinging the crate lid from side to side. She estimated that even the lid on its own would weigh several hundred pounds. Get in the way of that, and you would know about it.

"Society always turns on those who dare to think differently," Van Wick said, his voice gaining in strength. "But I will show everyone. When there's a Van Wick in the White House, there will be no denying."

Athena worked the control again, building up momentum as the lid swung like a wrecking ball.

"Hey! What's that!" One guard pointed up at the swinging crate lid.

Van Wick glanced up, the color draining from his face.

"Stop that!" Van Wick shouted, pointing a shaking hand

skyward. He turned to the lab workers. "Stop that now, before it does any more damage."

The men rushed forward, trying to stop the swinging steel slab. In their haste, none realized that Athena was using the concealed control to cause the movement.

Two of the guards jumped up as the lid swung above them. The steel brushed their outstretched fingers, but neither could grab hold.

"Don't you think the story is really a warning about the consequences of playing with science?" Eden said, eager to keep Van Wick's attention split. "I think the author is saying that there are some things that shouldn't be messed with."

One of the guards scrambled up on top of the crate. He crouched carefully on the open box and waited for the lid to swing past, then jumped. The guard landed neatly on top of the lid and clung on. The lid swung even further forwards, now driven on with the man's weight.

The guard's expression paled as he realized his plan had backfired. He was now swinging around the chamber, unable to get down, and unable to stop the movement.

"Absolutely not," Van Wick said. "In fact, the opposite. We have a responsibility to use all the tools available to us."

Still standing unnoticed at the back of the chamber, Athena shoved the controller to its maximum. The crane's motors droned. The heavy steel lid sliced through the air.

What happened next, did so in slow motion. The lid completed a wide orbit of the chamber. The guard on top flattened himself against the steel and clung on tightly. Then, in a dance of gravity, weight and momentum, the lid smashed through four of the tubes. A shattering, crashing and splintering noise filled the chamber as the lid passed straight through the fragile glass in the way a runaway freight train would take down anything in its path. Glass jingled against the concrete, and the viscous green goo spewed forth.

Van Wick Senior placed his hands over his face and howled like an animal in pain.

Athena glanced at Winslow. His tube remained intact. She would need to find a less dangerous way to break him out, and soon. The green liquid was almost at his neck. Time was clearly running out.

Liquid gushed from the shattered tubes, knocking three guards off their feet in a slippery, gooey mess. The four long-dead cadavers slithered out of the tubes and thwacked down to the concrete floor.

"Johannes, no!" Van Wick cried, watching the destruction unfold.

One cadaver collided with a guard, smashing him on the face and knocking him sprawling backward to the floor. The dead Van Wick came to rest on top of the guard, trapping him face down in the goo.

"What a way to go," Eden said, watching the action.

Another of the cadavers bounced across the floor and slid across the slick floor at quite some speed. Two guards, attempting to rush out of the way, were knocked flying by the rubbery corpse, their arms flailing wildly.

Another guard, seeing his comrades go down, tried to sidestep the human missile. The back of his boot met the wet surface. He teetered for a moment, arms windmilling, before falling backward. The sound of his skull cracking against the ground resounded in the din.

Further away, two scientists attempted to leap over the spreading pool. The first made it but just barely, with droplets splattering onto his boots. The second wasn't so fortunate. Mid-jump, his foot caught the edge of the liquid, slipping out beneath him. He landed off-balance, his legs splitting in opposite directions like a champion gymnast. The crunching noise of his tearing muscles demonstrated this was the first ever time he'd made such a stretch.

"There's something you've forgotten about the Frankenstein story," Eden shouted, at Van Wick who was now watching the pandemonium with a vacant expression. The old man appeared to have lost his vigor, like an inflatable toy with the stopper pulled out. He swiveled his gaze towards Eden.

"It's just a story, Eden. It means nothing." Van Wick shoved forward on the control. Sludgy liquid sprayed out beneath the wheels, getting him nowhere.

"Now you've changed your tune."

Van Wick tried again, yanking harder on the control in an attempt to get out the way of the chaos. He was too late, the thick substance had already expanded beneath the wheels of his chair, gumming up the mechanism.

"It might be a story, but there's one thing you need to remember," Eden said, continuing anyway. "Frankenstein dies, and the monster wanders away to live in oblivion. That's how this is going to end — with you dead and the Van Wick name obscured in oblivion."

Van Wick turned, fire burning in his eyes. "Never. That will never happen…"

"Eden! Duck!" Athena's voice cut though the bedlam like a gunshot.

"Not this again," Eden hissed, reacting immediately. She pulled herself down through Thorne's arms and then rolled to the side.

Athena pulled back on the controls, swinging the lid in a wide arc straight into the back of Thorne's head. A clunk reverberated through the chamber and Thorne fell forward, crashing to the floor.

Athena thumbed the release button on the control. The chain spooled out from the crane, dropping the lid directly down. The steel crashed down on top of Thorne, reverberating like a gong.

The impact of the lid against Thorne's skull sent the guard, who had been desperately clinging on, flying across the chamber. Landing neatly on one of the steel-topped tables, the guard reached out, attempting to stop himself. Covered in the liquid from the tubes, his hands just slipped uselessly across the polished steel. At the end of the long table, one scientist had been working on an experiment with a Bunsen burner and some brightly colored chemicals.

The guard's eyes bulged as he slid towards the flickering flame. His hands pawed frantically at the slick steel, but his pace remained unaffected.

In a cacophony of smashing glass and cries of pain, the guard collided first with the chemicals, sending them flying into the naked flame of the Bunsen burner, then fell from the table and collapsed to the floor.

A moment later, the chemicals ignited across the guard's once pristine uniform. The guard shrieked in terror. The sound echoed through the chamber as flames enveloped him. The bright orange and blue tongues of fire spread rapidly, consuming his clothes and the spilled chemicals that now coated his skin.

As this was all going on, Eden scurried across the floor and snagged up the small glass ball which Van Wick had dropped in the confusion. She stuffed the ball in a pocket.

The guard, now a human-fireball, leaped to his feet and ran blindly across the chamber. Every piece of equipment, every piece of cloth, every spilled flammable chemical, was instantly set ablaze by the fire dancing from his clothes and skin.

Scientists and guards alike tried to evade the moving inferno, knocking over equipment, shoving each other aside, and creating even more chaos. Tables overturned, experiments were ruined.

Van Wick, still immobilized in his wheelchair, screamed orders to put out the flames, but his voice was drowned out by the intense roar of the spreading fire and the general pandemonium.

Finally, one lab worker switched on a sprinkler system. Water sprayed from fixtures on the roof, but did little to dampen the flames fueled by spilled chemicals.

Using the chaos as a cover, Eden and Athena climbed to their feet and sprinted across to the tube in which Winslow was still imprisoned.

Athena snagged up a rifle which had been dropped by a fleeing guard. She did a three-sixty to check for the threats coming their way, but everyone was now too occupied by the commotion to pay them any attention. Flame spread throughout the chamber, churning thick black smoke into the air.

Water spraying from the sprinkler system, rather than dampen the flames, spread the slippery green goo further across the floor.

With her heart doing double-time and her lungs stinging, Eden reached the tube where her father was trapped. The green liquid almost filled the tube, now. Winslow stretched up on his tiptoes, fighting to keep his head above the goo.

Athena rushed up beside Eden and smashed the butt of the gun into the glass. The fragile tube shattered into a web of cracks. Two strikes later and the butt broke through. Liquid gushed out. Unable to control his fall, Winslow slithered out with the liquid, crashing to the floor. Eden rushed over to help her father to his feet. The pair fell straight into an embrace.

"Eden," Winslow whispered, coughing from the smoke. "What took you so long?"

"Had a few things to sort first. You can't be number one priority all the time," Eden replied, still holding her father close and not wanting to let go.

"We need to get out of here," Athena said.

"I've never agreed with you more," Winslow said, still out of breath. "Lead the way."

48
___

EDEN, Athena and Winslow looked out across the chamber. What had a few minutes before been a high-tech scientific laboratory, was now the scene of a hellish nightmare.

Smoke billowed from multiple fires, quickly filling the chamber with an acrid gas. Men, now just shapes in the gloom, ran this way and that, either attempting to put out the fires or helping their fallen comrades.

Water vapor from the sprinklers further clouded the air.

"I love what you've done with the place," Winslow said. He rubbed the back of his hand across his mouth. "Yuck, this stuff taste disgusting."

"I'm glad your sense of humor hasn't taken a beating," Eden said, fire dancing in her eyes.

"That'll be the day I die," Winslow said.

"Look!" Athena's voice once again cut through the melee.

Athena stepped forward and pointed across the chamber. In the center of the commotion, a colossal figure climbed to its feet, pushing aside a heavy object. The figure swayed from side to side as though re-calibrating its balance, then it shook each of its limbs individually. The man-beast moved his head from side to side, manually clicking his vertebrae back into position, then turned to face the assembled crew. Silhouetted against the roaring fire, the figure looked every bit the beast from hell that Eden knew he was.

"Thorne," Eden groaned, her lips forming into a scowl.

"This guy is really starting to get on my nerves." Athena swung the gun in an arc, sending a strafe of rounds directly across the big man's shoulders.

Thorne didn't move, his back the shape and size of an ox.

Blood splattered from craters on his back, but Thorne remained standing.

Thorne roared. It was the most pained, evil, and demonic roar Eden had ever heard.

Athena fired again, opening another series of wounds.

"They're not even getting though his muscles," Eden said.

The gun clicked empty.

"He's just not... human," Athena faltered, her hand slumping to her side. "I'm out."

No longer irritated by the onslaught of bullets, Thorne stepped forward, crouched, and scooped Van Wick from his wheelchair. In the grip of the giant beast, Ludwig Van Wick appeared no bigger than a child. The old man's pale skin was streaked with soot and his thin, gnarled limbs drooped.

Glancing back over his shoulder, the flames turning his eyes into a pair of coals, Thorne strode in the direction of the elevator.

"We are not letting him get out of here," Eden hissed. Her field of vision narrowed to the giant figure lumbering away through the smoke and her thoughts occupied by all the abhorrent things the small man cowering in his arms had caused.

A guard rushed forward out of the smoke and waved his gun towards Eden and the crew.

"You're way too late for the party." Eden hopped into a roundhouse kick, connecting neatly with the guard's neck. All the tension dropped from the guard's face as he folded into a heap on the floor.

Eden snagged up the guy's rifle and slid two spare magazines from his belt. She tossed one magazine to Athena, who caught it with one hand. Eden relieved the guard of his side arm too.

"Time you did some work," Eden said, passing the side arm to her father.

All armed and ready to fire, Eden led them through the mayhem. Each step they took revealed another horrific scene, like a tableau in a top-shelf horror flick.

Passing the second shattered tube, Eden noticed one of the guards trapped beneath a cadaver. The dead man had been huge, with giant rolls of waxy skin, which now pinned the poor guard to his back in the goo. The guard's struggling was now little more than a twitch as his consciousness ebbed away.

The sight sickened Eden to her stomach, as did the thought they could do nothing to help the man. Although he was working for the bad guys, he didn't deserve to die this way.

Eden turned and saw Thorne's shoulders swaying ahead through the smoke. Right now, they didn't have time to help anyone.

They passed the final shattered tube and stepped over the body of a guard lying face down in the green sludge.

"This guy's had a seriously bad day," Athena said, pointing at the bloody mess that was now the back of the guy's head.

Eden bent down and relieved the guard of his spare magazines. There was a firefight coming, and Eden expected it to be a savage one.

"Let's make a run for it," Athena said, pointing towards the door which lay somewhere behind the smoke. "There's no one around to get in our way and we don't have long."

Eden tried to speak, but it turned into a hacking cough. Her mouth tasted vile, and her lungs ached. Athena was right, the melee had died down as Van Wick's staff either ran for their lives or descended into unconsciousness.

The fires, however, were just getting started. With each passing minute, the smoke grew thicker and tasted more toxic. Whatever nasty chemicals Van Wick had been working with, they made a noxious cocktail.

Keeping their formation with Eden at the front, they darted towards the door. Eden crossed the last part of the chamber with an arm outstretched. The smoke was so thick now that she felt the cold concrete wall before she saw it. She shuffled to the right until she felt the door.

The door had been left ajar and Eden wasted no time tearing it open. The smoke in the passageway was lighter than in the chamber. Gathering up at the ceiling, the smoke muted the fluorescent lights into a dusky glow.

Eden slipped through the door, followed by Winslow and Athena. When they were all through, Athena pushed the door closed and snapped the bolt home.

The destruction from the chamber continued in the passageway. What had, less than an hour ago been a clear walkway, was now littered with slumped figures, broken glass, and gooey footprints.

Eden glanced down at the prone body of a guard lying to one side. She paused and looked more closely at him. Bullet wounds scarred his body.

"Thorne's idea of tidying up," Athena whispered.

A gun roared from somewhere further up the passage, reverberating harshly. The sound physically jolted the crew. They all stared in the direction of the elevator.

"He doesn't want any survivors," Eden said, her hands tensing around the rifle.

Eden and Athena shared a glance and then rushed forward.

Almost one-hundred feet further on, having passed several more bullet-riddled bodies, Eden signaled for them to stop. The passage curved a few feet ahead, beyond which they would be in full view of the elevator.

Eden approached the corner slowly and peered around.

Thirty feet away, Thorne strode towards the elevator. The elevator's birdcage door was closed, but Eden could see the elevator had yet to ascend. There were several men in the elevator. The doctor with the thick eyeglasses who had attached Thorne to the IV drip jabbed frantically at a button on the elevator's control panel.

Eden scanned the scene, looking for anything that could give them an advantage. The only cover in the passage were several large crates stacked against one wall.

Thorne strode towards the elevator. Holding Van Wick Senior in just one arm, he lifted the rifle towards the people inside the elevator. Without a pause, he squeezed the trigger and sent half a magazine tearing through the bars. The men howled, then slumped down inside the car. Either through luck or design, the doctor remained uninjured. The man looked fearfully towards Thorne.

Thorne let go of the gun, which hung on a strap over his

shoulder and tore open the door. Thorne stepped inside the elevator and, with surprising care, placed the old man against the back wall. He then turned and dragged the dead and wounded men out into the passage. One of the men had the misfortune to cry out. Thorne threw him hard against the wall, the man's head cracked against the concrete.

In the light of the elevator, Eden saw that the swelling to Thorne's face had gotten worse.

When the elevator was clear, Thorne stepped up to the doctor.

Watching from behind the wall, Eden had no idea how this was about to play out.

Thorne gazed hard down at the small man who was now physically shaking. Thorne punched the man so hard in the face that his spectacles smashed, sending glass fragments into his eyes. Thorne picked the man up by the neck and squeezed until bones broke.

"No survivors," Eden said again. "He's worried these guys know too much."

Thorne threw the doctor from the elevator car and then turned his attention to the control panel on the wall outside the elevator shaft. He tore the panel from the wall, exposing a nest of wires.

"What's he doing?" Athena peered around the corner beside Eden.

"He's making sure no one can follow him up there," Eden replied, her voice grave.

Thorne grabbed the wires, which sparked with electricity, and yanked them hard. Several feet of wire came out of the wall.

"He really doesn't want that going back together again," Athena said.

Thorne threw the wires and the switch inside the elevator car.

Eden's mind roamed for options and possibilities. Whatever their plan, they had to do it soon, before Thorne disappeared up the shaft and left them to die in the hellfire.

49

Huddled behind the wall, Eden, Athena, and Winslow watched Thorne step back into the elevator car and ram the door closed.

"A bullet in the eye gets my vote," Winslow said.

Eden glanced at her father, for a second not quite understanding what he was talking about.

"That'll be his weak spot. Not many people survive a shot to the eye."

"How do you know all this stuff?" Athena said, her hands on her hips. "Actually, please don't answer that."

"Surely a headshot will do the job?" Eden said, looking at the brute.

"This guy's strength is off the charts," Winslow said. "I'd say he's got some super strong bone structure. A bullet in the eye and it'll go straight into his brain."

Thorne stepped across to the control panel inside the elevator car which was clearly still operational. For a long moment he looked at the buttons as though it was a really difficult decision, then he jabbed one.

"Either way, we don't have time to talk about it." Eden took the rifle in both hands and charged out from behind the wall. "Let's give the eye shot a go."

Eden took aim at Thorne as the elevator started to ascend. She ran and fired at the same time. As the rifle howled, she closed the gap, sending shot after shot towards the giant.

Athena stepped out after her and joined in the assault. Bullet after bullet zipped, tracers scoring through the smoke.

Thorne locked eyes with Eden and then lifted his arms. He now held a rifle in each hand. The large guns looked like little more than a child's toy in his bear-sized paws.

Thorne tilted his head to the side as bullets tore up the back of the elevator car, somehow, so far, failing to hit home. He grinned and then fired both weapons at once.

Eden saw the muzzles flash and heard the report before she truly registered what was happening. The barrage from a rifle at such close range was eerily mesmerizing. Each discharge created a brilliant flash, illuminating the elevator car for the briefest of moments. Every ripple and flex of Thorne's powerful muscles became discernible as he expertly steadied the rifles between bursts.

Eden tore her eyes from the threat and glanced at the crates, which were now just a few feet away. Although her brain sent the 'change direction' message to her legs, it felt like an eternity until they obeyed. The whole brutish scene took on the appearance of an old film played in slow motion.

The elevator slid upwards, pulling Thorne and Van Wick Senior away from them. Bullets zinged and thwacked into the walls of the passage.

Eden tried to aim her rifle, but the gun spat wildly, the recoil distorting her aim.

Athena turned too, rushing towards the crates.

The elevator strained and groaned, now five into its ascent.

Thorne crouched down, improving the angle of his shot.

Bullets rebounded from the concrete, tearing lines and scattering dust. One of the fluorescent bulbs shattered into glittering pieces.

Eden's feet scraped across the ground as the bullets sizzled past her, by some divine intervention passing her skin with a fraction of an inch to spare.

Finally, after what felt like a long ordeal, she slumped in behind the crates. Athena joined her a heartbeat later.

Both women dropped to the floor, the bullets pinging from the crates and slamming into the surrounding walls.

For several moments, Thorne's gunfire continued and then that too stopped as the elevator dragged both monster and creator upwards.

Her heart in her throat, Eden checked her body for wounds and was surprised to find none.

The whirr of the distant winding mechanism continued as the elevator, their one chance to escape the chamber inferno, rumbled away.

Athena was first to her feet. She dusted herself down and looked around.

She paced towards the elevator's yawning mouth and peered up the shaft. Through the bars, the base of the shaft was gloomy.

"Are... are you okay?" Winslow said, sprinting forward.

"Miraculously, yes," Eden said, climbing to her feet. For a moment she felt shaky, her ears ringing from the gunfire in the enclosed space. She joined Athena at the elevator gate and assessed the scene.

An unknown distance above them, the winding mechanism stopped.

"They've reached the top," Athena said, trying and failing to see up inside the shaft.

Eden steeled herself and stepped away from the bars. "We need to find a way out of here, before this place fills up with smoke too."

"Agreed," Athena said, glancing at the passage behind them. Smoke wafted in great clouds now as fire engulfed more of the chamber.

"This shaft is the only option," Eden said. She tried to slide open the door, but without the elevator car in position, it was locked. "First, we need to get this open, and then we will find a way up there."

Although Eden tried to sound positive, all she could think about was Ludwig Van Wick and his genetically engineered brute slipping away above their heads.

Athena paced over to one of the crates. Torn to shreds by Thorne's bullets, Athena easily twisted out the locking mechanism and flipped open the lid. The box contained a mixture of tools and power equipment.

"Bingo." Athena pulled out a battery-powered angle grinder with a cutting disc.

"Nice of them to leave the skeleton key lying around," Eden said, stepping back from the door to make room for Athena. "This thing will open anything short of a vault."

Winslow stepped over to the box and retrieved a roll of sticky tape. "I'll get the cracks around the door taped up," he said. "Try to stop some of this smoke."

"Good idea," Eden said. "You've still got the gun?"

Winslow lifted the side of his shirt, showing Eden the gun secured in his waistband.

"Cover your ears folks, this is going to be loud." Athena flicked on the grinder and a whining shriek filled the passage. She stepped up to the door and angled the cutting edge against the lock in a bright shower of dazzling sparks.

Looking away from the light, Eden thought about the horrendous body count the Van Wicks had racked up with their unchecked ambition. She thought not just of the people who had died that day in the chamber, but of those poor souls on *The Titanic* who had lost their lives beneath the icy waves. There was no knowing how many others had fallen foul of the Van Wick family before and since.

"We're through," Athena said, clicking off the grinder and placing it on the floor.

Eden stepped beside Athena and together they heaved the door open and then stepped into the lift shaft.

Eden craned her neck, looking upwards. The elevator car sat over one-hundred feet above.

Athena scurried back to the crate and retrieved a flashlight. Using the flashlight's beam, Athena traced the inner workings of the elevator.

"These rails keep the elevator steady," Athena said, illuminating four thick rails which ran down the sides of the shaft. "And that's the counterweight." She pointed the light at a large metal oblong which hung at the side of the shaft about twenty feet to their left. Various cables ran to and from the counterweight.

Eden pointed at the counterweight, the situation finally starting to feel less helpless. "We can use those cables to climb all the way up, then slip past the elevator car and out through one of the doors above."

"In theory," Athena said. "It's a long climb, though. And if someone uses the elevator while you're halfway…" The words dried up in Athena's throat at the thought of either the fall back down the shaft or the possibility of being crushed between the moving counterweight and the elevator car.

"I'll go," Eden said, moving her neck from side to side, which was already starting to ache.

"You got it open," Winslow said, arriving back at the elevator shaft. He'd sealed the cracks around the door and already there was much less smoke coming through.

"Now we've just got to work out how to scale the shaft," Eden said, stepping out of the shaft's bottom and crossing back to the crate. Eden pulled out a pair of vice grips and held them up. "These could help. We'll attach them to the ropes as we ascend."

"I don't think you will," Winslow said, one ear cocked towards the shaft. "Listen to that."

Eden and Athena whipped around. The elevator's winding gear murmured in the distance.

Athena darted into the shaft and looked up. "Someone's coming," she shouted.

The elevator car slid laboriously down the rails. The counterweight began to grunt and groan as it rose.

"Thorne coming back to finish the job?" Eden said, looking around at the destruction.

"Maybe." Eden rushed across to the crates and started dragging at one of them. "Help me with this. Make a barrier. If it's Thorne, we'll be ready for him."

Winslow and Athena dived in to help, shoving the crates across the passage until they were in the center, about fifteen feet back from the elevator.

Guns ready and magazines replenished, Eden, Athena

and Winslow waited behind their makeshift barrier as the elevator grumbled downwards.

For several seconds, no one spoke. A fluorescent bulb somewhere further down the passage flickered numerous times.

Eden concentrated on taking long and slow breaths, tuning in to the surrounding situation. The acrid chemical zing of the fire burned her nostrils.

Nearing the bottom of the shaft, the elevator ground and clunked. Whispers of the cable and creaks from the pulleys became increasingly distinct. The shaft's bare-brick walls echoed the noise out into the passage.

"Maybe we should have looked for another way," Athena whispered, glancing over her shoulder.

"There was no other way," Eden grunted. "Unless you want to cook in there."

The noise increased further as the elevator reached the bottom of the shaft.

Eden's muscles tensed. Her shoulders hunched over, and her finger slipped across the trigger.

The base of the elevator car appeared, sinking steadily into the void.

With a grunt and groan, the elevator dropped another few inches, allowing the trio to see inside the car. In the firefight, the elevator's internal lights had been damaged and now the car sat in darkness.

Eden's finger tightened further around the trigger, just a hair's breadth from firing.

A figure stood inside the car, holding a flashlight. With the light shining out towards them, Eden couldn't identify the interloper.

The elevator finally groaned to a stop at the shaft bottom and a figure stepped out.

The trio tensed, ready to fire.

But the man who emerged from the smoky gloom, didn't have Thorne's hulking figure. The man was slimmer, more athletic. He was in his early middle age and, incongruously for the chaotic scene, wore a suit.

"Senator," Winslow said, standing up and letting the gun drop in the surprise.

"Yes," Senator Everett Van Wick said, beaming his thousand-watt smile. "I hear you need a ride out of here."

50

"I've always known that my father followed some unusual interests..." Everett Van Wick said when they were all assembled in the elevator car.

"Understatement of the century," Athena said.

Eden stood in the far corner of the elevator car. She continued to hold the rifle tightly across her chest. As far as she was concerned, Everett was a Van Wick, and trusting a Van Wick was like trusting a scorpion.

Everett Van Wick cast his eyes around the passageway. For a moment he just stood there, his eyes moving from the bullet ridden walls, to the crumpled figures of the Van Wick staff murdered in cold blood. "This is just... It's horrific."

"You've never been down here?" Eden asked.

Everett shook his head. "I heard rumors of secret bunkers and passages around this place as a child, but as I grew up, I thought they were just that... rumors."

Everett turned and eyed each of the group in turn. "You've got to understand, my father is as secretive with me as he is with everyone. I've no idea what he does in this house all alone. I've suggested he sell the place and come to Washington. But to my father, this place is part of the family."

"It's part of the family for sure," Eden grunted, her grip on the rifle relaxing slightly as she recognized the genuine shock in Everett's expression.

"How did you find us?" Eden asked.

"Let's talk upstairs," Everett said, stepping across to the elevator's control panel.

Winslow pulled the door closed and Everett thumbed one of the buttons. The elevator mechanisms moaned from somewhere high above.

Two minutes later, they stepped out of the car and into the main hallway, which was now brightly lit.

"I had no idea this elevator was even here," Van Wick said, looking at the painting which seamlessly covered the opening.

"Someone obviously left in a hurry." Eden's eyes traced set of bear size footprints on the marble floor.

Everett Van Wick led them through to the kitchen. Eden and Athena maintained their guard, scanning each room for movement. But, as they'd expected, Thorne and Van Wick Senior were long gone.

"Talk then," Eden said when Everett had positioned himself at the head of a giant oak table.

"This afternoon I got a call from my father asking me to come up here. I thought that maybe his health had taken a turn for the worse. Then, as I was arriving, I was almost run off the road by an SUV going the other way."

"How long ago was that?" Eden barked.

"Ten minutes, maybe. I arrived, parked up out front, walked in and found the place like this."

"That was probably Thorne leaving with your father," Athena said.

Everett suddenly stood upright. "Thorne has kidnapped my father? Why? Where has he taken him?"

"Not kidnapped, rescued from what went on downstairs."

The final bit of color drained from Everett's face. The man wilted right there in the kitchen. "I'm sorry, I don't understand. What went on downstairs?"

Eden's muscles slackened. Everett Van Wick was as much in the dark about this whole sorry mess as the rest of them.

"That's something you need to see for yourself," Eden said. "Shame we can't get down there because of the fire."

"I need to see it." Everett's hand crashed against the table and muscles in his face bulged. "I need to understand what my father has been doing all these years."

"It's impossible. The place is on fire." Athena said, the rifle now hanging at her side.

"I might have just the thing. Come with me."

Before anyone could answer, Everett jerked to his feet and marched off through the house. Eden, Athena, and Winslow glanced at each other and then set off at a jog to keep up.

After several turns, they passed through a heavy door. Even before Everett turned the light on, Eden got the impression that it was a big space. When countless bulbs burst into light, Eden saw that she was right. The room was the size of a small warehouse. Two large SUVs sat at one side and the equipment needed to maintain the grounds sat on the other. A lawnmower the size of a tractor and a large rack filled with gardening tools occupied a quarter of the space.

Everett Van Wick paced to a cabinet at the back of the room and swung open the door.

Inside the cabinet, rows of firefighting equipment were neatly organized.

"My father was always afraid that we'd have a fire up here. He hated the idea of the emergency crews coming on the property."

"I can understand that," Eden said.

"He had his own staff trained to fight fires. There will be enough here for us to deal with almost anything, I'd say."

Eden, finally reassured of Everett Van Wick's good intentions, swung the rifle around to her back and stepped forward to look at the equipment.

There were fire-resistant suits, helmets with built-in communication devices, and high-capacity oxygen tanks. Alongside these were racks of fire blankets, heavy-duty gloves, and specialized boots. There were also several compact, motorized water pumps, neatly coiled hoses, portable water tanks and large cylinders of carbon dioxide.

"Suit up then," Eden said. "It's time you learned a thing or two about your family."

AN HOUR LATER, Eden and Everett were back in the kitchen. Athena had taken Winslow out to the truck and Baxter had come inside to help decide what they should do now. Baxter had only just stopped freaking out about the long period of radio silence.

"I just couldn't stop thinking about the worst thing to possibly happen," Baxter muttered morosely.

"You imagine that worst thing," Eden said. "And I'm telling you that what actually happened was much more terrible."

In the kitchen, Everett Van Wick held his head in his hands.

"I can't believe this has been happening, right here, for all these years. It's disgusting."

Eden and Baxter nodded slowly.

"Your father and your grandfather before him have been messing with science," Eden said. "That's how Thorne, your brother, is so strong and powerful."

Everett Van Wick looked up at Eden, his gaze as hard as the bullets which had failed to penetrate Thorne's muscles a couple of hours before.

"My brother?" Everett's face tensed as though another piece of the puzzle clicked into place. "That makes sense," he said, barely above a whisper. "Thorne has been part of the security team for as long as I can remember. Then, when I decided to go into politics, father made him the head of my personal security."

"When you decided to go into politics?"

"Yes, I was at Yale when it really caught my interest."

"I doubt you ever had a decision," Eden said, laying her palms flat on the table. She was still wearing the firefighting suit down to her waist, although now it was charred and burned. "I'd say you were *set up* to go into politics," Eden said. "*Bred* to go into politics."

Once again, Everett Van Wick acted as though he'd been slapped. He stumbled over some words but couldn't pronounce a single one.

"Think about it," Eden said. "Everything about you is the respectable statesman. The way you look, the way you talk, your education, even your smile is too perfect. I bet from day one your father had you learning the specialist skills you would need to fulfill the desire he had for you."

Silence filled the kitchen for a long moment.

Finally, Everett spoke, although his voice was little more than a groan. "You're right." He looked morosely down at the tabletop. "You're totally right. I was groomed for it from the very beginning."

Eden nodded, feeling a welling grief for Everett Van Wick's lost childhood.

"While other kids were watching TV or playing games, I was watching and replicating the great presidential speeches of the past. My father would have me go over them again and again, ensuring every word, every gesture was immaculate."

"That doesn't sound like fun," Eden said, sympathy furrowing her brow.

Everett let out a dry chuckle. "It wasn't, but then, I suppose I never knew what *fun* was." He went quiet for a long time, lost in the memories of past times.

"That's not actually true. There were times when I felt like a normal child. During the summers, we would go to the lake house, and I would sneak into the woods. I'd climb trees, get muddy, and do the normal stuff... at least... I think that's the normal stuff that children do."

Again, Everett dropped into silence.

Eden eyed him, wanting to say something to reassure the man, but words failed her. She slid her hand across the table and placed it on top of his.

Suddenly, Everett raised his head, his gaze now hard and focused.

"That's where my father will have gone," he said, standing up and shuffling out of the firefighting gear.

Eden and Baxter glanced at each other to see if the other understood what Everett had just said. Neither did.

"My father will have gone to the lake house," Everett

said, his voice now booming like it did when he spoke to millions. "I'm going to finish this."

"You're wrong," Eden said, climbing to her feet. "We're going to finish this."

51

Lying on her stomach, Eden clamped the binoculars to her eyes and peered at the Van Wick's lake house across the calm waters of Lake Wenatchee. Behind the lake, the Cascade Mountains reared up, muscular and daunting in the moonlight.

Gazing up at the mountains, Eden remembered their skiing exercise on the slopes of Dragontail Peak just a few days ago. With so much happening, it felt like half a lifetime ago.

She adjusted the binoculars, and the lake house shifted into focus. In contrast to the men Eden suspected were inside, the lake house was idyllic. Nestled between tall pines and shimmering water, the only part of the building not constructed with traditional materials were the giant windows, which no doubt offered panoramic views of the lake and mountains.

As Eden swept the binoculars from side to side, one of the windows changed from a dark box to a brightly lit square.

"There's definitely someone at home," Eden said.

"There's light in the house and a vehicle parked beside." She re-angled the binoculars and focused on the vehicle.

"Cadillac Escalade," Baxter said, placing a hand on Eden's shoulder.

Eden peered at his hand and resisted her knee-jerk reaction to push it away. After a moment or two, she realized the touch was actually a nice thing.

"Ten points, Captain Baxter." Eden handed the binoculars to Baxter. He removed his hand from her shoulder and checked out the vehicle. "That's the one, alright. I saw it leaving the mansion just before the senator arrived."

"Do we have to call him that?" Eden said.

"What?"

"'The Senator', it just sounds weird. I mean, he's not here on 'senatorial duties,'" Eden said.

"Sure. Call him whatever you like," Baxter muttered nonchalantly.

"Will do, Captain," Eden mumbled.

A few seconds of silence swelled between the pair.

"This place is creepy," Eden whispered, peering out across the lake as Baxter scrutinized the scene through the binoculars.

"Creepier than a basement full of dead relatives?" Baxter said. On the drive from the mansion, Eden had described the Van Wick's Chamber of Horrors in graphic detail.

"Well, no. I suppose not," Eden replied. A chill swept across the water and shook the pencil-thin pine trees behind them.

"We've got them running scared now. Remember, Thorne took out most of their security team back there. They're here alone," Baxter said confidently.

"And so are we." Eden pulled her coat more tightly

around her to counter the chill. "And Thorne is a difficult man to kill."

Baxter removed the binoculars and glanced at Eden. "We've got this," he said.

Eden was suddenly aware of how close they were to the lake's lapping water.

"Sure. Don't let me down," she said, her face set in a scowl.

Eden shuffled backward, staying low to the ground in case anyone was watching. When she reached the tree line, she stood and paced back towards their borrowed Jeep Wrangler.

"It looks like we've got the right place," Eden said, sliding into the passenger seat.

Everett Van Wick glanced at her anxiously from the back seat. It was strange to see the man not wearing his suit. Raiding the guard's stores and the now abandoned Van Wick Mansion, Eden had found Everett a set of black fatigues and a baseball cap.

"You know they are there?" Everett said, his hands twisting together.

"Yes, they are there," Eden said, staring hard at the man. "Just as we knew they would be."

Eden turned and gazed out through the windshield. Incapacitating Thorne and capturing Ludwig Van Wick was now feeling like an impossible task.

Of course, they could just wait for more people to arrive, but Eden figured that disappearing for a man like Ludwig Van Wick would be all too easy. The guy had more resources than some world nations, and an obsessed son with superhuman strength to make sure he got what he wanted. This was a now or never kind of thing.

Baxter materialized from the darkness and stood in front of the Jeep's hood. He signaled for Eden to pop the catch.

Eden reached down, found the lever and pulled. The hood clunked.

Baxter lifted the hood and used a screwdriver to disconnect the Jeep's running lights. They could now approach the lake house without being seen.

A minute later, Baxter slid into the driver's seat and started the engine.

"Are you sure this is going to work?" Everett mumbled, his voice a soft shadow of its normal baritone.

"Absolutely," Eden replied. "My plans always work."

"Making it up as you go along doesn't constitute a plan," Baxter said, his amused tone cutting through the tension.

"Just because I'm gifted with the ability to create a fully formed idea..."

Baxter clicked the Jeep into drive.

"It will work," Eden said. "All we need to do is keep them in place. My father has some contacts in the F.B.I."

"Of course he does," Baxter said, eyes never leaving the road.

Eden shot him a glance but didn't rise to it. "He's in contact with them now and as soon as we're done, they'll be here. Van Wick Senior has a lot of questions to answer."

Eden and Baxter both leaned forward in their seats as though getting a few inches closer to the road would help them see. Above them, moonlight filtered in through the trees, illuminating the road like a grey ribbon.

Eden glanced up and saw the lake house through the trees. Again, she thought of the two men who were currently inside planning their next move. The abhorrent crimes of those men seemed a direct contrast to the beauty of the natural world in which they sought refuge.

Eden lowered the window and listened to the sounds of the Jeep blending with the distant calls of nocturnal animals.

They passed a thick section of woodland, which reduced the visibility even further. Baxter slowed the Jeep and relied on the well-worn ruts in the track to stay on course.

Finally, they reached a vantage point overlooking the lake house.

"Just here," Eden said, pointing to a ghostly clump of trees a few feet from the track.

Eden clambered out and carefully turned on a flashlight which she kept angled directly at the ground. Using only the light from the flashlight, Baxter turned the Jeep around and then reversed it out of sight.

Baxter killed the engine and silence sprung forth.

Eden turned off the flashlight. The lake house was now just a couple of hundred feet away. When she turned around, Baxter and Everett had climbed out of the Jeep. For a moment, they all stood in complete silence.

The sound of the wind rustling through the trees was accompanied by the distant hoot of an owl. Eden focused on the gentle lapping of Lake Wenatchee's water against the shore. She closed her eyes and inhaled deeply. When she opened them again, she could see each detail more clearly — the pine needles carpeting the forest floor, the silhouette of the lake house against the mountains, and Everett Van Wick, his face etched with fear and determination.

"It's time," Eden muttered, her voice ghostly quiet. "Let's finish this."

Eden paced across to the Jeep's trunk and pulled out a black kit bag. She passed the bag to Baxter and then hefted out a second, which she slung over her shoulder. Something inside the bag rattled.

"Stick with the plan." Eden pointed at Everett. "Get in position and wait for us to neutralize Thorne. Then you'll get your quality father and son time."

"How do you know Thorne will fall for it?" Everett said, talking quickly.

"I've met people like him before," Eden said, turning towards the woodland. "I know exactly what he'll do."

"You know where to wait?" Baxter said to Everett.

Everett nodded.

Baxter tapped the comms device in his ear. "Any problems, let us know."

Although the radios weren't as good as the usual near-invisible they usually used, they were good enough. Another donation from the Van Wick stores, they were very much appreciated.

Without another word, Eden turned and paced off through the trees.

Baxter glanced back at Everett Van Wick one more time and then followed.

After a minute, Eden held up a finger to indicate they should pause. Baxter sidled up beside her.

Eden glanced back the way they'd come. The senator, the road, and the Jeep were completely indistinguishable through the forest.

"Good," she said. Surprise was the only thing on their side right now.

Eden indicated they should continue. The pair pushed on for several minute. Weaving through the darkness on the uneven forest floor was slow going. The ground, covered with fallen branches, pine needles and animal burrows, created the ideal environment to snap an ankle. Eden thought about the frustration of going through everything they had, surviving near death on countless occasions, only to break an ankle walking through the forest. She grinned to herself — Indiana Jones certainly never had to worry about that.

After a few more minutes her eyes had further adjusted, allowing her to see the grey outlines of trees and the general descent of the forest floor towards the lake house.

She cursed the Van Wicks for not keeping night vision goggles in their stores.

Eden pushed through a thick clump of trees, sharp branches scratching against her skin, and emerged in a part of the forest which was less densely packed. Orange light spilled from the lake house, burning through the trees like some strange, otherworldly force.

She turned and signaled to Baxter. They were close. Baxter nodded once, without a break in his stride.

A few seconds later, the house came into view. The rear of the building was just as grand as the front, constructed from large stones and giant wooden beams. Fortunately for Eden and Baxter, though, the windows on the back were smaller.

Eden led them further through the trees. For what she had planned, she needed to get right up to the back of the house without being seen. It was a daring plan which required nerves of steel, precision, and a good deal of luck.

Eden reached the tree line and paused behind the trunk of a douglas fir.

"Looks good," Baxter said, joining her a moment later.

"I'm in position, waiting about two minutes out." Everett's nervous voice came down the radio.

"Understood," Eden said in reply. "We're just setting up Thorne's surprise now. Wait for our signal."

Eden clicked off the radio and then turned to Baxter. "Ready to catch a monster?" she whispered.

Baxter slung off his kit bag and placed it on the ground. "Ready as I'll ever be."

52

ALMOST TEN MINUTES LATER, Eden and Baxter returned to the tree behind which they'd paused on their initial approach.

"All good?" Eden said, glancing at Baxter.

Baxter nodded and passed Eden a remote control. "I'll let you do the honors."

"Why thank you." Eden turned the device over in her hands. "How many do we have?"

"Three, but let's hope it only takes one."

Eden thumbed one of the buttons.

Almost fifty feet away, the small explosive device roared, shattering the silent night. A fiery burst erupted from the tree where Baxter had stashed the device, sending pine needles shooting like darts in all directions. The ground trembled for an instant, protesting the violent interruption, and a harsh orange light flashed up into the sky.

Eden grimaced, pushing her back hard against the tree. The explosion had been louder than she'd expected.

"Sheeesh," Baxter hissed, pushing himself down into the

ground behind the tree. "We're just trying to get one man's attention, not the whole state!"

Eden grinned. "Sorry! I didn't realize it would be quite that loud."

The explosion reverberated across the lake and back again, causing a startled flock of birds to erupt from their roosts in nearby trees. Just as quickly as the noise had come, it faded back into the stillness of the wilderness.

Eden scrambled around the base of the tree, lifted the binoculars to her eyes and checked the rear of the house. "No change yet," she reported.

The device in Eden's ear crackled, and Everett's voice came through. "Was that supposed to happen?" His voice sounded like little more than a distant hiss after the roaring explosion. "It was very loud."

"Exactly as planned," Baxter replied. "Stay in position."

Eden saw movement inside the lake house. At first, the movement was just a shadow in one of the windows. Whoever was approaching was doing so carefully.

"We've got something," she whispered, describing the movement to Baxter.

For almost half a minute, the shadowy figure moved from window to window, assessing the scene outside. Eventually satisfied that no one was going to pepper the back of the house with lead, a shadow darkened the back door's glass.

With a burst of violent energy, the door swung open and smashed against the wall. Glass shattered down onto the stone. Then, his face set into his trademark snarl, Thorne paced out onto the rear porch. He panned a rifle from right to left, squinting into the darkness. The man moved with the confidence of a hunter who knows he's at the top of the food chain.

Eden signaled to Baxter, and the pair pushed themselves in close behind a tree. Even without the binoculars, Baxter could see the brute's movements.

Cloaked in the gloom of the forest, Eden was confident that Thorne couldn't see them from his position at the back of the house. Still, the guy creeped her out. She shuddered involuntarily.

Thorne wandered further out on to the porch. The man showed no signs of the ordeal his body had just been through. He moved like he'd never had an injury in his whole life, let alone taken several gun shots to the back just a few hours ago. Whatever genetic trickery Van Wick Senior had performed, Eden hated to admit, it was impressive. That was if you discounted the whole swollen face thing, which had got even worse since they'd last seen him.

Eden passed the remote control to Baxter and then pulled a second, similar device, from her pocket. This remote control was linked to the trap she'd set at the bottom of the porch steps.

"Come on, come on," Eden muttered, her finger hovering over the button.

"Not yet," Baxter replied, leaning forward to get a better view. "A moment too soon and the whole thing's a bust."

Eden pouted with concentration. Her finger hovered over the button.

"What's going on? Is it clear?" Everett's voice came through the comms.

"No. Not yet. Wait for our signal," Eden hissed through gritted teeth.

Thorne took another step forward, his rifle raised and ready.

Thorne reached a small flight of stone steps at the edge

of the porch and stopped. At the base of the steps, a well-preened lawn rose towards the tree line.

Eden instinctively held her breath, flattening herself against the tree.

Thorne completed another one-eighty of the scene, then lowered the rifle. The brute yawned, stepped back from the top of the steps, and turned back towards the house.

"Damn it." Eden's fist clenched and her fingers moved away from the remote trigger.

"What's going on?" Everett said, fear lacing his voice.

"Nothing yet. Stay in position," Baxter said.

"Give him another blast," Eden said.

Thorne took a step back towards the house and then paused. The giant man stretched, the muscles in his back standing out like hydraulic pistons.

"Do it now," Eden commanded, her voice sharp.

Baxter hit the button, and another explosion roared through the forest.

Thorne froze in position and then spun on his heel. This time he was in position to see how close the explosion was to the rear of the lake house. A light flared amid the trees, splashing the rear of the house in angular shadows, and sending several dozen birds into crazed flight.

Thorne moved quickly this time. He crossed the back porch in two giant steps, his eyes never leaving the site of the explosion. He took the stairs two at a time, running full pelt towards the forest.

Eden gripped the second remote control tightly. Her finger hovered over the button, waiting for just the right moment.

Thorne descended the final step, his rifle at the ready, eyes still scanning the shadowy forest.

Their whole plan hinged on whether Eden could press

the button at just the right time. In the next few moments, it would be over, one way or another. Eden drew another calming breath.

Reaching the bottom of the stairs, Thorne slowed.

With the light of the explosion already dying out, Eden wondered whether he was thinking twice about charging into the unknown.

Still, he took the next step. His giant foot thumped down on to the grass, followed by the second.

Eden pressed the button.

The hidden mechanism she'd laid there a few minutes before sprung to life. A taut cable snapped closed around Thorne's ankles. Placed perfectly, the cable forced Thorne's legs together and then locked in place.

Eden depressed the next button and a pulley system attached to one of the nearby trees, whined into action. The strong steel cable, which was now looped around Thorne's ankles, slid across the grass.

Caught off guard, Thorne let out a guttural cry. For a few moments, he tried to hop along with the sliding cable, but as the speed increased, he fell to the ground. The hulking man crashed down with an earth-shaking thump.

Despite his surprise and sudden loss of balance, Thorne swung around with the rifle and fired into the forest.

Eden darted around the back of the tree until she heard the magazine click empty. She waited a few more seconds, just to make sure Thorne wasn't carrying another weapon or a spare magazine.

When she was confident that he was well and truly out, Eden darted from her hiding spot and snapped on a flashlight. Baxter joined her a moment later, pacing across the lawn.

Thorne lay on the ground twenty feet away, twisting and

fighting against the thick cable which pulled him across the lawn. He scowled, his face distorting into a snarl of pure rage. He roared a feral beast.

Keeping a safe distance, Eden shone her flashlight down on the man. She kept the motor running as Thorne's legs were pulled against the tree and then up into one of the lowest branches. When he was angled upside down with his head just above the ground, Eden hit stop on the remote and the winch clicked off.

Thorne yanked at his restraints, growling. His muscles bulged, threatening to pop through his skin as he pulled against the cables. Blood oozed from his ankles where the cable dug into his skin. For a moment, the tree shuddered and shook at the force of his efforts.

"You think this will hold me?" Thorne spat, his voice tinged with both mockery and a boiling anger. "I'll pull this tree up from the roots."

Thorne thrashed violently, his body convulsing in powerful surges. The tree, a douglas fir, did nothing but wiggle.

Eden and Baxter kept a safe distance, their eyes never leaving the man-beast they'd finally captured.

Eden knew that underestimating Thorne, even for a second, could be a fatal mistake.

"You can struggle all you want," she said calmly.

Thorne continued wrestling with his restraints.

"You're not going anywhere. That cable can hold up to 6,000 pounds. And that system attaching you to the tree is secured with a military-grade padlock. It's virtually pick-resistant."

Thorne stopped struggling for a moment, as if considering the specifications Eden had recited. His eyes shifted to the padlock, which secured the winching mechanism in place, then to the cable, and finally back to her.

"You might as well save your energy," Eden concluded, locking eyes with him. "You're not breaking free without the key, and the key," she dangled it before dropping it into her pocket, "is staying right here with me."

Eden and Baxter turned and strode in the direction of the back steps.

"Is it done?" Everett's voice came through the radio.

"It's done," Eden confirmed. "Thorne is neutralized."

53

Eden slipped her Glock from its holster and climbed the stairs up to the rear porch of the lake house. She paused at the top for Baxter to join her. Shattered glass covered the slabs from where Thorne had smashed the door against the wall.

Eden glanced over her shoulder to see the monstrous man now hanging upside down from the tree. She hoped the authorities took her father's warning about how dangerous Thorne was seriously.

"Let's end this," Eden said, glancing at Baxter.

Although they were confident Ludwig Van Wick would now be alone in the house, they had no way of knowing whether he would be armed. As a gun was just as deadly in the hands of a frail old man. Eden intended to keep the Glock ready for action until she knew things were safe.

Eden led the way through the rear door, her boots crunching over shattered glass, and stepped into the kitchen. Granite worktops glinted beside high-end appliances. An empty fruit bowl and an absence of used plates or cooking equipment suggested the house was not often lived in.

Eden walked through a large dining room and into a double-height space at the front of the house. A large proportion of the house consisted of just one open space, a double height living area with a giant window overlooking the lake.

Baxter pointed towards a staircase, indicating that he would check the rooms upstairs and Eden should make a circuit of the large living area.

Eden paused and checked the room for movement. Lamps on side tables bathed the room in a gentle glow and an open fire twinkled from a stone fireplace. An impossibly large moose head watched the room, sharing the wall above the fire with dozens of pairs of antlers.

Several sofas the size of compact cars squatted in the gloom and on the far side a grand piano stood with its lid propped up as though ready for a concert. Lake Wenatchee glinted in the moonlight through the glass.

Eden glanced towards the staircase which wound its way up the far wall, allowing access to a landing which cantilevered across the back of the room, giving access to a row of bedrooms. Eden glanced up at the pitched roof high above them and estimated the average family home could fit into just this one space.

"I hoped I wouldn't see you again," came a weak and nasal voice from somewhere near the giant window.

Eden swung around, but still couldn't see the speaker. She took a step towards the noise and then noticed a pair of oxygen tanks and medical monitor standing beside a wing-backed chair. The chair, upholstered in red leather, was positioned to allow the occupant to gaze out at the lake and, as such, remain almost invisible to anyone inside the room.

Eden approached the chair slowly, gun outstretched. She kept her distance and rounded the chair carefully.

Seeing Ludwig Van Wick, Eden stifled a gasp. If she thought the old man had looked unwell before, now he was death re-animated.

His skin was now almost translucent. Tubes ran from the tanks to his nostrils, and the screen for the medical monitor flashed and flickered sporadically.

Ludwig Van Wick's colorless eyes assessed Eden, taking in her horrified expression, and then shifted down to the Glock.

He choked out a laugh, which sounded more like a cat trying to emit a hairball than real humor.

"You won't need that," Van Wick said, nodding weakly towards the weapon. "I'm an old man. I can barely lift a finger."

Eden scowled down at the man, keeping the gun squarely aimed at his narrow chest. She moved further around the chair, crossing an ornately patterned rug, and took a position where she could see him straight on.

Van Wick licked his lips in the way a lizard might, and then blinked.

"I can only assume, by the fact that you've walked in here, that you have somehow disposed of my wonderful Thorne?"

"He's currently engaged, yes." Eden took a step backward.

"Clever. I expect you realized that killing him was nigh on impossible."

"He does have the tendency to keep coming back," Eden said.

"He's a masterpiece of human engineering. Perhaps my

greatest invention. Thorne has been undergoing gene therapies his whole life." Pride laced the old man's voice.

"That sounds like a blast," Eden said.

Van Wick wasn't to be put off and continued with his explanation. "Nanobots circulate in his bloodstream, speeding up cellular repair. They're controlled by a subdermal implant that regulates his adrenal levels..."

"He's like one of those diseases that won't go away," Eden interrupted.

Van Wick Senior sputtered with laughter again. "He is so much more than that. He is a living, breathing, war machine. We could all learn a thing or two about his cellular composition."

Baxter walked down the stairs, his gun lowered. "The rest of the house is empty."

"Is... is... that the wonderful Captain Baxter?" Van Wick stammered, trying but failing to glance over his shoulder in the big chair.

Baxter padded across the room, moving like a big cat.

"It's so good to finally meet you. I've heard many things about you," Van Wick said.

Baxter glanced down at the little man with the curiosity a person reserves for mold growing on spoiled food.

At that moment, the door clattered open, and Everett Van Wick entered, his face red with exertion.

Eden glanced from father to son and back again. The two men couldn't have been more different — one shriveled and corrupted, the other a confident, collected statesman.

Everett Van Wick crossed the room and stared hard at his father. Fury burned in the younger man's eyes.

"This is a chance for you to clear the air with your father," Eden said. "After tonight, I don't expect you'll be seeing each other again for a long time."

Van Wick roared with laughter, sending a string of drool up in the air and then swinging down against his shirt. He clapped his hands like a child at a birthday party.

"Oh, are you going to have me arrested? How very charming! That will certainly be interesting. I haven't seen the Commissioner for a very long time, but I was a key supporter of his last campaign."

Everett Van Wick paced towards his father, his patience bubbling over into anger. His hands hung at his sides.

"I will make personally sure that you stand trial for the awful things you've done." He pointed at his father. "You will pay for the innocent people you've killed and the lives you've ruined."

Ludwig Van Wick tilted his head to the side and peered up at his son. "And risk your own position? You think the people of this great nation will want their next president to be the son of a criminal?"

Everett gazed down at his father. "I think they would rather have someone who's honest. Someone who's helped bring an abhorrent criminal to justice."

Van Wick roared with laughter again, clapping his hands like a wind-up monkey. "You are joking! You are joking! Where did you learn to be this funny? I certainly didn't teach you that." Van Wick's laughing died on the frosty expressions of the three people gathered around his chair.

"If you really believe that, then you are delusional." Ludwig pointed a bony finger up at his son.

"Enough!" Everett roared. "I saw your chamber. I saw the deformed figures you were experimenting on. I saw the bodies of your scientists and the staff. I know that you and my grandfather killed many times, not least the poor souls on *The Titanic*..."

"You know, do you?" The old man murmured, studying

his withered legs. "You know the pain I go through every day because of our steps forward in science? You worked out well with a strong body and a quick mind — I got one of those at the expense of the other."

"I will not... I cannot pity a murderer," Everett said. "What were you trying to achieve with all this?"

"Look at humanity," Ludwig slurred, his arms outstretched. "People are pathetic. They wander through life getting sick, getting injured, making no progress. And yet they want choice and control. This is about keeping power where it should be. In the hands of people like us!" He thumped the arm of the chair again.

Everett shook his head. "But at what cost? The end does not justify the means."

Ludwig Van Wick turned and pointed back through the house. "Consider Thorne out there. I created a man that can walk into gunfire, he can fall from trains... and survive. How much will governments pay to turn their armies into that?"

"To turn their soldiers into monsters?" Eden said, stepping forward, anger flaring.

Van Wick Senior grinned, showing tiny sharp teeth. "Yes. That's exactly what he is. He's a monster! That's because you don't control him."

"You intended to make more?" Everett said.

"Not make more, as such, but use the Thorne's program of therapy to make people stronger and more resilient. For a fee, obviously. Each generation will be smarter, stronger, and more resilient than the last. Slowly we will be able to remove some of the flaws."

"What flaws?" Eden said. "He's a killing machine already."

"Why thank you dear," Ludwig said, grinning as though

Eden's words were a compliment. "But he's not perfect. Aside from the lack of empathy we discussed, and the inability to fit in socially with other humans, try as we might, we can't seem to get him to adapt to water."

"What do you mean, adapt to water?" Eden probed, thinking about the giant man trussed up outside.

Ludwig Van Wick paused and scowled up at the ceiling. "The hyper-dense muscle fibers and bone structure that make him resilient on land effectively make him a lead weight in water. Put it in simple terms, he sinks like a stone."

"Enough of this!" Everett Van Wick roared, standing up at his full height and then pointing down at his father. "You did all this without considering the consequences."

"Of course, I considered the consequences, that's why I bred you. You were designed to be the president. When you were in office, we could take this mainstream. Imagine how much our government would pay for ten thousand Thornes on a battlefield? And if the United States didn't want to pay, once we'd developed the system, we could offer it to the highest bidder."

Everett Van Wick shook his head, his anger deflating into something akin to sorrow. "You're a fool, an arrogant fool. The world doesn't work like that. It's not just about war, and battles and conflict. It's about connection and understanding."

Van Wick Senior clapped his hands and laughed. "This is it... this is it... you have just perfectly illustrated the problem I've known about for years."

"What are you talking about?"

Senior controlled his laughter and eyed his son. "I've known for decades that there was something wrong in your conditioning. Now you've just proved it to me."

Everett Van Wick's eyes narrowed on his father.

"I knew it when you were a boy. You were just too soft!" Van Wick Senior bumped a fist against his chest. "For the success I have in mind you need to be hard. You need to be realistic. You need to know that whatever you do, people will suffer, and you need to close your heart to that."

"Nonsense!" Everett roared, angrier than ever. "I know that my decisions impact millions, but that doesn't mean it's bad to care. Caring about each other is what makes us human, and I will not..."

A thunderous boom echoed from the forest behind the lake house. Pictures rattled against their fixings. The moose head, antlers vibrating, threatened to crash down into the room.

Eden and Baxter eyed each other and then swiveled towards the back of the house.

"Go," Everett said, locking eyes with his father. "I'll be fine."

Father and son held a gaze for a long moment. Everett narrowed his eyes and took a step towards his father.

"Fine," Eden said, already moving towards the kitchen. "We'll be two minutes and then it's time to get out of here."

Baxter followed wordlessly.

Neither Van Wick man spoke until they heard Eden and Baxter move out through the kitchen.

"You know my biggest regret," Senior Van Wick said, wheezing with each word.

"The fact you've brought our whole family name into disrepute?" Everett snarled. "The fact you've killed countless people for personal..."

"No," the father said, interrupting his son mid-sentence. Somehow, he found more energy and his lips now quivered. "My biggest regret is that blasted assassin."

The younger man inhaled. His eyebrows inched together. A ghostly silence settled over the lake house.

"Why?" Everett said slowly, clearly not quite understanding. "I recovered fully, thanks to Doctor Hunter's quick thinking."

"Yes, you did." Van Wick Senior pointed up at his son. "That's the point. You survived thanks to that infernal doctor. How was I supposed to know you'd invite the local doctor to stand beside you and play the blasted hero!"

Silence returned as the two men locked eyes.

"I don't understand," Everett said, finally breaking the gaze with his father. "Why would that be of such disappointment..." A sledgehammer of realization slammed Everett Van Wick in the stomach, knocking the air from his lungs. All expression dropped from his face. He stepped backwards and steadied himself against the wall. He turned towards his father. The old man was grinning like an amused child.

"Tell me that's not true," Everett said, his jaw setting in anger. "Tell me I've got this wrong."

Ludwig Van Wick licked his lips, clearly enjoying every moment.

"I'm afraid you've got it completely right," Ludwig said. "I paid to have you killed. But the idiot failed."

Everett Van Wick took another step back as though the older man had just physically struck him again.

"Leavenworth..." Everett's arms hung limp at his sides. He slumped as the energy drained from his body. "That's why you insisted I made the presidential announcement in Leavenworth. You'd planned it all right from the start."

"Exactly. These big arenas with all their security checks make an assassination attempt so difficult. Not to mention the medical team that are always on standby. In a small-town theater, though, there are real opportunities." Ludwig Van Wick's voice was calm and emotionless. "If only that doctor wasn't there."

"But, why?" Everett said, gazing at his father.

"I needed you out of the way because you're too weak, don't you get it?" Ludwig Van Wick roared. "Even if you made the Oval Office, which I very much doubt, you would never have the strength to take my research mainstream. Progress like that takes strength and confidence, and you don't have either of those things."

"But... but... to have me killed. To order the death of your own son?" Everett's voice was barely above a whisper now.

"Ah yes, well that's the clever bit. There is one thing you are good at... getting people to like you." Ludwig paused to cough.

Everett rocked forward momentarily as though the slightest gust of wind could shake him from his feet.

"It was perfect you see," Van Wick Senior continued unabated. "But that presented me with an opportunity too. You die, and the country laments what a great president you might have been, given the chance. Then, I find another Van Wick candidate — a long lost nephew or something — and people will remember the president you might have been and..."

"And that justifies killing your own son?" Everett hissed through gritted teeth.

"Success is justified by any means. But, do you know the best thing?"

Everett scowled at his father. Ludwig gazed manically, his eyes glinting like the water through the glass.

"Now I will get another chance." Slowly, with the speed

of the changing seasons, the old man reached into the chair and removed a small handgun. He leveled the gun at Everett and slid a bony finger across the trigger. "And this time there's no one to get in the way."

54

Eden rushed out on to the back porch and then froze. She peered into the night, her eyes adjusting slowly. A thin blanket of cloud had slid across the sky whilst they'd been inside and dampened the light even further.

Eden slipped out her flashlight and clamped it to the bottom of the Glock. She swept the finger of light across the lawn and then gasped. It took her a few moments to piece together what she saw. The bough of the great douglas fir from which Thorne had been hanging, lay splayed across the lawn. Although almost a foot in diameter, the branch had been torn from the tree. The winching mechanism and the cable had fallen to the ground beside it, but Thorne was nowhere to be seen.

"Oh no," Eden said, slowly making sense of the scene. "He's gone."

Together Eden and Baxter surged across the lawn, their feet sinking into wet grass. Eden clasped the Glock in extended arms, sweeping left and then right for any sign of movement. She glanced down at the gun and realized how useless it would be against Thorne's super strong musculature, anyway.

Unperturbed, they ran on. Reaching the tree, Eden studied the winching mechanism which now lay mangled on the ground. Several cogs had been yanked from their housing and a bunch of wires hung loose. The device hadn't just been broken, but disemboweled.

"He's pulled the cable free," Eden said, focusing on the winching mechanism.

"It looks like he couldn't get the cable from around his ankle, though." Baxter turned and inspected the forest.

"He's just taken it with him," Eden said, her voice ghostly. She turned and followed Baxter's gaze, shining the flashlight through the trees. "We need to get after him..."

A great crashing noise reverberated from somewhere within the trees. Eden scanned the light from side to side, trying to pin down the sound. Without a second thought, Eden set off at a run through the trees.

Another crash thundered from somewhere ahead. Eden heard it above the sound of her ragged breaths and thumping heart. She paused and swept the light from right to left again. All she saw were the trunks of the trees standing like silent sentries.

"Eden, wait," Baxter said, charging up behind her and placing a hand on her upper arm.

"What are you doing? We need to get after him!" Eden pointed off into the forest. "This guy is dangerous!"

"Yeah, he's dangerous, but he's running away," Baxter said. "He's no threat to us right now. Right now, we get out of here and..."

Another noise jarred through the still night. It took Eden and Baxter a moment to realize what it was.

"A gunshot!" Eden shouted, instinctively leaping behind a nearby tree. When another gunshot didn't ring, Eden peered out, trying to work out where the sound had come from.

"I think it came from the house," Baxter shouted, pointing back towards the lake house which was now obscured behind a curtain of dense tree trunks.

"Oh no," Eden murmured. She swung back towards the house.

Running at full pelt, Eden and Baxter charged up the back steps.

Without breaking her stride, Eden sprinted through the kitchen and into the living area. She froze in mid stride, almost colliding with a table. The smell of cordite hung in the room.

Standing in the window, illuminated only by the dull light of the lamp nearby, Everett Van Wick pointed a gun into the chair where his father had been.

"No... no!" Eden shouted, picking up her pace again and rushing across the room. As she rounded the chair, her stomach felt as though it were knotting itself into a ball and climbing its way up her throat.

"This was not what we agreed," Eden roared. "He was supposed to face charges."

Rounding the large wingback chair, Eden saw exactly what she feared. Crumpled in the center of the red leather upholstery, taking up no more space than a child, sat Ludwig Van Wick. Blood bloomed from the front of his shirt, dripping down and pooling on the floor.

Eden froze and then stepped close to the man. Her fingers touched his neck but found no pulse. The old man was gone.

She shook her head and turned back to face Everett, her rage boiling over.

Everett Van Wick let the gun slip from his fingers, it thumped to the floor and the sound boomed through the quiet house like a death knell.

"We never should have brought you here," Eden snarled. "This man was not a threat. It was not supposed to end this way."

"He... he... I didn't mean..." Everett pointed with trembling fingers towards his father's body.

Baxter stepped forward and slipped a gun from Ludwig Van Wick's dead fingers. "He was going to shoot his own son." Baxter held up the gun. An image of a golden eagle glittered on the barrel. "Is this your father's gun?"

Everett nodded. "He kept that gun wherever he went. It's a Walther PPK Royal Eagle Edition."

Out of instinct, Baxter released the catch and the magazine slid into his palm. Baxter examined it closely, his eyebrows arching.

"What is it?" Eden said, sensing Baxter's intrigue.

Baxter didn't answer. Holding the gun securely, he pulled back the slide and checked the chamber. That was empty too.

"He couldn't have killed anyone with this." Baxter held up the PPK. "The gun's empty."

Baxter, Eden, and Everett Van Wick exchanged a long glance.

Eden then turned to look out through the door. She shook her head.

"Thorne," she muttered, almost under her breath. "I think we've underestimated him."

THREE MINUTES EARLIER, as Eden and Baxter turned and ran back towards the lake house, a cloud, exhausted from dumping its rain on the high mountain slopes, dissipated into nothing. Without the dampening effects of the cloud, light from the full moon beamed across the landscape once again.

As the milky-white light spilled through a crack in the canopy of the thick forests which lined the foothills, it illuminated a figure crouching out of sight behind the thick trunk of a pine tree.

Hearing Eden and Baxter's retreating footsteps, Thorne turned and peered from his hiding place. The last two minutes had been a nervous wait for the man, as he'd crouched out of sight. Of course, Thorne knew that he could have overpowered his pursuers in a single swipe, but he didn't want to.

As Eden and Baxter disappeared back towards the lake house, Thorne glanced down at his hands. His thick fingers were bloodied from his attack on the machine.

Thorne struggled to his feet. The shooting pain of his dislocated ankles, which would incapacitate any normal person, was little more than a tingle.

He glanced down at his feet. Deep gashes were cut into the skin just beneath his shins and his feet splayed outwards at a strange angle. They would heal soon enough.

He peered at the bloodstained coil of cable on the forest floor next to him. Smashing up the winching machine and pulling down the branch had all been for show really. Thorne just needed to get Eden and Baxter back out of the house.

"I told you," Thorne said, his voice now soft and almost amused. "You couldn't keep me locked up like some common animal."

He stood motionless, staring out into the forest for

several seconds. He took a deep breath of the damp night time air and, for a moment, just reveled in it.

Hearing Eden and Baxter run up the stairs at the back of the lake house, Thorne pictured the scene inside.

Thorne knew that his father would finish the job he'd begun, and he knew that Everett wouldn't go anywhere unarmed. People were so typical, Thorne had realized many years ago. They were so predictable in both their actions, and their assumptions about him.

Thorne slipped a hand into a pocket and felt the contents, cold and smooth against his fingers. He pulled his hand out and raised it to his face. Six rounds glittered on his palm like magic beads.

Thorne exhaled and threw the rounds down to the forest floor. In that moment he thought through his life so far and then considered the future.

"This isn't over," Thorne muttered. "But now I do it on my own terms."

Thorne exhaled, his breath came out like a jet of steam. Then, Thorne made one of the first decisions of his life. He chose a direction and hobbled away through the forest.

55

The British Museum, London, England. Five days later.

"I just don't get it," Eden said as Alexander Winslow paid the driver and they scrambled out of the bulbous London Taxi. "Eww, it's still raining," Eden said, crossing the cobbles and peering through the high iron bars at the porticos and columns of The British Museum. Although the museum had closed its doors to visitors several hours ago, lights still illuminated the impressive structure.

"You don't get why it's always raining in London?" Winslow said, flipping the collar of his coat up against the chill and striding towards the museum's main gate.

Although darkness now cloaked the streets of London, it had in truth been one of those English winter days when it never really got light to begin with.

"I don't understand that either," Eden giggled. "But that isn't my main concern right now."

"You've clearly been away too much. Londoners don't even notice the rain." Winslow pointed at a pair of people sitting outside a pub opposite and wearing summer clothes.

"What I don't get is why you think the *Lady of Leone* is still here," Eden said, steering them back to the topic at hand. "I wish I'd never shown you that marble," Eden groaned. Winslow had been teasing his daughter about her having not figured it out for the last five days.

"It's obvious, isn't it?" Winslow said, stepping up to the gate and pressing the button on an intercom system.

"Well clearly not, or I wouldn't be asking."

"Where else do you think she would be?"

"She could be anywhere. The moon. Outer Mongolia. Timbuktu," Eden said.

"Now you're just being silly." Winslow flicked his eyes towards his daughter.

Eden shrugged. "Yeah, agreed. But just because she wasn't in the crate, doesn't mean she's still here. Maybe someone could have got her out during the voyage to show a few passengers, and never put her back."

The intercom system buzzed, sounding like it was trying to connect with someone on the other side of the planet.

"It's not as simple as just pulling her out of the case," Winslow said. "Remember, they also kept her off the cargo manifest because they thought it might give people the heebie jeebies."

"Dad, I really wish you wouldn't use terms like '*heebie jeebies*.'"

"The willies, then" Winslow said, waving a hand.

"That's even worse," Eden groaned.

"You get my point, though," Winslow said. "There are several things to consider here. If the *Lady of Leone* wasn't in the crate, the chances are that she wasn't on the ship at all. Remember the chain that Van Wick's goons had to cut away?"

Eden nodded. She didn't think she'd ever forget the events of that harrowing night.

"There was only one man on the ship who had the key to unlock the crate."

"... so no curious ship workers could have got in there."

"Exactly," Winslow continued. "And that lock was place on the case, in this building..." He pointed through bars.

"At the Museum," Eden answered, stamping her feet in an attempt to stave off the cold.

"Then there's this," Winslow removed the marble from his pocket and held it up.

"That's the marble that *was* inside the crate." Eden took the small glass ball and peered inside. "Wait a second, there's a small figure inside the glass."

Winslow grinned. "Up there," he said, pointing to the figures carved in the portico of the British Museum.

"No way!" Eden said. "They're from the marble."

Far beneath the portico, Eden noticed a small figure wearing a parka coat step from one of the museum's side doors. The figure glanced up into the rain and then shoved the parka's fur-lined hood up over their head.

With the intercom still buzzing, Eden doubted that was the person they were waiting for. She reached around her father and jabbed at the button again. The buzzing noise continued to sound from the speaker.

"Almost the same," Winslow said, pointing at the marble. "The picture inside the marble is actually a replication of one of the statues which are displayed in this museum. Part of the Parthenon Marbles collection."

"A Parthenon Marble, inside a marble," Eden said playfully, before hardening her tone. "But the Parthenon is in Athens, Greece, right?"

"Yep, but for all sorts of horrible colonialist reasons, the statues are here." Winslow said.

Eden reached forward and pressed the intercom harder this time. "Come on. Don't you know it's cold and raining out here."

"It's always cold and raining in this country," Winslow muttered. "That's why we drink so much tea."

"I don't follow," Eden said, her brow furrowed in thought.

"It warms you up doesn't it. A nice cup of tea after you've been out in the rain."

"No, not that!" Eden playfully slapped her father on the shoulder. "How do the Parthenon Marbles link to the *Lady of Leone?*"

The figure approached the gate. Eden and Winslow stepped to one side, assuming the person was probably just a member of staff making their way home.

"Well," Winslow said, huffing out a breath almost impatiently. "That all comes down to a man called…"

"Marcus Nettleby, pleased to meet you," the man wearing the parka coat said. He swung open the gate and peered up at Winslow and Eden.

Winslow turned and grinned at his daughter. "It all comes down to him." Winslow smiled, clearly enjoying Eden's confusion.

Ten minutes later, Marcus Nettleby opened the door of his office and beckoned Eden and Winslow inside. The small room, hidden deep within the bowels of the grand building, shared none of the structure's opulence.

"I was very excited to hear from you," Nettleby said, he turned to face Winslow. "I must say, it's an honor to finally meet you. I've followed your work for as long as I can remember."

Winslow thanked the curator, nodding deeply.

"Come in... come in... may I take your coats?" Nettleby wriggled out of his parka and hung it, still dripping from the rain, on the back of the door.

"It's fine," Eden said, slipping out of hers and placing it beside the museum curator's.

"Thank you for seeing us at such short notice," Winslow said, glancing around the office. "Great place you've got here."

"The pleasure is all mine," Nettleby said.

Eden glanced at the man, seeing him clearly for the first time. Probably in his sixties, he had the appearance of a man whose work came first. Several days of silver stubble clung to his chin like mountain snow and his hair was long and scruffy. He appeared to be every bit the museum curator.

Nettleby turned and swept a hand from left to right. "My office. I'm sorry it's not as grand as you'd expect. I'll make tea and then we'll get down to business." Nettleby shuffled towards a kettle set up on a simple wooden desk in the corner.

"I told you, tea is a necessity," Winslow whispered.

Eden's gaze swept through the room. A wooden desk, which could have been a museum piece in its own right, occupied the bulk of the space. The desk sagged under the weight of several giant tomes and stacks of paper. To one side, almost forgotten about, waited a laptop computer with its screen off.

"That's a beautiful piece," Winslow said, stepping towards a clock on the wall of the office. "Sir John Bennett made such wonderful pieces. The craftsmanship is something to behold."

"Yes, it's wonderful." Nettleby turned away from the

kettle and looked proudly at the clock. "It's been keeping time since my grandfather bought it from Bennett himself."

"Okay, okay!" Eden said, her impatience bubbling over. "I need to know what's going on here. You've told me how the *Lady of Leone* could still be here, that sounds reasonable. But you say this guy is responsible for that." Eden pointed at Nettleby who poured boiling water into three cups. "I mean, for this guy to have been involved diverting the *Lady of Leone* from *The Titanic*, he'd have to be almost a hundred and fifty!"

Nettleby laughed and turned to face his guests. He pointed at a stained G Plan coffee table surrounded by a cluster of sagging chairs.

"Young lady, don't you know that tradition dictates us not to get to the point of the conversation until the tea is ready and served," Nettleby said, shuffling towards the table and placing down three mis-matched mugs.

Winslow sunk into one of the chairs, Eden followed.

"I've told her this many times," Winslow said, tutting and shaking his head.

"But I can see you're eager to know, so I won't stand on ceremony any longer. I'm Marcus Nettleby the third. The man you're referring to is Marcus Nettleby the first, my grandfather."

Eden picked up one of the mugs with a faded Rosetta Stone design. "Okay, that makes sense. You've all worked here, at the museum?"

"Archaeology is something of a family curse, I'm afraid." Nettleby pointed at Winslow and then Eden. "As you are both proof of."

Not to be put off, Eden leaped straight into the next question. "What did your grandfather do with the..."

Winslow raised a finger, silencing Eden, then removed

the marble from his pocket. He placed it on the table between them. "We wondered what you'd know about this."

Nettleby studied marble sitting perfectly still on the worn surface. He picked it up between his thumb and forefinger and peered through the glass.

"Well, I never," he said, inhaling. "It really is!" He looked at Eden, then Winslow, then back at the marble.

"This is one of those things that I'm going to have to show you," Nettleby said, launching back to his feet. "We need to go for a walk."

Eden for the tenth time in the last five minutes, rolled her eyes.

56

"A MARBLE WITHIN A MARBLE. It really is very clever," Nettleby said, leading Winslow and Eden out of his office and down another of the museum's subterranean corridors. They reached an elevator and ascended to the next level.

"But what does it mean?" Eden said, struggling to keep her patience under wraps.

"For that, we must travel back in time," Nettleby said, a whimsical tone in his voice. "When my grandfather took over as curator, he had the issue of too many artifacts and not enough space to display them in." Nettleby pushed them through a set of double doors and into a vast dark room. Following him inside, Eden felt cold air pass her skin.

"One moment," Nettleby mumbled, bumping around somewhere nearby. "There you are. I give you, the Parthenon Marbles." Nettleby clicked several switches and light flooded the room.

Eden drew a sharp intake of breath at the sight. Surrounding them on all sides, displayed carefully against the walls and on various pedestals, stood the world-renowned Parthenon Marbles. Eden stepped up close to one of them. The chunk of rock was around the size of a refrigerator, with various figures carved into the front. These objects were clearly beautiful, but there was also something slightly melancholy about them — like a great animal in a zoo — they felt so far from their rightful home.

Nettleby gestured toward the marbles, as if presenting them to his guests for the first time.

"The Parthenon Sculptures, previously known as the Elgin Marbles, are steeped in historical, artistic, and, unfortunately, political significance. You see, these pieces were originally part of the Parthenon in Athens, built in the 5th century BC. Then, Lord Elgin, who was the British Ambassador to the Ottoman Empire — then the rulers of Greece — acquired them at the start of the nineteenth century. The manner of this acquisition remains... questionable." Nettleby shrugged and then let his hands fall limp to the sides. "But, we are not politicians. So, here they are."

Eden spun around to face the curator. "Okay, but that was one-hundred years before *The Titanic* set sail without our *lady* on it. How does it all fit together?"

Winslow and Nettleby shared a glance. Winslow nodded in a gesture that said, *'you tell her.'*

Nettleby's eyes twinkled. Clearly the curator was delighted to delve into his knowledge with a captive audience.

"Right, yes. The Marbles were officially given to the museum in 1832, and for a long time were stored in another, much inferior, gallery. It was clear they would need to expand the museum to house these, and many other artifacts. But, as with all projects like that, it took a long time, a very long time. Almost one-hundred years, in fact." Nettleby removed his spectacles and cleaned them with the speed of a man who had nothing better to do.

Eden tensed her leg to prevent her foot from tapping impatiently.

"The result of that long-awaited expansion was this." Nettleby raised a hand towards the ceiling. "The Duveen Gallery, in which we're now standing. Named after Lord Duveen, the art dealer who funded its construction. The idea for this whole wing of the museum was first officially proposed at the end of the 19th century, although they'd already needed it for decades by then."

Winslow stepped across to one of the sculptures and examined it closely.

"This wing was designed as a grand, dedicated space for these wonderful things." Nettleby swept his arm in a flourish, indicating the spacious hall around them. "The project faced various delays and interruptions, including the First World War. Eventually, construction began in the late 1920s, and it was opened to the public in 1939."

Nettleby glanced from Eden to Winslow, then back at the marbles. "So, you see, when *The Titanic* set sail in 1912, plans for the Duveen Wing were already in motion, even though it would be years before construction began."

"I see," Eden said, holding the marble to her eye. "It's a shame that your grandfather never got to see it."

Nettleby clasped his hands together in front of him and stared down at the floor. "Yes, indeed it is. But his passion and dedication live on right here..." He made another sweeping gesture with his hand. "...and his sense of humor lives on too." Nettleby smiled, his eyes glinting in the museum's overhead lights.

"What do you mean?" Eden asked.

"Well, building the new wing gave the planners the unique chance to create some spaces, how shall I put it, that were off the books. If the rumors are to be believed, that is."

Eden pursed her lips and then her smile broke free.

"After my grandfather died, my father went back through his journals. Although he doesn't mention any specifics, he alludes to the inclusion of rooms beneath these floors that are not public knowledge."

"Why would they do that?" Eden said. "This is a museum, not a place for spies."

Nettleby and Winslow shared an amused glance.

"Oh, my dear, the worlds of archaeology and espionage are far closer than you might think. If these chambers exist, then they were designed to move things — be that artifacts or information — in and out of the museum without anyone noticing." Nettleby pointed at the marble which Eden still held between her thumb and forefinger. "That's why I was quite so excited when I heard from your father. I think that marble may tell us where to look."

Nettleby strode across to Eden and took the marble, then held it up to the light. "Interesting." Nettleby extended the word so that it was several syllables longer than normal. "You know, twenty years ago I would have been able to see this from an arm's length. Now I can't even make it out from here."

"I know the feeling," Winslow said, removing a leather pouch from his pocket. The Key to the Nile symbol glimmered from the worn leather. Winslow slipped a jeweler's loupe from the pouch and handed it to Nettleby.

"Perfect!" Nettleby said, excitedly. He fitted the loupe into his eye and then held the marble up towards the light. He turned the marble slowly while they all stood in silence. "Gosh this really is something. The detail is incredible, especially considering it must have been painted by hand."

Silence descended once again. Eden glanced from side to side, still trying not to tap her foot. She'd frequently spent time with her father's archaeological friends and knew that people like Nettleby just could not be rushed. They did things in their own time, or not at all.

"Ha!" Nettleby bellowed, his voice echoing through the gallery. "Of course, it is! Of course!" He removed the loupe and turned excitedly from Eden to her father and back again.

Eden shrugged as though to say, *'come on then.'*

"It's Dionysus of course! Hearing the tales of my grandfather that makes perfect sense — Dionysus was the god of wine after all! This way!" Nettleby scuttled off across the gallery. He stopped a few moments later in front of the statue of a reclining man.

"What now?" Eden stepped forward and stared intently at the figure. The statue's hands and feet were missing, but what remained was incredibly detailed.

"This is what my grandfather wanted us to see," Nettleby said, stepping forward and using the loupe again to examine the statue.

Nettleby's eyes scrutinized the statue through the loupe, sweeping meticulously over every detail. After what seemed like an eternity, he sighed, stepped back, and removed the loupe from his eye.

"This sculpture is a masterwork of Hellenistic artistry," he said, gesturing to the marble figure. "The precise chiseling that defines the musculature and drapery. Such anatomical fidelity." He leaned in close again.

Eden inhaled, it felt as though they were on the brink of discovering something.

"Even the high-relief carving of the hair is a testament to the craftsmanship. It beautifully captures the aura of Dionysus in stone. Sublime." Nettleby scowled, his expression turning dejected. "But despite its artistic splendor, it offers nothing that we didn't know already. Dionysus is exactly as he's been since my grandfather studied him all those years ago. Puzzling, truly puzzling."

Nettleby removed the marble from his pocket and examined it again. "When you get stuck, as my father used to say, go back to the beginning, and start again. Well..." Nettleby twittered.

Eden stepped forward just as Nettleby turned, the loupe once again clamped to his eye. The pair collided, and then both took a step backward.

"I'm so sorry," Nettleby murmured. "I was just involved in..." he raised his fingers, but the marble wasn't there.

"Where is it?" Eden asked.

"I don't... I had it a moment ago..."

"There!" Winslow said, pointing at the marble which Nettleby had dropped and was sitting on the polished stone floor at their feet.

"There you are!" Nettleby said, crouching down to retrieve the marble.

Then, Eden saw something. "No stop!" She shouted, seizing Nettleby by the shoulder.

The curator acted as though an electric shock had just moved through him and shot back up to his feet.

"What is it?" he muttered.

Eden pointed down at the marble. "It's moving!"

All three of them gathered around the marble. Sure enough, it had started to roll. With the highly polished floor of the museum offering little friction, the marble accelerated.

"I don't understand, surely this floor is level?" Eden said.

"Worn by the shoes of millions of visitors a year," Nettleby said, dismissively. "I suppose it wouldn't take much of a descent for a glass ball to roll on polished marble." The curator bent to pick up the marble again.

"Wait," Eden said, a thought striking her like a physical blow. "What if the movement isn't an accident? Maybe this is what your grandfather is trying to tell us. Maybe the uneven floor was designed twenty years before this place opened."

The curator glanced up at Eden. His bushy eyebrows slid up his forehead, giving him an owl-like appearance.

"There's one way to find out." Winslow stepped back out of the path of the marble which was now picking up speed towards the center of the room.

Eden shuffled after the marble, keeping her eyes locked on the speeding ball. Reaching the gallery's center, the marble swung to the left. The movement was uncanny, appearing as though the thing was controlled by an invisible hand.

Eden watched it go, her eyes never leaving the tiny glimmering ball.

After making the turn, the marble straightened up and whizzed through the ghostly shadow of the 'Sculpture of Venus.' Scurrying past the sculpture, Eden couldn't help but glance up at Venus. The sculpture regarded the scene, as though judging these mortals for their strange behavior.

The marble accelerated again now, down the center of the gallery, causing Eden to break into a run. Two steps behind Eden, Winslow easily kept up the pace. A few feet behind Winslow, Nettleby huffed and puffed his face already glowing like a beetroot.

The marble rolled on, faster and faster towards a large horse's head. Expecting the marble to slow or turn, Eden decelerated into a walk. But the marble did no such thing.

In fact, the tiny ball accelerated and then struck the pedestal on which the horse's head was displayed.

Leaving the floor completely, the marble pinged to the left. It bounced twice and then rolled again, tracing a wide arc to the right. As though running on an invisible track, the marble veered around an ornate vase.

Watching the marble move, Eden thought it looked like one of those weird optical illusions.

Finally, the marble's course straightened up as it set off back in the direction of Dionysus.

Eden glanced behind her and noticed that her father was still on her tail, with Nettleby grunting further back.

As the marble honed back in on their starting point, Eden felt a sinking feeling. Maybe they had just been chasing a small lump of glass around the natural undulations of the gallery's floor.

At the last second, the marble swerved hard and made a beeline for the far corner of the gallery. Eden peered in the direction the ball was now running. There were no exhibits or lights positioned in that corner.

The marble slowed now, turning at such a speed that Eden could see the flickering picture deep inside the glass.

Eden slowed in pursuit, now just walking alongside the ball. She jogged a few paces and reached the corner before the marble. Then, she crouched down and watched the marble roll towards her. The miniature image of Dionysus spun head over heels three more times before the ball stopped dead against the wall.

Eden held her breath, listening for any sound that might give her a hint of what to do next.

When nothing happened, Eden stood, and took a step backward.

Winslow crouched down and studied the marble in

silence. Eden figured he was playing his cards close to his chest so as not to embarrass himself in front of the curator. She knew these academic types were always trying to "out knowledge" each other.

Nettleby bumbled up beside them, wheezing like a steam train.

"This is it," Eden said, her tone dry. "The secret we've all been waiting for." She pointed at the section of wall before them.

"But... I... that's just a section of wall," Nettleby said, stepping up to the wall.

Eden stepped alongside the curator and studied the plaster too. She ran her hands up across the wall, checking for indentations. She also poked at the floor just beneath to make sure it wasn't some kind of well-hidden trap door.

"Hmmm, the road to success is fraught with wrong turns," Nettleby said, placing his hands on his hips and stepping away from the wall.

Winslow cleared his throat. "Maybe it was just an uneven floor after..."

At that moment, a cold breeze ripped through the gallery. The hairs on the back of Eden's neck rippled with a sensation she was all too used to.

"And I think this is where we take over." Came a voice Eden recognized without having to turn around.

"Thorne," Eden whispered.

57

Although hearing Thorne's voice from the gallery's entrance, Eden continued staring at the wall. In that moment she realized that her first assumption had been correct, but the builders had done an incredible job. To the untrained eye, the wall was like any other in the gallery. But now, having noticed what she had a moment before Thorne's entrance, it screamed at her like a thousand-watt loudspeaker.

Eden felt the familiar excitement of a discovery flutter within her.

"Like the rest of the world, you have underestimated me. That was a mistake," Thorne said, his voice resounding through the gallery. He took a step forward and glanced around the room. "I knew you were going to discover something of mine... my family's... I want it now, to continue my father's work."

"Thorne plus four men," Winslow hissed, telling Eden what they faced. "All armed. Experienced mercenary types, I'd say."

"I'm sorry, but you have no business being in here,"

Nettleby said, striding forward as though addressing a group of unruly school children.

Winslow lunged forward, attempting to stop the curator, but Nettleby was already out of reach.

Thorne grinned down at the little man, treating the interruption like that of an irritating fly.

"You must be the curator here," Thorne sneered. "For a century you've gotten away with hiding something of ours. Not anymore."

"Yes, I am one of the hardworking people who keep the heritage of the world safe for the next generation." Nettleby seemed to grow in stature as he addressed the beastly Thorne. "I'm afraid you won't be taking anything out of here tonight, or at any time. And, right now, you're going to have to leave and come back during the proper opening hours."

Thorne's rubbery lips twisted into a cruel smile. The brute nodded and his men raised their weapons and fired. The deafening sounds of gunshots filled the gallery. Strobing muzzle flashes illuminated Thorne's twisted snarl.

Nettleby cried out in pain clutching his chest. He glanced up at the ceiling, his eyes as round as those of the surrounding statues. The curator crumpled to the floor. Blood ran through his fingers and spiraled across the tiles.

Eden spun around upon hearing the gunshots. She screamed for Nettleby to move, to seek refuge behind one of the statues, or at least dive to the floor. But she knew that her warning was already too late.

Eden rushed forward, grabbed Nettleby by the shoulders, and dragged him back to their position by the wall.

"Take this," Eden said, forcing the marble into Winslow's hand. Then, very quickly explained what she'd realized the moment before Thorne had arrived. "I'll distract Thorne. You get ready to move, okay?"

Winslow nodded and rolled the marble between his thumb and forefinger.

"It doesn't have to be this way," Thorne said, taking a step forward and levelling his gun at Eden.

The gallery now reeked of cordite. A cool breeze blew through from whatever window or door Thorne had smashed on his way in.

"You take me to the *Lady of Leone*, then my men and I will be on my way. I am not like my father, I don't kill for sport."

"You think I trust you?" Eden shouted.

Nettleby groaned softly from the floor as the last bit of color drained from his face.

"If I show you to the *Lady of Leone*, you'll get what you want, then kill us all anyway."

Eden noticed that the swelling in Thorne's face had receded. She wondered whether that was because he was unable to get dosed up on whatever drugs they gave him back at the mansion.

"No," Thorne said, mockingly. "I'm not a reckless murderer. I'm doing this for science."

Winslow took a step backwards towards the wall.

Noticing one of the guards eying her father, Eden laughed out loud and then clapped her hands. The jarring noise had the desired effect, and all eyes were now on her. So was the ugly snout of each rifle.

"They really don't make bad guys like they used to," Eden said, taking on the persona of a playground bully. "Nowadays you people are all so sensitive, you all claim to have a *mission* and a *purpose*." Her fingers became quote marks. "It's all rubbish. You're just a thug using some fictional lofty goal to make what you do seem less barbaric."

Thorne's leathery tongue moved around his lips.

"Nonsense." Thorne pulled the rifle tight against his chest. His muscles bulged, threating to bend the gun out of shape. "The Van Wicks have been working on this for centuries. I am part of our body of work, so is my brother, and so was my father. We all know our place within the family."

"Your father didn't seem happy with it when you engineered your brother shooting him," Eden quipped.

Winslow took another step backward. The heel of his left shoe tapped against the wall.

Eden took a small step to the left to cover her father's movements.

Thorne smiled more widely then ever at the mention of his father's death. "My father's time was over. Now, thanks to you, a new Van Wick dynasty has begun."

"We've ended your family," Eden said. She stared deep into Thorne's oil-colored eyes and prepared to move.

Winslow turned around and noticed instantly what Eden had described. There was a tiny hole in the plaster about four feet above the floor. The hole was so small and insignificant that it was unlikely to be noticed by someone just passing by. Anyone who did notice it would probably just think it was an imperfection in the plaster.

Winslow extended his arm and placed the marble inside the hole. As Eden had described, the marble fitted perfectly.

"Nonsense," Thorne said, his lips jutting out like a bullfrog. "This is just the beginning. With the *Lady of Leone*, and my father's plans, I can create everything I need."

But Eden wasn't listening to Thorne, she was tuned in to her father's movements.

Winslow gave the marble a shove and it disappeared out of sight. The marble rattled down a series of channels deep inside the wall.

"Then what?" Eden said. "Let me guess, you're going to take over the world?"

Eden heard the sound and lowered her center of gravity by leaning forward and bending her legs. She expected something to happen but had no idea what it might be.

"That's none of your business right now." Thorne studied Eden as though she were little more than a curiosity. "But I could get you a front row seat. Having someone like you around could be helpful."

Eden didn't respond as she was listening to the marble rattle down below the level of the floor. Then, all went silent.

Thorne raised an eyebrow.

The moment of silence stretched into an eternity.

Then, a low rumbling echoed through the gallery. It sounded as though it was coming from deep beneath the floor, like an earthquake several miles away. The exhibits vibrated on their pedestals and the lights on the ceiling shuddered.

Eden felt the floor tremble beneath her feet. The vibration increased until it felt like the earth was preparing to swallow them whole.

"What have you done?" Thorne roared, his face turning ashen. Not wanting to waste another second, the giant man lunged forward, his private army following. Thorne sprinted across the gallery like an angry bull. Although the gallery was large and Thorne was probably forty feet away, Eden knew it wouldn't take him long to close the gap.

"Come on, come on!" Eden shouted, crouching now, and shuffling towards the wall. Then, as though obeying Eden's instructions, the floor below them gave way.

"We're going down!" Eden shouted, gripping onto her father with one hand and Nettleby with the other.

The giant marble slab which they were standing tilting down at the end nearest the wall. The lowering slab revealed a passage, which would usually be hidden beneath the floor.

"That way," Eden roared, pointing at the opening.

Winslow launched himself into the void first. Eden slid Nettleby inside and then ran through herself. Once they were no longer on the moving section of the floor, the great marble slab rose again. Eden watched the gap close just as Thorne appeared, his face now an angry purple.

The sound of gunfire tore through the grinding of the moving floor. Eden pushed further into the passage, until she was out of harm's way.

Then, in the total darkness, Eden felt herself falling. She was slipping forward and then sideways, picking up speed, sliding down a slick surface. She scrabbled around, trying to grab something to arrest her fall. Everything she touched was smooth, offering nothing to hold on to. Eden gave up trying to stop and leaned forward, grabbing hold of her father with one hand and Nettleby's coat with the other. The three of them spun and twisted further into the void.

58

THORNE STARED at the spot where a moment ago a passage had been. The brute snorted out a breath, his nostrils flaring like a bison.

"Open that up," he growled, pointing a finger at the wall. "I don't care how you do it, but open that up!"

The men swung the rifles towards the section of the floor which they'd seen rise to block the passage. Without waiting for a command, the men fired into the floor. Chips of marble and dust wafted into the air, scattering around the room. Several rounds ricocheted away into priceless artifacts.

When the guns had clicked empty, Thorne stepped forward to examine the mess. Although the floor's marble slab now lay in tatters and the wall was shredded into blocks of plaster, the door remained stubbornly shut.

"Use the tools," Thorne roared. "Don't waste time. I need that open, now!"

Two men retrieved a pair of duffel bags from the corridor. The men unzipped the bags and distributed an assortment of pry bars, sledgehammers, and electric drills around the group.

Armed with their tools, Thorne's men rushed to the site of the sealed door. They wedged pry bars into the cracks in the shattered marble, and smashed sections to bits with the hammers. The careless thumping and grunting noise of demolition filled the gallery.

Thorne watched it all in silence, his anger slowly bubbling into full-scale rage.

Thirty seconds later, Thorne reached boiling point.

"Give me that," Thorne snapped, striding forward, and snatching a sledgehammer from one of the men. The man fell to one side under the force of Thorne's shove. Thorne marched forward and swung the hammer high and hard, lacing the blow with all his pent-up rage. The impact reverberated throughout the chamber, sending a spiderweb of cracks radiating out from the point of contact.

Thorne pulled out a chunk of marble the size of a washing machine with his bare hands and threw it to one side. He stared down into a small opening.

"Flashlight, now!"

One of the men passed him a flashlight and Thorne shone the beam into the hole.

"That's it," he grunted, then he lifted the hammer again. "Get this opened up, now."

∾

SLIDING THROUGH OBSIDIAN DARKNESS, an unknown distance below, Eden heard Thorne yelling orders to his men. The sound of gunfire rang down the shaft, the rounds thudding uselessly into rock, or wood, or whatever the structure was constructed from.

In the confusing blackness of the descent, Eden's mind remained sharp. She figured that even though the floor had closed behind them, Thorne knew where they had gone, and it wouldn't take him and his men long to smash their way through. For now, though the balance had tipped both literally and figuratively in their direction.

Sliding further downwards, Eden noticed a change in the air. It was cooler and more humid down here.

Eventually, and as quickly as their movement had begun, they slowed and then came gently to a stop.

Not losing a moment, Eden scrambled dizzily to her feet. She patted herself down and was relieved to find that she still had her flashlight. She turned it on and swept the beam around their new surroundings.

The descent had deposited them in a cavernous underground vault. Built in the same style as the gallery upstairs, the vault had Grecian columns reaching up to a ceiling twenty feet overhead.

As Eden moved her beam around the space, the light danced across elaborate friezes on the walls which mimicked those in the museum above.

"I don't think I've ever seen anything quite like this," Winslow said, sidling up beside his daughter. "In this frieze they've mixed divinity with humanity, that's very unusual."

Eden checked out the figures for a moment, then turned her attention to the columns which punctuated the space every six feet or so. She ran a finger across the marble and noticed it came away damp.

"The humidity is good for storing artifacts. It's actually much better than at ground level, because it's constant all year round."

Eden spun around on hearing the voice and saw

Nettleby sitting up and rubbing a hand on the back of his head. The curator then groaned and grasped at his chest.

Eden stared at the man for several seconds as though he had just come back from the dead.

Nettleby slipped a hand inside his parka coat and withdrew a small hip flask. "My grandfather's flask. Marcus Nettleby the first always claimed that carrying a flask brought him good luck. Strangely, he forgot it the day he left for *The Titanic*." Nettleby ran a hand across his shirt and jacket which was now slick with the spilled wine. "He used to fill it with claret too. Apparently, it's better for you than whisky, and keeps the chill off just the same."

Winslow crossed the vault and plucked the flask out from between Nettleby's fingers.

"Your grandfather's investment in high-grade stainless steel was a good one," Winslow said, examining the flask which was dented and cracked. "I'm afraid you won't be using that again, though." The Nettleby crest which adorned one side had been distorted by the impact. Winslow sniffed at the flask. "Let me guess, Chateau Bateaux?"

"The very same," Nettleby said, glancing up at Winslow. "I wouldn't leave the house without it." Nettleby tapping the ground around him. "Now, where are my specs?"

Using the flashlight, Eden found Nettleby's eyeglasses on the floor nearby and passed them across. Nettleby fitted them back into position and then gasped as though he was now the one to see a ghost. The small man struggled to his feet and turned one way and the next, his eyes bulging with amazement.

"My word, my word!" he mumbled. "I've heard rumors of such places, sure, but never expected this place to actually exist. This is something... something incredible."

Nettleby darted across the room and started searching the various alcoves set into the walls. Eden followed Nettleby's gaze with the beam of her flashlight and noticed the alcoves housed artifacts like the museum upstairs. Unlike the museum, though, these weren't behind glass or ropes.

"Well.... I never thought I would..." he stuttered, clearly unable to formulate his words. He turned towards Winslow and then Eden. "Do you know what this is?"

Eden turned towards an object which sparkled in the beam of her flashlight.

"It's an astrolabe," Nettleby said, leaning in close. "It's an ancient instrument used for solving problems related to time and the position of stars. But this one ... this one is unlike any I've ever seen..."

Winslow crossed to another alcove which contained a set of stone tablets. "I think this is Sumerian," he said, scratching his chin. "But it's not just a recounting of trades or laws. This seems to be a narrative, a story of some kind."

"Could it be another version of the Epic of Gilgamesh?" Eden asked.

"No," Winslow shook his head. "At least I don't think so. I don't think I've ever seen this phrasing before."

Like a child at Christmas, Nettleby moved on to another alcove, this one containing an elaborate golden mask. "From the Mycenaean period, I think." He pointed at the object with his little finger. "The craftsmanship! Masks like this were made to honor great kings or warriors. I've never seen one quite like this before."

"There are a lot of secrets down here." Eden examined a golden sphinx which reminded her of a similar, although much larger vault which they had discovered beneath the Giza Plateau.

"It's astounding," Nettleby muttered. "The scope of these

objects extends much further than any collection I've seen before."

Eden glanced around, her flashlight beam playing over countless treasures that defied explanation.

A crash echoed down the entrance shaft, jolting them all back into the urgency of their situation.

"It sounds like we don't have much time." Eden turned back towards the shaft and inspected it with the beam of her flashlight. A spiral ramp, like a chute, ran around the outside of the shaft, with steps on the inside. The system was clearly designed for people to use the stairs, and larger objects or artifacts to be lowered down the chute.

Another boom reverberated down, followed by the sound of shattering rock.

"There's more," Winslow said, pointing at an opening at the far end of the vault. "I think it's probably a good idea that we aren't still down here when they get that door open."

A louder crash came, followed by a splinter of light which cut through the gloom.

"I agree," Eden said, watching the light from above increase. "I don't think they'll be very long, either."

Another crash followed, sending a cloud of dust drifting down into the vault.

"They're here for the *Lady of Leone*," Eden said, turning back to the chamber. "Thorne won't be interested in any of this other stuff."

"And, I expect this is her," Nettleby said, pointing at a the largest alcove in the room.

"Really?" Eden said, suddenly excited, although not quite believing it to be true. Finding this artifact had involved so many red-herrings and obstacles, Eden had started to doubt they would ever actually find the *Lady of Leone*.

Winslow and Eden stepped up to the alcove. Eden shone the light inside.

A long, thin crate was positioned sideways in the alcove.

"It's similar to the one we recovered from *The Titanic*," Eden said, touching the cold metal.

"Perhaps a bit thinner. I suppose this one wasn't designed to withstand the bumps of the journey."

"We should open it, right?" Nettleby said.

"Absolutely," Winslow replied, without even thinking.

Winslow ran his fingers across the front edge. "There's a joint here. It opens like a freezer."

Winslow and Nettleby gripped the lid.

A thunderous crash rolled down the shaft, followed by the distant sound of raised voices. Eden's muscles tensed — soon it would be time to fight or fly.

"On the count of three," Winslow said, before counting down. The two men heaved open the lid and a cloud of frozen air drifted into the vault.

"She's... she's still frozen?" Nettleby said, in amazement.

"This must be attached to some power source," Winslow said, examining the crate. "Very impressive engineering for the 1930s."

"I'm glad I'm not paying to keep the freezer on for one-hundred years," Eden muttered.

"Shine the light inside," Nettleby beckoned Eden across.

Eden held the light high and directed the beam inside the crate.

"Oh my... just..." Nettleby stuttered.

"And there she is," Winslow said.

Eden shuffled between the men and gazed into the crate. Lying inside, looking as though she were just asleep, was the *Lady of Leone*. Amazingly, she looked just as she had in the photograph from all that time before.

"They were a prudish lot back then." Nettleby pointed at the white cloth, which was wrapped around the body, the color almost matching her skin. Her long black hair swept down across her chest.

Eden felt the chill from the crate sting her face.

"The trick to preservation is the cold," Nettleby said, his teeth chattering. "My grandfather's journals said that she had to be kept at a very cold temperature all the time. It made working on her a challenge but was worth it. I studied my grandfather's journals, you see. He gave a detailed account of her, and of course there are the photos."

"There was a time when I didn't think we'd find her at all." Winslow stared fixated at the frozen body.

"This certainly is no ordinary artifact," Nettleby murmured, captivated by the sight.

"No," Eden said, inhaling.

Another crash echoed from the shaft followed by a bright light streaming down into the vault.

"But, I'm afraid our time is up. We've got to go." Eden locked eyes with Winslow and then Nettleby.

"What are we going to do about her?" Nettleby said, pointing at the *Lady of Leone*. "After all these years we've found her. We can't just leave her here for those... those mercenaries!"

The curator was clearly much more worried about losing an ancient artifact than his own safety, a fact that Eden deeply respected.

"I've got at idea," Eden said, glancing at Nettleby's stained shirt and coat. "But I'm going to need you to get undressed."

59

"Your time is up. Your only chance of survival is to give me what is mine." Thorne led his men slowly down the spiral staircase.

Before stepping into the opening, Thorne and his men had clipped flashlights to the barrels of their rifles. These lights now swept through the shaft as they picked their way down the narrow stairs.

"If you surrender now, and hand over what I want, then I will let you live."

Reaching the final curve in the spiral staircase, Thorne held up a hand and commanded his men to stop.

Without warning, Thorne leaped down the remaining staircase and into the vault. He landed deftly in the center of the room, sending a shudder through the ancient stones. Thorne completed a full three-sixty of the room. Besides several glimmering artifacts, the room was empty.

Thorne growled and then beckoned his men down. The men moved into position behind their leader, fanning out to cover the full width of the room.

"Search for the *Lady of Leone*," Thorne instructed. "If you see any of them, shoot to kill."

The men made quick work of the search, sweeping their flashlights through the various alcoves.

"Sir, sir, look at this!" One of the men waved Thorne over to the crate.

Thorne peered inside the crate, a vein in his temple throbbing with frustration.

"She was here," he grumbled. "They have her. They can't have got far."

"Sir, the body of that guy we shot," another man said, pointing at a prone figure right at the back of the vault. The body was lying in such a position the men had missed it as they came down the stairs. The man had landed face down on the floor, his long parka coat covering the back of his head.

"Shall I check him for vitals? He might still be alive."

"No, leave him," Thorne snarled. "He's of no use to us."

"There's another passage, sir. And there's a light."

Thorne charged forward and saw the faint light moving in the distance down the passage. Eden and Winslow were on the move.

"It's them," Thorne snarled, recognizing the unmistakable sound of fleeing footsteps. "After them, now!"

The men broke into a sprint, their boots thudding against the stone. Thorne pushed his way to the front, his eyes narrowed. No one was escaping, not today.

∼

"ARE you sure we should have left the *Lady of Leone* there," Nettleby said, as Eden met them further down the passage, thirty seconds later.

Maneuvering the frozen corpse out of the freezer had been easier than Eden imagined, using Nettleby's thick parker coat as insulation. Slipping Nettleby's clothes around her and arranging her at the bottom of the stairs as though Nettleby had fallen that way, was easier still.

The curator shivered, now just wearing underwear and a vest. He had given his clothes willingly, though, saying it was a small price to pay for the *Lady of Leone's* safety.

"Absolutely," Eden said, not breaking her stride. "We'll lead them off into the tunnels and then you can head back and get her back in the freezer. We can't stop now, though, they're coming this way." Eden quickened her pace.

Nettleby broke into a run, his little legs struggling to keep up.

The sound of running footsteps came from somewhere behind them.

Eden led them into a narrow passage, barely wide enough for them to walk shoulder-to-shoulder. Angular shadows danced on the walls around them as they pushed forward, listening to the rumble of feet somewhere behind them.

"Do you know where this goes?" Nettleby said, panting.

"No idea. As long as it's away from them, that's good enough."

Eden swept her light around the tunnel, trying to figure out where they might end up. Constructed from bricks, with pipes and wires winding their way along the ceiling, the tunnel gave no indication of its destination.

"Electrical wires are a good sign," Winslow said. "It means this tunnel connects up to somewhere."

Eden kept the light low. Having drawn Thorne away from the vault, Eden hoped they could lose him in the tunnels and then find a way back up to ground level.

The further they ran, the more the walls felt as though they were closing in. The air became heavy, and Eden had the awful sensation they were heading towards a dead end.

After they'd been on the move for nearly five minutes, a curve appeared in the tunnel ahead. Without a backward glance, Eden ran around the bend. It felt good to put a couple of twists and turns between them and their pursuers.

They emerged into a broader, arched tunnel. The scent of mildew and rust became stronger. Eden swept her light around and recognized the iconic wall tiles which lined so many of the London Underground stations. The light played over a pair of 'Keep Calm and Carry On,' war-time propaganda posters pinned high on the wall. Another poster gave directions to a first aid post. Eden paused and glanced back at her father and Nettleby.

"What is this place?" Eden asked. "It's like we've stepped back in time."

"This is the disused British Museum Underground Station," Nettleby said, panting. "It's a ghost station. I've known for a long time that it was here but didn't know it was directly accessible from the museum."

"It is pretty haunting," Eden said.

"It was used as an air raid shelter during the Second World War too," Nettleby continued, his voice little more than a whisper. For a moment Eden imagined what that must have been like for the people of London — hearing bombs raining down on their homes above, and not knowing what would be left when they returned.

The station platforms and tracks had been removed in this section, making the entire space one level.

"We've got to keep moving," Winslow said, striding forward.

Eden swung her flashlight towards a faded, peeling sign

that read 'British Museum' above the iconic London Underground blue and red sign.

"It was closed down in the 1930s. Part of the Central Line," Nettleby added. "It's now used as a maintenance depot. I had no idea it connected to the chamber we were just in. That's some crazy planning or an incredible coincidence."

Eden glanced at a set of posters advertising plays and products from decades past.

"There's no such thing as a coincidence," Eden said as they pushed on through the empty station. "Whoever designed that vault, did this on purpose."

"It sounds very convenient that they closed down the station at the same time the new museum wing was opened." Winslow said. "This is the perfect way to get things in and out of the museum without being noticed."

A distant rumble reverberated through the tunnel, causing the trio to pause again. This noise wasn't coming from the direction of their pursuers, though. It came from the other way entirely. The noise grew progressively louder, hissing and groaning as metal scraped against metal.

Eden recognized the clatter of wheels on tracks and the whoosh passing air. Somewhere up ahead, a train thundered along the rails.

"This connects to a live line somewhere up ahead," Eden said. "It sounds close too."

"That's Holborn Station," Nettleby said. "It's less than a hundred feet away. That's why the British Museum station was closed."

"That's our way out," Eden said, charging forward. "We need to get on that train."

The noise of the rumbling train turned into a hiss and then a screech as it slowed for the station.

"Quickly!" Eden shouted, setting off at an all-out sprint.

"Not more running," Nettleby sighed, grimacing behind her.

A few feet further on, Eden could see the glow from the station. They pushed on and arrived at a junction in the tunnel. The tracks of the working underground train sparkled in the light.

Eden turned and saw the train idling in the station just twenty feet away.

"Go, go, go!" Winslow shouted, already sprinting down the tracks.

Eden pulled a deep breath and set off after her father. The tunnel reeked of engine oil. The ground between the tracks was uneven, slowing progress.

Nettleby panted from the rear. Eden turned around, grabbed the small man by the hand, and pulled him on.

"I swear, if I get out of this," Nettleby hissed between gasps. "I'm going to the gym."

For some reason, Eden found the comment especially amusing. She grinned, pulling the curator on.

They reached the rear of the train and heard the station's public address system.

"Mind the gap," the operator said. "This train is ready to depart."

An electronic beeping noise sounded, indicating the doors were about to close.

Winslow was already up on the platform and closing in on the nearest door. The bright lights of the station dazzled the trio.

"Go!" Eden shouted, pushing Nettleby up and on to the platform with all her strength. Nettleby ran as fast as he could, slipping between the doors as they started to close.

Eden hoisted herself up the platform and charged full

pelt for the doors which were now closing. Her toes dug into the solid ground of the platform, pushing her, urging her forward.

What happened next, did so in slow motion. The door of the train slid shut with a thump. Eden stopped herself a moment before colliding with the train. She tried to claw at the gap, but the doors remained locked.

Winslow paled and then ran across to the emergency stop lever. Eden banged on the side of the train and then shook her head. Getting Nettleby and her father out of here safely was a blessing. For a long moment she peered through the door at her father, bedraggled but safe. Then glanced at Nettleby, just wearing his vest and underwear having given his clothes to the *Lady of Leone*.

"A true gentleman," Eden muttered, stepping away from the train.

With a hiss of hydraulics and the whine of electric motors, the train slide from the platform. It picked up speed, and a moment later Winslow and Nettleby were out of sight.

Eden turned and gazed into the now empty, yawning mouth of the tunnel. There in the tunnel, five flashlight beams whipped from side to side. Thorne and his men were closing in.

"Why won't you just die," Eden groaned, spinning back around and again watching the lights of the train slide away.

60

Panic beating in her ears, Eden sprinted down the platform. She heard the raised voices of Thorne's men as she fled. Five against one wasn't just bad odds, it was a massacre. Eden wished she'd been able to bring a weapon. This was supposed to be a simple meeting with a museum curator, not an all-out firefight.

Thinking she might be able to call for help, Eden pulled out her phone. An icon flashed at the top of the screen warning that she had no signal.

"Damn you, London Underground," Eden said, running down the platform. "How does every other metro system on the planet manage to have a phone signal?"

At that time of the evening, the platform was empty. Passing beneath a large digital display, Eden glanced up. The last train of the day was due to arrive in three minutes. If she could survive three minutes, Eden figured, then maybe that train would be her chance to get away. The other option was a game of cat and mouse through the streets above.

A bullet streaked forth and Eden instinctively swerved

for a small passageway to her right. She got inside the moment before three more bullets smashed into the tiles. Eden spun around and stared carefully back down the platform.

Thorne led his men up onto the platform, firing haphazardly towards Eden. Another barrage of gunfire boomed through the tunnel, chipping away a row of tiles a few feet away.

She glanced the opposite way down the platform and saw the signs guiding passengers to the street exit. She checked out the passageway in which she was sheltering. It was one of the short tunnels that led from one platform to the other. Twenty feet away she could see the platform for trains going in the other direction.

Another flurry of gunfire boomed through the station. Eden ran down the passageway. Like most stations, Holborn Underground Station was a network of interlinking tunnels and passages — at the very least she wasn't cornered.

Eden picked up speed. She needed to reach the other platform before the men arrived at the end of the passage. Running past a small metal door set into the sidewall, an idea occurred to her. She glanced at the door and then stopped running, her feet sliding for a moment. She took a step back. A 'staff only' sign was pinned to the door. Her mind spun with ideas. The first thing she needed was a weapon. Failing that, she could do with a place to hide.

Another boom of gunfire echoed from behind her.

Eden grabbed the handle. The door was locked, but the mechanism felt worn out. She tugged at the handle hard. Something inside the lock clicked and then the door swung open. Eden ducked inside the room just as the first group of men rounded the corner and into the passage.

"Two of you that way." Thorne shouted instructions to his men. They were splitting up — that was good news.

Eden glanced around quickly. Her heart sank. The room was a cupboard for cleaning supplies. A few mops and buckets were piled up in one corner and a large shelving unit stored bottles of cleaning liquids.

Footsteps pounded past the door.

Eden checked out at the objects again. She would make do with what she had. Eden snagged up one of the mops and tested the strength of the handle. It was a solid length of metal. She pulled off the mop head and swung the handle around, testing its weight. Then she crossed to the shelving unit and inspected the various chemical cleaners. She grabbed one with skull and crossbones on the bottle and removed the lid. Whatever was in the bottle smelled dangerous.

Back at the door, Eden peered out into the passage. The men were now just reaching the other platform. Thorne and the other two were nowhere to be seen.

Eden slipped out of the store room with her makeshift weapons and moved silently towards the men who had just passed. They were closer, and Eden decided the longer she could put off dealing with Thorne, the better.

Up ahead, the men split up, heading in different directions down the platform. Without drawing attention to herself, Eden closed the gap.

At the end of the passage, Eden paused and glanced from one man to the other. Both stepped further down the platform, their guns raised, ready to open fire on anything that moved. Fortunately, both had their backs to Eden.

Eden turned right, coming up behind the man in just two paces. She drew back the metal handle and swung, aiming at the back of the man's knees. The man yelped as his legs buckled beneath him, causing him to drop to the floor. The man splayed out with his gun jammed beneath him and his hands outstretched.

Eden forced her heel between his shoulder blades.

The man squealed again, this time like a stuck pig.

Hearing the noise, the other man spun around, his gun raised. Eden reacted without hesitation and hurled the bottle of chemicals in the man's face. The bottle spun three times, sending an arc of the liquid splashing across the man's face. The man cried out, clawing at his eyes as the caustic substance burned.

Eden stepped off the first man's back and kicked him hard in the temple sending him into unconsciousness with a grunt.

With that man out of the game for a while at least, Eden seized her momentary advantage with the other. She spun the mop handle like a staff, striking the wrist of the hand that held the gun. The weapon clattered to the ground. She then shoved the man hard.

Still not able to see because of the chemicals in his eyes, he stepped back, his arms flailing. In what felt like slow motion, he stepped backward towards the platform edge. Still unable to find his balance, the man stepped back again. Out of space on the platform, his foot hit nothing but air. The man shouted in surprise and fell backward, crashing on to the tracks and bashing his head on the electric rail. Electricity sizzled and screams filled the station for a moment. Then all went silent.

Two men down, two more to go... and then Thorne. Although Eden wasn't sure that brute counted as a man.

Eden glanced at the overhead screen, wondering whether the next train in this direction might provide her ticket out of here. Although the body on the tracks probably ruled that out.

A flurry of gunfire reverberated down the passage, starting Eden back into action. The rounds hammered into the wall opposite, tearing a poster for a West End show into shreds.

Eden ran back towards the passageway, collecting the fallen man's rifle as she went. She swung the weapon around the corner and opened fire. After a quick burst of gunfire, Eden pulled the gun back and stepped away from the opening.

Footsteps echoed down the passage, but no one appeared.

Eden counted to three and then swung out around the corner and into the passage, rifle raised and ready to fire. There was no need. One man lay bleeding out in the center of the passage, and another sprinted away in the direction of the first platform.

Eden took aim carefully and sent a bullet through the fleeing man's thigh. He cried out in pain and sprawled to the floor ten feet from the passage end.

Not willing to lose her advantage, Eden dashed forward. She closed the distance between herself and the groaning man in just over a second. The man struggled up into a crawling position and tried to move out of her way.

"You're dead," he grunted weakly.

"You're entitled to your opinion," Eden replied, sending him into unconsciousness with a kick to the neck.

She snagged up the guy's full magazines and then kicked his gun out of his reach should he wake up before nap time was over. She refreshed her magazine and then stepped out onto the platform.

Twenty feet away, Thorne stood at his full height,

grimacing at Eden. In the brightly lit confined space, the man appeared even more beastly than Eden remembered.

"I'm going to enjoy this," Thorne said, his hands hanging limp at his sides like sleeping vipers. Although Thorne had a rifle, the weapon hung from a strap at his back.

Eden suspected that meant Thorne intended to kill her with his bare hands. She swallowed, but her throat tasted like dust.

"I'm pleased to see your face has cleared up," Eden said. "It must have been a reaction to the stuff that creepy doctor was giving you."

Thorne clenched his fists and his knuckles cracked.

Eden glanced up at the large electronic sign overhead. The train was due at any moment.

"I mean, you're still look like the Hulk, but..."

Eden was interrupted by the thundering of wheels on the rails from the open tunnel. Eden thought about the train speeding their way, but with Thorne so close, getting on the train wouldn't help at all.

"Enough. The time for talking is over. You had your chance." Thorne placed one fist inside the palm of the other and cracked his knuckles again.

Eden rolled her eyes. "Could you get any more clichéd? Is there a *'how to be a bad guy'* book that you all read with chapters on knuckle cracking and ominous things to say?"

Eden glanced up at the screen. The train was one minute away. Then, she noticed the system on which the screens were mounted. The whole thing was set inside a large metal and glass box with the screen system and a pair of security cameras attached and, most importantly, it was positioned right above Thorne's head.

"Any last words before I end this?" Thorne grunted.

The rumbling from the tunnel grew as the train neared. Wheels ground against rails. Brakes screeched. Air hissed.

"That's exactly what I mean!" Eden said. "You just said, *'the time for talking is over'*." Eden mimicked Thorne's deep voice. "Then you ask me a question. Is it any wonder people struggle to take you seriously?"

Eden swung the rifle up and fired into the mount that secured the sign to the tunnel's ceiling.

"Looking like a pig doesn't help, either. But if you were a nice guy, at least you'd be likeable."

Sparks flew as the bullets punctured their target. Eden kept pressure on the trigger, punching countless holes through the sign's wires and mounting. The screen strobed and wires snapped. The sign juddered.

Behind Eden, the train roared into the station. A wall of warm wind tumbled in ahead of it.

Eden kept her finger pressed on the trigger. Finally, the sign broke free of its supports and swung down.

Thorne raised his head a moment too late. The heavy sign smashed into his skull and shoulder. He took a step sideways to counter the blow.

The roar of the approaching train filled the station. Headlights swept across the tiles, making sharp shadows out of Eden and Thorne.

Now the brakes screamed.

Thorne took another step sideways, balancing like a top-heavy ballerina. He reached out, trying to grab something to steady his fall. His fingers groped uselessly, reaching towards nothing.

The train roared closer, sliding into the station.

Thorne stepped again, still out of balance. Eden watched the giant man teeter towards the rails and the speeding train.

Thorne took another step and almost caught his balance, but not quite.

The train whipped past Eden, sending her hair into a frenzy. She watched the scene, her body tense and her breath held.

Thorne teetered again, his immense bodyweight fighting against gravity like an ice-skating mammoth. He twisted away from the train and managed to hold his balance for another second as the train slid past him. Thorne visibly relaxed and fell against the side of the speeding train. Glass shattered and something inside Thorne's shoulder cracked.

Although the step a moment before saved Thorne from falling on the tracks, the impact of the speeding train sent him into a spin, cartwheeling across the station. He thumped against the wall, hard, dislodging several tiles which rained down on top of him. Thorne groaned, his eyes opening and closing several times.

Eden wasted no time. She spun around and dashed for the exit.

61

EDEN DREW out her phone as she ran up the escalator. Two things happened when Eden reached ground level. First, her phone chimed to inform her that she now had signal. Second, a large hulking figure lumbered towards the bottom of the escalators.

Eden locked eyes with Thorne — this guy was seriously getting on her nerves.

Then, Eden remembered something Van Wick Senior had said. She berated herself, frustrated that she'd not picked up on it at the time. All at once, a fully formed plan appeared in her mind. A plan which, if it worked, would deal with Thorne once and for all.

Eden leaped over the turnstile and took the final few stairs towards the street slowly — she wanted Thorne close behind.

Her phone buzzed and bleeped as notifications flooded in. There was no time to check them now.

At the top of the stairs, Eden glanced over her shoulder just in time to see Thorne reach the top of the escalator, break into a run and then leap over the turnstile in one stride.

Eden darted out into the street. It was now late in the evening, but the hustle and bustle of London continued.

A red double-decker bus, filled with people heading to the bars of central London, swished through a puddle. A pair of pedestrians hurried past, raincoats swinging around their ankles.

Eden strode into the road and flagged down a taxi. The car stopped immediately, and Eden climbed in.

"Tower Bridge, quick as you can," Eden said, taking a seat and then removing her phone.

She turned and watched the station exit. A few seconds after she'd leaped inside the taxi, Thorne appeared. The big man stepped out into the rain, water sloshing across his taut muscles.

Thorne turned one way, then the other, then noticed Eden's taxi splashing away. The brute stepped out into the traffic and forced a car to stop. The vehicle skidded to a stop, missing Thorne's shins by a few inches. Thorne rounded the front of the car and yanked open the driver's door. He tore the driver from the seat and threw her, sprawling and screaming to the road. Thorne climbed in and set off after Eden's taxi.

A moment later, two police cars slewed to a stop right outside the station. Their red and blue light bars glittered across the wet asphalt.

Eden minimized the notifications on her phone, and then called Baxter.

"Where are you?" he said, the relief in his voice palpable.

"Just leaving Holborn Station. Thorne's right behind me. Don't worry, I've got a plan."

"You and your plans," Baxter muttered, clearly knowing better than to make alternative suggestions.

Baxter listened silently as Eden explained what she needed him to do.

"I'll be there," Baxter said when she'd finished. "Stay in touch, okay?"

As the taxi powered through the streets, Eden scrolled through the messages on her phone. She read the final one, and then froze. It was a message she'd been expecting, and if she was honest, it was the result she was expecting too. She pushed it from her mind for now. That was something to deal with later.

Fifteen minutes later, the taxi rolled on to Tower Bridge. Eden turned and saw Thorne's car cutting through a large puddle right behind them.

"Just here, thanks." Eden handed over a note and sprang from the vehicle.

Eden stepped out onto the wet cobblestones and gazed up at the iconic bridge rising in front of her. The rain fell in sheets now, soaking the Gothic turrets and obscuring their reflection in the inky-black river.

At this time of night, the bridge was mostly empty, save for the occasional car that sped by.

Eden ran, crossing beneath the first tower and on to the bridge's central span. She reached the midpoint and turned around to face her pursuer.

London's skyline surrounded her on all sides. In the distance, The Shard's glass façade gleamed, and right beside the bridge the grim outline of the Tower of London squatted beside the water.

A car powered along the bridge and then screeched to a stop. The car's engine continued to run, headlights blazing.

Eden didn't have to see through the smeared glass to know who was inside.

The driver's door swung open, and Thorne stepped out. The vehicle's suspension howled in distress.

Eden took a few steps backward, edging further across the bridge.

Rain bounced from Thorne's shoulders as though he were made from stone. The brute paced towards Eden. With his clothes soaked through, Eden could see the movement of each muscle as the giant man closed the distance.

"Enough running," Thorne shouted, his voice rising against the hammering rain and the distant growl of the city. "You should have done what you were told when you had the chance."

"What, and miss having all these special moments with you?" Eden said in return. "It's this quality time with genetically engineered meat-head cyborgs that I live for."

Thorne took another two steps forward. Just fifteen feet away, Eden already had to crane her neck to lock eyes with the man-mountain.

Thorne's giant shoulders tensed giving Eden the impression that she was about to go head-to-head with a highly trained buffalo.

"Say what you want." Thorne pointed at his chest with a finger about as thick as Eden's wrists. "I am the future. You have no future."

"Ha! That's pretty funny for someone with your intellect. Did you read that in a book?"

Thorne charged forward, his feet thundering against the cobbles. He pulled back his right arm and swung a freight train of a hook directly at Eden's face. For such a giant man, he moved with surprising speed.

Fortunately, Eden was quicker. She saw the punch

coming and sidestepped, pivoting backward. The first shot passed her head, sending Thorne out of balance.

Eden rose nimbly on her toes and sent a flurry of kicks into Thorne's stomach. Sharp pain jarred through her shins as though she'd just kicked a brick wall. Although the attack caused Thorne no visible pain, it pushed him back half a step.

Thorne swept an open hand in a downward arc, clearly intending to grab Eden's ankle while she was mid kick. If he managed that, Eden knew he would throw her to the curb like a stuffed toy.

Eden aborted the kick, hopped backward, and dropped into her fighting stance. Her legs felt like white-hot steel was searing through her muscles.

"Quick feet," Thorne said. "But can you keep this up? I can do this all night." Thorne lunged forward again, this time abandoning his fighting technique and attempting to grab Eden between his giant hands.

"You really know how to get a girl excited," Eden said, kicking up with one leg and jabbing a knee into Thorne's face. She felt her kneecap strike his nose, but again it was like hitting rock.

Eden grunted in pain, but Thorne barely reacted. Eden pushed backward, just evading the swipe of his hands again.

As Thorne lunged forward, Eden saw her chance. She darted to the left and sent a succession of punches into his abdomen, before darting again out of the way.

Thorne grunted and retreated a whole step. It wasn't much, but it was the closest thing Eden had gotten to a reaction. In contrast, her body ached, both from the exertion of the fight and the constant striking against Thorne's rock-hard muscles.

Thorne straightened up and tensed. A clicking noise came from somewhere deep inside his neck.

"The problem is, I am designed to do this, right down to the nanobots whizzing around my bloodstream," Thorne said. "I could do this hour after hour, day after day." The brute grinned, showing a set of teeth and protruding jaw muscles that could probably chew through iron.

"You said that already," Eden said. "And I'm sure it's true. Should we just skip this and head home?" Eden stepped backwards, preparing for another impact. Over Thorne's shoulder she saw lights in the river below. A great barge, sitting low in the water and carrying several shipping containers slid, slowly and silently, upriver.

"Good work, Baxter," Eden murmured, watching the vessel slip beneath the bridge.

Eden pulled her attention back to Thorne and grinned.

"What?" Thorne snarled. "Baxter isn't here to help you now. Once I've dealt with you, don't worry, I'll be tracking him down too."

Eden glanced at her nails, then eyed at Thorne as though he was a minor inconvenience. "Yeah, sure, you *say* that. All you've done so far is stand around chatting."

Thorne roared, the sound came from deep down in his body, almost rumbling the old cobbles of the bridge beneath their feet.

"I'm right here." Eden held out her hands like a bull fighter. "If you want to finish it, now's your time to shine."

Playing right into Eden's plan, Thorne charged forward, both hands like battering rams.

This time, however, Eden had no intention of taking on the brute. She stepped to the side and broke into a run.

Thorne spun around and made a grab for Eden, but she was just out of reach. She charged on, extending her lead to several feet. Eden ran a few more steps, closing in on the edge of the bridge.

Across the ornate blue barrier, London's skyline shimmered in the falling rain. A few feet from the edge, Eden paused and glanced over her shoulder.

Thorne spun around, caught his balance, and then gave chase.

Eden waited a second or two for Thorne to close the gap. Just as he was about to make a grab for her, she turned, sprinted, and launched herself clean over the side of the bridge.

For a moment, Eden felt weightless, suspended above the river's churning waters. The rain slowed, each drop glittering like a tiny jewel.

Then the barge came into view. The hunk of metal was almost invisible against the pitch-black water. Eden landed in a crouch on the first container. Her feet clunked onto the slippery wet metal. Eden turned, stood up and stared at the bridge behind her.

Thorne remained standing on the roadway, his great shoulders silhouetted against the streetlights. Above him, the Gothic towers loomed into the sky, soaring over the scene like monsters themselves.

"Come on then!" Eden shouted. She unfurled her arms and stood like the Redeemer, peering down on Rio de Janeiro. "I thought you wanted to finish this."

Thorne looked down at the barge, fighting against the current. He nervously considered the water before glancing side to side down the bridge.

"Your call big boy!" Eden shouted. "Finish it now or..." She pointed at the distant flicker of police strobes. "After that mess you made in the tube station, they'll be calling in half the force."

Thorne glanced at the incoming lights. His facial expression hardened as he made up his mind. In one swift move, Thorne placed a hand on the barrier and swung his legs across. He dropped like a cannonball before colliding with the barge, two containers down from Eden. A clang reverberated through the hull and the boat rocked forward and backward.

Thorne stood, his face set in a grim mask of determination like nothing Eden had seen before. She wondered whether luring the deadliest man she had ever met out to the middle of the river on her own was a bad idea.

Eden's mind filled with two thoughts. On one side she thought of all the people Thorne had mercilessly killed. On the other side she thought about all the awful procedures Thorne's father had put him through to make him that way. He was a monster, yes, but not by his own failings. She wished there was another way do to this, but she couldn't see one.

Before Thorne even took a step forward, the roar of a high-powered engine cut across the river. Eden glanced towards the noise and saw one of London's fireboats racing towards them. Lights blazed from the bow, illumining the raindrops like crystals.

"Good timing." Eden turned back towards Thorne.

Thorne remained stationary, standing tall on the barge. If he knew what was about to happen, he showed no sign of fear.

The fireboat slowed, moving parallel to the barge.

Then Eden saw Baxter, standing on the fireboat's front deck, manning the water cannon.

Baxter and Eden locked eyes and then Eden nodded. Baxter clicked a switch and the powerful water cannon roared into life. A thousand liters of high-powered water cut through the air like a javelin.

Baxter swept the cannon carefully up across the side of the barge, and then hit Thorne square between the shoulders. The water jet delivered the blow with the force of a tidal wave.

Thorne dropped into a crouch, trying to withstand the powerful jet. He clawed pathetically at the container, but the slick wet steel offered him no help. He tried to roll to the side and get out of the jet's force, but Baxter tracked his every move with minor adjustments to the cannon.

Eden watched the scene, her body tensed, her heart in her mouth.

After what felt like an incredibly long time, Thorne lost his footing and skidded uncontrollably across the container. The brute emitted a guttural, animalistic roar which cut through the noise of the water cannon, the rain, and the chugging engine of the barge. The noise cut right into Eden's chest and for a moment she felt like they shouldn't do this. But talking to Thorne was futile. He was too far gone. Too damaged.

As though in slow motion, Thorne scrabbled around, trying desperately to find his grip. His thick fingers swept across the container one more time and then the water jet swept him from the side of the barge and into the swirling waters of the Thames.

Eden signaled to Baxter, and he shut off the water cannon.

The crew maneuvered the fireboat alongside the barge and Baxter scrambled across.

"You took your time," Eden said, helping Baxter up on top of the container. Together they crossed to the position where Thorne had disappeared.

"Well, it does help if you tell me where you are," Baxter said. "I'm not a mind reader."

"Oh really?" Eden placed her hands on her hips and looked up at the man she had come to rely on almost as much as her father. "Well, you should try a bit harder next time."

Baxter pulled out a flashlight and the pair studied the water. There was no sign of Thorne. After almost half a minute, a series of bubbles rose to the surface.

"You're not going in to get him?" Eden said, pointing downwards. "Or shall we let him sleep with the ducks?"

"Not this time," Baxter said, gazing up at Tower Bridge. "And, by the way, it's fishes."

"What?" Eden said.

"That phrase. It's from the film The Godfather, and it means to be murdered."

"Don't worry," Eden sighed, slipping her arm through Baxter's.

EPILOGUE

One Hyde Park Residence, London, England. The Following Day.

"I just can't believe we left her there, lying on the floor," Nettleby said, his voice carrying across the hubbub of activity in their penthouse apartment.

Several people were clearing away computer equipment and setting the table for the team to eat a meal together.

"Who are you talking about?" Athena said, walking up to the table with a stack of plates. "I don't remember anyone lying about. I haven't been to bed in so long that I think I'm going to have to read the instructions next time."

"No, no, no," Nettleby said, taking on the color of the claret he was sipping. "Not you. Your team have worked tirelessly. I mean the *Lady of Leone*."

"I know," Winslow replied, placing a finger on the curator's arm. "But she was back in the freezer within what, an hour?"

"Yes, absolutely," Nettleby said, pausing to take another glug of wine. "She didn't seem to have defrosted at all, which is good. I say, the discoveries in that vault will keep me and my team busy for months, if not years."

"I'll toast to that," Winslow said, raising his glass. Winslow turned to Doctor Hunter who arrived at the table with a fresh bottle of wine. "I hope this place hasn't been uncomfortable for you."

"All things considered, it's not been the worst." Hunter scanned the luxurious apartment with its view of Hyde Park and top of the range facilities.

"Well, the good news is, with Thorne out of the way it's safe for you to go home," Winslow said.

"That is good news," Hunter said, popping the cork and refilling Winslow's glass. "And I'll rush straight back there, in a few more days."

Laughter filled the room. Hunter topped up the rest of the glasses.

"I expect your patients are missing you," Athena said, taking a sip.

"I expect so too, but even a doctor has to have a life," Hunter said. "I haven't had more than a weekend off in over a decade, you know. Every time I'd go away, I'd feel guilty about Mrs. Maggoty and her bunions. That needs to change."

"What, Mrs. Maggoty and her bunions?" Athena said.

"Oh, I'm fairly sure that will never change. But I will be going taking more vacations from now on," Hunter said.

"I'll drink to that," Nettleby shouted, slurping at the wine again.

"Food E.T.A. two minutes," Baxter said, glancing up from his phone.

Nettleby's eyebrows rose as though Baxter was speaking a totally different language.

"He means the take away will be here in two minutes," Athena said. "This guy always thinks he's on a mission."

"Now that is clever, how can you possibly know that?" Nettleby asked, pointing up at Baxter. "Don't tell me. You've hacked into the city's camera system and are following the delivery driver through the streets?"

Baxter shook his head.

"Okay. Maybe you went into the restaurant earlier today and planted a tracker!" Nettleby's eyebrows appeared to bounce on his forehead.

Baxter shook his head again and went to speak, but Nettleby interrupted him.

"Maybe an informant! Someone is tracking the poor guy. I haven't seen Eden in a while…"

"Much simpler than that." Baxter spun his phone around and showed Nettleby the delivery app tracking the driver.

Nettleby scoffed and leaned back in his chair. He shook his head so violently that his hair became even more tangled than usual.

"In fact," Baxter said, pointing up at the ceiling. "I think food will be here in three, two, one…"

The chime of the doorbell cut through the room. Baxter turned on the spot, paced across the luxurious apartment, and swung open the door.

"Room for one more?" boomed Nora Byrd. She held up two bags of takeout food as though she were a prize game hunter. "Don't worry, I saw the young delivery guy in the elevator."

"You're always welcome," Baxter muttered, stepping aside to let the larger-than-life character in.

Nora placed the various tubs in the center of the table before introducing herself to Nettleby and Hunter.

"No Beaumont and DeLuca?" Byrd said, scanning the assembled people.

"You know," Winslow said, climbing to his feet and welcoming Nora with a peck on the cheek. "After what they're now calling the *Atlantis Episode*, they decided they needed some time away."

"To make up for those lost years." Athena's eyes glinted with layers of meaning even she was too polite to verbalize.

"And where's that wonderful daughter of yours," Byrd said to Winslow. "I hear she's, once again, the hero of the hour."

"Indeed so," Winslow said, nodding deeply. "I'll go and get her, I know she'd love to thank you personally for your daring rescue in the mid-Atlantic..."

"A daring rescue, is that what she's calling it? It was nothing, really. A bit of fun." Byrd turned her attention to the food. "What have we got here then?"

∽

"Food has just arrived," Winslow said, stepping out on the balcony and crossing towards his daughter. "I know you'll be hungry."

Eden didn't move, her eyes locked on the skyline. The rain which had pummeled the city continuously for several days seemed to have burned itself out now, leaving a cold clear sky.

After a long moment, Eden shook her head as though returning herself back to the present.

"Absolutely," she said. "Let me guess, chicken korma with boiled rice."

"Am I that predictable?" Winslow said, rubbing his hands together as an instinctive reaction to the cold.

Winslow stepped up to the railing and then turned to face his daughter. He swallowed twice and then cleared his throat. "Before we go down, there is something I've been meaning to tell you for a while..."

"I've got a question to ask you, too," Eden said, staring out at the city.

Winslow stepped back as though startled. "Right, okay... You go first, if you'd like."

"I've been thinking about this a lot over the last few days," Eden said, turning to face her father. Although Eden was now looking at her father, in her mind's eye she saw Thorne struggling to stand on the top of the barge and then sliding into the water.

Eden glanced down at her hands for a long moment before speaking.

"How do we make sure that what we create in this world is for good? I can't seem to stop the events of the last few days going through my mind. Too many monsters causing too much pain."

Winslow stepped towards his daughter and put his arm around her shoulder then together they surveyed the skyline.

"This, I suppose, is the problem that we all have to face at some point in our lives. It's not just a problem for us, doing what we do. Everyone out there has these questions..."

"Dad, listen, you know I love chatting with you, but for once I'd just like a straight answer. No questions. No knowing looks. Just an answer."

Winslow dropped into silence for almost half a minute. Traffic rumbled from the street far below.

"Ultimately, I suppose it comes down to faith," he said. "I

have faith that I know you have a good moral compass, and you'll always do what you think is the right thing."

"But that's the problem," Eden said. "Thorne thought *he* was doing the right thing. He had been brainwashed to such an extent, that he didn't even know what was right."

"Yes, that is the problem," Winslow said. "Ultimately, I suppose there is no way you can know for sure. You've just got to do what you feel is right, at the time."

Eden nodded slowly and then straightened up, as though shaking off the melancholy which had hung like a physical weight on her shoulders.

"What was it you wanted to talk to me about?" she said, glancing up at her father.

Winslow gazed stoically out at the city. He swallowed, his Adam's apple bobbing. "Oh, we can do that another time," he said finally, his voice thin.

Eden tilted her head as though wondering whether to question her father further. The moment of silence swelled between them.

"Okay," Eden muttered, barely a breath above the city's noise below them. Eden pursed her lips together and then drew a deep breath.

"I know you're not my father by birth," she said.

The words hung for far longer than any words have the right to.

Winslow seemed to sway back on his heels as though physically struck by what she'd said. When he turned to face his daughter, his face was ashen.

"How did you find out?" he said, his voice cracking.

"I've known for a while that you've been keeping something from me, despite promising that you wouldn't. It took me a while to figure out what it might be, but then, it just clicked. That is the only thing that I could think of that would affect you this much."

"But how did you *know*?"

"That's a bit sneaky. When we sent Everett Van Wick's blood off to be tested, I sent yours too. I actually got the results while I was in the taxi leading Thorne to Tower Bridge."

Winslow's eyes sparkled now, although Eden couldn't tell whether it was from emotion or relief.

"I should have told you before," he said slowly.

"Why? It really doesn't matter," Eden said. "You're my father, and you'll always be that whether you like it or not."

Winslow sighed and then pulled Eden close. "Talk about creating a monster," he muttered, into her hair.

"I heard that," Eden said, unable to prevent the laugh brightening up her voice.

Winslow held his daughter at arm's length. "Do you think we ought to go and get some food before those gannets eat it all?"

"Absolutely," Eden said. "You lead the way."

∼

"Eden!" Nora Byrd shouted as Eden and Winslow descended the stairs.

Eden greeted Byrd with a kiss on each cheek before turning to face the table. "Thanks for saving us a few scraps." Eden pointed at all the empty tubs which had a few minutes ago been brimming with luscious curries.

"There's loads left," Athena said, pointing at a couple of the dishes in which a few scraps remained.

"Around your mouth maybe," Eden muttered. "It's

alright. We'll order some more. First, I wanted a drink anyway. Did you bring it?" Eden said to Nora.

"Of course." Byrd lifted her rucksack and removed a bottle. "Personal air mail from the States."

"You mean you flew all the way here just to deliver that to Eden?" Baxter said.

Byrd crossed the room and stood behind Baxter who was still sitting at the table. "And to see you, of course, Captain" She placed her hands on Baxter's shoulders, then leaned over and kissed him on the cheek.

Baxter turned beetroot red, which almost concealed the lipstick mark on his cheek, but not quite. The room again descended into hoots of laughter.

Eden collected the whisky glasses from the kitchen. She lined them up on the table and then removed the bottle from the carrier Byrd had given her.

"Before we have this," Athena said, reading something on her phone. "Senator Everett Van Wick is on the news."

"Put it on the screen," Winslow said.

Athena tapped a button and Everett Van Wick's thousand-watt smile filled the giant TV screen.

"In light of the developments with my father, I feel it would be inappropriate for me to proceed as a candidate for the presidency. I will of course continue to work tirelessly as your senator, and maybe next time around... who knows."

Journalists sitting at the press conference shouted their questions.

"Give him three years," Byrd said. "He'll be back."

Athena tapped the phone, and the screen shut off.

"Yeah, we've not seen the last of him," Winslow said.

"And that's not a bad thing," Eden said. "He's a good man. Maybe even too good for politics. Anyway, turning to more important matters, this is possibly the rarest bottle of Whisky in the world," Eden said, pulling out the cork.

"How did you get it?" Winslow asked.

"I think I know," Baxter muttered, standing from the table.

Eden silenced him with a look.

She poured a measure of the golden liquid into each glass and distributed them around.

"Put it this way, it's been chilled for over one-hundred years."

Everyone shared a disbelieving glance.

"It can't have. How did you..." Winslow paused midsentence. He picked up a glass and sniffed. "In fact, don't tell me."

Eden looked at Nettleby who was examining the glass as though it was a relic itself.

"Would you like to make a toast, for your grandfather perhaps," Eden asked the curator.

Nettleby pointed a finger at his own chest as though not believing what was happening. Then realizing that Eden did, in fact mean him, he stood a little straighter and held his glass aloft.

"Everyone, please raise your glasses. Tonight, we toast not just to those who are here with us, but also to those who are not. To the mothers, fathers, sons, daughters..."

As Nettleby began to speak, Eden turned from one member of their crew to the next.

"In their honor..." Nettleby continued, now warming to his theme. "Let us remember not just the ending, but the whole voyage — the laughter and stories they shared, the chances they took, the love they carried, and the lives they touched. May their spirits find safe harbor... To memories that were never sunken... To lives forever cherished... To *The Titanic*... and to friends. Cheers"

"Cheers!" Everyone roared in unison.

THE TEMPLAR ENIGMA

AN EDEN BLACK THRILLER
LUKE RICHARDSON

Eden Black returns in The Templar Enigma!

Search online for 'The Templars Enigma' by Luke Richardson or visit this website: www.lukerichardsonauthor.com/templar

A TEMPLAR CURSE
AN ANCIENT PROPHECY
A PULSE-POUNDING RACE AGAINST TIME

In 1314, Jacques de Molay, the last Templar Grand Master uttered a curse as he burned at the stake. Within months, both men responsible for his downfall, the King of France, and the Pope, lay dead.

Centuries later, a Templar descendant discovers the key to unleashing the curse's power: The legendary Seal of Solomon. Learning of the relic's power, he plans a cataclysmic event which will return civilization to the Dark Ages.

Enter Eden Black. As the countdown begins, Eden is thrust into a web of intrigue that spans centuries, from the final days of the Knights Templar to the shadowy activities of a modern secret society.

But, learning just how deep this conspiracy goes, and who exactly is involved, Eden realizes things are much more deadly that she first thought.

From the crypt of a long-dead templar knight, to the shifting sands of the Sahara, and on to the palaces of Portugal, she uncovers shocking truths about her own destiny and the role she must play in the coming apocalypse.

With heart-pounding action, characters you'll fall in love with, and a plot that will leave you breathless, The Templar Enigma is a must-read for fans of Dan Brown, Steve Berry, Ernest Dempsey, and Nick Thacker.

Search online for 'The Templar's Enigma' by Luke Richardson or visit this website: www.lukerichardsonauthor.com/templar

AUTHOR'S NOTE

To watch me reading this author's note on YouTube visit: www.lukerichardsonauthor.com/titanicnote

Thanks so much for reading The Titanic Deception. It's been my pleasure to entertain you for the last few hours. Producing a book like this is the work of many months — sharing it with you makes it all that labor worthwhile

Travel is an incredibly important part of my writing process. In fact, I don't think I would be a writer if I wasn't first a traveler. Sometimes that comes through in the settings of my stories. I work hard to make you feel like you're right there in the mess with my characters. Other times that's because when I travel, I'm away from my desk and life's never-ending to do list. This distance allows my mind to roam, and ideas to form.

The Titanic Deception came to me in this way. In January 2023, Mrs. R and I took a trip to Egypt to research The Giza Protocol.

As an aside, it was such a fantastic trip. I've written

about it in detail here: https://www.lukerichardsonauthor.com/egypt

While we were in Egypt, we took a guided tour to the Valley of the Kings, just outside Luxor. The tour guide kept our interest for several hours, explaining how the tombs were built and the lives of the people inside. Then, he started talking about the mummy trade.

The mummy trade, called 'mummia,' is a dark, and pretty weird part of history. It's one of those stories that are great to cite when a clueless friend rants about the failings of the modern world with claims like, *'things were better back then.'*

During the Renaissance and later, Europeans developed a fascination with ancient Egyptian mummies, not for their archaeological significance, but for their supposed medicinal properties. Ground-up mummy powder, known as 'mummia', was believed to help all sorts of ailments, from headaches to stomach disorders. This macabre trade led to a high demand for mummified remains, which, in turn, spurred grave robbing and the counterfeit mummy industry. As medicine improved — and maybe as people realized how weird consuming corpses was — the practice and demand for mummia dwindled.

"There's even a legend that says a number of mummies from the British Museum were transported on *The Titanic*," our tour guide explained, claiming that by the start of the twentieth century people had started believing that mummies were able to bestow misfortune on people nearby. As such, the British Museum had sold some mummies to someone in New York and arranged passage across the ocean.

My mind was racing by this point. I saw in my mind's eye the scene with Marcus Nettleby rushing through the stricken *Titanic* on the way to see his beloved artifact one more time.

The idea for The Titanic Deception had arrived.

Later, I learned that it wasn't in fact a mummy that was supposedly transported on *The Titanic,* but a mummy board. The artifact is actually called the *Unlucky Mummy* and remains in the British Museum to this day, so wasn't on *The Titanic* at all! That said, *The Titanic* was a big ship, who's to know exactly what was in her many holds and cabins...

Okay, let's address the elephant in the room here. Did *The Titanic* hit an iceberg?

The answer I've come to is... probably, yes. However, there a many different facts that allow some room for doubt.

The Titanic was travelling through unusually still waters in the middle of the night. That means the men on watch wouldn't have been able to see very well. Bear in mind, electric lights weren't as good then as they are now, obviously, and the men on watch were just watching with the naked eye — they didn't have any binoculars or anything else to help them spot these giant chunks of ice. Also, as the great idiom tells us, most of the iceberg is below the water. What I'm getting at here is that it's very possible that no one actually saw the iceberg clearly. If no one saw the iceberg, then this leaves a whole world of possibilities, right?

The sinking of *The Titanic* also isn't without its conspiracies.

Was it really *The Titanic* at all? One of the most well-known conspiracy theories suggests *The Titanic* was switched with its sister ship, *The Olympic,* as part of an insurance scam. These ships were built side by side in the same dockyard and were almost identical — a couple of tins of paint to change the names and no one would know the difference. Proponents of this theory claim *The Olympic*, which had been damaged in a collision, was intentionally sunk to collect insurance money.

The US Federal Reserve theory. Central to this theory are the untimely deaths of three of the ship's prominent passengers: John Jacob Astor IV, Benjamin Guggenheim, and Isidor Straus. These wealthy men, theorists argue, opposed the creation of the US Federal Reserve. Their deaths, so the theory goes, cleared the path for the Federal Reserve Act to be passed. Adding some weight to this, J.P. Morgan, who was a key player in the establishment of the Federal Reserve was one of the owners of White Star Line, and *The Titanic*.

My books come to me as I'm writing. I don't know the end when I start. I don't know where the story is going to end up, or what twists and turns we might make on the way. I have tried planning before I begin, but invariably end up changing things when another, better, idea arrives. It wasn't until I was chatting with a friend who happens to have Rh-Negative blood, that idea for the *Lady of Leone* and the Van Wick's Xero+ blood appeared.

About 15% of people have Rh-Negative blood, and the other 85% are Rh-Positive. Interestingly 35% of the people in the Basque Region of Spain are Rh-Negative, which is the highest concentration in the world. This is quite a big thing, though, and can cause health complications. If an Rh-Negative mother is carrying an Rh-Positive fetus, her body can think the baby's Rh-Positive red blood cells are foreign and develop antibodies to fight them. There is also evidence which claims Rh-Negative people have lower than normal blood pressure, a slower pulse, and in some cases, people are known to have an extra vertebra in their spine. Further to this, it seems that no one really understands where this difference came from. Some suggest it could be a mutation, others propose this indicates the human race has more than one origin.

Here's the thing that really piqued my interest. In the general world population, Rh-Negative is low, yet a surprising number of powerful and important people have Rh-Negative blood. This number include countless US politicians and several presidents, the British Royals, numerous musicians, sports people, and loads of other people of note. That really got me thinking — for a trait that consists of small percentage, they really do have a lot of very wealthy and powerful people! This stuff is like rocket fuel to an archaeological thriller writer like me.

Towards the end of the story, Eden and Winslow go to see The Parthenon Marbles in the British Museum. This is a real exhibit and is on display in their specially designed gallery which was finally completed in the 1930s after several decades delay. Whether there are secret rooms beneath the building, I don't know, but I would love to think so. The way these sculptures came to be in the British Museum, when they are really part of the Parthenon in Athens, is a shady one. Lord Elgin, who was the envoy to the Ottoman Empire at the time when the Ottomans ruled Greece, got a license to do some research on the Parthenon. He ended up removing loads of the statues and causing a lot of damage. Towards the end of his life, Elgin got into financial trouble and had to sell the sculptures to pay his debts. The British Government bought them and then placed them in the museum. Greece have asked the British to return their sculptures so that they can be displayed in Athens, but the British have refused.

Maybe one day I'll write a story about a crack team of archeological thieves who go around stealing all the artifacts that have been looted during the colonial period and returning them to their places of origin.

I was also very pleased to feature The London Underground in this book. Although there are several similar metro systems around the world, I've always found the London Underground (we don't call it the metro!) fascinating.

The disused British Museum Underground Station is totally true, and still exists deep beneath the streets. Located on the Central Line between Tottenham Court Road and Holborn stations, it operated from 1900 to 1933. Over the years, various redevelopment proposals were put forward for the disused station, including transforming it into an air raid shelter during World War II, but none came to fruition. Today, it remains one of London's 'ghost stations.'

Ghost station is a suitable phrase for it because supposedly the abandoned station tunnels are haunted! The tale goes, the ghost of Amen-Ra, an Ancient Egyptian princess or high priestess, wanders the platforms wearing a loincloth, headdress, and screaming at the top of her voices. The legend gained traction in the 1930s when stories circulated of the ghost's apparition being seen by construction workers and night watchmen. More recently, late night travellers on other nearby stations report to have seen and heard her wandering the tunnels. In an interesting twist, it was the mummy board from Amen-Ra's sarcophagus that was supposed to be on board *The Titanic*. Sometimes these legends are crazier than my stories!

As always with my books, I intend for you to come for the action, and leave having made some good fictional friends along the way. I hope you've enjoyed getting to know Eden and her crew better within these pages.

It has occurred to me recently that I always seem to write

characters who are "outsiders." What that says about me, I don't really want think, but in all my books the main character is a bit of a lone wolf trying to fit in with the world around them.

In Eden's stories, while having a great adventure, she finds the engagement with other people a challenge. You may have noticed that she often hides behind humor when things get personal.

I love addressing topics like this, because although most of us won't face genetically engineered bad guys, I expect we all know what it feels like to be the odd one out at some point.

This book also sees the men in her life, her father and Baxter, start to open up a little more. How either of these relationships will develop, I'm not at liberty to say. You'll have to join me on the next one to find out!

Once again, thank you for your company and can't wait for our next adventure together.

Luke
October 2023

CAN A PRICELESS PAINTING VANISH INTO THIN AIR?

Eden Black meets Ernest Dempsey's Adriana Villa

Ten years ago, Bernard Moreau baffled police by stealing a Picasso from the Modern Art Museum. He was arrested and imprisoned, but the painting was never found.

Now, back on the streets, all eyes are on Moreau. But he's a skilled thief and isn't going to make it easy.

EDEN BLACK can't stand corruption and the theft of priceless art. This case reeks of them both. Heading to Paris, she vows to return the Picasso to its rightful home as soon as possible.

ADRIANA VILLA works alone, always, that's the rule. So, when she sees another woman following her mark, things get heated.

To find the painting before a dirty police inspector with a score to settle, the pair must put their egos aside and work together. What they discover shows that nothing is as simple as it first seems.

THE PARIS HEIST is an up-tempo novella which will keep you pinned to the pages until the very end. If you like the sound of a race against the clock, action packed, adventure thriller, set amongst the blissful Parisian streets, you'll love THE PARIS HEIST.

Read The Paris Heist for FREE today!
https://www.lukerichardsonauthor.com/paris

BOOK REVIEWS

If you've enjoyed this book I would appreciate a review.

Reviews are essential for three reasons. First, they encourage people to take a chance on an author they've never heard of. Second, bookselling websites use them to decide what books to recommend through their search engine. And third, I love to hear what you think!

Having good reviews really can make a massive difference to new authors like me.

It'll take you no longer than two minutes, and will mean the world to me.

Thanks :D

THANK YOU!

Books are difficult to write.

Not a month goes by where I don't think it's "too hard," or "not worth it." Every time this happens — as though by magic — I get an email from a reader like you.

Some are simple messages of encouragement, others are heartfelt, each one shows me that I'm not doing this alone. Those connections have kept me going when all seemed lost, and given me purpose when I didn't see it myself.

A special heartfelt thank you to those who support me on Patreon. These people support me with a few dollars, pounds or euros a month. In exchange it's my pleasure to share my travels with them through postcards and other random gifts from the road.

Some Patreon supporters even get the opportunity to read my books early. If that resonates with you, check out my Patreon here:

https://www.patreon.com/lukerichardson

Don't feel obliged, the fact you are here is more than enough.

Thanks goes to (in alphabetical order):

- Allison Valentine and The Haemocromatois Society
- Anja Peerdeman
- Chris Oldfield author of 'The Less Years' series
- David Berens (for the cover)
- Fritzi Redgrave
- James Colby Slater
- JazzLauri
- Mark Fearn from the Bookmark Facebook Group
- Marti Pannikar
- Melody Highman
- Ray Braun
- Rosemary Kenny
- Tim Birmingham
- Valerie Richardson

LEND ME YOUR NAME AND I'LL KILL YOU (IN FICTION!)

Although my books aren't gory, and don't have a lot of swearing and extreme violence, quite a lot of people die!

That's not a reflection of me and my hobbies (at least I hope it isn't), I think it just makes for an exciting story.

Anyway, always on the lookout for names for these short-lived characters, I've got "name bank" on my computer. Whenever I hear an interesting name, I add it to the "name bank". Then when I need to name someone, I'll open the list and find one that fits.

Of course, I do a similar thing with main characters too, but they take a lot more time as their name has to really suit them.

My question for you is: do you have a name you would like to add to my "name bank?"

You could suggest your name, the name of someone you know, or just a name you like the sound of. They can be of any origin, but I do love to use less common names - sorry Dave!

Be aware, though, this character may die! I've had people offer the names of their grandchildren, before changing their mind as they wouldn't want to see that character fall from a tall building, or be crushed by falling rocks, or jump from a moving train.

Join my mailing list and maybe you'll end up dead: www.LukeRichardsonAuthor.com/mailinglist

HAVE YOU READ MY INTERNATIONAL DETECTIVE SERIES?

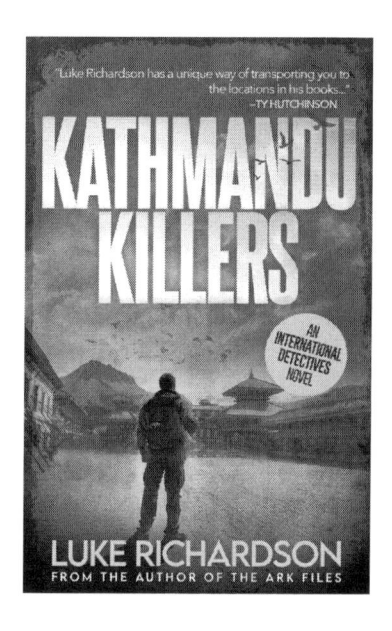

You visit a restaurant in a far-away city, only to find you're on the menu.

Leo Keane is sent abroad to track down Allissa, a politician's daughter who vanished two years ago in Kathmandu. But with a storm on the horizon and intrigue at every turn, Leo's mission may be more dangerous than he bargained for... A propulsive international thriller!

READ TODAY

https://www.lukerichardsonauthor.com/kathmandu

Printed in Great Britain
by Amazon